"Do you know, sweetheart, that there are times when I wonder if your undeniable charms are worth putting up with that waspish tongue of yours?"

"You could always change the terms of our bargain," Arabella suggested demurely. "I shall be happy to oblige you."

"No," Tony said flatly. "The bargain stays." And catching her off guard, he pulled her into his arms. His mouth found hers, and there was nothing gentle or teasing about the kiss he gave her this time. The kiss was hungry and demanding, a man's kiss for a woman he desired, a woman he intended to have.

Arabella could not fight him. In the secret places of her heart, she did not want to fight him. Her entire body rejoiced in the plundering kiss. . . .

❧ ❧ ❧

"I have always loved her novels . . . intricately woven, deeply romantic, and spellbinding."
—Rosemary Rogers

"One of the best romantic writers of our time."
—Affaire de Coeur

Also by Shirlee Busbee

Lovers Forever

A Heart for the Taking

Love Be Mine

For Love Alone

SHIRLEE BUSBEE

At Long Last

WARNER BOOKS

A Time Warner Company

WARNER BOOKS EDITION

Cover design by Diane Luger
Cover illustration by Franco Accornero
Hand lettering by David Gatti

Warner Books, Inc.
1271 Avenue of the Americas
New York, NY 10020

Visit our Web site at
www.twbookmark.com

W A Time Warner Company

Printed in the United States of America

First Paperback Printing: December 2000

10 9 8 7 6 5 4 3 2 1

To John Westlund, the original family storyteller
and legendary jokester. And to Rachel,
his charming wife and a long-suffering victim of some of
his more imaginative pranks, such as the
April Fool's diamond brooch.

AND

To Howard, for all the things you are
to me and all the things you do for me.

Chapter One

❧

"*Y*ou did what?" exclaimed Arabella Montgomery, her voice a mixture of horror and incredulity.

Across the brief distance that separated them, her younger half brother Jeremy would not meet her eyes as he muttered, "I gambled away the plantation. Everything. We have nothing left."

As Arabella stared at him transfixed, he sank down into a chair near her desk and buried his blond head in his hands. "Dear God, Bella, we are ruined! What am I to do?"

Telling herself not to let blind panic seep in, Arabella took a deep breath. This particularly lovely April morning, she had been seated behind the desk in the small room she used as an office, humming happily to herself and looking for a recipe for making rose water. The mundane tranquillity shattered by Jeremy's announcement, she carefully laid aside the scrap of paper she held in her hand, and in a surprisingly calm voice said, "Tell me what happened."

"I don't really know," Jeremy replied despairingly. "I was too drunk."

With an effort Arabella bit back the angry recriminations that sprang to her tongue. Now, she reminded herself grimly, was not the time to take him to task. She would see to that once the current crisis was past!

Suppressing a sigh, she stared at his bent head, not really seeing him as her thoughts turned to all the other crises they'd faced in the past few years. The sudden death of their father, William, just barely two years ago had been by far the hardest to bear and overcome— there were still days that she longed painfully for his calm, steady guidance and affection.

Besides Arabella, his eldest child and the only issue of his first marriage, at the time of his death, William had left behind five minor children and a widow—his second marriage over twenty years ago, to the young Miss Mary Kingsley, having proven to be quite fruitful. Arabella had been ten years old when William married his second wife and after an initial stiffness between the two females, she and Mary had become increasingly fond of each other. As for her half siblings, Arabella simply loved all of them.

In addition to the now twenty-one-year-old Jeremy, there was seventeen-year-old Sara, a budding blond-haired, blue-eyed beauty, who already had the young gentlemen falling over their feet in their haste to become part of her court. Fourteen-year-old Jane, her hair still in long braids, thought that Sara was too puffed up with herself and could not understand what all the fuss was about. Nine-year-old George and seven-year-old John were still too young to be more than a pair of limpid-eyed mischievous little imps whose antics left Arabella uncertain upon occasion whether to smack their bottoms or laugh aloud—laughter won more often than not.

There were times, however, when she wondered what life would be like if her father had never remarried and there was only herself to worry about. She made a face, attractively wrinkling her saucy nose. She would probably go mad from boredom within a week.

William's tragic death falling from his horse had only been one more crisis for the family to bear—although, by far, it had been the most painful and hardest to overcome. For many in the Natchez area, the years from 1789 to 1796 had been difficult, anxious ones, the tobacco depression reducing most planters to near ruin—including the Montgomery family. Only the invention of Eli Whitney's saw gin in 1795, the year William had died, had given them a glimmer of hope. The following year, nearly everyone with any sense had planted cotton, and for the first time in years, the planters felt that they had a future.

Arabella smiled sadly. She wished her father had lived long enough to see the near-miraculous profits of his five far-flung plantations last year. But having overcome one hurdle, another loomed—one that not only touched the Montgomery family but encompassed the whole Mississippi Territory.

For as long as Arabella could remember, Natchez and the surrounding lands had belonged to the Spanish, and while she and her family were English, as were many of the other inhabitants in the area, they had lived well and prospered under the rule of the Dons. But that was to change. Last year all the lands east of the Mississippi River and above the thirty-first parallel claimed by Spain, which included Natchez, had been transferred to the control of the young United States. The entire territory was currently a hotbed of intrigue. Despite the treaty, Spain was showing a strong reluctance to turn the land over to the Americans. The Americans were grimly persisting in their efforts to oust the stubborn Spaniards, and rumors of an English invasion from Canada had lately been sweeping through the district.

It was an unsettling time. There had already been riots, and amongst some of the rougher element of the town there was loud talk of attacking the Spaniards. Intrigue and plots were everywhere—Arabella was never certain when she woke in the morning if she would find herself and her family in the midst of a war, or if they were to be greeted by another day of surface placidity. And now this, she mused uneasily, her gaze sharpening as her thoughts turned once again to the present.

"Whom were you gambling with, Jeremy?" she asked quietly. "I cannot think of any of your friends who would allow you to play for such high stakes."

Unhappily his blue eyes met hers. "It wasn't a friend; it was Daniel Leyton."

Arabella's breath caught sharply. "Daniel Leyton! Oh, Jeremy, how could you? You know that he is the most unscrupulous gamester in Natchez. You should have known that the only reason he would play with a stripling like you was because he knew you were easily duped! What were you thinking?"

As soon as the words left her lips, she bit back further

recriminations, cursing her unwise tongue. Having turned twenty-one only three months previously and having come into control of his inheritance at that time, Jeremy was painfully conscious of his youth, and he tried to compensate for that fact by attempting to act far more adult and mature than he was. Behind his back, Arabella and Mary smiled fondly at his posturing. Arabella rested assured that, since he generally had a good head on his shoulders, he would soon enough become less sensitive about the issue and return to his easygoing self. But chastising him and pointing out his youth just then were the worst things she could have done.

Jeremy stiffened, and resentment was obvious in his expression. "Thank you very much! I come to you for help with the disaster we are facing, and all you can do is criticize me." But his resentment did not last, and, sounding very young, he muttered, "Oh, Bella, do not scold. I know I was a fool. What are we going to do?"

"Well, I suspect that the first thing we need to do is get our property back," Arabella returned coolly—far more coolly than she felt.

"Can that be done?" Jeremy asked with a frown. "A gentleman does not go back on his word, and I would never fail to pay my debts. I signed the vowels." He grimaced. "At least I think I did. It was all very hazy to me."

Arabella rather thought that it would be. Jeremy was not prone to drink, and Daniel Leyton and his cronies were known for their hard drinking and less-than-fair play. Jeremy was just one of many young men who had come to grief at Leyton's hands. Only last year a neighbor's son had shot and killed himself over his gambling debts—gaming debts owed to Leyton. Her soft mouth tightened. That was not going to happen to Jeremy, Arabella swore fiercely to herself. They were going to get back those vowels if she had to steal them back!

A little appalled at her own thoughts, she looked at her brother and decided there was no reason to involve him in whatever she finally decided to do. She asked simply, "Do you want to tell me all about it?"

Jeremy nodded. His eyes everywhere but on hers, he began, "Uh, we started in, uh, a little place on, uh, Silver Street."

"Silver Street, Jeremy?"

He nodded again, a flush on his cheeks.

Wisely Arabella made no comment about his presence in the notorious area known as Natchez-under-the-hill. Its reputation was legendary up and down the Mississippi River, and the stories of knifings and killings, eager whores, free-flowing drink, and cutthroat gambling were more understated than not.

"Did you go there by yourself?" she inquired. Silver Street was not a place that she thought Jeremy would gravitate to on his own. He was, in his way, a rather innocent young man and much preferred his horses and hunting to drink and loose women. In fact, she had seldom known him to partake of much more than a glass of hock before dinner. And as for women—he still blushed when addressed by the sisters of his friends.

Jeremy tugged at his neatly tied stock. "The first night there were several of us—Tom Denning, James Gayle, John Roache, and Edward Crocker," he said, naming his usual quartet of friends. Arabella knew them all—every one of them a nice young man about Jeremy's age and station. She could not picture any of them leading him into the kind of situation in which he had apparently found himself.

When Arabella said nothing and merely regarded him with a slightly raised brow, he added with obvious reluctance, "And, uh, Vincent Walcott."

"Ah," Arabella said softly, much suddenly becoming clear. Vincent Walcott was as nasty a piece of goods as it had been her misfortune to meet; but as is often the case with impressionable young men, Jeremy and his friends thought him to be a model of sophistication. Older than Jeremy and his cronies by nearly a decade, he was closer to Arabella's age than Jeremy's. He was a handsome man, tall and urbane, and came from a respected family, but his predilection for scandal and unsavory pursuits had made him somewhat of an outcast amongst the more staid planters and their families. Which, of course, coupled with his easy charm, elegant dress, and fine eye for beautiful women and horses, made him quite alluring to the younger set.

Vincent's family had quietly disowned him years ago. These days he managed to live on a small inheritance from a great-aunt, supplementing it by methods that were not discussed in polite circles. Winnowing young fools into Leyton's net was only one of the ways that Vincent managed to maintain a facade of wealth. Jeremy was not the only green youngster Walcott and Leyton had befriended, fawned upon, then ruthlessly ruined.

"What do you mean by that?" Jeremy demanded defensively. When Arabella looked innocent, he said, "You know what I mean—that 'ah,' you just gave."

Arabella shrugged her delicate shoulders. "Only that Vincent's addition to your party explains a great deal."

His defensiveness fading as quickly as it had come, he sighed, and said morosely, "I've made a fool of myself, haven't I? And ruined us in the bargain."

"We are not precisely ruined and although your losses will certainly hurt us, the family does have a few other assets. You *were* reckless, but you've done nothing that half your friends wouldn't have done in the same situation," Arabella said gently. "You were flattered and excited by the attention that a pair of older, worldly men paid you, and they took blatant advantage of that fact. You are not to blame."

"But I am," Jeremy said miserably. "I knew that Vincent was friends with Leyton, and everyone knows his reputation. And I knew that I should not have gone back the next night. Tom and Edward tried to dissuade me, but Vincent . . ."

"But Vincent mocked their efforts and made them look young and foolish, and so you went."

"Yes, that's exactly what happened!" Jeremy replied, much impressed by his sister's quick grasp. "I thought I was being singled out by Walcott and Leyton because I was so much more sophisticated than my friends. I was quite puffed up with myself, believing that I was so much more mature," he said with loathing. "I realized late yesterday—when the enormity of what I had done became clear—and my head had stopped aching—that they had only befriended me to take advantage of me. And fool that I was, I let them."

Arabella frowned. "This did not happen at one sitting? But several?"

Jeremy gave a bitter laugh. "Oh, yes, indeed—I've been gambling with them off and on for nearly a month. I can see now that they played me skillfully. Teasing me, letting me win occasionally, letting me think that I was this incredibly lucky gambler as they baited their hook and lured me to strike. It wasn't until Sunday night—or rather the early-morning hours of yesterday, that they set the hook and landed me." He shook his head. "I should have known better, but I was caught up in the excitement of it all. We were drinking and we played for hours and hours—I lost all idea of the time—and how deeply I was plunging. On the last hand, I pledged everything on the turn of a card, encouraged by the pair of them to believe that I could win back all that I had lost that night—and other nights." Dully, he added, "Instead I lost everything, Bella. Everything." His voice muffled, he hung his head again and said, "Finally realizing what I had done, I lay awake all last night bracing myself to tell you and wondering if it wouldn't be easier just to kill myself."

"Well, that would have been silly in the extreme—and cowardly. It was very adult of you to decide to accept your responsibilities," Bella said carefully, trying to assess just how serious he was about the latter half of his statement. Leaning forward, she said urgently, "Jeremy, we need you now more than ever. You are the head of the family and do not forget that your mother and brothers and sisters look to you for guidance. They would be devastated if anything were to happen to you. They need you, Jeremy."

He looked up smiling faintly, and the hard knot of fear in her breast eased. "You are the one everyone looks to when there is a problem, and you know it," he said mildly, "so don't try to bamboozle me, my girl."

She grinned at him, her cat-slanted eyes crinkling at the corners, golden lights dancing in their sherry-colored depths. "Now who is bamboozling whom, my good young man?"

A crack of laughter came from Jeremy. "Oh, Bella! What would I do without you? I was certain my life was over, and now you have me laughing." He sobered immediately, and asked, "But what are we going to do?"

"I've already told you—we'll get the vowels back . . . some way." When Jeremy started to argue, she said quickly, "And if the worst happens and we do not, we shall not be as bad off as you think. If you will recall, I have my mother's fortune and the plantations left to me by my grandfather. Fortunately," she said dryly, "those you could not pledge because they do not belong to you. We may have to practice a few unpleasant economies, and, of course, Greenleigh is not as grand or as lovely as Highview, but we shall survive. We shall not be destitute."

Relief flooded Jeremy's face, and he stood up and took a few steps around the small room. Looking back at Bella, he said, "I had forgotten about Greenleigh—it is rather small, but it would do. And I should have known that you would find a way to save Mother and the children. They were my first concern." His young face hardened. "As for me, you do not have to fear that I shall expect you to see to my welfare. I shall find some way to support myself and then, even if it takes me my whole life, I shall repay you whatever it costs to take care of the family." He straightened his shoulders.

"It is my fault that we are brought to this point, and I shall do my best to see that the others do not suffer unduly from my mistakes—I swear it to you, Bella!"

He looked very young and proud as he stood before her, and Bella's throat suddenly closed up with emotion. Keeping her voice as even as she could, she said, "Admirable sentiments—and I would not have expected any less from you, but for the time being let us keep this matter between us. I do not want your mother and the others upset until it is absolutely necessary."

Jeremy looked puzzled. "But Bella, there is no other solution. Do you not understand? I lost Highview and all the land I inherited from Father." He dropped his gaze and admitted painfully, "Even the lands and monies held in trust for the others—I have ruined their lives as well. We shall have to leave—although I am certain that even Leyton will give us a few weeks to depart the premises. Mother must be told."

Bella rose to her feet and came around the end of her desk. Grasping Jeremy's arm, she guided him to the door. "Ah, yes, but she does not have to be told today, does she? Let us not worry her until we have no choice. We do not want her upset and anxious until we have everything worked out. You and I shall think on our problem for a few more days, and once we know precisely where we stand, we shall explain it all to her. Don't you think that would be wise?"

Jeremy stared down at her, a little frown creasing his forehead. "What are you planning, Bella?" he asked suspiciously. "Moving to Greenleigh is our only option. We have no choice. Mother should be informed as soon as possible about our change of circumstances. There is much to be done to move a household of this size."

"Yes, yes, I quite agree," Bella said soothingly, patting his arm lightly, "but I still think it would be wise if we waited a few days before disrupting the entire household." She smiled conspiratorially at him. "You know how your mother worries. Wouldn't it be better if Greenleigh were all prepared for her and the children before we told her? Greenleigh has sat empty these past years, except for the Tidmores, who keep the house up. There is much to be done before the house is ready for us. Wouldn't it be wiser to wait . . . just a little while?"

Half-convinced, but still not entirely won over, Jeremy regarded her narrowly. Of all the siblings, despite the eleven years that separated them, he and Bella were the closest. He knew her well, and there was something about her manner that made him wonder just what she was up to. Aware that she would tell him nothing until she was ready and that her arguments had some merit, he reluctantly gave in. "Very well," he said. "We shall wait—but only until Thursday morning."

Arabella considered pressing for more time, but hastily discarded the idea. She knew that stubborn look on his face, and, if pushed further, Jeremy was likely to stalk from the room and blurt out everything to his mother. In the meantime, she needed to distract him and keep him busy—too busy to pay attention to her activities. A plan was forming in her mind, and she smiled sunnily up at him. "Very well, Thursday morning it shall be. Meanwhile, why don't you ride over to Greenleigh and assess what needs to be done?" As if the idea were spontaneous, she added, "It might be a good idea if you stayed the night there, so that time will not be wasted riding back and forth between the plantations." Something occurred to her. "You lost the plantations, but what about the slaves and other personal possessions? Did you pledge them, too?"

Jeremy grimaced. "I think so. I don't really know— you have to remember, I was very drunk."

If Jeremy had indeed pledged the plantation slaves, their loss would almost be worse than the loss of Highview. Without the slaves, they would not be able to work the remaining lands, and her fortune, while considerable, could only be stretched so far. It would be completely depleted if she had to spend it on replacing slaves, as well as using it to support Mary and the children.

She took a deep breath. It didn't really matter she reminded herself grimly. She had every intention of getting Jeremy's vowels back. Forcing a smile, she said, "Well, let us hope that it is only your plantations that have been lost. Now, why don't you get ready to go to Greenleigh? If you hurry, you will be there in less than an hour. I shall tell your mother that you are doing me a favor by seeing how the house and lands are faring."

His hand on the door, Jeremy halted and looked back at her. The sun shining through the window behind her turned her bright red hair to fire and bathed her in a golden glow. With her small stature and lively, fey features, she looked, he thought fondly, almost like a little fairy princess standing there. Despite approaching her thirty-second year, she did not look much older than Sara did—much, he knew, to her chagrin. This morning she had certainly been his fairy godmother, he admitted

gratefully. Without her he probably would have put a
period to his existence. Still, he didn't quite trust her.
When Arabella got something in her mind, there was no
swaying her, and he could not help thinking that she had
something planned he would not like. He knew very
well that he was being sent to Greenleigh to get him out
of the way, and it made him uneasy.

A little frown creasing his brow, Jeremy said, "I may
have been duped, but I did lose Highview to Leyton.
There is nothing that can undo my foolish actions—and
I do not want you doing anything that might be equally
foolish."

Arabella opened her eyes very wide, and, looking as
innocent as she knew how—which was very innocent
indeed—she murmured, "Why Jeremy, how you do run
on. Of course, I will not do anything foolish."

Her reply did not satisfy him, but he knew it was all
he was going to get from her. "Very well, I shall have a
horse saddled and leave for Greenleigh. I will be back
either tomorrow night or Thursday morning—and we
will tell Mother then. Correct?"

"Of course. We agreed."

After sending her one last searching glance, he finally left, shutting the door quietly behind him.

Alone once more, Arabella began to pace the small
room, her small face scrunched up into a fierce scowl.
Thursday morning did not give her much time, but she
was sworn to have Jeremy's vowels back by then, and
by Gad, she would!

She waited impatiently until she knew that Jeremy
had well and truly departed for Greenleigh. Then she
called for her cart to be readied, not fifteen minutes be-

hind Jeremy, and drove in the opposite direction, to Natchez. Once in town, she went quickly to the family attorney and, without explanation, despite his grave misgivings, retrieved the documents she wanted from his safe. Placing them carefully in the small portfolio she had brought with her for that purpose, she turned to face Mr. Haight. Flashing him an impish smile, she said, "You are not to worry. I know precisely what I am doing."

Mr. Haight, bald and bespectacled, regarded her soberly. He had known the family since they had arrived from England nearly fifteen years previously and had considered William Montgomery a personal friend. "I hope you do," he said, his brown eyes concerned. "I have heard some disturbing rumors recently about young Jeremy's doings. I trust you are not going to ruin yourself while trying to save him from the folly of his ways."

Arabella opened her eyes very wide. "Why, Mr. Haight, whatever do you mean?"

He snorted. "And don't try that innocent look on me, miss!"

Arabella laughed, a seductively throaty sound, so at odds with her puckish features. "Very well then, I won't. Good day to you, sir, and my best to your wife."

Thoughtfully, Mr. Haight watched her drive away in her jaunty dark green and yellow cart pulled by a gleaming black mare. What that little minx needed was a husband. A strong-willed husband who would not be distracted by those laughing eyes or become helplessly twined around one of her slender, dainty fingers.

It was a shame that young lieutenant of hers had

been killed back in '87, when she had been only twenty-one. As he recalled, they had planned to marry that fall. Lieutenant Stockdale had seemed a nice young man when he had come to visit at Highview in the summer of 1786. Damned shame, Mr. Haight thought again. Instead of gallivanting about and risking her own fortune for that silly young fool, Jeremy, she would by now, no doubt, be surrounded by her own brood of children.

His gaze still on Arabella's disappearing cart, he frowned. Of course that business five years earlier with Tony Daggett would never have done. It had been bloody bad luck that Dagget had returned from London just as she finally put aside her grieving for her dead fiancé. Dagget was a libertine of the worst sort, with two dead wives to his credit, wives that most people believed he had murdered. Haight could understand William Montgomery's vigorous objections to the match. Fortune and family aside, Mr. Haight certainly would not have wanted a daughter of his to marry Tony Daggett. It was a dashed good thing that Arabella had for once shown some sense and followed her father's dictates.

Arabella's cart completely disappeared from sight, and, with a shake of his head, Mr. Haight turned to go back inside his office. He'd said it once and he'd say again—that little baggage needed a husband!

Smiling to herself, Arabella tooled happily down the dirt track leading away from Natchez, having a fair idea of Mr. Haight's thoughts. Nearly everyone was convinced that she should marry. Even her stepmother bewailed the fact that Arabella was approaching thirty-two and still unmarried. And just then, it was a good thing, Arabella thought to herself, that she wasn't married. No husband would allow her to do what she had every intention of doing!

and still murmured. And just then it was a good thing. Arabella thought so herself, that they hadn't married. No husband would tolerate what she had every in-tention of doing.

Chapter Two

ಶಿ

*D*aniel Leyton's plantation, Oakmont, lay about ten miles from Natchez, and the afternoon was growing sultry by the time Arabella turned her mare onto the winding track that led to the main house. The badly rutted road meandered about a mile through small patches of woodland and green cotton fields before ending in a circular driveway in front of an imposing house with wide, shady verandas surrounding it.

Pulling her mare to a stop in front of the house, Arabella noted that she was not the only person to call that afternoon. A rakish scarlet-and-gold curricle hitched to a pair of restive grays was already standing on the far side of the circular drive. She did not recognize the vehicle, and its presence disheartened her. Leyton would be less inclined to see her if he was entertaining guests. Well, guests or not, she would just have to make certain that he did see her, she thought firmly. Jeremy had not left her much time in which to maneuver.

At the sound of her vehicle a pair of round-faced

black boys came running from around the corner of the house. Tossing the reins to one of them, Arabella alighted and left the cart in their care.

Not giving herself a chance to consider the wisdom of what she was doing, portfolio and reticule in one hand, the hem of her pale yellow muslin skirts in the other, she quickly ascended the broad steps. She had barely crossed the wide front veranda and rapped smartly on the door when it swung open.

Brushing artlessly past the startled butler, she said brightly, "Will you tell Mr. Leyton that Miss Montgomery has come to call?"

"I'm sorry, Miss Montgomery, but Mr. Leyton is not receiving visitors this afternoon." The butler, a grizzled-haired black man in worn blue breeches and white shirt, waited patiently in the open doorway for Arabella to leave.

"Very well, then," she said amiably. "I shall wait here until he *is* seeing visitors." And she proceeded to cross the hall and seat herself on one of the delicate satinwood chairs along the east wall of the lofty entry hall. Smiling sweetly at the wide-eyed butler, she murmured, "Never mind me—you just go about your business. I shall be fine right here until Mr. Leyton is agreeable to seeing me."

"But miss, you can't—"

Arabella flicked a brow. "I certainly can. And I certainly shall. You may tell Mr. Leyton that I have no intention of leaving the premises until he sees me. Now run along and tell him that I am here."

He hesitated, eyeing her uneasily. She smiled sunnily

back at him. Shaking his head, he finally ambled off down the hall and disappeared.

While she waited, Arabella glanced about her. The once-fine hall was almost shabby. The cream silk-hung walls were faded and worn, and there were paler marks on the fabric where pictures or other decorations had probably hung. Her eyes fell upon the green-and-cream marble-tiled floor, noting the grime and dust that clouded its beauty, and a look upward revealed an equally dirty chandelier, a plain pewter affair that looked oddly out of place. The entire room was clearly neglected and in need of, if nothing else, a thorough cleaning. Perhaps, she thought slowly, Leyton's finances were far worse than anyone realized.

Her heart sank. Her task was going to be difficult enough, but if Leyton was desperate for money, it was highly unlikely that she was going to be able to convince him to release Jeremy's vowels—even with the offer of Greenleigh and her own lands to make it more palatable.

Hearing the sounds of returning footsteps, she sat up straighter and forced a serene smile onto her face. As the butler motioned for her to follow him, she rose to her feet and sedately followed him toward the back of the house. So far, so good, she told herself.

Walking behind the butler, Arabella discovered that the signs of neglect that she had first noticed in the hall were everywhere. Traversing a long, wide hallway that ran the entire length of the house, she was greeted, as they passed by, with glimpses of echoing, empty rooms, or rooms ghostly with dust-covered furniture. It seemed that Leyton had abandoned most of the house and only lived in a few rooms at the rear.

Stopping, the butler threw open a handsome paneled door, and announced glumly, "Miss Montgomery to see you, master."

Arabella took a deep breath and, like a small frigate armed for battle, canvas spread, sailed forward to meet the enemy.

It was a surprisingly pleasant room in which she found herself, the walls wainscoted in oak, a fine rug in tones of russet and gold lay upon the floor. Leyton, an annoyed expression on his pale features, was seated behind a large, untidy desk at the far end of the room. Behind him was a table littered with decanters and glasses; a comfortable leather chair was situated in front of the desk. To Leyton's left, a pair of French doors were half-open allowing the warm afternoon air to drift inside; heavy, gold damask drapery hung on either side of the doors.

Making no effort at politeness, Leyton, a compactly built man of thirty-five, remained lounging in his chair. From his manner, it was apparent that he was extremely annoyed by the interruption. Arabella snorted to herself. She couldn't see why he should be annoyed—Jeremy was the wronged one, and it was clear from Leyton's casual garb, white shirt opened at the throat and breeches and boots, that he wasn't going anywhere.

Arabella had only met him once or twice. Surreptitiously, she studied his features and concluded that while not unhandsome, his predilection for drink and self-indulgence had definitely left its mark on his face,

giving him a sulky look. He was also, she realized unhappily, going to be difficult.

His careless position did not change even when she
finally stood in front of his desk, but a disagreeable
smile did cross his face. "You've wasted your time,
Miss Montgomery—and mine," he said bluntly. "I assume the reason for your call is Jeremy's vowels. I tell
you right now that I cannot give you those vowels."

"Not even if I am willing to give you the deeds to my
grandfather's home and the two other plantations that I
inherited from him?" she asked quietly, as she quickly
set the portfolio and her reticule upon his desk. Opening
the portfolio, she laid the documents on the desk in front
of him. She was not going to let his boorish manner or
discouraging attitude dissuade her from plunging forward with her plan.

Leyton did not even look at the deeds or offer her a
seat, but merely continued to stare at her in a decidedly
unfriendly fashion. There was a tense air about him that
puzzled her. She was the one who should be tense! She
had not expected him to be very happy to see her, but
she had thought that he would at least listen to her. Was
his surly manner simply because she had compelled him
to see her? Remembering the curricle outside, she wondered suddenly if his previous visitor was the cause of
his decidedly unpleasant mood. And where, she mused,
was his visitor?

Ignoring his lack of welcome, she causally seated
herself on the other side of the desk from him, yellow
muslin skirts fluttering about her ankles. So far they had
not gotten off to an auspicious start, and there was an

anxious knot in her stomach. Jeremy faced ruin—as did the rest of the family.

She had put a good face on in it in front of her brother, but the truth was the family would be hard-pressed to maintain any semblance of gracious living if she did not get those precious vowels back from Leyton.

The fortune she had inherited from her mother was generous, and for a single woman, was more than adequate for her needs—even the occasional extravagant splurge. But all her resources would be perilously strained to maintain even a modicum of the manner of life the Montgomery family was used to. Nor was her grandfather's house going to easily accommodate all of them. Greenleigh, though charming and comfortable, was only half the size of Highview. It had never mattered before that she had been more of a "comfortable" heiress than a great one. She had viewed her inheritances as merely precious little pots of gold that kept her independent and able to do as she wished. And if she wished to trade her fortune and independence for Jeremy's vowels, that was her business!

Her lips thinned as the minutes spun out and Leyton let her offer simply hang there between them. He seemed distracted, she thought curiously, his gaze flitting constantly around the room, but why? The other visitor?

She brushed the thought from her mind, growing impatient with the situation. "Well? What do you think?"

"I am a very busy man and I do not have time to discuss this matter with you right now—besides which, there is the fact that we have nothing to discuss."

Tamping down the despair that threatened her, Arabella leaned forward, and said urgently, "Mr. Leyton, I know that I have burst in on you without warning, and for that I apologize most sincerely, but my need is desperate. It is not just Jeremy you have ruined, but my family as well. My stepmother is a widow, and she still has four minor children to care for—not an easy task. She and the children do not deserve to be thrown from their home because of a foolish act of Jeremy's." He appeared unmoved by her plea, his hazel eyes not meeting hers, an almost sullen cast to his lips.

There had to be some way for her to convince him to return the vowels. She took a deep breath. "I am not so green as to beg you to return the vowels simply out of the goodness of your heart," she began earnestly, her golden brown eyes soft and pleading. "Remember, I do offer you something in exchange—not the fortune that Jeremy's vowels would bring you, but certainly a substantial addition to your holdings. Won't you please consider it?"

Leyton snorted, his fingers moving restlessly through the scraps of paper on his desk, halfway brushing against the deeds. "It is a bad bargain you are putting forth, Miss Montgomery."

Disappointed but not surprised that her pleading had not moved him, Arabella immediately tried another tack. "Is it?" she asked, leaning back into the chair and affecting a careless manner. "At least you would get some recompense for your efforts. Otherwise . . ." Her voice trailed off.

His fingers stilled and his gaze narrowed. "Otherwise?"

Appearing to become extremely interested in the folds of her yellow gown, she said coolly, "Why, only that if you do not accept my offer, I shall be forced to bring action against you for the way in which you cheated my brother out of his fortune." She crooked a brow. "I wonder how many other unwise young men you will be able to relieve of their wealth if your name is bandied all over the territory as a man who deliberately gets his victims drunk and then proceeds to ruin them?"

Leyton jerked as if she had stabbed him, and leaning forward, he spit, "If you were a man, I would run you through for what you just said! As for the other, it is Jeremy's name, my dear young woman, that will be bandied about." His flash of temper lessening, he warned, "Bring action against me, and it is your brother who will be shunned and disgraced for going back on his word as a gentleman and for not honoring his debts. A gentleman's word is his bond, and if he goes back on it, it is your brother who will suffer."

"Will he?" Arabella asked interestedly, her eyes innocent as she considered her next move. Inwardly she was quaking at her boldness. Jeremy would kill her if he ever found out what she was doing. She bit her lip, reminding herself that it had to be done—else they would all suffer the consequences. "I wonder?" she mused aloud. Shrugging her shoulders, she murmured, "Of course, you may be right, and naturally I would hate to put my family through all the scandal such an action would bring."

She smiled benignly at him. "Fortunately, Jeremy would not be the only one to suffer. The notoriety would certainly do you no good—your reputation is already somewhat, ah, tarnished." She tapped her lips consideringly with one gloved finger. "It will definitely be fascinating to see what does happen, don't you agree? I suspect that the community will rally behind Jeremy and that he will garner a great deal of sympathy. You, naturally, will be painted quite a villain. Who knows, Jeremy's action may cause others that you have duped in the past to come forth. What do you think?"

"Are you blackmailing me?" he demanded, clearly astounded at her audacity.

Arabella shook her head, the vibrant red-gold curls peeping out from around the broad-brimmed straw hat she was wearing. "Not exactly. I am offering you a bargain: Greenleigh for my brother's vowels and our silence."

"This is ridiculous!" he snapped, running an agitated hand through his tawny hair. "Even if I were in a position to make such a bargain, I would be mad to do so. Highview and the other lands are worth ten times what you are offering. You have come to me with a damned paltry exchange." His face darkened, and his expression was suddenly furious and resentful. "The Montgomery slaves alone are worth a small fortune."

Something in his words made Arabella's heart sink. She had never considered that he would just flatly refuse her offer, and yet that was precisely what he was doing. And yet why did he seem so angry? He held the power.

Trying to understand his manner and also to give herself time to think, she glanced around the room. She saw nothing that gave her clue, just a genteelly shabby room with faded draperies that needed a good airing. Her gaze suddenly paused as she stared at the drapes hanging on the right side of the French doors. A pair of gleaming black boots was protruding from the beneath the hem of the gold fabric. *Someone was hiding there, listening to them!*

Her breath caught. Leyton's visitor had not left! He had been concealed all this time behind the drapes. No wonder Leyton had been so uncomfortable—he knew someone else was privy to this unpleasant conversation.

Agitated now herself, not liking the notion of being spied upon, she stood up. There was something nasty and sinister about the odd situation that made her eager to be gone from the room. She wasn't afraid, exactly, but she was definitely wary. Hands clenched tightly together, she forced herself to make one last plea. "Mr. Leyton, won't you please reconsider? It is not the act of an honorable man to make an entire family suffer for the folly of one young fool. You are partially to blame for what happened; left to his own devices, you know that my brother never would have gambled for such high stakes, nor have gotten so drunk that he did not even realize what he was doing. You and Walcott deliberately set out to fleece him. And, unfortunately, Jeremy was silly enough to let you."

Her words stung him, and Leyton sprang to his feet and fairly shouted, "Don't you understand? I *cannot* return the damned vowels even if I wanted to—I do not have them any longer!"

Stunned, Arabella stared at him. "W-what do y-you

mean you do n-not have them?" she finally managed to stammer.

"Because, you stupid little chit, I lost them in a card game!"

"B-but how can this be? Jeremy only pledged his vowels Monday morning. You can't have lost them so soon."

Leyton sank back down into his chair. Sardonically he muttered, "But I did indeed, Miss Montgomery. I was unwise enough to gamble last night with a man who possesses the devil's own luck, and I ended up throwing Jeremy's vowels on the table." He smiled nastily. "You will have to make your pretty little speech to him. Perhaps he will prove more amenable. Now, for God's sake, leave me in peace! And take your damned deeds with you." He made an angry gesture that sent the opened portfolio, her reticule, and a cloud of paper spinning to the floor. Her reticule flew open, spilling its contents across the scattered documents.

Arabella stared at him dumbfounded, and then at the mess upon the floor. Obviously there was no dealing with him. Eager to be gone from his unpleasant presence—and the hidden listener—wordlessly she began to gather up the scattered documents, heedlessly stuffing them into the portfolio and her reticule.

Her jaw set, ready to leave, she looked at him and forced herself to ask, "Who? Who has the vowels now?"

Malice glinted in his hazel eyes. "A gentlemen you once knew very well—Tony Daggett."

How she remained upright, she never knew. Leyton's words hit her like a blow. Tony Daggett! If he held Jeremy's vowels, they were well and truly ruined.

With a great effort she kept her expression fixed, though she knew her face was white with shock. "I did not realize that he had returned," she said with what composure she could summon. "Where is he staying?"

"At Sweet Acres. Allow me," he added with malicious enjoyment, "to give you the directions." And began to scrawl something across a scrap of paper.

"That won't be necessary," she said stiffly.

"Oh, but I insist," he said almost gaily, and thrust the paper into her nerveless hand. "Go see Daggett. I am sure that he will prove far more amenable to your offer than I ever would—even if I still possessed the vowels. After all," he added cruelly, "you *do* have a history together, don't you?"

Her back ramrod straight, she turned and walked swiftly to the door. She hurried from the house, dazed and shaken, hardly able to understand the ramifications of the calamity that had overtaken her. She had been so certain she could get the vowels back. So certain she could save the family from ruin. So certain she could convince Leyton to prove himself an honorable man that she had never considered what failure would mean. And if Tony held Jeremy's vowels, then she had truly failed.

The room was silent for a moment once the door had closed behind Arabella's departing form. Then Leyton sighed heavily, and said, "You can come out now. She is gone."

A tall, slim man garbed in the height of fashion strolled out from behind the drapes. A smile on his mouth, he murmured, "Such a passionate little creature, I am surprised you were able to withstand her pleas."

"You know very well that I had no choice," Leyton snarled. "Daggett has the vowels."

"Um, yes, that is so. It was very stupid of you to gamble with him last night. You know that he always wins."

"Have done! And get on with your bloody errand. I am in no mood to be polite."

"So I see. Very well then." The man steepled his long slim fingers, and said, "A curious thing has occurred— someone actually tried to extort money out of me the other day."

"Really? What have you to hide?"

His eyes watchful, the other man said slowly, "It seems a letter that I was foolish enough to write some years ago has come back to haunt me." He looked thoughtful. "It was, I admit, silly of me not to have made certain it was destroyed, but at the time I did not think that someone would be stupid enough to keep it." He glanced across at Leyton. "I want the letter back. It would no doubt cause me some—er—embarrassment if it were shown to a certain person. I am sure you know of whom I speak."

Leyton looked bored. "I am afraid that you are talking Greek to me. And I fail to see why you think I should care about your problems—I have enough problems of my own."

"Well, you see that is the odd thing about it," the gentleman said gently. "It was unfortunate for the—er— blackmailer, but I happened to be home when the message arrived and had the good sense to immediately send my man to follow the boy who delivered it. The boy was very good in making certain that he was not followed when he left my place, but . . ." He smiled. "My man knows it is worth his very life if he fails me, and so of course, he did not."

Leyton shrugged. "I still fail to see why you think I should be interested in this tale."

"Ah, well you see, this is where it gets most interesting. My man followed the messenger here to your plantation."

"And you think I had something to do with it?" Leyton demanded. "This is an outrage! Are you accusing me of trying to blackmail you? Only our long friendship prevents me from calling you out this very minute for such a statement."

The other man continued to stare at Leyton for several seconds, then he sighed. "Very well, have it your way. I apologize. But I should tell you—I intend to have the letter back. And attempting to blackmail me could be dangerous—it could even prove fatal."

Their eyes met and held, but it was Leyton's gaze that fell first. Shuffling some of the papers on his desk, he said carelessly, "It is an interesting tale, but I still fail to see how it affects me. Your man was, no doubt, mistaken."

"Unlikely, but I believe we have lingered enough on unpleasant subjects and should move on to more diverting topics." Leaning comfortably back in the chair and crossing his legs, he murmured, "That was a most entertaining interview between you and the fair Arabella. Ah, what I wouldn't give to be a fly on the wall when the sprite confronts Tony and demands those vowels back. It should be most amusing, don't you agree?"

* * *

Arabella was never certain how she managed to get out of the house and into her cart. Instinct must have guided her because she had left the track to Oakmont behind and was driving down the main trail to Natchez before she even became aware of her surroundings. Suppressing a sob, she pulled her mare over to the side of the road and halted the cart.

Dear God! she thought painfully. Tony Daggett. Just his name still had the power to fill her with the most exquisite longing and despair—and five years had not lessened the pain of his betrayal.

Blindly, Arabella stared into the lush, green undergrowth that pressed close to the dusty trail. When Thomas Stockdale had died a decade ago from an infected wound suffered in a skirmish with Indians, she had thought she would never love again. Her life, she had been certain, was over. At barely twenty-one she had been determined to spend the rest of her days as a spinster, her heart buried in Canada with Thomas.

Thinking back on her reaction, Arabella smiled faintly. What a dramatic little twit she had been. But her feelings for Thomas had been real, and his unexpected death, only weeks before they were to wed, had devastated her.

She had loved Thomas for as long as she could remember. The Stockdales had lived next door to the Montgomerys in Surrey, England, and even her father's decision to emigrate to the Americas in 1783 at the cessation of the American war with England had not lessened the affection between the families. All his neighbors and friends had thought her father mad for leaving the safety of England for an uncertain future in the New World. But William had been adamant—he wanted broader horizons and so, having sold all his holdings, placed his family on a ship sailing for America. The move had not broken the bond between seventeen-year-old Arabella and twenty-one-year-old Thomas. They wrote to each other incessantly, declaring their undying love and, with both sets of parents' blessing, when Arabella turned eighteen, they had become engaged.

But while both families welcomed the engagement, the elders urged the young couple to wait until Thomas was better situated in his chosen career in the Army. Since they had weathered the previous separation, and there was a great deal of wisdom in their parents' urgings, Arabella and Thomas had reluctantly agreed to wait to wed until she became twenty-one and came into her mother's fortune. Neither of them ever dreamed what that delay would cost them.

Arabella's expression softened as she thought back on the bittersweet memories of Thomas. Their love, she realized now, had been a gentle, undemanding emotion and, no doubt, if Thomas had lived they would have enjoyed a comfortable marriage. Certainly she would never have known the whirlwind passion and fierce ardor Tony Daggett had aroused within her heart.

A shudder went through her. Tony. Of all the people in the world, why did it have to be *him* who held Jeremy's vowels? She would rather be confronted by a horde of painted, howling savages than face him. Her generous mouth twisted. And she would probably receive more kindness from savages than she would from Tony Daggett.

Oh, what a fool she had been over him! And it wasn't as if she hadn't known his reputation—everyone in Natchez did. His dead wives and scandalous behavior were the topic of conversation everywhere one went. And, of course, he couldn't have cared less—which only infuriated everyone and made them gossip more. If anything, he baited the polite folk of Natchez with his outrageous antics—driving his horses up the steps of the governor's residence on a wager, and engaging in a drunken shooting contest right in the middle of town.

There had been nothing gentle or comfortable about Tony Daggett, Arabella admitted with an odd little smile. He entered a room like a March wind, full of power and promise, his indigo blue eyes glittering brightly, his black hair wildly tossing, and his hard, arrogantly carved features alight with expectation.

Why his fancy had alit on her, Arabella had never known. But once he had set his sights on her, she had been lost, totally overwhelmed by him, dazzled by his handsome face and tall, lean form, just a little excited by his reputation and utterly beguiled by the way a single touch of his hand could transform her entire body into a vibrant flame.

Of course, she should have listened to everyone who warned her about him. Her father had nearly had a fit of apoplexy when it had dawned on him that his daughter was being pursued by Tony Dagget and that she was not trying very hard to escape. Even Tony's cousin, Burgess, had tried to steer her away from certain disaster. But she had been in love, she thought disgustedly. The emotion she had felt for Thomas was a pale weak thing compared to the way Tony made her feel.

Even now, nearly five years later, she couldn't believe that she had been so mad, so reckless, and so very, very foolish. At twenty-seven, she had been well on her chosen path to becoming a sedate spinster—much to her father's dismay. There had been a few young men who had paid court to her in the years following Thomas's death, but Arabella had gently repulsed their advances, determined to be true to Thomas's memory. Until Tony Daggett.

Tony had not been the least repulsed by her aloofness, in fact, she had discovered afterward, it had been a challenge—a wager between him and his good friend, Patrick Blackburne, whose reputation was almost as notorious as Tony's. Her eyes darkened with remembered pain.

It had been bad enough that Tony had captured her heart simply for his own amusement and to win the wager. But did he have to also declare himself wildly in love with her and beg her to marry him, knowing full well that he had no intention of ever wedding her? Had it been part of that infamous wager to seduce her? To take her innocence? To leave her nothing?

Miserably, Arabella reminded herself that it had all happened a long time ago, that it shouldn't matter any longer. But she lied, and she knew it; there were still nights when she lay alone in her bed, her body burning for Tony's urgent caresses, on fire to experience again the pleasure of being possessed by him. Oh, she couldn't deny it—despite all the reasons not to, she longed most fervently to know again the heart-shaking pleasure she had discovered in his arms one, unforgettable time. She had eagerly given him her innocence, and he had thrown it away—for a wager!

Angry with herself for mooning over a man who had proven himself to be a cruel betrayer, who had chosen the most brutal way possible to reveal to her just how little she had meant to him, she picked up the reins and urged her mare forward. She would have much preferred to drive immediately to Highview and accept defeat, but she could not. She really only had once choice, painful and uncomfortable though it would be—she had to see Tony and try to get back Jeremy's vowels.

A crackle of paper caught her attention, and she stared down at the slip of paper still clutched in her hand. She snorted. She needed no directions to Tony Daggett's plantation. Contemptuously tossing the paper onto the cart's floorboards, she slapped the reins and urged her mare into motion.

Though she tried to remain calm and focused on what she had to accomplish, with every mile that brought her closer to Sweet Acres, she could feel herself growing tenser and more nervous.

By the time the drive to Sweet Acres came into view, the place she had once thought to come as a bride, Arabella had herself whipped into a fine temper. *You silly chit!* she chastised herself angrily. *You were the one who was wronged. Why should you be agitated about seeing him again? He is the one who should be uncomfortable! He is the one who wooed and seduced you for sport! And let you discover how little you meant to him by allowing you to find him in the arms of his mistress!*

Thanks to Tony, she was no foolish virgin to be snared by a flashing smile and teasing indigo blue eyes, she told herself fiercely. Oh, no. She was thoroughly immune to the many charms of Tony Daggett. She knew him for what he was—a blackhearted scoundrel, and he would never take advantage of her again!

the told herself fiercely. Oh, no. She was thoroughly
immune to the many charms of Tony Daggett. She knew
him for what he was . . . . and he
would never take advantage of her again.

Chapter Three

❧

As Arabella was reluctantly wending her way to Sweet
Acres, Tony Daggett, his booted feet propped up carelessly on a fine mahogany table, was staring moodily at
the charming expanse that greeted his eye. Until it disappeared into the tangled wood on its border, a broad,
gently sloping lawn, interspersed with live oaks and
magnolias, flowed almost endlessly before him. There
were patches of gaily colored flowers planted here and
there, and, from the open French doors of the study
where he was sitting, the heady scent of roses, he-
liotrope, and pinks wafted to him. The handsomely ap-
pointed room was silent except for the sleepy drone of
insects, but Tony found no pleasure in their song or the
scent of the flowers, nor even the sight of the agreeable
view before him.

Quite frankly, he was bored—and restless. Taking a
long swallow of his ale, he admitted that it had been a
mistake to return to Natchez. He would have been wiser

to have remained in England. At least there, he wasn't haunted by memories.

He scowled. He hadn't been back in Natchez a fortnight, and already he had fallen into his old profligate habits—and with bad company. Last night's gambling with Leyton and Walcott had been unwise at best and at worst . . . He shook his head, not wanting to think about the worst. Of course, he had risen from the gaming table the winner. And he had not compounded his error by ending the evening in the arms of a nameless, faceless whore as had been his wont previously. That should have given him some comfort, but did not.

The days when he had found pleasure in pitting his skill against a pair of scoundrels like Leyton and Walcott were long past. As were the nights, when he came home too drunk even to remember where he had been or what he had done—or with whom. If he came home at all. At least these nights he came home reasonably sober and slept in his own bed. *Age and experience,* he thought with a cynical lift to his lips, *have some virtues to recommend them.*

He glanced at the pile of vowels he had thrown on the table early this morning when he had returned home. He supposed at some point he should find out the extent of his winnings, but at the moment he found the task oddly distasteful. The thrill of winning, even against Leyton and Walcott, did not fill him with any joy.

In fact, Tony conceded uneasily, very little gave him joy these days. It was why he had left England and finally returned to Natchez after an absence of five years. He had hoped being back in the land of his birth and amongst his old friends would help dispel the growing

feeling of dissatisfaction with his life. But so far, all it
had done was increase his boredom and indifference to
life in general. Why he had thought he would find a solution to his queer moodiness at Sweet Acres escaped
him for the moment.

The extensive lands and grand mansion in England,
inherited from his mother's family, were certainly
everything a man could want. And God knew, he had
fortune enough and friends aplenty to amuse him in
England. But for all his great wealth and many friends,
he had been restless, and had found that places and people who had once given him enjoyment seemed oddly
flat and insipid. To his surprise, Tony had recently discovered an odd longing to return to the land of his birth.
Without dwelling on it, he had immediately closed up
his country house, as well as the town house in London,
and along with a few longtime, trusted servants, had
boarded a ship sailing for America. And despite his
boredom that afternoon, he couldn't deny that he was
glad to be back at Sweet Acres once again.

Tony had grown up at Sweet Acres as an only child.
He could not remember either of his parents, which was
no surprise, since his mother, Susan, had died birthing
him. His father, Ramsey, distraught over his wife's
death, had died three months later in an accident as he
rode home drunk from a night spent drowning his sor-
rows.

It was both fortunate and unfortunate for Tony that
his father's parents, Sidney and Alice Daggett, had
mainly raised him. Fortunate, because they adored him;
unfortunate, because they denied him nothing, and he
grew up believing that the world revolved around his

own perfect self. And since he had been blessed, or cursed, as the case may be, with strikingly attractive features and a tall, loose-limbed, athletic body to match his indigo-eyed, black-haired handsomeness, it wasn't very surprising that he had come to expect no less than the adulation of all around him.

Worse yet, he was also heir to two great fortunes: his father's and his mother's. His mother, an only child herself, had been an English heiress of substantial wealth, and, as her son, Tony had inherited the fortune that had come with her when she married Ramsey. Under the terms of his maternal grandfather's will, he would also, in good time, inherit the wealth of her father, the Baron Westbrook.

It was considered by some a piece of good luck that Tony's father, Ramsey, had been a twin, else poor Tony would have been heir to the entire Daggett fortune—which everyone agreed would have been his ruin. Upon his grandfather's death, since Ramsey had been the eldest son, if only by a scant five minutes, Tony had, following the English manner, inherited the majority of the Daggett fortune; half then, the other half when he reached thirty. His uncle Alfred had inherited a handsome fortune, too, but Alfred had always felt that once Ramsey had died *he* should have been the principle heir—not his nephew!

Fortunately for Tony's character, before he died lord Westbrook had come to realize just how outrageously spoiled his beloved grandson had become. Consequently, he had tried to make amends by ensuring that not all of the immense Westbrook wealth came into Tony's careless hands at once. And Tony *had* been careless in those days—a reckless, spendthrift gambler in fact.

Baron Westbrook had been a shrewd old man, and, upon the baron's death, Tony had come into a decent portion of the estate; but the bulk of it was safely beyond his reach. Of course, Tony had the use of the various homes scattered about England, but, no doubt hoping that age would bring his beloved grandson wisdom, the baron had craftily set aside the largest part of his fortune to be doled out in specific amounts as Tony reached various ages. But with his father's fortune already at his fingertips, something the baron had known when he had made his will, lack of money had never been a problem for Tony.

Nor had women. In addition to a parade of fancy pieces, he had had two wives to his credit. His mouth twisted. Two dead wives. The first, Mercy, whose death had been accidental, although there were plenty who believed otherwise, had been his bride for only eight months before her tragic death. And the second . . . Tony's eyes grew bleak. The second, Elizabeth, had been brutally murdered, and there existed an even larger part of the population convinced that she had died by his hand.

Tony sighed. He had married both times for a proper, if not exemplary, reason—to please his grandparents by providing the next generation. Both sets of grandparents had pleaded with him to marry and settle down, and because he loved them, he had tried to give them what they wanted—to no avail and a great deal of scandal.

His early life had been dominated by his two sets of grandparents—the Daggetts in Natchez and the Westbrooks in England. He had spent a great deal of time with the Westbrooks in England and in due course had attended school there at Eton. It didn't help his character any that Lord and Lady Westbrook continued the ruination begun by the Daggett grandparents. The Westbrooks, with the best of intentions, encouraged his pride and smiled fondly at his youthful arrogance and recklessness, instilling within him at an early age the notion that there was nothing that he could not have—that his own way and his own pleasure came first.

Tony did have some saving graces. Along with his handsome face and lithe body, he had also inherited the Devil's own charm and grace, a lively sense of humor, and, as time passed, the ability to laugh at his own foibles. Despite his wealth and attractiveness, there was not a conceited bone in his body. He was considered a loyal and true friend by those upon whom he bestowed his affection—something he did these days with great caution—having also learned that his fortune attracted too many "friends" whose only interest in him was his wealth.

His father's twin, Uncle Alfred, had also been able to bring it home to Tony that the world was not his for the taking. Alfred heartily disapproved of him and said so, frequently and loudly. In his youth, Tony's cousins, Franklin and Burgess, had done him the favor of habitually bloodying his nose. Franklin in particular had brutally taught him that he could not be cock-o'-the-walk all of the time.

Considering everything, what was surprising, as Tony had neared his majority, was the fact that he was not thoroughly despicable. Eton had helped—there was no favoritism there! And Tony was not unintelligent. As he had ventured farther and farther out from the ruinous cocoon of his doting grandparents and begun to rub shoulders with others—some who had an even higher opinion of themselves than he did—he began to realize that he was not quite the perfect being he had been led to believe and that life was not his to command.

It had been, he thought with a wry smile, something of a shock to discover that as far as most of the world was concerned, he was simply an arrogant young puppy with more hair than wit. *And I was,* he admitted, taking another long swallow of his ale. *An arrogant, selfish, puppy.* But that, he reminded himself quickly, was a very long time ago and now, at the age of thirty-eight, he was able to view some of his early antics with something approaching astonishment—and bitter regret.

Finishing his ale, Tony put the tankard down on the table and reached for the thick, black-velvet rope that hung nearby. Giving it a hard yank, he waited for a servant to appear. When his English butler, Billingsley, arrived, he waved his tankard in the air, and said, "I think I need another—you might as well fill a pitcher and bring it back with you. It will save you several trips to the cellar."

Lyman Billingsley, thin and lean as a hickory stick and with a beaklike nose that could frighten impressionable children, gave him a long look down that same nose. They had been together nearly twenty years. Tony had hired Billingsley on a silly wager that he could pick out a felon from Newgate and make a decent servant of him. Tony had been very drunk at the time, a state he seemed to continually inhabit in those far-off days.

But it had worked out well, owing more to luck than any brilliance on the part of young Tony. Billingsley, originally a highwayman by trade, had taken a considering look at the young swell who had rescued him from certain hanging and decided that this was an opportunity too good to miss. His days of crime were behind him— well, except for the occasional gold watch or jeweled pin that had caught his eye. But in the main, he had given Tony his loyalty, and over the years had actually turned into a fairly good butler. He had not, however, ever learned to view his employer with the reverence accorded by most servants to their master, much to Tony's relief and delight.

Picking up Tony's empty tankard and slapping it down noisily on a tray he had brought with him, Billingsley said tartly, "Seems to me, guvnor, that you've been drinking a mite too much lately. And since when have you ever worried about how many steps you save me?"

Tony grinned. "Of course I've been drinking heavily—haven't you learned yet? It's what gentlemen of my class do when they have nothing else to do. And as for saving you steps . . ." His eyes gleamed. "You are getting on in age, you know."

"Is that so? I may have twenty years on you, but I ain't in my dotage yet!" Billingsley returned with relish. "And as for getting on in age, I ain't the one who needs a wife and some little Daggetts to terrorize the country-side—and inherit Sweet Acres and your bloody great fortune!"

"I think you're forgetting my cousins," Tony said with a lazy smile, putting his hands behind his head and leaning back in his chair. "They will be only too happy to step into my shoes."

"Indeed they would," Billingsley replied sharply. "That stiff-rumped uncle of yours, at the snap of a finger. But do you want 'em to? That's the question, my lad."

Tony shrugged. "It doesn't matter. When I am dead I'll be beyond caring."

Billingsley drew himself up, his brown eyes snapping. "Well, if that don't beat the Dutch! And what about me?" he asked in scandalized accents. "What'll 'appen to me if you cock up your toes sudden-like?"

"Ah, I see, I am to marry and beget heirs to ensure the well-being of my butler?"

"You should think about it," Billingsley said virtuously. "And while you do, I'll fetch another tankard of ale, but no pitcher—you've been drinking alone too often these days."

Used to being bullied by his butler, Tony waved him away with a grin. But his expression was thoughtful after Billingsley had left the room. If Billingsley was worried about him, and Tony recognized that his long-time servant was, then it was time to do something about this pool of melancholy he seemed to be falling into. But what?

The cotton crop was planted. Besides, he had a very able plantation manager, John Jackson, to oversee the running of the various plantations he owned. He also had an extremely astute business agent both here and in England. His house ran to his liking. John Osgood, his head stable man, another of the servants he had brought with him from England, kept a gimlet eye on the horses—and anything else he took a notion to interest himself in, Tony thought with a grin.

His grin faded. Which left him with damn little to do but brood over the hand that fate had dealt him. Or rather the fate he had regrettably fashioned for himself.

Irritated by his mood, he stood up decisively. If he was so bloody bored that he was actually feeling sorry for himself, then by heaven, he had bloody well better do something about it! But not, he reminded himself firmly, anything that smacked of his old dissolute life. He had sworn to himself that those days were behind him. But were they? The previous night would certainly give the lie to that!

Scowling, Tony wandered to the French doors and stared out at the beguiling view. Perhaps it had been a mistake to come back to Natchez. In England, he spent much of his time in the country, safely away from temptation, able, for long periods of time, to convince himself that he had exactly the life he wanted. Which was, of course, why he was so restless and thought he needed a change.

With relief he heard the door open behind him. However, the expression of barely suppressed excitement on Billingsley's face halted whatever Tony had been about to say.

Drawing himself up grandly, Billingsley announced, "A lady to see you, sir."

Billingsley instantly stepped aside, and into the room swept Tony's dearest dream and worst nightmare. Arabella Montgomery.

Almost smirking, Billingsley asked, "Will that be all, sir?"

Tony visibly started, and, tearing his stunned gaze from Arabella's set face, muttered, "Yes, of course, leave us."

Arabella's heart was pounding like a war drum, and she was furiously aware of the maddened leap her pulse had given at the first sight of those once-beloved features. The years, she thought waspishly, had treated him well—he was still the most attractive man she had ever met. Blast him!

Though his features remained composed, Tony was uneasily conscious of the fact that he was suddenly invigorated in a way he had not thought possible. He motioned to a lovely channel-backed chair covered in coffee brown silk. *By heaven,* he thought dazedly, *she hasn't changed a bit.* She was still as vital and vibrant as he had remembered. And yet it was as if he were seeing her for the first time, those mysteriously slanted golden brown eyes, the saucy nose, and full mouth. And that hair! Had it always been such a vivid shade of red? So brilliant and bright that it looked as if a touch would sear flesh.

Unable to help himself, his gaze flashed over her with frank appreciation. He noted the trim little figure, the surprisingly voluptuous bosom he had once tasted and teased, the narrow waist his hands had eagerly clasped, and the lush hips that had cradled him as he had brought them both ecstasy. Dear God! How had he managed to stay away from her for five long years?

Deliberately reminding himself of the precise reasons he had left Natchez all those years ago, Tony forcibly pushed away the painful memories. She had made her feelings for him quite clear, and he was not about to let himself in for that type of anguish ever again.

Determined to remain indifferent to her presence in his house—the house he had once hoped she would inhabit as his bride, he asked politely, "Will you have a seat?"

Arabella gave a stiff nod and sat down. She had not missed his swift appraisal, and she told herself that she was insulted and outraged. And her heart had not leaped with pleasure! Keeping her eyes fixed on a spot above his head, she said crisply, "You are no doubt surprised to see me."

Tony's long mouth quirked at the corner. "Surprised? Oh, I don't think that begins to describe what I am feeling."

She shot him a glance from under her long lashes. She reminded herself that her history with Tony Daggett had nothing to do with that day's meeting. The return of Jeremy's vowels was the only reason she was there. He was a lying scoundrel and less than dirt beneath her feet! He had bewitched her once and made her love him, then thrown it all back in her face. She loathed him.

But confronted by the flesh-and-blood man who had haunted her dreams, face-to-face with the sweet lover who had taught her the joys of passion, she discovered that her heart and brain were in decided conflict.

Angry at her unruly emotions, she focused on the task in front of her. Taking a deep breath, she said bluntly, "I have just come from Oakmont. Daniel Leyton informed me that you are now the owner of Jeremy's vowels. Is this true?"

Whatever Tony had expected her to say, it certainly

hadn't been that. Frowning, he glanced at the pile of vowels and miscellany lying carelessly on the mahogany table where he had so recently rested his feet. *Jeremy? Who the devil is Jeremy and, more importantly, why do his vowels matter to Arabella?*

An icy chill went through him. Not, he hoped with a fierceness that startled him, a husband. But if not a husband, then what?

When he remained silent, Arabella continued uncertainly, "You do remember Jeremy? My brother?"

Her brother. Thank God! He did vaguely remember a blond-haired stripling, a pleasant youth.

"Er, yes, I do, now that you mention him. It is his vowels that Leyton lost to me last night?"

"Yes, and I want them back," Arabella said grimly. "Leyton and that blackguard Walcott had no business seducing Jeremy the way they did. They cheated him."

"Ah, and Jeremy has, of course, accused them of this?" Tony inquired silkily, deciding that fate had finally dealt him a most interesting hand—*most* interesting. His boredom was gone. The feeling of melancholy that had lately assailed him vanished, and, inexplicably, he felt like laughing out loud. Life was suddenly extremely enticing. And he was going to see that it stayed that way!

"Well, not exactly," Arabella admitted. Her expression earnest, she added, "You see, they induced him to drink too much, and then they encouraged him to gamble."

One of Tony's slimly arched brows rose. "Their actions may have been objectionable, but unless, er, Jeremy, has some sort of proof that they actually, ah, fuzzed the cards, I don't see what you expect me to do about it."

As he had known she would, Arabella rose to the bait. "I expect," she said through gritted teeth, her fingers tightly clasping the portfolio she held in her lap, "you to return his vowels to me."

Tony sat down in a matching chair across from her, his long breeches-clad legs stretched out in front of him. His black boots rested not two inches from the flounced hem of her yellow gown.

With an effort Arabella resisted the urge to jerk her feet away as one would from a flame that had burned too near. She suddenly felt too warm, and wondered again if confronting him had been her wisest course. And again she reminded herself it had been the only course.

"Just like that?" Tony asked idly, once he was comfortable. "You just expect me to turn over the vowels?"

"Yes, yes I do." She hesitated. Nobility had never mattered to Tony, but she had to try. The family was dependent upon her. "It would be the noble thing to do."

Tony snorted. "And when, my dear little Elf, have you known me to do the noble thing?" His gaze hardened. "In fact, I think that it was my lack of nobility that caused you to end our betrothal, was it not?"

"I do not want to talk about that!" Arabella snapped. "Our history has nothing to do with this."

"Oh, I beg to differ with you, my sweet. I think it does. I doubt very much that you approached Leyton and simply demanded the vowels back from him. Only to me would you dare such a thing."

Arabella flushed. "You're right. I didn't. I offered

him a trade, and, naturally, I am willing to make the same trade with you."

Tony looked interested. "And? This trade is?"

"Greenleigh and my other lands for Jeremy's vowels."

"Just what the devil has that young fool brother of yours been up to?" Tony demanded with a frown, aware that she had just offered him everything she owned. "Does your esteemed father know what you are up to? What his son and heir has been doing?"

Arabella felt her eyes sting and she looked down at her hands. "My father is dead. He d-d-died two years ago."

"I'm sorry to hear that," Tony said quietly, his face softening. He resisted an urge to touch her. "I know that you were very close. You must miss him a great deal."

Arabella looked away. "Yes. It has been difficult for us."

Something occurred to him, and, rising to his feet, he leafed through the papers on the table. Finding what he was looking for, he whistled under his breath when he realized the enormity of Arabella's plight. No wonder she had come to him. That damn silly brother of hers had lost Highview! He glanced through the vowels again. And nearly all of the Montgomery fortune, if he remembered correctly.

Impetuously, he swung around, his first instinct simply to hand her the vowels that she so obviously wanted. His mouth twisted. *And she had to want them most desperately if her need has brought her to me!* he thought cynically.

But before he could act, Arabella straightened in her

chair, and, opening the portfolio, said briskly, "I know that Greenleigh cannot compare to Highview, but I am willing to trade you for Jeremy's vowels." As his expression darkened, she added gamely, "It w-w-will not be an even trade, but it will a-a-at least give you some recompense." Her eyes unknowingly pleading, she held out a sheaf of folded papers with a hand that shook slightly.

Tony was furious. Did she really believe that he was such a villain that he would allow her to beggar herself to save her family? Well, why not? he reminded himself viciously. Hadn't she refused to marry him five years ago because she believed him the blackest villain alive?

"Put your bloody deeds away!" he said savagely. "I don't want them—and I damn well won't take them."

Already shaken and distressed, his words flicked her on the raw, and before she could stop herself, she burst out bitterly, "I should have known you would act this way! You never cared who you hurt as long as you got what you wanted. I can see that you haven't changed." She flashed him a contemptuous glance. "Will it pleasure you to see us thrown out of Highview? Will you come and oversee our removal from our home yourself. Or will you simply send one of your minions to do the task?" She made a sound, more sob than laugh. "Or will you make another wager with your friend Blackburne? Betting on how long it will take us to leave?"

Tony's face went white. He snarled something under his breath and, his eyes glittering dangerously, strode up to her. Catching her shoulders he roughly shook her. "You dare," he said thickly, "you dare say that to me?"

Stonily she met his fierce gaze. "Why not? Wagering

seems to give you great pleasure. Especially wagers that bring others personal pain."

His nostrils flaring, he took a deep breath and deliberately removed his hands from her. Glancing at her with open dislike, he growled, "Despite my many sins, and I will not deny that there are many, do you know that I have never laid hands on a woman in anger before in my life? And considering the provocation, you are damned lucky I did no more than shake you."

"Very well, I will consider myself lucky," she said stiffly, conscious of the shameful pleasure that had knifed through her at his touch. Conscious, too, of the heat and vitality radiating from his big body as he remained standing in front of her. He was wearing a white-linen shirt, carelessly opened at the throat, and the evocative sight of that strong brown throat, a throat she had once pressed wild, hungry kisses upon, and the well-remembered scent of his body was almost more than she could bear.

Tony was assailed with memories as potent as hers, and he ached for all that he had lost through his own foolishness. She would never forgive him, and he doubted that his own considerable pride would ever allow him to ask for forgiveness. After all, he *had* made that damned wager with Blackburne.

Fearful that she would give way to the powerful emotions that curled and clawed through her, Arabella took several steps away from him. Turning her back, she asked painfully, "How soon do you wish us to vacate Highview?" She swallowed back a sob. "It w-w-will take my stepmother several d-d-days to pack."

Tony's hands clenched into fists. He took a steadying

breath. "I never said that you had to leave Highview," he muttered, his thoughts racing.

Her eyes wide, hope brimming in their golden brown depths, she swung around to look at him. "You'll make the trade?" she asked breathlessly.

Tony bit back a curse, on the verge of grabbing the vowels and thrusting them into her hands, when a decidedly reprehensible idea flitted through his mind. But, if he were to propose it, reprehensible or not, it would give him something he desperately, passionately wanted. The thing he wanted most in the world. Arabella in his arms once more.

Assessingly he eyed her, a painful ache in the region of his heart. Was he really that base? he wondered. To use her unfortunate circumstances for his own needs? And if he did not, if he simply handed her the vowels, she would thank him and then be gone again. Out of his life once more. Oh, she might think kindly of him for the moment; no doubt she would even feel gratitude. But gratitude was the last thing he had ever wanted from Arabella Montgomery.

As Arabella waited expectantly, her lovely eyes fixed on his, Tony swiftly considered his next move. She already thought him a most-despicable creature, and if he made the outrageous proposal, it would only confirm her worst opinion of him. So what, he asked himself harshly, did he have to lose?

Recklessly, not giving himself time to think, he said, "I am willing to make a trade."

A blinding smile lit Arabella's expressive features. "Greenleigh for Highview?"

Tony shook his head. "I said *a* trade, not that trade."

Puzzled, her smile faded. "Then what? I have nothing else of value."

A distinctly sensual spark lit his blue eyes. "Ah, Elf, you are wrong there. You do have something of great value to offer me—your own sweet self."

Arabella looked blank. "W-w-what? You want to m-m-marry me?"

Tony's lips curled. If he thought he could really blackmail her into marrying him he would, but he doubted that she would tie herself to him for the rest of her life, even to save her family. No. She'd not marry him. But she might be willing to put herself in his hands for a specific period of time. And though he knew it was base and dishonorable, he was willing to risk it. For a little while at least, she would be his.

But he was curious and he asked, "*Would* you marry me? For Jeremy's vowels?"

Arabella gaped at him, hardly daring to believe what he was proposing. Could she marry him? Live the rest of her life as his wife? The memory of the pain and humiliation of their last meeting came rushing back, and she put out a hand as if warding off a terrible fate. No, she could never face that sort of anguish for the remainder of her life. "Do not ask that of me," she whispered. "I could not bear it."

Harshly, Tony said, "You have nothing to worry about; marriage between us is out of the question. We trod that path once before, and it brought us both misery. No, what I am proposing is a far different arrangement this time."

Arabella paled, her skin starkly white against the flaming red of her hair, her eyes dark with shock. His meaning was clear, and she could not believe that even Tony could stoop so low.

But apparently he could, for he closed the distance between them and pulled her into his arms. Brushing his warm, knowing mouth against hers, he murmured, "My mistress. Become my mistress, and the vowels need never be called in."

Chapter Four

❧

*H*eld firmly in Tony's strong embrace, his warm lips sliding lazily against hers, the taste and scent of him making her dizzy with remembered passion, for one dangerous moment Arabella forgot the past. Mindlessly, she let him kiss her as he willed, her mouth soft and sweet under his, as the portfolio dropped forgotten to the floor, she flung her arms wildly around his neck.

Tony made a muffled sound when her arms enclosed him, and his embrace tightened. He teased them both by his restraint, his mouth moving seductively across hers, his teeth nipping arousingly at her bottom lip. Arabella sighed, filled with longing. It was only when she caught herself desperately clutching his dark head that reality exploded in her brain.

As if bitten by a copperhead, she leaped out of his arms. Cheeks flushed, her straw hat askew, she glared at him. "Why you devious, ass-eared, underhanded beast! How dare you!" she exclaimed furiously.

Feeling oddly pleased with himself, Tony propped

his hips against the mahogany table. Crossing his arms over his chest, he said mockingly, "Oh, come now, Elf, you can do better than that! I seem to recall that the last time you called me names, it was something to the effect that I was a 'lying, scheming, despicable, blackhearted, pigheaded beast.'"

Instantly recovering herself, Arabella lowered her eyes, and said demurely, "You are mistaken. I did not call you a beast that time. I called you 'a lying, scheming, despicable, blackhearted, pigheaded, *dung-cock.*'"

Tony suppressed a laugh. Blue eyes gleaming, he replied, "Do you know, I think you are right. It was dung-cock—that lamentable memory of mine."

Arabella looked at him. "I do not think that there is a thing wrong with your memory."

Tony nodded, his expression unreadable. "I remember everything about you," he said softly.

"If you do," she said sharply, "then you must recall that I loathe you. And I am sure that you would not enjoy a mistress who shudders with revulsion at your very touch."

Tony's brow rose. "Did you shudder just now, my sweet? I don't seem to remember that particular reaction from you."

Arabella gritted her teeth. "You caught me by surprise."

"Ah, and so, if I gave you fair warning that I was going to take you in my arms again and kiss you as I just did, you would—er—'shudder with revulsion'?" He smiled cheerfully at her. "Shall we try it and see?"

As he started forward, Arabella cried, "Stay where you are! Don't touch me!"

Tony sank back into his original position, looking extremely satisfied with himself. "Well, that is an experiment we shall have to try soon, but not right now. Right now we have a proposal in front of us." He reached around and picked up Jeremy's vowels. "I put these in my safe where they stay until . . . oh, shall we say, until I grow tired of your shudders?"

"You are undoubtedly the blackest, the vilest—!"

"Dung-cock?" Tony supplied helpfully.

"Worse!"

"That may be true, sweet, but you still haven't given me an answer."

Indecisively she stared at him.

"You're very sure that you won't just take Greenleigh in exchange for Jeremy's vowels?" she asked.

Tony shook his head, his blue eyes locked on hers. "No. I don't want Greenleigh. I want you."

"As your mistress," she said tightly.

He nodded. "As my mistress." Softly he added, "Since our liaison would be secret, as I am sure you would demand, you have no fear of your reputation— only the two of us would know of our intimate relationship. My intention is not to ruin you, or create more scandal." He smiled grimly. "You can continue to disdain and loathe me in public to your heart's content . . . provided in private you are in my arms."

Arabella could not meet his gaze. She was so angry and yes, she would admit, hurt by his suggestion, that she wanted to do nothing more than slap his arrogant face and storm out of the room. But that was not the only emotion which churned in her breast. She was also unwillingly intrigued by the suggestion. He wanted her . . . as his mistress.

Turning away from him, she stared out the window. She didn't know what she wanted to do at that moment, but she was certain that she did not want to walk away from Tony Daggett, beast that he was. Glancing back at him, she asked, "May I have time to consider your, um, offer?"

"No," he said bluntly, his indigo blue eyes unfathomable. He was not going to give her time to consider all the implications of his offer. And he certainly didn't want to give her enough time for that clever little mind of hers to consider the possibility that he might be bluffing. At the moment, he had her trapped and thoroughly convinced that he would coolly toss her family out of its home, and he was going to take full advantage of the situation.

Arabella showed him her back, thinking hard. Becoming Tony's mistress, she admitted reluctantly, did have some merit to it.

It was a shocking thought, but Arabella was not shocked. She was, in fact, increasingly fascinated by the idea. A mistress had so much more freedom than a wife. As Tony's wife, she would have belonged to him as much as any of his possessions. Her lands and fortune would have become his; he could do as he willed with them, and her. But as his mistress . . .

She realized that she was already halfway to agreeing to his disgraceful bargain. If Tony hadn't stated that their relationship would be private, her decision would have been much more difficult to make. Could she trust him to keep his word?

She had trusted him once, and look where it had got her. But in this instance, it would be as much to his advantage to keep their relationship a secret as it was to hers. He might turn an indifferent shoulder to most scandal, but one of this magnitude would turn even his most loyal friends against him. Why, she thought acidly, he might even be forced to marry her. And he wouldn't want that! So, yes, she trusted him to keep her name pure and unsullied.

Thoughtfully she tapped a finger against her lips. She and Tony both agreed that marriage to each other was not for them. She was not a silly young maid. She was thirty-two years old, and she had already given this man her virginity. It was highly unlikely that she would ever marry, so there was not the problem of offering a husband soiled goods.

As Tony's secret mistress, she would, she supposed, continue to live her life just as she did now. Her money and plantations would still be hers. To the world and her family, she would still simply be Miss Arabella Montgomery of Highview. But there would also be secret times that she would share Tony's bed, times that they would meet privately, and he would show her again the pleasures to be had between a man and a woman. A funny little knot clenched low in her belly, and she was aware of a sudden heat between her thighs.

She was, she decided, quite wanton—and probably wicked in the bargain. But wicked or not, she rather thought that she would enjoy being Tony's mistress. And of course, she reminded herself wryly, she could always soothe her conscience by telling herself that she had sacrificed herself for the family.

Straightening her shoulders, she swung around to face him. "Very well," she said, "I shall become your mistress."

A crooked smile on his lips, he murmured, "A wise decision, Elf." His eyes darkened. "One that I will take great pains to make certain you find pleasure in."

Pushing away from the table, his intention obvious, Tony walked toward her.

Suddenly nervous about what she had let herself in for, Arabella took a step backward, and asked uneasily, "Oh, do we have to, um, start right now?"

Tony grinned. "I was merely going to kiss you to seal our bargain—not toss you on the floor and make love to you." His gaze ran appreciatively over her neat little form. "Although," he murmured, "that isn't such a bad idea."

"Oh, please wait!" Arabella protested, discovering that she wasn't quite as blasé and brazen as she had thought. "I have agreed to become your mistress; isn't that enough for you for one day?" Her eyes darting around the room, she muttered, "Shouldn't we discuss the terms or conditions of the, ah, trade, first?"

"There is only one condition—you, in my bed," Tony answered bluntly.

"But you said you would keep my reputation safe!" Arabella protested. "You said I could trust you! I mean, I can't—! There is my family to consider!" Her hands tightened into fists. "I'll not face another scandal because of you!"

Tony was willing to be generous. It was obvious that she was having second thoughts, and he didn't want to frighten her into changing her mind—and he *had* promised to keep her reputation safe.

Taking her arm, he led her back to her chair. Sitting in the chair across from her, he said amiably, "I agreed to keep our arrangement secret, and I shall. To avoid scandal and gossip we shall have to be very discreet."

Arabella nodded, "Very discreet," she breathed fervently, thinking of her stepmother and the children.

While he had maintained mistresses in the past, this was an entirely new situation for Tony. Previously, he had simply set up a nice little house in a pleasant part of town, installed his current high-flyer, and paid her visits whenever the mood struck him. Or, when his mistress had been someone of his own class, she had been a sophisticated married woman or widow, who had known precisely what she was about. Arabella was none of those. If their liaison became known, it would ruin her. She needed, he thought with a flash of protectiveness, shielding. Above all, her reputation must be safeguarded.

His jaw tightened. He wouldn't like having to kill any man who dared to make a disparaging comment about her. But he would.

"It is obvious that, for the most part, our meetings will have to be in the afternoon. There would be too much speculation if you suddenly began to go out at night alone. And then there is the problem of a proper place to rendezvous. We cannot use any public tavern or inn—and you obviously," he said slowly, thinking aloud, "cannot come here very often for an afternoon of trysting. Nor can I march into Highview whenever I like and go upstairs to your bedroom."

Arabella shut her eyes and muttered, "Merciful heavens, no!"

"So we will have to find a place that is easily accessible to both of us, but, er, discreet."

Tony rapidly considered and discarded several locales. "Ah, I have it," he said suddenly, an odd expression in his blue eyes. "The hunting lodge at Greenleigh. I'm sure you remember it."

"You really are a cruel beast, aren't you?" Arabella said quietly, her eyes dark with pain she could not hide. It had been at Greenleigh's hunting lodge that they had met and he had seduced her. And it had been at that same hunting lodge where she had found him in bed with another woman, and all her dreams had ended.

He shrugged, his features unreadable. "It is the best place—private, secluded, and very comfortable as I recall. And since you own it, no one will think it strange that you visit the place."

Not willing to give him the satisfaction of learning that even five years after the fact the lodge still held unbearably painful memories for her, she said stiffly, "Very well. The Greenleigh hunting lodge. And how do you intend to let me know when you . . ." Her face burned fiery red, and she cleared her throat before she managed to add, "When you decide you, um, need me." She could hardly believe what she had just said. Could hardly believe the entire situation. It seemed incredible, a bad dream, that she was calmly sitting here cold-bloodedly discussing the place and manner in which she would toss away the precepts of a lifetime and become Tony's mistress. Not his wife, she reminded herself painfully, but his mistress.

Tony suddenly reached across the short distance that separated them. Taking her hand in his, he lifted it to his lips and pressed a gentle kiss into the palm. Slipping to his knee in front of her, he said huskily, "It will not be so very bad, Elf. I will treat you gently, and I swear to you that I will allow no shame to come to you."

"You swore once to love me—how can I believe you now?" Arabella asked unhappily.

His mouth tightened. "I seem to recall that you did some swearing of your own—you swore that you loved me and also that you would marry me."

Arabella snatched her hand away from him and sprang to her feet, nearly knocking him over in her agitation. Glaring at him, she snapped, "I think, considering the circumstances at that time, that it was only wise and prudent of me to change my mind. There is hardly anyone who would disagree that finding my fiancé in the arms of his former mistress wasn't reason enough to cry off."

Tony rose to his feet, his face hard and set. "I was drunk! I don't even know how she came to be there—I had broken off with her months previously."

Arabella gave an angry titter, her heart squeezing painfully as the vivid memory of Tony lying in bed with that, *that* creature flashed across her brain. "And that is your excuse for making love to Molly Dobson, and I might add, in the very same bed where I had given you my virginity—that you were *drunk*?"

Wearily, Tony replied, "It is the truth."

Aware that there was nothing to be gained by raking over the bitter coals of the past, Arabella said, "It doesn't matter. It is over and done with, and we should both be grateful that we came to our senses before it was too late."

Tony's mouth twisted and he turned away. "Yes, of course," he said dryly. "We are to be congratulated on our narrow escape."

She should have been happy that he was following her lead, but his words left her oddly dissatisfied. She picked up the portfolio where it had fallen on the floor when Tony had kissed her, and muttered, "I must be leaving. It will be dark soon."

Tony glanced over his shoulder at her. "I suppose my offer of escort would be immediately thrown back in my face?"

"How clever of you to guess," Arabella returned sweetly, making a halfhearted attempt to straighten her straw hat.

Walking over to her, Tony undid the green-satin ribbon from beneath her chin and, arranging the wide-brimmed hat on her head to his satisfaction, deftly retied the ribbon into a saucy bow. "There," he said with a lopsided smile, "you look presentable again."

They were standing only inches apart, their eyes locked on each other. Unhappily, Arabella searched his features, wishing that he did not still hold a great deal of fascination for her. She should loathe him, yet she knew she would be lying to herself if she said that she did.

Prompted, perhaps, by the memory of that magical time when she had believed fiercely that he loved her, that all the gossip and stories about him were a gross exaggeration, she asked in a little voice, "Are you really going to force me to become your mistress?"

Tony gently tipped up her chin. "I would rather not have to use force, but since you leave me no other way, yes, I am," he said softly. "I would prefer that you come to me willingly, but since that occurrence is highly unlikely . . . There is only one way, sweetheart, that you can have Jeremy's vowels—and you know what it is. The choice is yours."

Jerking her chin out of his hand, she said bitterly, "There is no choice, and you know it."

"Well, you could call my hand," he said without thinking.

Arabella's eyes narrowed. "You mean refuse your infamous offer and wait and see if you carry through on your threat to leave my family homeless?"

Despite the yawning hole that had suddenly appeared in front of him, Tony nodded. "Do you want to risk it?" he asked carefully, his gaze cool and indifferent. "We can certainly do it that way if you like."

Arabella shook her head. There was a time she would never have believed him capable of such a cruel act, but that had been before the debacle with Molly Dobson.

"No. I will become your mistress." She hesitated and glanced at him uneasily. "But before our, um, liaison is begun, I would have you give me some sort of written assurance that at some point in time"—her mouth curved downward—"after, naturally, I have served my sentence as your paramour, that Jeremy's vowels will be given to me."

It was all Tony could do not to smash a fist into the table. She believed him that base! To force her to become his mistress and then renege on returning the vowels! Stiffly, he said, "Of course. I shall write a letter stating something to the effect that the vowels are yours . . . after a period of time." He cast her a bitter look. "Since it is well-known that my affairs do not last long, shall we say, six months from today? And of course, there should be a provision, dangerous for me should you decide that six months is too long to suffer my attentions, that if I should die, the vowels are yours. I will give the document to you when we next meet."

"I would not murder you," Arabella shot back, furious and hurt that he believed her capable of such a dastardly act. "Although it is a wonder that someone hasn't murdered you long before now!"

He bowed, a twisted smile upon his hard mouth. "So. We are agreed. Now we have only to decide when we are to meet at the lodge. Are there any days that are impossible for you?"

Arabella swallowed. This was really happening. She was going to be Tony's mistress! And they were discussing it with the same cool demeanor as persons merely agreeing to meet for tea! "S-S-Sunday would be difficult," she finally managed to say. "The family always spends the day together."

"Very well, we shall not meet on Sundays." He glanced back at her. "Friday. We shall meet this Friday at two o'clock. It will probably be easier if we have no set time and day. On Friday we can decide on the next time. Will that suffice?"

Her throat tight, Arabella nodded, clutching the portfolio for dear life. Merciful heavens! What was she doing? Was saving the family worth what she had agreed to do? To become Tony's mistress? Had she gone mad?

Those questions were still whirling around in her mind when Tony tossed her up into the cart a few minutes later and bid her farewell. Dazedly, she picked up the reins and urged her little mare into a gentle trot. *She had agreed to become Tony Daggett's mistress!*

Tony watched her drive away and once she had left the circular drive and started down the long, winding trail that led to the main roadway, he turned and bounded quickly up the steps. Inside the house, he snapped to Billingsley, who was hovering nearby, "I shall be gone for a while. Expect me back when you see me."

Not ten minutes later, he was astride a powerful, blaze-faced chestnut stallion jestingly dubbed Sugar. Tony directed his mount into the woods that lay to the east of the stables. There was just one more little task at hand and then . . .

Nervously Arabella noticed that dusk was rapidly falling, and she clucked to the mare, gently tapping her with the whip she held in her hand. Obediently, the little black horse, Sable, lengthened her stride.

Arabella was not more than forty minutes from home, but darkness was falling rapidly. She bit her lip, wishing for the first time that she had brought a servant along with her. She should have done so for propriety's sake alone, never mind that she would be less apprehensive at the prospect of driving in the dark if someone had been with her.

In the fading light, she glanced at the lamp that hung at one side of the black-leather dash and decided that it would be prudent to light it immediately, while she could still see. Pulling her mare to a halt, she wasted precious seconds getting the carriage lamp lit.

The flickering yellow glow from the candle in the lamp made her immediately feel better, even if its small dancing beam of light did not travel farther than the vicinity of the cart and the horse. Telling herself that she had nothing to fear she once again set the mare into motion.

Yet tales of Samuel Mason and his gang of cutthroats, or the terrible Harpe brothers and the unspeakable things they did to those unfortunate enough to cross their path, flitted through her mind. Even reminding herself that she was miles from the Natchez Trace where they preyed did not lessen her growing unease.

Almost immediately there was a loud, terrifying crashing in the underbrush to her right and a horse and rider suddenly plunged onto the road right in front of the cart. Sable instantly shied and reared.

Frightened, but busy with controlling her startled mare, it was a few seconds before Arabella could consider her own peril. Having gained some control of her horse, heart slamming painfully in her chest, she squinted into the darkness.

The fitful light from the carriage lamp dimly revealed the newcomer and he seemed huge, a scarlet scarf covering the lower half of his face and a black hat pulled across his forehead. He was seated astride a large, dark horse; his mount was positioned sideways across in the road in front of her, blocking her path.

"Your valuables," barked the man upon the horse. "Give them to me."

Hardly able to believe that she was actually being robbed, Arabella stared dumbfoundedly at the man before her. There was just enough light from the carriage lamp for her to see that a long black pistol was leveled at her. He waved the weapon slightly, and snapped, "Give me your valuables. Now!"

Not about to argue with a man holding a pistol aimed at her, Arabella instantly transferred the reins and whip to one hand and with the other reached for her reticule and the portfolio, which was lying on the floor of the cart near her feet. Her fingers had actually touched the portfolio when she remembered, with a spurt of panic, the precious deeds it contained.

If her heart had already been banging frantically away inside her chest, it now felt as if it had fallen to her toes. She could not give up the deeds! She could not!

She straightened back up and facing the robber, she said breathlessly, "I have nothing. I am wearing no jewels, and I have no money with me."

The man swore and snarled, "If you do not wish to have me put a bullet through you, Madame, you will give me your belongings and let me satisfy myself as to their contents."

"No," Arabella replied stubbornly, her fingers unconsciously tightening on the reins, causing the mare to dance and jib. "Go away and let me be," she said with more confidence than she felt.

"By God, you're a stubborn baggage! Hand me your belongings. Now!"

Suddenly Sable struck out at the horse in front of

her. The bigger horse squealed and wheeled away, startling the robber. His pistol went off. The boom and distinctive smell of black powder exploded through the air.

Arabella paid the shot no heed—she was too busy fighting to keep Sable from tangling in the traces.

The other horse was rearing and wheeling in fright, the rider swearing and sawing at the reins. Just as it dawned on Arabella that this was a perfect opportunity to attempt an escape, the rider got his horse under control. Swinging around, he positioned the big horse at the side of Arabella's cart. Staring down at her, he said with an ugly note in his voice. "The next bullet will not be wasted. Give me your belongings, or I shall kill you and take them off your dead body. The choice is yours."

It was sheer temper rather than reason that prompted her next actions. She'd already been forced to make one earthshaking choice that day, and she was damned if this vile robber was going to force her to make another. Besides, everything she owned in the world was represented by the contents of the portfolio.

She struck out blindly with the small whip, its lash catching the robber full on the side of the face. He blinked and swore at its vicious bite, and Arabella immediately struck again putting all the force of her own small body behind it; this time her objective was the hand that held the pistol. A yelp came from the robber, and the pistol went spinning.

"Why you little—you're going to pay for that!" he growled, reaching out for her.

"Touch the lady," suddenly drawled a new voice

from behind them, "and I am very much afraid that it will be the last thing you ever do."

The robber froze, and Arabella's head whipped around to stare behind her. Peering into the darkness, she could barely make out the white blaze of a horse and the tall form upon it. But she would have known that voice anywhere, and she stammered, "T-T-Tony?"

Chapter Five

His heart began to beat again as he realized that Arabella was safe, that he wasn't too late. After one brief, all-encompassing glance over her, Tony bent a cold eye on the would-be robber as he said dryly, "Yes, it is I. I trust you were not expecting anyone else?"

Despite the gravity of the situation, Arabella squelched a mad urge to giggle. "N- N-No," she choked out, torn between fear and nervous amusement.

Arabella's features were clearly agitated, her golden brown eyes huge in her white, strained face, but it was obvious to Tony that she had not been physically harmed. Having satisfied himself that she was safe, Tony turned his full attention on the robber and, bringing his horse alongside the other man's, he reached across, intending to snatch away the face-concealing scarlet scarf. But the robber had other ideas and jerked his head violently away and flung up his arm even as he gave a frightful shout.

Already spooked, Sable lunged forward and Arabella

frantically clutched at the reins, which had been resting limply in her lap. Tony's stallion, Sugar, snorted and tossed his handsome head, taking a half dozen swift, choppy steps backward. It all happened in a split second, enough time for the robber savagely to dig his heels into the flank of his horse and put several yards between himself and the others.

Swearing under his breath, Tony immediately fired, but the shot went wild, Sugar's continuing antics spoiling his aim. As the shot echoed through the night, Sugar and the little mare danced uneasily, and Tony and Arabella were as much concerned controlling their animals as about the escaping robber. But the incident was over almost before it began. By the time they had their animals safely under hand, the robber and his horse had disappeared into the forest, leaving Tony and Arabella alone on the road.

There was silence for a moment, Tony glaring into the darkness where the robber had last been seen. "The Devil! I should have been prepared for some sort of trick."

"It doesn't matter," Arabella said. "We are neither one of us hurt, and he rode away empty-handed."

Tony nodded and brought Sugar alongside her cart. He asked gruffly, "He did not harm you? You are not hurt in any way?"

She smiled mistily up at him and shook her head. "No. I was frightened, but that was the worst of it."

"Then I suggest, before who knows what else befalls us, that we get you safely to Highview. Your friend may have companions."

More shaken than she cared to admit, Arabella

agreed, and a moment later, with Tony riding beside the cart, they began to move down the road at a quick pace. There was a frown between Tony's eyes as he kept a prancing Sugar beside the cart, and after a moment he said, "I know I have been away for several years, but I do not remember that this particular road held much allure for bandits and the like. Does this sort of thing happen often?"

Arabella shook her head. "No. There are robberies and murders regularly along the Trace, and there is a large, lawless population in the area. Robberies do occur somewhat frequently, but most of the roads near Natchez itself are reasonably safe. This road is not heavily traveled—mainly those of us who live on it use it. I would not think that it would be a profitable area in which to wait for suitable victims." She frowned. "It was extremely odd."

Damned odd, he decided as he glanced at her, taking in the cart, the mare, and Arabella's apparel. There was nothing obvious that he could see which would have tempted a robber. Unless the thief had been after something not so obvious? "It certainly was not a very bright thing for him to have done," he said slowly. "Even a dunce would have been able to see that you were unlikely to be carrying anything of value."

Arabella nodded, sending him a rueful smile. "I will confess that I had been thinking of Mason and the Harpes, but I never truly expected to be accosted that way. I cannot imagine what he thought he would gain."

"Unless," Tony said thoughtfully, "he already knew that you had something that he wanted."

Arabella gasped, her eyes wide. "You mean he was waiting specifically for me?"

"It is a distinct possibility and makes as much sense for what happened as anything else. We must assume that he was not after jewels and such since you are not wearing any. And there is only one thing of value, besides your own sweet self, that I know of that he could have been after."

Arabella couldn't help flushing at Tony's reference to herself, but she caught her breath in alarm as his words sank in. "My deeds!" she nearly squeaked.

"That would be my surmise, and if we go on that assumption, I rather think it narrows down the list of people who would have attempted to rob you. Who knew, besides myself, of course, that you had the deeds to Greenleigh with you?"

"Well, Mr. Haight, our attorney knew, but I cannot imagine Mr. Haight deciding to rob me. He did not even know where I was going today." Her gaze narrowed. "Besides, the robber was too tall. Haight is rather a small man and wears spectacles. Which leaves only Daniel Leyton. He knew about the deeds because I made him the same offer I did you, Jeremy's vowels for the deeds to Greenleigh."

"From what I recall of Leyton, he was always on the brink of ruin," Tony said slowly. "And he is the right size for our would-be thief."

They rode along in silence as they both considered the situation. "But the deeds themselves would do him no good." Arabella said eventually. "He could not attempt to take Greenleigh from me without exposing the fact that he was the one to steal them in the first place."

Tony flashed her a look. Dryly he asked, "Hasn't the notion of blackmail crossed your mind, sweet? Once he had the deeds, he could easily extort money from you for their return. And since Leyton is always just a step ahead of the moneylenders, I wouldn't be at all surprised if that was his plan."

"Oh! I hadn't thought of that."

"Well, it is high time you start realizing that not everyone is the honest little citizen that you are!"

The moment of camaraderie between them was gone, and Arabella shot him a frosty look. "Of course, you are absolutely correct, I *should* have been aware of that fact—especially after this afternoon and the deplorable bargain you forced upon me."

"I did not force you, Elf. You made the decision to become my mistress."

Her temper sparking, she glared at him. "You left me no choice—it was either that or see my family thrown out of their home and reduced to poverty."

Tony chuckled, his dark blue eyes dancing. "Oh, sweetheart! Only you would consider it poverty to be compelled to live at Greenleigh and make do on the comfortable fortune your mother left you."

"Do you know," she said sweetly, "that you are the most disagreeable, rude, detestable creature I have ever known? And do not again explain to me the alternative—I might change my mind."

Tony abruptly reached down and effortlessly plucked Arabella from the cart. Despite her protests, he deftly positioned her on the saddle in front of him and proceeded to kiss her soundly. Lifting his hard mouth from hers a long, dizzying moment later, he stared down into her dazed features, and said softly, "But you will not, will you?"

Her head spinning, her lips still tingling from the warm imprint of his, Arabella slowly shook her head. "No. I gave my word."

Depositing her back in the cart, he flashed her a bone-melting smile. "It is a good thing that one of us has ethics, is it not?"

"Oh, hush, you wretched beast!" she said crossly. She picked up the reins from the floor of the cart and, clucking softly to Sable, urged the mare forward once again.

Riding alongside of the cart, Tony sent Arabella a surreptitious look, noting in the pale flickering light of the cart lamp that her cheeks were flushed with what he suspected was temper and that her lips were set in a rebellious line.

She was obviously thoroughly incensed with him, and he smiled. Good! He had ruffled her feathers quite enough for one night and once the white frightened look was gone from her face, Tony let her simmer in silence. That was far better for Arabella than being frightened. His mouth thinned. As for Daniel Leyton, that was another matter entirely, and just as soon as he saw Arabella safely to Highview, he was going to pay him a visit. A visit, he rather thought, that Mr. Leyton would find most unpleasant.

Arabella was busy with her own thoughts. Tony had been right; she was extremely annoyed with him and not the least frightened anymore. He was the most outrageously vexing man she knew but, she supposed darkly, she should be grateful for his convenient arrival. Certainly the situation might have had a far different ending if he had not come along when he had. She frowned suddenly. How was it, she wondered suspiciously, that he had just happened to be in the right spot at the right time?

Abruptly she demanded, "What were you doing on the road so opportunely?"

"Following you," he returned easily, having expected the question, once she'd had time to consider the situation. "And I cannot tell you how very much I regret the fact that I had not yet caught up with you before your, er, meeting with the robber." His face grew grim. "I do not ever want to feel as I did when I heard that shot ring out, knowing you were on the road alone."

She thought about his explanation, stubbornly ignoring his words of concern for her safety. Finally, nodding, she came to a conclusion. "I refused your escort home," she said resignedly, "and you, in your usual high-handed, arrogant fashion, decided to escort me to Highview anyway."

"Ah, there you have it, my sweet."

Beyond flashing him an exasperated glance, Arabella said nothing. With no little aggravation she recalled that blithely going his own way, no matter what others may have wished, was one of Tony's most vexing traits—that and not being the least regretful or contrite about it. Arabella's teeth ground together almost audibly. He was indeed the most exasperating, annoying, and enraging man she had ever come across. She slanted him a glance. And the dearest, whispered her heart.

The gleaming lights of the big house at Highview came into view from between the trees, and once they had turned their horses down the long, gently curved carriageway, Tony pulled Sugar to a halt. "I suspect," he said, "that you would prefer to arrive alone. I shall wait here, out of sight, until I see you mount the steps."

Having also pulled her mare to a stop, she sent him a searching look. "How can you be so thoughtful one minute and the next so, so—"

"Provoking? Vexing?" he supplied helpfully, a little smile lurking at the corner of his lips.

"All of those!"

He bent down and brushed a kiss across her mouth. "'Tis part of my great charm, Elf."

Willing to die rather than admit agreement, she snorted, and said, "Well, I must thank even an abominable rascal like you for your efforts this evening."

"Accepted," he replied with a mocking gleam in his eyes.

She gave him a stiff nod, undecided which she would like to do most—slap his handsome face or kiss that taunting mouth. "Very well then. Good evening."

"Until Friday at two o'clock," he reminded softly. "Do not forget that."

"I have not," she snapped, finally deciding that there would be much satisfaction in slapping that provoking face. She started to drive away when she remembered uneasily another of Tony's traits. Pulling Sable to a stop, she glanced back at him.

"You are not, I trust, going to do something silly like calling upon Daniel Leyton?"

He smiled, and she was not at all reassured. "Now why would I do that?" he asked silkily.

"Because you probably have this ridiculous notion

that someone should punish him for what he did—if he did it—and that you are the only person who can do it."

"Go home, Arabella," he said gently. "Do not worry overmuch about Leyton's hide."

It wasn't the answer she wanted, but she was well aware that it was the only answer he was going to give her. "I just wish for once," she snapped as she turned away and slapped the reins against Sable's haunches, "that you would meet your match and come across someone you cannot charm, bully, or buy!"

"But I already have, sweetheart," he muttered under his breath as he watched her speed down the carriage-way, the light from the cart lamp bobbing and blinking in the darkness. An oddly vulnerable expression on his face, he waited a few minutes longer until he saw the cart stop in front of the house and her small figure dart up the broad steps of Highview. "Believe me," he repeated again, "I already have."

As he turned Sugar away, his vulnerable expression disappeared and was replaced with one that would have given Arabella much to worry about. *And now,* Tony told himself grimly, *for Mr. Leyton.*

Mr. Leyton had troubles enough already without any help from Tony Daggett. The side of his face stinging painfully from the blow from Arabella's whip and his temper sorely tried by the failure of the robbery, he was in an ugly mood when he finally returned home. He tossed the reins of his lathered horse to the sullen-faced slave who met him at the stable door and, without a word, stalked away in the direction of the main house. Entering the house through a side door, he made his way to the large room where Arabella had found him earlier in the day. The house was quiet; despite the earliness of the hour, the few servants had been dismissed before he had departed on his mission. His failed mission, he thought with a scowl.

The scarlet scarf was still around his neck, and, with an angry movement, he ripped it off and threw it on the floor. The hat followed. *Damn and blast!* he thought furiously. Bad enough that the little shrew had held him at bay, but for Daggett to arrive! He was lucky to have escaped with his hide still intact.

The room he entered was in near darkness, the only light coming from a pair of candles burning fitfully in matching brass holders placed on the front edge of his desk. His thoughts as shadowy as the room, he considered what he'd like to have done to that little bitch Arabella as he strode to a long narrow table littered with bottles of liquors and various kinds of glassware. Pouring a snifter of brandy, he quickly downed it and poured another.

Had Daggett recognized him? He doubted it. In the darkness, he would not have even realized that it was Tony Daggett if it had not been for Arabella's calling out his name and the distinctive markings of the horse. Though Sugar had been in the district only a few weeks, the stallion's wide blaze and four high white stockings made him a notable animal, easily remembered and recognized. As for anyone recognizing his own horse, he was not worried—he had ridden a swift, nondescript bay gelding.

Still, he was uneasy. Daggett was unlikely to overlook the incident, and he cursed himself for not remembering Tony's penchant for meddling in affairs that were none of his business. He reminded himself with growing disquiet that Arabella could be considered Daggett's business. Unfinished business at that.

He felt relatively safe. If Tony did confront him, well, he was not unknown for his art of bluffing. As for the telltale whip mark on his face, it would fade in a day or two and, in the meantime, he would make himself unavailable for any meeting with Tony.

Feeling a little better, Leyton shrugged out of his dark gray coat, carelessly dropping it onto a chair. He caught sight of the scarf and hat lying where he had thrown them on the floor and stuffed them out of sight in one of the drawers of the handsome sideboard against the far wall. Except for the red welt on his face, and he could think of a dozen innocent reasons to explain its presence, there was nothing to connect him with an attempted robbery.

His mood lightening, he poured himself the third brandy in five minutes and sprawled comfortably in one of the chairs. He had failed. He could always try again. Although, he admitted, his task would be harder now.

The faint whisper of the French doors as they opened to admit a cloaked figure made him jerk uneasily in his chair. Recognizing his guest, he gave a nervous laugh, and said, "Devil take it! I wish you would not creep up on a fellow like that!"

The visitor shrugged and, after throwing his cloak on top of Leyton's jacket, casually helped himself to a snifter of brandy from the table. Gently swirling the amber-colored liquor, he sniffed the bouquet appreciatively and sank down in a chair across from Leyton.

Taking a sip of the brandy, he drawled lazily, "I have just had a most . . . interesting experience. Would you like me to tell you about it?"

Leyton stiffened, uneasiness filling him. "Why," he asked with more indifference than he felt, "do you think that I would be interested in your activities?"

"Oh, I just thought you might like to know that your little, ah, masquerade tonight was not unobserved." He smiled as the color drained from Leyton's face. Nodding at the expression on Leyton's face, he added, "Oh, yes. I followed you. Did you think I would not?"

"You followed me?" Leyton repeated dully.

"Indeed I did and as I said, your actions were most revealing." He smiled, a smile that sent a chill down Leyton's spine. "Now, would you like to tell me what it was that you were so desperate to have from Miss Montgomery that you stooped to robbery? My letter, perhaps? Did you write the directions to Sweet Acres on the back of it? Did you congratulate yourself at the way you had gotten rid of it, right under my very nose?" He laughed nastily. "I am sure that Tony's interference tonight must have given you pause."

Slumping back down in the chair, Leyton muttered. "I do not know what you are talking about."

"Do you not?"

Something in the other man's voice made him nervous, and Leyton added quickly, "I swear to you that I know nothing of any damned letter!"

"I wonder? Surely you were not so stupid that you thought to redeem your current money problems by stealing her deeds?"

His eyes narrowed as something occurred to him.

Amusement flickering across his face, he asked incredulously, "Do not tell me that you planned to extort money from her for their return?"

"I do not know what you are talking about," Leyton insisted sullenly. "What is more, I find your attitude bloody insulting."

"Do you? Well, I suspect that you are going to find Tony's attitude a damned sight more insulting than mine." He took a swallow of his brandy. "How long," he demanded, "do you think it will be before Tony realizes that there is only one person who would have known that Arabella would be out alone tonight?" He laughed contemptuously at the look on Leyton's face. "Hadn't thought of that, had you? You should start. I would be willing to make you a wager, that even as we speak, Tony is planning on paying you a visit this evening."

Suddenly deciding that there was no use pretending that he had not attempted to rob Arabella, Leyton asked aggressively, "What if he does? He can prove nothing."

"You are a fool, my friend," drawled the visitor. "And you are making a bad mistake in underestimating Daggett. Tony, unfortunately, has an uncanny way of discovering just what one would rather he did not— believe this. As for not suspecting you, who else would have known where to lie in wait for her?" He sighed. "You know it occurs to me that you are rapidly becoming a distinct liability to me. Once Tony starts sniffing around there is no telling where his nose will lead him."

Leyton got up and, with jerky movements, poured himself another brandy. His voice slightly slurred, he muttered, "I can handle Daggett."

"Just as you did last night?" the other man taunted.

"It was stupid to play against him—I could have told you that!" His gaze cold and considering, he added bitingly, "You know you have made several miscalculations lately, but the worst was trying your hand at blackmailing me."

"And I tell you that you are mistaken," Leyton persisted doggedly. "I did not try to blackmail you."

"And I do not believe you," snapped the other man.

Leyton took a long swig of his brandy, bitterly aware that denial was gaining him nothing. Leyton knew the other man too well, had watched him with others and knew that his visitor had him caught like a rat in the coils of a snake and wasn't going to let go—he never did.

Sighing defeatedly, Leyton finally admitted, "Oh, very well, you were right. I did try to blackmail you." A whine in his voice, he added, "I had no choice! I was desperate."

"And the Montgomery vowels? Was your need so great that you thought to steal that fortune as well as part of mine?"

"I had set the wheels in motion to blackmail you before it was clear just how thoroughly the Montgomery boy could be plucked," Leyton admitted sulkily.

"But you no longer have the vowels, do you?"

Leyton's mouth thinned. "No."

"And so we have come full circle, have we not?"

Leyton did not answer. From the beginning he had known that it was dangerous to try to blackmail the man before him. When the letter had fallen into his hands, it had seemed worth the risk, and it had never occurred to him that his intended victim would ever lay the crime at his door. He glanced thoughtfully at the other man. Everything had gone wrong, and it wasn't likely that he would have such a seemingly easy opportunity again. He decided that his best option would be to cut his losses and try to repair the damage his unwise actions had caused.

It seemed his visitor had come to the same conclusion, for he suddenly smiled, and said amiably, "Since your plot came to nothing, I am inclined to forgive you. But I would warn you, I will not be so forgiving in the future."

Leyton nodded, vastly relieved. His guest made a bad enemy.

"Well, now," said the other man, "let us put the matter from us. Pour me another brandy, and we shall consider how to deal with Tony."

Leyton eagerly complied. Having taken the snifter from his visitor's hand, he turned back to the sideboard and reached for the crystal decanter that held the brandy. "Let me reassure you that you will have no reason to doubt me in the future. My actions were stupid and unworthy."

Concentrating on what he was doing, his back to the room, Leyton was not aware of the other man's swift, silent approach. It was only when the man spoke mere inches from his ear that he was startled by his nearness.

"Indeed they were," purred the visitor. "Pity."

Leyton did not even have time to react as the thin, wicked stiletto slid neatly between his ribs and unerringly into his heart. He gave a little choked sound, his eyes wide with astonishment, then slowly crumpled to the floor, the brandy spilling from the snifter he still held in his hand.

Surveying his handiwork, the visitor almost absent-mindedly wiped the blood from his stiletto on the faded gold drapery and deftly replaced the knife in his boot. Plucking the snifter from Leyton's limp fingers, he swallowed the scant remains which had not spilled, then wiped the glass dry on the same drapery he had used to clean his knife. Replacing the snifter on the tray, he glanced carefully around the room. There was no reason to search it again. He had done that earlier and was confident of one thing—the letter was not there.

Except for his cloak—and poor Leyton, of course—there was no other sign that he had been here. Crossing the room, he put on his cloak and, after one more look around the room, glided to the French doors and slipped outside.

His horse had been hidden in a small copse not far from the main house, and it took him only a few minutes to reach the animal. A moment later, he was gone, melting into the night.

Tony's arrival was nearly half an hour later, and his approach was cautious, though he expected no trouble. There was little moon, but the faint, silvery light allowed him to pick out the main house and the outbuildings. Coming upon the house from the front, all was in darkness. It didn't surprise him, although considering the hour, it would have been more normal for some signs of light to have shone out of one or two windows of the house.

As he rode silently by the main house, he noticed the

faintest hint of light coming from one of the rooms at the rear of the building. Good. Leyton was no doubt inside gleefully congratulating himself on his narrow escape. Before confronting Leyton, however, Tony wanted something a little more tangible than a hunch and mere suspicion with which to confront his target.

Halting Sugar before the dark stable, Tony dismounted and quietly entered the still building. Moving like a cat through the almost utter blackness of the interior, he used touch as sight to find his way. Fortunately, and he had already suspected it given Leyton's precarious financial state, there were only four horses in what had once been a fine, extensive stable.

Just as well, Tony thought to himself as he listened to their soft blowing and restive movements; otherwise, his task might have taken all night. Entering the various stalls one by one, he quickly ran a sure, questing hand over each of the animals. The third animal he touched gave him the information he had hoped to find. Despite the passage of time, the animal's coat was scratchy and sticky where the lather and sweat had begun to dry and the horse was still faintly damp under the area where the saddle had been, indicating that it had been ridden hard not too long ago.

A lathered horse was little to go by, but increased Tony's confidence that Leyton had been the robber. Remounting Sugar, he guided the stallion toward the big house. Leaving his mount tied to a small, ornamental bush near the pair of French doors from which the fitful glow of light shone, Tony brazenly walked into the room.

At first glance the area appeared empty. Idly his gaze

slid over the dark gray jacket thrown carelessly on the chair. The candles were guttering in their holders, and there was an unpleasant odor in the room.

Tony halted just inside the French doors. He had not been in the presence of many dead bodies, but he instantly recognized the smell. Swiftly crossing to the only place hidden from his sight, the area behind the desk, he wasn't surprised to see the body of a man lying on the floor.

Though there was little blood, only a small patch where the knife had gone in, he surmised from the foul smell and the eerie stillness of the body that the man was dead. Gingerly, Tony turned him over. As he had expected, it was Leyton, and the welt on his face told Tony he had found Arabella's would-be robber.

Gently repositioning the body, he glanced around the room. Except for Leyton's body there was nothing out of place. He stood there a moment indecisively, his brain racing. Under normal circumstances, rousing the house would have been the thing to do, but with his reputation, Tony didn't think that he wanted to be the one to have discovered Leyton's body. His lips thinned. There were already enough people convinced that he had murdered two wives, and he didn't want Leyton's death laid at his door.

Concluding that a silent retreat was the best course for him, Tony left. A moment later, he was riding away from Oakmont.

Tony had little remorse about Leyton's death or the violent manner of it—the man had been without honor, a parasite, and it had been generally agreed that he would come to a bad end. He grimaced. Which half the population of Natchez firmly believed about him.

Leyton's connection to Arabella, however, bothered him. It was too coincidental that Leyton should die almost immediately after attempting and failing to rob Arabella.

Leyton's death, and the whip mark, only intensified Tony's certainty that Leyton had indeed been the bandit. Besides himself and Arabella, Leyton had been the only other person who had known that Arabella had carried the deeds to Greenleigh with her that afternoon, and would be driving home from the direction of Sweet Acres. Granted the attorney, Haight, had known she had taken the deeds with her, but unless Haight had followed her or hired someone to follow her—in which case, he had changed drastically since Tony had known him—the attorney had had no way of knowing her destination.

Thinking of the bespectacled, eminently admired Mr. Haight, Tony dismissed all notion of his having had anything to do with that night's events. No. The identity of the robber could only have been Leyton. But then who had killed Leyton, and why?

Chapter Six

*I*t wasn't to be expected that Arabella's arrival home would go unnoticed, but she was surprised to be greeted by the entire family and several servants when she entered the house. In the act of removing her bonnet, she stared in astonishment at the crowd that was gathered in the middle of the elegant rose-and-cream hallway. From the anxious expressions on everyone's faces, she feared that a calamity had befallen the house. Had something happened to Jeremy on his way to Greenleigh?

Arabella's stepmother, Mary, whose fair head had jerked around at the sound of the opening of the door, spied her and gave a shaken cry of relief. As one, the crowd surged in Arabella's direction. Instantly engulfed by the family, her ears assaulted by the babble that arose around her, she was tightly clasped against her stepmother's bosom. "My dear," exclaimed Mary in agitated accents, "you are alive and safe! Thank heavens! I have been beside myself with anxiety once darkness began to fall and I learned that you had not yet returned home. Where have you been?"

Embarrassed to realize that she had been the cause of their distress, Arabella gently extricated herself from Mary's frantic embrace and smiled reassuringly at the worried faces clustered around her. In addition to her tall, slender stepmother, Mary, there was Sara, as golden and ethereal-looking as her mother; clearheaded Jane; exuberant and mischievous George; and, hanging on to her skirts for dear life, the angelic-faced baby of the family, John. Beyond them hovered the butler, Lawrence, his usually austere features creased into a wide smile. Just behind him stood his wife and the family housekeeper, Mrs. Lawrence, her plump form appearing even plumper as she stood beside the cook, Mrs. Hickman, who was stick-thin despite all the delicious meals she prepared day after day for the family.

John tugged impatiently at Arabella's skirt. "Bella," he cried. "George said that a bear had eaten you. Did you see a bear, Bella?"

Arabella laughed and bent down, pressing a kiss to John's pink cheek. "Indeed I did not! George," she said warmly, "was only teasing you."

Blue eyes gleaming, John glanced triumphantly back at his nine-year-old brother. "See, I told you! I knew that Bella was too smart to be eaten by a bear!"

"Well, she could have been," George insisted stubbornly, his lower lip jutting.

"Don't be silly," chimed in Jane. "It would be highly unlikely that Bella would be anyplace where she would meet a bear."

"Children, children," scolded Mary gently. "Shall we

forget about the bear for a few minutes and see that our Bella really is safe?"

"We were so concerned," said Sara, her celestial blue eyes wide in her delicate face. "No one knew where you had gone, and when dusk came and there was still no sign of you, we all became quite anxious about you. Even the Lawrences and Mrs. Hickman. We were so frightened that something had happened to you. Mother was on the point of sending a servant for Uncle Richard to implore him to go look for you."

Arabella kept her face blank as she sent a rueful look around the hall. Mary's brother, Richard Kingsley, was not one of her favorite people. In fact, she often wondered how someone as vain and conniving as Richard could be related to her own sweet stepmama. And the thought of Richard finding her with Tony made her shudder.

Richard Kingsley had been one of the most vociferous opponents of her engagement to Tony five years before, and she was certain half of her father's and Mary's objections to Tony had been because Richard had filled their heads with every vile story he could recall. Arabella's mouth twisted. Not that most of the stories about Tony didn't hold some kernel of truth.

Unhappy at having caused such worry amongst those she loved, Arabella murmured, "I apologize for alarming all of you. My errand took longer than I expected it would. There was nothing for anyone to worry about—after all, I am a grown woman. Not," she said affectionately as she gave Sara's chin a gentle pinch, "a flighty little chit like some I could name."

Sara giggled, but it was Mary who asked the question

that Arabella had hoped to avoid. "But where did you go?" Mary inquired, clearly perplexed. "It is not like you to leave without telling anyone where you are going—or without a servant with you."

Arabella had not planned to return so late and had hoped that she would be able to pass off her absence as having merely gone for an impetuous pleasure drive. Obviously, without some swift improvisation on her part, that excuse was not going to pass muster.

Stripping off her driving gloves, she said carelessly, "Oh, nowhere in particular. There were a few things I wished to discuss with Mr. Haight so, on a whim, I drove into town. When I was finished with Mr. Haight, it was such a beautiful day, I decided to take a drive along the bluff and look at the river." She laughed deprecatingly. "Would you believe that I managed to get the cart stuck when Sable took exception to a blue jay and shied? I do not know what I would have done if some very nice strangers hadn't happened along eventually and freed my wheel from where it had lodged between a half-rotted log and a small sapling." Arabella knew she was elaborating too much, so she quickly finished her mendacious tale. "And there you have it, nothing very exciting at all and certainly nothing for any of you to be worried about."

Mary was not a suspicious person, and she readily accepted Arabella's story. "It must have given you a start when you discovered your predicament," she commiserated, her affection for her stepdaughter obvious.

"Indeed it did," Arabella replied. Looking in the direction of the servants, she asked prettily, "Dear, dear Mrs. Hickman, would it be possible for you to make up a plate for me? I know that everyone else has eaten, but I am absolutely famished."

Recalled to their duties, the servants quickly reverted to their usual roles. "As you wish, miss," said Mrs. Hickman instantly and darted into the nether regions of the house. Mrs. Lawrence, realizing that there was no longer any reason for her to stand gawking about, added briskly, "And I shall go up and see if your bed has been turned back."

When the two women had bustled off, Lawrence bowed, and murmured, "If you will hand me your hat and gloves, miss, I shall put them away for you."

Arabella smiled at him and, though she was perfectly capable of putting away her own things, meekly handed him the hat and gloves. "Oh, thank you so much. I do not know what I would do without all of you. You pamper me shamelessly."

Many of the Montgomery servants were English which was rare amongst the majority of the wealthy planters in the Natchez area. When William Montgomery decided to leave England and settle in the New World, most of his existing staff had opted to come with the family—which wasn't surprising, since many of them were third and fourth generation in service to the Montgomerys. The very real concern of the Lawrences and Mrs. Hickman for the missing Montgomery member was understandable; they had seen Arabella grow up from a chubby baby to the woman she had become.

When the servants departed, Arabella and the others immediately made for the large, untidy room on the second floor where the family usually gathered on quiet evenings at home. It was a pleasant place with high airy ceilings and plenty of space for the family to spread out, yet it still retained a feeling of intimacy. The furniture had comfort more in mind than style and was arranged haphazardly. The effect was welcoming and charming.

Seating herself on one of the long sofas that faced its twin near the hearth of a brick fireplace, Arabella looked around and smiled. It was obvious from the scattered rods, that George and John had been playing Pick-up Sticks before the growing anxiety over Arabella's absence had interrupted them. Jane had been painting, her small easel and tray of watercolors near one of the long windows, which opened onto a small balcony at the far side of the room. An embroidery frame had been left on the seat of a chintz-covered chair, and a Gothic novel by the English author Ann Ward Radcliffe, *Mysteries of Udolpho* was lying nearby on the gaily painted carpet: Sara had been practicing her stitiches and Mary had been reading.

Leaning back against the couch, Arabella asked, "Did anything interesting happen while I was gone?"

"I found a bird's nest this afternoon," piped up George, as he settled himself on the floor near the couch. "There were four eggs in it."

"I trust you left it undisturbed," Arabella commented dryly. George's penchant for dragging home various bits of nature could be unsettling, especially since he had once brought home a baby skunk and let it loose in the nursery.

After a few minutes of desultory conversation, it was as if Arabella had never been away. Sara had picked up her embroidery and begun to ply her needle; Jane had started again on her painting, and the boys were once again engrossed in their game. Only Mary had not yet picked up her novel and begun to read.

Fixing her stepdaughter with a stern eye, Mary asked quietly, "What is all this nonsense about Jeremy going to Greenleigh for you? He was extremely vague about it when he came to bid me farewell this morning."

Arabella sighed. When she had left Highview this morning, she'd had a very simple plan: get her deeds from Mr. Haight, come to some agreement with Leyton, and be home before anyone even realized that she had been gone. She had also planned on having enough private time in which to formulate a reasonable excuse for Jeremy's sudden visit to Greenleigh. Nothing, she thought with a grimace, had gone as she had hoped.

Rapidly considering and discarding a dozen little white lies to throw Mary off the scent, she finally settled upon something that had some basis in truth. Shrugging casually, she said, "I know that he is a grown man and can do as he wishes, but it seems to me that of late he has been spending too much time in, ah, unhealthy pursuits. I thought that enlisting his aid in seeing how Greenleigh was being maintained was an excellent way to wean him away from dangerous pastimes for a while."

Mary nodded. "I wondered if it wasn't something like that. I have not been happy about his late nights, but I felt that commenting on them would only cause him to puff up like a toad and be more determined than ever to show me just how very adult he is." She smiled fondly at Arabella. "You are so clever, Bella, always seeming to anticipate trouble before it actually occurs. I do not know what we would do without you. Your father would be proud of you and the way you always watch over us."

Arabella flushed and glanced away. She felt mean-spirited deceiving Mary thus and had the lowering feeling that the ugly sensation was only going to grow worse as she embarked upon her career as Tony's mistress. She was, she realized sickly, going to be put to a great deal of subterfuge in the following months, and lying was, no doubt, going to become second nature to her. How else was she going to keep her liaison with Tony a secret?

The enormity of what she had agreed to do had not really sunk in and it was only when she was finally alone in her own bedchamber, lying sleepless in the big bed with its pale yellow silk canopy, that she perceived the trap she had set for herself. Tonight had been just a little example of the deception that lay before her.

She did not, she admitted with brutal candor, even have the comfort of putting a noble face on her actions. Her first instincts may have had some nobility about them—after all, she had been willing to give up her own fortune to secure the fortune of her family—but once that particular plan had fallen by the wayside . . . She swallowed painfully. Tony's teasing comment that only she would consider living at Greenleigh to be comparable to abject poverty rankled and cut a little too close to the bone.

If she had thrown his disgraceful offer back in his face, it was true that the family's great fortune would be lost, and that the younger ones would have a hard time of it when they reached adulthood, but it was not as if they would have been reduced to living on the streets and begging for crusts of bread from strangers. She made a face. And of course, Richard would have no doubt come to the aid of his sister.

The problem was, she would rather die than have the family beholden to that pompous ass. Richard was thirty-six, a determined bachelor, used to pleasing only himself. He tolerated his nieces and nephews and treated his sister with affectionate contempt. He would never, Arabella knew, let Mary forget that she and her children owed their financial well-being to him. Money would be a powerful weapon in his hands, and he would not be averse to using it. No. Whatever other foolish decisions she may have made that day, not going to Richard Kingsley had been wise. And, she admitted wearily, agreeing to become Tony's mistress had been most unwise. . . .

She tossed restlessly in the bed. Faced with the choice between the loss of the family fortune or becoming the mistress of a man who had betrayed her—yet who still held a mesmerizing fascination for her—had not seemed like such a bad trade at the time. Tony Daggett had been her first and only lover. She had loved him once, and perhaps in a tiny corner of her heart she still did, so it wasn't as if she were giving herself to a man who filled her with revulsion. And that, she admitted, was the sticking point.

Only with Tony would she have made the deplorable bargain, and that knowledge filled her with disgust. She had tried to cloak her actions today in nobility, but the plain and simple truth of the matter was that she wanted to be in Tony's arms again. Her eyes stung with unshed tears. And having been offered a way to do just that she had lunged at it, regardless of the cost.

Feeling like the lowest creature in nature, Arabella twisted in her bed. She had called Tony a wretched beast, but she was one, too. That she had, in fact, saved Highview and the Montgomery fortune, did not give her much comfort. She saw only her own ugly bargain with a Devil in the far-too-attractive shape of Tony Daggett.

On Wednesday morning, Arabella woke scratchy-eyed and exhausted. After her morning ablutions, she ruthlessly secured her bright, curling hair into a spin-sterish bun at the back of her head and chose to wear a rather plain gown of fawn muslin.

Her intention was to leave for Greenleigh as soon as she could—once she had concocted another lie for Mary's delectation. Her spirits sank. Would the lying never stop?

Glumly she descended the grand, curving staircase, realizing that she was going to have to lie to Jeremy, too. If he had the faintest inkling of what she was up to, he would be at Sweet Acres demanding Tony's blood before she could blink. Unfortunately, she reminded herself drearily, it would probably be Jeremy's blood that would be spilled in any confrontation between the two men. Tony's handiness with both the sword and the pistol was legendary.

As she entered the breakfast room, she hadn't de-cided precisely on what she was going to tell Mary to explain her sudden desire to go to Greenleigh for a few days. She was both relieved and dismayed to discover that the entire family had arrived ahead of her and was scattered along either side of the long table.

Breakfast was always a casual affair at Highview,

and there was no set menu, nor a time for eating. One arrived when one felt like it and a black servant or Lawrence conveyed one's wishes for breakfast to the kitchen and Mrs. Hickman. A heavy silver urn with hot coffee was always kept on the mahogany sideboard, as well as some fruit and freshly baked biscuits to sustain those who could not wait for more substantial victuals.

After greeting everyone, and not particularly hungry, Arabella selected some early strawberries and a cup of coffee. There was the usual morning chatter, George declaring that he was going to ride his pony to the small creek that traversed the plantation to look for tadpoles, and John immediately insisting that he be allowed to tag along. Sara and Mary had already made plans to be driven into Natchez to select a pattern and material for a ball gown for Sara; Jane was leaving on Friday to stay for a few days with her bosom friend, Edith Gayle, at the Gayle plantation.

Idly listening to everyone's plans, Arabella sipped her coffee and picked at her strawberries. She wondered bitterly what sort of lie she could concoct for Mary's benefit to explain her sudden desire to stay at Greenleigh, especially since she had just sent Jeremy there to look the place over for her.

"And have you no plans for today?" Mary asked her lightly, interrupting Arabella's unpleasant thoughts.

Arabella stared at her, her brain absolutely blank.

Mary smiled. "I thought for certain that you would have come up with a reason to visit Greenleigh by now."

Arabella nearly choked on her coffee and sent her stepmother an alarmed glance. "R-R-Really?" she finally managed to stammer. "Why is that?"

Sara and Mary exchanged a glance, and both burst out laughing, their blue eyes sparkling as they stared at her.

"You have forgotten," crowed Sara.

When Arabella still looked utterly at sea, Mary asked with amusement, "Have you forgotten that Cousin Agatha is coming to visit? Remember, she always comes this time of year and stays for a few months. In her last letter, she wrote that if the journey upriver went well, she hoped to arrive sometime today or tomorrow. I know I told you about it last week when her letter arrived." Her amusement deepened. "Since then I have been waiting for you to suddenly come up with a reason why you simply must be away from Highview for at least a few weeks. Never tell me that you have had a change of heart about Cousin Agatha."

Arabella's lack of affection for Mary's only cousin, Agatha Rutledge, was only equaled by Agatha's blunt manner toward Arabella. Several years older than Mary and Richard, Agatha was a childless widow of long standing, who also had a decided penchant for sticking her nose where it wasn't wanted. Ruling her own household with an iron hand, she was of the notion that there was only one way of doing things—hers. In her favor, she was genuinely fond of Mary and Richard and fairly doted on the children. It was privately understood that Agatha meant well.

Two years ago, when word of William's death had reached her at her home in Walnut Hills, Agatha had immediately hurried upriver to give solace to her dear cousin. It took all of Mary's persuasive powers to prevent her from moving permanently to Highview. She had been convinced that Mary and the children needed her to run their lives for them and was quite resentful that it was to Arabella they turned in their hour of need.

Not surprisingly, Agatha's bossy manner grated on Arabella. She tried to make excuses for Mary's cousin, but the plain fact was that she and Agatha simply did not get along. Arabella had little patience with Agatha's forceful ways, and Agatha resented Arabella's influence over the family.

Grasping the lifeline Mary had unknowingly tossed her, Arabella put on a shamefaced expression. "I was just this very morning, uh, trying to think of a reason to go to Greenleigh that wouldn't sound too mendacious to you," Arabella muttered, aware she was telling the truth yet not telling the truth.

"Do not worry about it," Mary said lightly. "Go to Greenleigh and see how well my eldest son is carrying out your charges. Cousin Agatha will be disappointed that Jeremy is not here to greet her—you know how she dotes on him—but the knowledge that she will be able to rule Highview without interference from you will be more than adequate compensation for his absence.

Free to leave for Greenleigh with Mary's blessings, Arabella felt like the lowest worm on earth. "Are you certain that it will not be terribly inconvenient for you?" she asked earnestly. "Cousin Agatha sometimes bullies you unmercifully. Are you positive that you want to face her alone?"

"Agatha does not bully me quite as much as you fear, my dear. But if she insists upon my doing something that I do not want to, I shall," she added with a twinkle, "tell her that you have absolutely forbidden me to do it and that I have promised you that I shall not."

Arabella choked back a giggle. "You would hide behind me?"

"Without compunction," Mary replied promptly, her blue eyes glinting. "Go to Greenleigh, Arabella. You know that you are eager to do so. Let Cousin Agatha settle in and have the time in which to explain to the children and me all that we are doing wrong. Once she has shown us the error of our ways, she will relax and not be so inclined to find fault with everything. You know how she is." She smiled gently at Arabella. "She is not a bad person, just slightly autocratic."

Arabella nodded glumly. "I know she means well, but I cannot seem to help bristling at her manner. We are like chalk and cheese."

"Oh, I wouldn't say that," Mary argued. "You both have my best interests at heart, and while it is your nature gently to suggest things to be done, Agatha tends to demand they be done. She cannot help it."

Arabella made a face, not liking the comparison. Deciding she'd have to examine that idea more deeply at a later time, she set down her cup, and said decisively, "Well, as long as you have no objections, I think I shall see to my packing and leave just as soon as I can for Greenleigh. I shall send Jeremy back in a few days, but I will probably remain at Greenleigh for most of Agatha's visit."

"I rather suspected that would be your plan. I shall tell Agatha that you have been thinking of making renovations to the place and that the project could not be put off." She smiled impishly at Arabella. "I shall also tell her how very dreadful you felt when you realized that you would miss her arrival."

Both Sara and Jane, who had been listening to the exchange, laughed aloud.

"Oh, Mama," exclaimed Sara. "What a bouncer! You should be ashamed of yourself."

"And I am," Mary added hastily. "But it is far kinder to tell a tiny little lie than to give Cousin Agatha another crime to lay at Arabella's door."

The threat of Agatha's impending arrival lent wings to Arabella's feet. Not two hours later, she pulled away from Highview driving a high-stepping brown gelding with a black male servant perched behind her on the cart for the sake of propriety. Her maid would finish her packing, and arrangements had been made for her things to be driven over to Greenleigh. But before she set off to Greenleigh she had one last errand to run: to deliver the deeds safely into Mr. Haight's hands.

Remembering the previous night's attempted robbery and even knowing that it was highly unlikely she would find herself in the same situation today, and in broad daylight, Arabella was taking no chances with the deeds. The precious documents, still in the portfolio, were safely hidden under the seat of the cart.

The visit with Mr. Haight took only a few minutes. Handing him the portfolio once she had been shown into his office, she said, "You see, you had nothing to fear. Here are my deeds returned safely to you. I would suggest we leave them in the portfolio for the time being."

Mr. Haight laid the portfolio on the edge of his desk

and regarded her over the rims of his spectacles. "I do not suppose you will tell me why you needed them?"

Arabella dimpled at him. "Indeed not, kind sir. You would only scold."

"No doubt," he returned. Rising to his feet, he walked over to a big black iron safe that sat in one corner of the room. He unlocked it, and placed the portfolio on one of the shelves inside the safe. He then shut the heavy door and relocked the safe.

Looking back at Arabella, he smiled. "Now they are truly safe."

With the deeds delivered, Arabella's cares seemed to lift, and it was with relief that she finally guided her horse from the jessamine-lined streets of Natchez and began the journey to Greenleigh.

The road was fairly busy, and they passed several pedestrians, vehicles, and horsemen on their way into Natchez as they drove away. After the first few miles traffic became nearly nonexistent, and giving the gelding his head, Arabella let the animal set the pace and settled back to watch the passing countryside. Deliberately, she did not let herself think of Tony Daggett.

Greenleigh was situated nearly two hours from Natchez, and Arabella planned to use the time in concocting some sort of story for Jeremy's edification to explain her unexpected arrival. For once she was grateful for Agatha's annual visit—it gave her an excellent reason for beating a hasty retreat to Greenleigh, but that still left her searching for an explanation for the return of Jeremy's vowels.

Her nose wrinkled. Technically the vowels had not been returned, but there was no longer any danger of the family being tossed out of Highview. Jeremy's fortune was safe, and with it, Mary's future and those of the other children.

Their problems were over . . . once Tony gave her the letter relinquishing his rights to the vowels. Her heart gave a painful little thump. Until she had that letter safely in her hands the family was still in danger, and an unpleasant thought suddenly occurred to her. If something were to happen to Tony, if an accident should befall him or some terrible tragedy overtake him before he wrote the letter . . . Her stomach felt hollow, and she was aware of a feeling of light-headedness.

Telling herself that her reaction had nothing to do with the idea of a world without the aggravating Tony Daggett in it and everything to do with her family's future, Arabella calmed herself. Nothing was going to happen to Tony, at least not in the next few days. Of course, once he had given her the letter, she thought grimly, he could bloody well go hang!

Chapter Seven

It was midafternoon before Arabella finally turned the brown gelding down the long tree-shaded driveway that led to Greenleigh. Like many of the plantations in the Natchez area, the main house was built on a bluff overlooking the turbulent Mississippi River.

Greenleigh was not a grand house, but it was charming and welcoming, with its wide, shaded verandas draped with fragrant honeysuckle and graceful arched windows. An extensive stretch of lawn sprinkled with magnolias and oaks surrounded the pale green and cream-colored two-story house on three sides. From the front veranda, there was an excellent view of the river. Behind the house lay the many outbuildings; the office, the kitchen, the dairy, slave quarters, and stables. Beyond them lay the green cotton fields, with their rose-and-white blossoms and, in the distance, the untamed woodland.

Pulling her horse to a halt in the circular carriageway, Arabella stared with dismay at the horses that were tied to the various black-iron hitching posts in front of the house. Jeremy, it appeared, was entertaining friends and was certainly not going to be expecting a visit from his sister. She supposed she should be grateful as it put off the need for immediate explanations.

Samuels, the black servant she had brought with her, saw to the horse and cart, leading the horse away in the direction of the stables. Taking a deep breath, Arabella slowly mounted the broad front steps.

Greenleigh was maintained by a minimum of staff, and so Arabella was not surprised that there was no one to greet her as she entered the main hall at the front of the house. A swift glance around revealed that the older couple she had placed in residence to see to the upkeep of the place did their job well. The oak floor gleamed, and the delicate brass-and-crystal chandelier in the center of the high ceiling glistened. There were several doors that opened off the main hall, and at the far end was a winding oak staircase that led to the upper floor. The hall narrowed at that point and continued along the left side of the staircase, leading to the back of the house.

For a moment Arabella stood in the middle of the hall, uncertain in which direction to look for Jeremy. A crack of laughter and the sound of masculine voices came from behind a pair of double doors to her right. Walking to the doors, she gave a gentle tap since after all, she was unexpected, but without waiting for a reply she pushed open one door and entered the room.

There were six gentlemen in various relaxed poses scattered around the main saloon, and at Arabella's entrance conversation ceased.

"Bella!" Jeremy exclaimed, as he left his position near the gray-marble fireplace and hurried in her direction. "What are you doing here?"

Smiling as she stripped off her tan driving gloves, Arabella said teasingly, "Well, it is my house, you know."

"Dash it all! That is not what I meant at all, and you know it! Is all well at Highview?" he asked anxiously, his blue eyes full of questions. "It is nothing, er, urgent that brings you here?"

Arabella shook her head. "Not exactly." Sending Jeremy a look, she added succinctly, "Cousin Agatha."

Jeremy laughed. "Oh, gad! I forgot that she is due to arrive any day now."

"Yes, she is—today or tomorrow. And I thought that it would be, ah, more comfortable for everyone if I came to inspect Greenleigh and see for myself how the Tidmores were doing."

Glancing beyond Jeremy, she smiled warmly at Tom Denning and James Gayle, Jeremy's closest cronies, who had risen to their feet upon her entrance into the room. She was quite familiar with both young men and treated them with the same easy affection that she did her brother. It was James's sister, Edith, whom Jane was going to visit on Friday.

Having acknowledged the hasty bows of Denning and Gayle, her smiling glance fell upon another young man she recognized, although at twenty-five, Morgan Slade was a bit older than Jeremy and his friends. Now that she thought of it, he was married and the father of a young son. What, she wondered, was Morgan doing there? He was not part of Jeremy's usual circle.

Walking up to her, Morgan bent over her hand. "Miss Montgomery. A pleasure as always." A smile lurking in his piercing blue eyes, he added, "Allow me to introduce you to my friend, Jason Savage, and his companion, Blood Drinker."

Arabella's eyes widened as the two men came forward. Savage was a tall, broad-shouldered young man with the most striking emerald green eyes she had ever seen in her life. While Blood Drinker . . . She swallowed. Blood Drinker was an Indian, his swarthy skin and unfathomable black eyes gave away his heritage, as did the pair of thick shining black braids that hung halfway down his back. They were both dressed in well-worn fringed buckskins and moccasins and looked decidedly out of place in Greenleigh's elegant salon.

"H-h-how do you do," Arabella replied politely, wondering again what was going on. "It is a pleasure to meet you."

Jason's handsome face was full of amusement at her restraint. Many a gently reared woman would have fainted dead away if she had been suddenly confronted in her parlor by two such rough-looking characters as him and Blood Drinker.

"You are no doubt," Jason said lightly, "wondering what we are doing here."

Arabella arched a slim brow and sent him a look.

Jason laughed at her expression. "There is a very innocent explanation, I assure you. Your brother and his friends met us on the road while they were out riding this morning. When Morgan introduced us and mentioned that Blood Drinker and I had traveled across the Sabine River into the Territory of Texas with Philip

Nolan on some of his horse-gathering expeditions, nothing would do but that we return here to talk about our adventures."

"Bella, Savage says that there is a fortune to be made in Texas," Jeremy broke in excitedly. "He says that there are tremendous herds of wild horses just waiting to be captured and resold in Natchez or New Orleans. Tom and James and I are thinking of joining Nolan the next time he goes west. It will be a great adventure, and just think, I could come back with a fortune in horseflesh."

It was as well, Arabella decided wryly, that she had already taken matters into her own hands to save the family fortune, else she had little doubt that at the first opportunity, Jeremy would be heading out into the untracked, hostile wilderness of Spanish Texas determined to risk his neck. A little shudder went through her at the dangers he would have faced. Not the least would have been falling into the hands of the hordes of savage Indians who roamed those high plains—even in Natchez tales of their terrible deeds were occasionally mentioned.

"Er, how exciting. Is Mr. Nolan planning a trip soon?" she asked, hoping her face displayed appropriate enthusiasm for a project that filled her with dread.

Jason shook his head. "Nolan is at present in New Orleans, and Blood Drinker and I have just returned from Texas only a few days ago." He glanced at Morgan and smiled. "Before heading home to New Orleans, we decided to inflict ourselves upon Morgan for a brief visit."

"And you were lucky to find me at Bonheur and not Thousand Oaks," returned Morgan, grinning.

"Oh, that's right," Arabella said, turning to Morgan Slade almost with relief. "I remember hearing of Thousand Oaks—your father gave you the land upon your marriage a couple of years ago, didn't he?" At Morgan's nod, she added, "But isn't it quite a distance from here?"

Morgan nodded again. "Indeed it is—Thousand Oaks is situated almost halfway between Natchez and Baton Rouge. It is at present very wild country, I can tell you that! My wife, Stephanie, is not at all happy about the proposed move from Bonheur. She likes being close to Natchez." He smiled. "I hope to convince her to change her mind. Civilizing the land is satisfying work, but it has been lonely. I miss her and my son, Phillipe."

Jeremy was not the least interested in Morgan's domestic arrangements, and he said airily, "Oh, I am sure once you have finished the house, she will be very happy there." Turning eagerly to Jason, he asked, "Do you have any idea how soon it will be before Nolan goes again to Texas?"

Jason shrugged his shoulders. "Nolan's current reason for being in New Orleans is to meet with the Spanish officials to get permission for a new trip to Texas." Jason made a face. "But I think that any journey to Texas by him—or anyone else, anytime soon—will depend upon how quickly the situation here in Natchez is resolved."

A strained little silence fell.

Though Spain had agreed under the terms of the Treaty of San Lorenzo, signed the previous year in

1796, to give up her claim to the lands east of the Mississippi River above the thirty-first parallel, which included the Natchez District, she was proving maddeningly reluctant in actually relinquishing control.

Andrew Ellicott, whom President Washington, before he had left office last year, had selected to survey the new boundary line between Spanish territory and the United States had arrived in Natchez in February. Initially, the American had been greeted cordially by the district's Spanish governor, Manuel Gayoso, but to Ellicott's requests that Gayoso and his garrison of sixty regulars depart for New Orleans, Gayoso had turned an amazingly deaf ear. At present, Ellicott and his small band of Americans were camped on a knoll overlooking the bluff where Natchez lay. During the ensuing weeks since his arrival, Ellicott had made no overt moves to physically dislodge the stubborn Spanish, but he had defiantly raised the United States flag above Connelly's Tavern, where it could be clearly seen by the Spanish from their fort at the south end of the esplanade. Gayoso had, of course, demanded that the flag be removed. Ellicott had bluntly refused.

At the moment, no one was certain how the standoff was going to end. Tension was mounting daily and had not been eased either by Gayoso's call for the loyalty of the local citizens, or Ellicott's recent circular urging the inhabitants of Natchez to join him in pressing the Spanish to leave. The arrival a few weeks earlier of "Crazy" Percy Smith Pope with his troop of soldiers to reinforce Ellicott's small band only increased the volatile and strained situation. The hope was that one side or the other would blink before outright battle commenced.

The current standoff between Gayoso and Ellicott was bad enough, but there was also a faction of planters and land speculators who were quietly pushing a separatists' movement. They wanted neither Spain nor the United States to rule the district. It was their hope to create a third entity, and their machinations only added to the rumors and tensions permeating the area.

"I suppose you are right," Jeremy said glumly, breaking the silence.

"And I think on that note we should be leaving," said Morgan. Jason concurred, and a few minutes later the three, Morgan, Jason, and Blood Drinker, had left the house and ridden away.

There was a little more conversation between Arabella and the others, then Tom and James also took their leave.

They had hardly left the room before Jeremy said, "Bella, don't you think that if I were to join up with Nolan that it would be an excellent way in which to recoup our fortune?"

Arabella had only met Philip Nolan once or twice, but she did not like the man. He was clearly an adventurer, and while she could not give any examples of untrustworthiness, she did not trust him. He seemed to be well connected and brushed shoulders with Governor Gayoso and the New Orleans governor, Baron de Carondelet, and others of that ilk. He was also considered to be the protégé of General James Wilkinson, one of the top-ranking officers in the United States Army, but since Arabella was not particularly impressed with Wilkinson either, this connection did nothing to improve Nolan in her eyes. And if there were any likelihood that Nolan could entice Jeremy to leave the safety of Natchez and hie off to chase wild horses, he would certainly top her list of people she detested!

Reminding herself that her bargain with Tony made any scheme of Jeremy's to recoup the family fortune unnecessary, she took a deep breath, and said calmly, "There is no need for you to consider such extreme measures. I was very busy yesterday, and I can assure you that your vowels are safe—your fortune and the family are saved. You have nothing to worry about anymore. I have taken care of everything."

"Bella! What have you done?" Jeremy demanded, his young face tense and uneasy.

"Oh, nothing for you to worry about," she replied. Turning away from him, she added casually, "I did speak to Leyton, but it was a futile effort on my part—he had already lost the vowels to someone else."

Jeremy blanched. "Someone else! Good gad! Who?"

"Er, Tony Daggett."

"Tony Daggett! And you tell me that the vowels are safe? Have you gone mad?"

Turning back to face him, she said levelly, "No. Tony is not quite the dishonorable wretch others would have you believe." And that, she admitted to herself, was a great bouncer considering what he had demanded of her for the return of the vowels.

Jeremy looked worried, He had only been sixteen that summer, when the engagement between Bella and Tony Daggett had ended, but he remembered vividly the heated arguments between Bella and his parents. He particularly remembered Bella's strained, pale appearance for weeks after the abrupt end of the engagement.

She had been like a little wraith, drifting ghostlike through the house, her ready laugh vanished and the expression in her eyes making his heart ache for her.

He had been too young at the time to know all the details, but he'd learned bits and pieces over the years. He knew from his own observation that Daggett had cruelly broken his sister's heart and that it had taken her a very long time to recover from it. He knew, too, of Daggett's reputation—everyone in Natchez did! And that many people, including their uncle Richard, had been adamantly against the match. His lips twisted. Considering how the affair had ended, they'd apparently had good reason to oppose Bella's choice of a husband.

"Are you telling me," he asked quietly, "that when you approached Daggett and requested the return of the vowels—and I'm assuming that is what you did—that he simply gave them to you?"

Her eyes not meeting his, she muttered, "That is exactly what happened. When I explained the circumstances of Leyton's winning the vowels in the first place, he understood completely." Meeting his skeptical gaze, she added defiantly, "He was, in fact, a perfect gentleman about the entire affair."

"And I do not believe you," he said softly, his tone of voice and the expression on his face reminding her uncomfortably of their father.

Her jaw set. "Are you accusing me of lying? What reason would I have for doing so?"

He hesitated. "I do not know. But from what I know of Daggett's reputation, it seems highly improbable that he would just give what is a very large fortune to you." Deliberately, he added, "Especially to you. Considering the past that lies between the pair of you, he has no reason to show you a kindness."

Arabella ignored the stab of pain that slashed through her at his words. But they had given her an idea. Her chin lifted, and she said, "Not kindness, I agree. But has it occurred to you that the man might feel guilt, perhaps even remorse, for what happened? And that feeling guilt, he might be willing to do something to lessen that feeling?"

It was a notion that had obviously not crossed Jeremy's mind, and he stared at her, dumbstruck. "Are you telling me," he finally got out, "that he gave back the vowels because he felt *guilty?*"

Arabella shrugged her slim shoulders. "Perhaps. I do not know—nor do I care. I only know that when I confronted him and told him of the manner in which Leyton had tricked you he offered to return the vowels."

Jeremy stared at her, his indecision plain. He desperately wanted to believe her; he had no reason to believe that she was lying, and it was possible that Daggett had felt guilt and remorse over their broken engagement. Yet something was not quite right.

"Bella, did he really give you the vowels back?"

"Yes, dear brother, he did indeed give the vowels back."

"You already have them?"

"Uh, well, no. Not yet," Arabella admitted reluctantly. "He has only promised to return the vowels."

Jeremy's eyes narrowed. "Do my ears deceive me? You are willing to trust the word of a man accused of killing not one, but two wives? A man who has already betrayed you once?"

"He didn't kill Mercy!" Arabella said sharply. "If she hadn't been so stupid as to try to run away with James Terrell, Tony wouldn't have been chasing after them and their vehicle wouldn't have plunged over the bluff into the river. It wasn't Tony's fault that she drowned! He tried to save to her—and James, too."

"So he said," Jeremy replied dryly. "We have only his word for it. Besides, there are plenty who believe that it was his actions that drove her to run away from him in the first place." Seeing that Bella was ready to leap once more to Daggett's defense, Jeremy added hastily, "But even if we set aside the death of his first wife, what about his second, poor Elizabeth Fenton? Do you really believe that it was some robber who broke into the house and shot her? I know that was the ruling at the time, but no one honestly thinks that it was a *stranger* who killed her. Everyone says that she and Tony were fighting like savages. And don't forget, he only married her because of a wager—there was no love lost between the pair of them."

At the stricken expression on Arabella's face, Jeremy cursed himself. Crossing to her, he put his arm around her shoulder, and muttered, "Gad! I am so sorry, Bella. I forgot. I never should have said such a thing."

Her eyes suspiciously bright, Arabella said, "It doesn't matter. Tony does seem to have a penchant for making foolish wagers, doesn't he? First Elizabeth, and then me." Flashing him a smile, she said, "I cannot argue with you about Tony's past, but I do not believe that he cold-bloodedly shot Elizabeth—do not forget she was carrying his baby at the time. No matter how much he may have hated her, he would not have murdered his own child."

In a far more adult voice than she had ever heard from him in the past, Jeremy said, "If it was his child. And if it wasn't, it gave him good reason to want her dead."

Tiredly, Arabella said, "You seem to have heard a great deal about Tony's past. I would remind you that much of it is gossip and that there has never been anything proven." She met Jeremy's gaze steadily. "I would never have thought myself in love with him if I had the slightest suspicion that he had murdered Elizabeth—or Mercy, for that matter. No one will ever convince me that Mercy's death wasn't a tragic accident. Remember he was only twenty-one, just your age, and they had been only married for six months when she tried to run away with Terrell." She smiled sadly. "There is no pretending that Tony had not been spoiled and petted all his life, or that he has a formidable temper. I'm sure that he was furious when she left him. It doesn't surprise me that he went charging after them—pride alone would have demanded that he do so. I am also certain that he never meant for her and James to die."

Arabella paused and took a deep breath, before going on softly, "And as for Elizabeth, he swore to me that he had nothing to do with Elizabeth's death. Besides, he had dined at Blackburne's place that evening and was not even at home. It was his butler who heard the shot and found her dead. I believe Tony—he may be a blackguard, gambler, and ne'er-do-well, and I cannot deny that he has acted reprehensibly, but he is no murderer.

Hotheaded, arrogant, impetuous, careless upon occasion, even foolish, but not a murderer."

Jeremy wasn't about to argue with her. It was obviously she felt deeply about these matters, but he could not help saying, "Even if I were to agree with you—and I don't—what makes you so positive that we can take his word on the vowels?"

Arabella sighed and slipped out from under his arm. Walking over to a pair of French doors that opened onto the small rose garden at the side of the house, she pulled aside the gauzy drape which covered the glass, and said, "You gentlemen will forgive each other many things, but the one thing that labels a man beyond the pale, a veritable pariah, is not keeping his word. No one has ever questioned Tony's word." She smiled faintly. "It is the one thing everyone agrees upon. For all his faults, Tony Daggett would never go back on his word. Believe me, you shall have the vowels."

Jeremy wasn't happy with the situation and sensed that there was a great deal his sister had not told him. But she seemed very confident that Daggett would return the vowels, and for the moment, he would have to accept her word.

Deciding that nothing would be gained by further discussion on the morals and manners of Tony Daggett, he asked, "Did he tell you when he would return the vowels?"

Arabella nodded, her gaze on the roses beyond the French doors. "In six months. But to—"

"In *six* months!" Jeremy exclaimed, his blue eyes kindling. "That's nonsensical. If he means what he says, why doesn't he just hand over the vowels immediately?"

She had hoped that Jeremy wouldn't ask that question, but anticipating that he might, she said coolly, "He, er, we, felt that you needed to be taught a lesson. Simply having your vowels returned to you so quickly and easily, might not make you fully appreciate just how unwise you were." Not meeting Jeremy's outraged stare, she continued gamely, "We decided that, um, having possession of the vowels denied you for six months would teach you to be more cautious in the future."

"And if something were to happen to him during that time?" Jeremy asked grimly. "What then?"

"He is writing a letter to the effect that the vowels are yours and that if anything unforeseen should happen to him prior to that time, they are to be returned to you immediately." She glanced back at him, her expression wry. "I am not a fool, Jeremy. I did not just take him at his word."

"Well, then," Jeremy muttered unhappily, "it seems as if our troubles are behind us, doesn't it? Or will be in six months."

Arabella nodded. "So it would seem—and I hope you have learned a lesson from all this."

"I'll have six months to find out, won't I?" Jeremy replied almost sullenly.

Annoyed with herself for having slipped in that little homily, Arabella smiled, and said, "It shall not be too bad. No one except the three of us knows that Tony is holding the vowels for you. On the surface, everything will be as it was—the bank accounts, everything are still in your name and will remain so. Tony will not change anything."

"I suppose so," Jeremy admitted unhappily, "but I do not like it. I feel as if I have a sword hanging over my head. I tell you, Bella, I will not rest easy until those vowels are back in my hands."

"Once we have the letter you may rest easy. We will then have proof that Tony means to do as he says. Even if he were so inclined, he will not be able to refute his own words."

Jeremy nodded, his mood lightening a trifle. "That's true. His letter will be almost as good as actually having the vowels themselves." A little glimmer of anxiety in his blue eyes, he asked, "Er, when will we have this letter?"

"Friday afternoon." And she refused to think about what else was going to happen on Friday afternoon.

Jeremy took an agitated step around the room. "I shall feel like I am in a state of limbo until then, I can tell you!"

"I know precisely how you feel," Arabella said in a hollow voice, reality and the knowledge of what she had committed herself to hitting deep. Once she actually became Tony's mistress, she hoped that she would feel more confident about the decision she had made.

"So, what are we to do in the meantime?" Jeremy asked uncertainly.

"What we do," Arabella said lightly, "is go on as if everything is progressing as it should." Taking a deep breath, she added, "Since the vowels are to be returned and we are no longer in danger of losing Highview, there is no real reason for you to remain here at Greenleigh. In fact, in view of Cousin Agatha's impending arrival, I think that you should go home and be there to greet her when she arrives. If she has already arrived"—Arabella's eyes danced—"you shall tell her that as soon as you remembered that she might actually arrive today, that nothing could keep you at Greenleigh—you felt compelled to ride home posthaste to greet her."

Jeremy laughed. "Oh, Bella! No one can tell a whisker like you can."

"Which is not a talent one should be proud of," she replied with a twinkle.

They spoke desultorily for a few minutes longer, and then Jeremy, too, departed Greenleigh. Arabella promised to have his clothing sent back to Highview, along with his servants.

After Jeremy left, Arabella was busy for some time. A meeting with the Tidmores immediately followed Jeremy's departure, and if they were surprised to find that young Master Montgomery had returned home and that Miss Montgomery would be staying indefinitely at Greenleigh, neither gave any indication of it.

The Tidmores, Ann and Thomas, were related to several members of the staff at Highview and had, like the others, followed the Montgomery family from England. Having watched Arabella and the younger Montgomerys grow up, there was a degree of intimacy between them that was not usually found between master and servant.

When Arabella explained that her stay would be a lengthy one, Ann Tidmore, her sweet, round face alight with pleasure, exclaimed, "Oh, miss! I am so happy to hear you say so. Thomas and I have long thought that it would be the best thing for you to have the ordering of your own household."

"Indeed, miss, we were talking of it only the other day." A spark lit Thomas's gray eyes, his short, wiry form almost quivering with excitement. "Will you be expanding the staff, miss? Mrs. Tidmore has long had her eye on a strapping young woman she'd like to hire as cook, and I know of at least half a dozen slaves who are wasted in the fields; they would make excellent house servants. Shall we see to it?"

Arabella smiled at them fondly. Ann Tidmore had been her grandfather's housekeeper for a number of years before his death, and Thomas, his butler. As their gray hair and lined faces testified, neither was a day under sixty-five, and she had left them at Greenleigh more as a form of semiretirement than anything else. Yet she sensed that they were eager to expand their duties, and while she had considered hiring other staff to replace them and to settle them in a nice little cottage of their own on the plantation, the expressions on their faces put that thought instantly from her mind.

"Er, yes, if you would not mind?"

"Mind? Bless my soul, child, it will be a pleasure!" said Thomas Tidmore. "The missus and I were nigh to dying of boredom with just the two of us rattling around in this place together. Our only pleasure was the spring and fall cleaning, when we had a proper staff in residence for a few weeks."

"I see," Arabella said teasingly, "that I have used you shamefully. Go. Go and find all the servants you think that we will need."

The afternoon that followed was a busy one. Mrs.

Tidmore insisted that Arabella eat a nice little meal she prepared for her; she had hardly finished her repast, when her clothing and maid arrived from Highview. After selecting a room for herself and seeing to the placement of clothes and other personal articles, nothing would do but she allow the Tidmores to take her on an inspection of the house and grounds. They had kept the house in immaculate condition and were rightfully proud of their work. By the time Arabella had viewed everything from the attics to the kitchen and the cavernous storerooms, darkness had fallen. She was longing for her bed, but Mrs. Tidmore tempted her to eat a bit of broth and a nice ham sandwich before she retired for the night.

While she had stayed often at Greenleigh, and the bed in which she lay was certainly comfortable, she still had trouble falling asleep that night. It seemed incredible that it had been only the previous morning when Jeremy had dropped his fireball at her feet and her world had turned topsy-turvy. So much had happened since then, but more alarming—in less than forty-eight hours, she was going to become Tony Daggett's mistress!

Determinedly Arabella wrenched her mind away from that fact and concentrated on trying to fall asleep. But her mind was too full of everything that had transpired, not the least her removal to Greenleigh. She had always been happy at Highview; it had been her home, but even after just a few hours at Greenleigh, she sensed the difference. Highview actually belonged to Jeremy. It had been her father and Mary's home. Greenleigh was hers alone.

For the first time in her life, she would be able to

please only herself when she made decisions; she did not have to consider or consult with anyone else no matter what she decided to do with the place. A little giggle shook her. Why, she could paint the place with stripes and no one would argue with her. Perhaps, she thought sleepily, there were advantages to having one's own household.

Despite being certain that she would not sleep a wink, Arabella eventually fell asleep, her mind filled with the notion of making Greenleigh her home permanently. How long she slept, she never knew. She only knew that she woke terrified.

Her heart was pounding, her breathing labored, and it took a moment for her to get her bearings, to remember that she was at Greenleigh. Then to her horror she became aware of the heavy weight on the bed next to her and the soft, whispery breathing of another person. *Another person lying beside her.* Her mouth opened to scream, but a hard, brutal hand clamped her lips shut.

"None of that," murmured a voice, a man's voice she didn't recognize. "Keep quiet and nothing will happen to you." She felt the prick of a knife at her throat. "I believe," went on the voice silkily, "that you have something of mine. I want it back."

Chapter Eight

❧

*H*er heart banging like a war drum, Arabella lay frozen, unbearably conscious of the knife at her throat. Her mind worked frantically, trying to make sense of what the man had said. She had something of his? What? And what was so compelling about the object that he couldn't have simply asked for its return?

"Now then," said the man, "I am only going to ask you once for its return. You tell me where it is, and as soon as I lay my hands on it we're quits. Play clever with me, and you'll regret it." She felt the knife prick her throat just a little. "Understand?"

Mutely Arabella nodded, terror rising through her. She had no idea what he was talking about, and it didn't appear that he was going to believe her if she said so.

Lying beside her on the bed and feeling her nod in the darkness, the intruder smiled to himself. It had been risky for him to do this, but he had decided that it was riskier still to think that the letter would simply vanish. He'd thought that once and damned if it hadn't resurfaced and given him a leveler he wasn't likely to forget. He'd taken care of Leyton, but it still gave him an unpleasant feeling whenever he thought of how helpless he had felt when Leyton had first tried to blackmail him. He had to find the letter and, this time, make certain that it was destroyed.

He was positive that Arabella had the letter even if she didn't know it; Leyton's aborted attempt at robbery had convinced him of that. Besides, he'd not found it during a rather thorough search of Leyton's things. He didn't believe that Arabella was a danger to him, even if she read the letter. If she were the only one he had to worry about, he would have let the matter rest. It was the fear of Tony's seeing the letter that motivated him. Arabella might not make the connection, but Tony undoubtedly would. His smile faded as he considered what that could mean: All his patient waiting and scheming would have been for naught.

Softly, he asked, "Now where is it?"

Arabella swallowed again. "You must believe me," she implored. "I swear to you that I do not know what it is that you seek."

He was silent as he turned her words over in his mind. She could be telling the truth. For a moment, he wondered if he had been mistaken. It was possible that she didn't have the letter, that Leyton had hidden it somewhere else, but he swiftly dismissed that idea. She had to have it—he was convinced of it. But there was a reasonable explanation for her denial. He wasn't certain how she had gained possession of the letter, so it was conceivable that she had not found it yet. Then again, she could be lying. So which was it? Truth or lie?

As her first terror ebbed and Arabella began to think more clearly, there was one thing she had determined upon; she had no plans simply to lie there and be slaughtered like a sheep. She lay stiff and unmoving beneath his knife, desperately seeking a way to defend herself. But search her mind as she might, no brilliant thought came to her, until with a leap of her heart, she remembered the heavy glass pitcher filled with water that was sitting on the small table next to her bed. Mrs. Tidmore, bless her! had pressed it and a glass upon her when she had retired in case she should become thirsty during the night.

Surreptitiously Arabella slid one arm toward the table and the precious pitcher. Second by second, inch by inch, her questing fingers grew nearer their goal.

The man sighed suddenly, and Arabella froze.

"I find myself," he admitted, "in a most peculiar position. If what you say is true, I have wasted my time. However, it is also possible that you are lying. But my real problem is what to do with you now that we have had this little conversation. I could, I suppose, take you some place private and make certain that you are telling the truth."

The knife slid stingingly along the side of her throat, and Arabella felt the warm wash of blood flowing in its wake. There was a roaring in her ears and she was conscious of a great rage welling up inside of her. He had cut her! How dare the cowardly scoundrel treat her thus! How dare he!

Unaware of the fury building within Arabella, the man sighed again. "This is becoming so much messier than I expected," he said more to himself than Arabella.

"Unfortunately, I am afraid that I cannot simply take your word for it, my dear—you'll have to come with me. We can, er, talk more easily away from here."

Arabella had absolutely no intention of going anywhere with him, especially since she had a very good idea he did not intend for her ever to return alive. She concentrated on laying her hands on the only weapon available, the heavy glass pitcher.

More to give herself time in which to reach the pitcher than because she was interested in what he was saying, Arabella asked, "What do you mean?"

Confident that she was thoroughly cowed, he lessened the pressure of the knife against her throat, and said, "I mean, my pretty, that whether you know what I am talking about or not, you now know too much. It was, I realize, a mistake coming here like this, but it is a mistake that I can easily rectify. So come along and don't give me any trouble."

Arabella barely heard him. With the knife no longer touching her, she concentrated on getting her fingers around the handle of the pitcher. To move was dangerous, but she sensed the moment to strike was then or never—and at that moment her fingers brushed the pitcher.

There was no time for finesse. Heedlessly she reared up, the pitcher in her hand, and swinging wildly, she cracked it savagely against the side of his head. The knife slashed viciously, but missed its target, and her assailant fell back groaning.

Soaked by the water that sloshed out of the pitcher, Arabella forcefully shoved away his heavy form. She scrambled from the bed and flew across the room to the door. Half-sobbing, she flung open the door and ran into the main upper hall. She took a deep breath and screamed like a banshee. It was quite a satisfying sound.

Down the stairs she stumbled, fright now that she was free mingling with the fury that churned in her breast. Braced to feel the hand of her assailant closing around her, she fled pell-mell, her feet barely touching every third step. Never stopping her headlong rush, the moment she hit the entrance hallway of the first floor, she sprinted off in the direction of the Tidmores' rooms, shouting at the top of her voice. This was no time to worry about dignity.

The blessed sound of anxious voices and the flicker of light came to her and a moment later she was clasped against Mrs. Tidmore's bosom.

"There, there, lovey," soothed Mrs. Tidmore. "Whatever is the matter?"

"A man," Arabella gasped. "There is a man in my bedroom—he was going to kill me!"

"Never say so!" exclaimed Mr. Tidmore, his expression shocked, as he held his candle higher to get a closer look at Arabella.

"It's true, I tell you!" Arabella insisted, her eyes huge with fear. "He had a knife at my throat."

Mrs. Tidmore smothered a shriek, her eyes widening as she took a second look at Arabella. Arabella's gown was wet and stained unmistakably with blood. Along her neck there was a thin, terrifying gash.

It took a bit for the Tidmores to assure themselves that Arabella was not fatally wounded. The wound was surface, hardly a scratch, but it bled profusely and when mixed with the water from the pitcher it looked like there was much more blood than there actually was. Mrs. Tidmore was all for cleaning and caring for the wound immediately, but Arabella impatiently brushed aside her concerns.

"I am not going to die, or even faint," she muttered, touched by their concern, but aware that the seconds were fleeing—as was, no doubt, her assailant. "It is the veriest scratch, and in the meantime, the devil who did this to me is getting away. There is not a moment to lose."

Seconds later, an old-fashioned flintlock rifle held tightly in his hands, Mr. Tidmore began a stealthy climb to Arabella's bedroom. He was closely followed by Arabella, who carried a lamp in one hand and one of her grandfather's dueling pistols in the other. After Arabella came Mrs. Tidmore, a solid maple rolling pin gripped menacingly in her hand. Pressing close in the rear was Arabella's maid, Martha, also carrying a lamp, and crowded behind her were the two young housemaids who slept in the house.

Throwing wide the door to Arabella's room, Mr. Tidmore called out, "Come out. Come out or I shall shoot."

Only silence greeted his words. Motioning Arabella to cast the light of her lamp more fully into the room, they slowly crept forward.

"He's gone!" Arabella cried with dismay, when a swift search of the room revealed no hidden assailant. The wide-open French doors that led out to the upstairs veranda showed his avenue of escape.

"That may be," replied Mr. Tidmore grimly, "but he left behind his little toy."

The "toy" was a wickedly curved knife of fearful

size. Staring at the long, gleaming blade in the candle-light, and remembering the feel of it against her throat, Arabella swallowed.

The crisis over, Mrs. Tidmore put down her rolling pin and set the girls to changing the soaked bedding. Clucking to herself, she picked up the empty pitcher, which miraculously had not broken. "There is a smear of blood on the rim. You must have struck him soundly."

"Not soundly enough," Arabella half snarled as she slipped a yellow-cotton wrapper over her damp night-gown.

Further inspection of the room revealed no new clues, and a search through the rest of the house and the grounds turned up nothing new. Having sent the other servants off to their beds, the Tidmores and Arabella settled comfortably in the Tidmores' neat little parlor at the rear of the house.

Arabella's wound had been tended to Mrs. Tidmore's satisfaction and, in view of the circumstances, Mr. Tidmore had broken out a bottle of brandy laid down by Arabella's grandfather over a decade earlier. All of them were partaking.

As the liquor slid warmly down her throat and settled comfortably in her stomach, Arabella felt some of the last vestiges of fear and fury dissipate. Besides, it was difficult to feel the least fearful sitting in the Tidmore's cozy parlor with the pair of them happily sipping their own brandies just as if this were a normal evening rit-ual. But it wasn't.

After a moment, Arabella looked across at Mr. Tidmore, and said, "At first light, I want you to select four of the stoutest men we have and, until I say differently, have them patrol the exterior of the house during the hours of darkness." Her fine mouth tightened. "I do not want to wake up and find a stranger with a knife in my bed again." She made a face. "*Anyone* with a knife."

"I just don't understand it," Mrs. Tidmore said anxiously, her ruffled nightcap slightly askew. "We've never had such an incident before. Why, I've never heard of anything like this happening to anyone we know. If it weren't for that knife we found on your bed and the wound on your neck, I would almost think you had a bad dream."

"It was no dream," Arabella replied grimly. "But like you, I find it nearly inconceivable that such a thing could happen. I would much prefer that it had been simply a nightmare!"

Mr. Tidmore shook his gray head unhappily. "Makes my blood boil, it does, to think that a respectable young lady like Miss Arabella can't even sleep safely in her own bed! Shocking."

"I just can't understand what he was after," mused Mrs. Tidmore. "If he was just a common thief, why did he attack you?"

Arabella shook her bright head. She had not told the Tidmores everything. Until she had time to think things through, it had seemed wiser to keep quiet about the fact that the intruder had been after something specifically that belonged to him, an item he'd been convinced that she possessed. Better to let them think it had been just a queer happenstance.

"I have no idea why he acted as he did," Arabella finally said. "I am only happy that I managed to escape."

That set Mrs. Tidmore off into exclaiming over Arabella's bravery and an agitated recounting of everything that could have gone wrong. There was more speculation about the man's motives and it was a while before Arabella was able to be alone with her thoughts.

There was no question of Arabella's returning to the bedroom where the attack had taken place. Despite her brave front she found herself, at least for that night, a trifle uneasy at sleeping alone on the upper floor. Taking a few quilts from a protesting Mrs. Tidmore, she waved them away and proceeded to make herself a bed on the sofa in the main saloon.

Sleep took a while in coming to Arabella. Her nerves were still jangled and taut and for several minutes after the Tidmores had departed and the house began to settle back down, she started at every sound. Her grandfather's dueling pistol lay by her side, and she took comfort from its solid presence. Next time, if there ever *was* a next time, she would have a most unpleasant surprise for anyone who thought to attack her while she slept.

Eventually she did sleep, though it was broken and restless, and she woke at first light and, for the second morning in a row, out of sorts. However, having enjoyed a relaxing bath and a tasty breakfast, and having been petted and fussed over by Mrs. Tidmore and Martha, she was feeling much more herself. She was even able to dismiss Martha's concerns about the attack the night before.

"The man must have been mad," Arabella said calmly. "I can think of no other reason for what happened. And you needn't worry that it shall happen again—Tidmore has arranged for the house to be watched at night. Put it from your mind. I have." Which was not strictly true, but the explanation seemed to satisfy Martha. And following her own advice, Arabella did not allow herself to think overmuch about what had happened. But despite her best efforts, the incident nagged, lurking all the while at the back of her mind as she went about the day.

Living at Greenleigh was a new experience for her. It seemed very strange to be the only one in residence except for servants. She was used to the boisterous household at Highview and in comparison Greenleigh seemed, well, quiet. She missed her usual routine, the excited chatter of the children, Jeremy's laughing banter, and Mary's light manner. She was, she realized, a trifle homesick, and she had only been away from Highview for twenty-four hours.

Telling herself not to be a ninny, Arabella threw herself into tasks of the day. After the previous day's brief tour, she began to familiarize herself more thoroughly with the running of the household and the estate. She approved the new additions to the staff that the Tidmores presented to her and began to make lists of items that needed to be purchased in order to make Greenleigh more suitable for her permanent occupancy. She even started to consider changes she wanted to make in the arrangements of the various rooms, as well as methods by which to increase the productivity of the plantation.

By one o'clock that afternoon, she was eager to take a break from her tasks and asked Mrs. Tidmore to have a picnic basket packed for her. She prepared to leave the house to view the lodge where she would meet Tony the next afternoon. All through the morning, she had tried to push away thoughts of Tony and the bargain they had made, but she knew that it was a futile effort. As the hours passed, it was more and more difficult to keep her mind on the matters at hand. Images of Tony and memories of previous intimate meetings at her grandfather's hunting lodge drove everything else out of her mind.

At least, she told herself grumpily as she walked away from the main house, when she was thinking of Tony, she wasn't thinking of the previous night. But the shocking events of that night had not gone far from her mind, and as she carefully picked her way along the narrow, almost overgrown path that led to the hunting lodge, they came back to bedevil her.

The day was warm and humid. Insects droned sleepily through the verdant forest, and there was the occasional cry of a bird on the heavy, scent-laden air. Normally Arabella would have taken delight in such a day—the sky was a brilliant blue with nary a cloud in sight, and the sun was a burning golden orb beaming high overhead—but her thoughts were on other things. Beyond making certain that she did not stumble over a root or step upon a snake as she followed the trail, her attention turned inward.

The previous night's attack still seemed incredible to her. All morning, she had refused to think about it, refused to remember the terror she had felt—and the rage. Or the knowledge that there was a man, whose identity she did not at present know, who was convinced that she had something that belonged to him, something he was willing to kill to get back. She didn't delude herself that she had seen the last of him; her grandfather's dueling pistol, currently resting carefully on top of the neatly packed lunch, proved that.

It was possible that she was wrong about the man's continued interest in her. After his failure last night and her honest mystification about what he was after, he might have decided that it would be wiser to leave well enough alone. Except, she thought with a frown, he had to know that she would be curious about what it was of his that he thought she had.

She made a face. This was the second time in two days someone had tried to rob her. Both incidents were freakish and it seemed likely that both attempts were done by the same person. What could be so important that someone, a man, was willing to take such risks? And why did he think that she had whatever it was he was missing? *And how,* she suddenly thought with an ominous drop in her stomach, *did he know I would be sleeping at Greenleigh last night?*

It wasn't a secret, but only a handful of people knew she had driven over from Highview and would be remaining at Greenleigh. The idea of Jeremy attacking her she brushed away as utterly ridiculous, and it was difficult, if not impossible, to picture Tom Denning or James Gayle threatening her with a knife. As for Morgan Slade, Jason Savage, or Blood Drinker . . . Her brow furrowed. They were strangers to her, but it couldn't have been one of them. The notion was outrageous. She'd only met them the afternoon before. And she certainly didn't have anything that belonged to one of them!

So who then?

There had been nothing familiar about the man who

attacked her. She had not recognized his voice or anything about him. The knife? No, she hadn't recognized it either; nor had the Tidmores. Which, of course, proved nothing.

She suddenly became aware of her surroundings and looked around in surprise as she realized that she had reached her destination. Before her, in a small clearing, sat the lodge.

It was a quaint-looking building, not very large, made from roughly hewn cedar logs. Its steep roof had a wide overhang. There were heavy shutters at the two windows that faced her, and she was surprised to find that they had been flung wide, as had the wide door in the center of the front wall.

The whicker of a horse from behind the lodge, where she knew there was a lean-to shelter made her heart leap uncomfortably. It was obvious that she was not the only visitor to the lodge.

Quickly she opened the picnic basket and took out the dueling pistol. After last night, she was not as inclined to give whoever was inside the lodge the benefit of the doubt. His reason for being here might be perfectly innocent, and then again . . .

A large man in a shirt with rolled-up sleeves suddenly filled the doorway, and, recognizing him, Arabella's expression was one of wary surprise.

"What," she asked, as she lowered her pistol, "are you doing here?"

Tony smiled at her, and she was annoyed at the rush of warmth that spread through her body.

Stepping out into the dappled sunlight, Tony said easily, "I thought that I would make certain that no, er, wildlife had taken up residence, and perhaps lay in a few supplies." His gaze dropped to the pistol, and he quirked a brow. "Is that for me?"

Arabella shook her head. "No, although I cannot deny that there have been times that I would have gladly used it on you."

Tony strolled up to her, his movements like a big African cat patrolling his domain. Stopping a scant few inches from her, with warm, strong fingers, he lifted up her chin. "But not today," he stated calmly, and brushed his mouth against hers.

Arabella's fingers involuntarily clenched around the pistol at the teasing pressure of his lips against hers, but she managed to reply with commendable calm. "No, not today."

He smiled and tucked her hand under his arm. "Excellent! I knew I could rely on your good sense. And now shall we inspect our soon-to-be boudoir?"

"This is just a jest to you, isn't it?" she said angrily. "A pleasant way to waste away a few hours."

Tony stopped, the expression on his dark face suddenly fierce. "Nothing," he said harshly, "that pertains to you has ever been a jest to me."

"You'll never convince me of that!" she shot back, the memory of a time when she believed him, when his promises had filled her with joy, knifing through her and making her cringe at her own stupidity. Tony Daggett would never deceive her again. Never! "You courted me and became engaged to me all because of a wager! So don't try to pretend now that I, or my feelings, ever meant anything to you."

"That damned wager!" he growled, temper sparking in

his indigo eyes. "Are you ever going to forget about it? Are you ever going to give me a chance to live down the follies and mistakes of a time that I am not proud of?"

Feeling oddly pleased that she had nettled him, Arabella's nose went up in the air. "No. I am not."

Tony's mouth tightened. "Do you know, sweetheart, that there are times that I wonder if your undeniable charms are worth putting up with that waspish tongue of yours?"

"You could always change the terms of our bargain," Arabella suggested demurely. "I shall be happy to oblige you."

"No," Tony said flatly. "The bargain stays." And catching her off guard, he pulled her into his arms. His mouth found hers, and there was nothing gentle or teasing about the kiss he gave her this time. The kiss was hungry and demanding, a man's kiss for a woman he desired, a woman he intended to have.

Arabella could not fight him. In the secret places of her heart, she did not want to fight him. Her entire body rejoiced in his plundering kiss, in the hard crush of his lips against hers, the demanding thrust of his tongue and the remembered taste that was uniquely Tony's. Held tightly against his tall body, she was buffeted by a powerful surge of naked desire. Her nipples ached, her arms longed to embrace him, to hold him close, and the heated, almost painful throb between her thighs drove coherent thought from her mind. Helplessly she arched up to him, the pistol falling unheeded on the ground beside them.

Tony muttered something unintelligible; his hands dropped to her bottom, and he yanked her firmly against the rigid bulk of his erection. Pleasuring them both, he moved her erotically against himself, the rhythmic pressure of her soft warm body, even with the layers of clothing between them, almost bringing him to the point of disgrace.

Unable to bear it a moment longer, he tore his mouth from hers, and muttered, "The hell with this!" And swinging Arabella up into his arms, he strode swiftly to the lodge. A sharp kick of his heel slammed the door shut behind them.

Her senses reeling, Arabella was tossed down onto a tumble of quilts and the next instant she was crushed beneath Tony's body. He found her lips and just as if there had been no break in the original kiss, took up where he had left off, his tongue taking blunt possession of her mouth.

The inside of the lodge was gloomy and shadowy, and small dust motes floated lazily in the few shafts of sunlight that permeated the area. A faint musty smell lingered on the air, but the quilts were clean and fresh, and for Arabella, Tony's demanding mouth and hands blotted out everything but his urgent caresses. Hungers she had forgotten awakened with a ravenous appetite for the touch of this one man; memories of Tony's lovemaking and the sweet ecstasy she had once known in his embrace had her clinging mindlessly to him, her body pliant and yielding beneath his questing hands and mouth.

Tony was as blind to his surroundings as Arabella. All his senses, every fiber of his being focused on the soft, voluptuous form before him. He hadn't planned this, hadn't planned to fall upon her like a starving man upon a lush, ripe peach, and yet that is exactly what he did. His mouth ate hers, his lips and tongue tasting and relishing its sweetness, his hands delighting in the firm, resilient flesh of her generous body.

His lips dropped to the full breasts still covered by her gown, and his mouth fastened hungrily upon them, heedless of the material that denied him access. He suckled fiercely, leaving damp patches on her gown, but it wasn't enough. A rough downward yank and her breasts suddenly spilled over the top of the gown. With a heartfelt groan, Tony's mouth captured a naked nipple, feasting on the plump nub.

Arabella gasped at the searing, demanding touch of his mouth on her breast. Her fingers clenched in his hair as she arched up uncontrollably at his caress, unconsciously urging him to greater excesses. He did not disappoint her.

Stunningly, she was suddenly aware that his hands were moving up her legs, pushing aside the enveloping garments that impeded his way. His hands slid along her thighs, caressing and exploring, and Arabella made a muffled exclamation when at last he reached the mound of crisp curls between her legs. When he touched her, when his fingers petted and parted the soft, damp flesh he found, Arabella shuddered, violent need clawing through her.

"Oh, please," she moaned, thrashing wildly beneath his stroking fingers. "Please. Please. *Please.*"

She wasn't even certain what she was pleading for; she only knew that she was desperate for succor from the ache that was centered there beneath his fingers.

Tony kissed her deeply, his hand fumbling with the opening of his breeches. Against her mouth, he muttered, "Sweetheart, I have every intention of pleasing us both."

Sighing as his swollen member leaped from his breeches, he sank back down onto her. His sigh changed to a soft, shaken groan of utter pleasure as unerringly, his shaft pierced the satiny flesh between her thighs. She was tight, so tight and hot, that Tony thought he would explode at the moment of entrance. But he did not. Trembling at the sweetly carnal sensation of being inside her once more, of thrusting heavily again and again into those silken depths, Tony fought to prolong the pleasure. It was a battle he would lose.

Arabella thought that she remembered what it felt like to make love to Tony, but she discovered that memory had lied. That memory could never compare to reality.

Her whole body seemed possessed by him. His scent was in her nostrils, his flesh was warm beneath her caressing fingers, his mouth locked on hers, just as lower, their bodies were locked together in an ancient melding. Emotions, sensations, as old and primitive as the act itself roiled up through her, but it was the sweetness, the incredible sweetness of being in Tony's arms once again, of knowing the joy of his possession once more, that pushed her to the edge. Ecstasy caught her, rippling up through her entire body, and she cried aloud at the power and wonder of it.

Tony captured her cry with his mouth, his own body racked suddenly by pleasure as fierce and powerful as hers as he emptied himself into her. And then there was the sweetness. The sweetness of lazily kissing her as passion ebbed, of holding her soft, generous form next to him, of lying bonelessly complete at her side.

Chapter Nine

Tony could have lain forever with Arabella cradled next to him, but all too soon she stirred in his arms. His mouth twisted. And now she had another sin to lay at his door.

If Arabella was thinking of sin, it certainly wasn't Tony's. She was appalled by her own actions, stunned to realize how swiftly passion could blind one to everything but the clawing need for release from the demands of the flesh. Embarrassed and ashamed of herself, shaken that she could act so lewdly and wantonly, she struggled away from the comfort of Tony's arms and sat up.

With shaking hands she pushed her rumpled skirt modestly over her thighs, and with fumbling movements stuffed her naked breasts back into the demure bodice of her gown. She was burningly conscious of Tony lying at her side, but she could not look at him, shame keeping her gaze firmly averted from his long body.

I have made love with Tony! she thought dazedly. She had been as willing as any common lightskirt, as eager as any bold-faced whore, and she could not deny her own actions or pretend that it had been entirely Tony's fault. She would have liked to blame what had happened on Tony, but her innate honesty forbade it.

She flashed him a resentful glance from beneath her lashes. It really wasn't fair that he should be so attractive, with that tall, lean body of his and those mocking indigo blue eyes. His physical attractions aside, it was also monstrously unfair that there was something about him that one look from him, one touch, turned her silly, yearning body into a mound of quivering mush. *And with as much backbone,* she thought waspishly.

Studiously avoiding looking at him, she got to her feet. Silently she concentrated on setting herself to rights, unwilling to think about what had just transpired between them. Her gown shook out fairly well, but her hair was a tumbled mass that defied her efforts to push it into something resembling the neat little bun she had started out with.

Watching her as she tried to force the fiery curls into some semblance of order, Tony got up from the pile of quilts. Calmly refastening his breeches, he walked over to a scrubbed-pine table that sat in the middle of the room and, selecting an item from the group of oddments scattered there, turned and walked back to her.

"If you will allow me?" he asked lightly, holding out a silver-backed brush.

Arabella nodded and turned her back to him. "You planned for everything, didn't you?" Her voice was not friendly.

Tony sighed. "No, sweetheart. I didn't. I certainly didn't plan for what just happened between us." When

Arabella remained silent, he added gently, "Don't repine over it, Elf. All we did was consummate our bargain a day earlier, and more, er, spontaneously, than planned."

Gratefully she seized upon his words. Telling herself that Tony was right, that they had only done what she had agreed to do on the morrow, Arabella struggled to regain her composure. It was not easy. Not with Tony's warm form standing so close to hers and her body still tingling from the aftermath of their passion.

Reminding herself that she was a grown woman and not some simpering maiden who had just been tumbled for the first time, Arabella finally managed to say with a commendable air of nonchalance, "I had not considered that aspect of it."

Behind her, his hands busy with the fiery mass of tangled curls, Tony smiled. "Well, you should have. In fact," he went on in a teasing tone, "you should thank me."

Outraged, Arabella spun around to glare at him.

"Thank you!" she snapped, her golden brown eyes bright with temper. "Why should I thank you?"

He grinned and ran a caressing finger down her straight little nose. "Because now you won't spend the night tossing and turning worrying about tomorrow."

"You flatter yourself!"

"Hmm, perhaps. But I think it is just as well that things worked out as they did. Our bargain has been struck, and there is no going back."

"Except," Arabella said sweetly, "that I have paid the price, but you have not—unless of course, you have brought the letter resigning all rights to Jeremy's vowels with you?"

"You know I didn't," Tony said dryly. "I think we agreed that what happened was not planned. I had no reason to bring the letter with me. I did not even know that you would be here. Do not worry, Arabella, you will have your damned letter." He cocked a brow. "And why are you here?"

Arabella made a face. "The same reason that you apparently came, to see what condition the place was in and to see what was needed to set it to rights." She glanced around. "I see that you have already been at work."

It was true. The open beams and corners had been swept clean of cobwebs and debris. The heavy wooden mantel of the fireplace looked as if it had recently been dusted; the hearth was clean, the kindling for a fire neatly lay in the center. But Tony's industry had not stopped there. The bed, and she couldn't help the blush that burned her cheeks when she glanced at it, appeared to have been freshly made, or had been before they had set the quilts all askew by their activities. From the pile of dust and grit near the doorway, and the straw broom resting nearby, it was obvious that she had interrupted him sweeping the floor.

"I generally," Tony said mockingly, "try to provide some degree of comfort for my, ah, ladies."

Arabella rounded on him. "Do you know that you are the most odious man it has ever been my misfortune to meet?"

Tony laughed and pulled her against him. "And also, I trust, the most fascinating."

Swooping down on her mouth, he kissed away the angry retort that rose to her lips, and it was several long moments later before Arabella managed to extricate herself from his embrace. Head spinning, pulse pounding, she put a little distance between them, and muttered, "Oh, definitely fascinating, if you remember that one can find even a rattlesnake fascinating."

He laughed again, and, putting out a hand, said, "Come, let us cry quits. I did not come here to be wounded by that sharp little tongue of yours. Let us see what has to be done to make our abode comfortable."

It was easier to go along with him than argue, especially since that was the reason she had come to the lodge in the first place. They worked together quietly for several moments, Arabella remaking the rumpled bed while Tony finished sweeping the floor. He had brought some candles and pewter holders, and she placed them on the mantel for future use, and put a pair of long-stemmed glasses and a half dozen or so bottles of wine in the rough pine cupboard that sat on the wall opposite the bed. There was even a matching washbowl and pitcher sitting on the pine table, and her lips tightened: he had planned well. Picking up the silver-backed brush and the matching comb and mirror, she stared consideringly at them. Tony was either being thoughtful, or he was very practiced in arranging trysting places. The latter, she decided unhappily, remembering the night she had found him naked, here in this very place, on that very bed with an equally naked Molly Dobson beneath him.

Tony caught sight of her expression and, setting aside the broom, crossed to her. His hands on her shoulders, he said perceptively, "Don't, sweetheart. Don't think about the past. Forget what lies behind us. Let us begin anew."

She gave him a sad smile. "I cannot. I believed you once. I do not think that I ever shall again."

"Then I shall just have to change your mind, won't I?" he said, his gaze locked on hers.

"Do you think you can?" she asked, curious in spite of herself, angry at the leap of hope in her breast.

"I only know that I am going to try my damnedest to do so," Tony vowed softly. He bent his head, clearly intending to kiss her, but he stopped abruptly, his gaze fixed on the wound on her neck.

"What is this?" he asked, tracing the mark with one long finger. "If I did not know better, I would swear that it is a knife wound."

Instinctively Arabella's hand, went to cover the nasty slash along her neck. When she had dressed that morning, she had arranged a soft scarf around her neck to hide most of the evidence of the previous night's horrifying attack; she had still been wearing the scarf when she had arrived at the lodge. During their lovemaking Tony must have tossed the scarf aside.

Turning away from him, she said, "It is. Someone broke into Greenleigh last night and threatened me. He used a knife."

Tony's hand closed painfully around her arm, and he swung her around to face him. The fierce expression on his face startled her, the look in his eyes making her mouth go dry.

"Someone attacked you?" he asked with quiet savagery.

Mutely, Arabella nodded, her eyes wide with astonishment. She had never seen him this way before, so dangerously intent, so full of grim purpose. There was a lethal air about him, the set of his chiseled lips and the inimical gleam in the depths of his dark blue eyes in stark contrast to his usual mocking, teasing manner.

Aware of Arabella's astonishment, Tony fought with the blind fury that coursed through him at the knowledge that someone had dared harm her. Normally he prided himself on his cool head and iron will, but where Arabella was concerned, he'd never had much control, never since the first moment he had laid eyes on her. To know that someone had threatened her, had actually harmed her, filled him with a volatile mixture of stark fear and cold rage. Someone, he thought fiercely, was going to be very sorry. Very, *very* sorry.

Taking a deep breath and forcing himself to act rationally, Tony guided her to one of a pair of stout oak chairs in the lodge.

"Tell me about it," he said as he settled her in one of the chairs.

Arabella did, leaving nothing out. It was a relief to share her fears with Tony, to share with him the whole incredible story.

By the time she finished speaking, most of Tony's initial rage had abated and he was able to view the incident with some, although not complete, objectivity.

"It is a wild tale you tell, my dear," Tony admitted, as he paced the floor in front of her. "A tale, that were it not for the mark on your neck, I would have trouble believing."

"Thank you very much," Arabella said dryly, irritated that it was only the wound on her neck that convinced him of the truth of her words. "You have as good as admitted that you would think me a liar."

Tony winced. "That was not my intention. I only meant that it is such an unlikely happening, that it is difficult to believe that someone actually went to those lengths in order to retrieve something he claims you have. You have no idea what he was after?"

Arabella shook her head. "None. Except for seeing Leyton and you on Tuesday afternoon, I have been nowhere except Highview and Greenleigh. I took nothing with me from Leyton's and"—she shot him a look— "I do not believe that it was you who held a knife at my throat last night."

Ignoring the jab, Tony muttered, "Well, your unknown guest last night certainly wasn't Leyton."

"What do you mean? How do you know that it wasn't Leyton?"

Cursing his own clumsy tongue, Tony said bluntly, "Leyton is dead. He was murdered Tuesday night."

Arabella paled. One hand at her throat, she asked, "And how do you know this?"

"Because," Tony said wearily, as he threw himself down in the chair beside Arabella, "I saw his body."

"You went to Oakmont after you escorted me home to Highview?"

Tony nodded, pretending not to hear the accusatory note in her voice. "After what happened to you on the road, it seemed a logical move." At the expression on her face, he said hastily, "I wasn't going to harm him. I just wanted to assure myself that Leyton couldn't have been the man who tried to rob you."

"And were you assured?" she asked sharply.

Tony shook head. "No. In fact, what I found convinced me that my suspicion of Leyton had been correct."

"You found proof that he tried to rob me?"

"Yes," Tony admitted. "I found proof that Leyton, or at least someone from Oakmont, had been out that night and had returned not too many minutes ahead of my arrival there. One of the horses had obviously been ridden hard—the animal was still lathered and damp. And Leyton had a welt on his face, where you whipped him."

Arabella frowned. She rather thought that she would have preferred some nameless individual who just happened to have tried to rob her on Tuesday night than to know that it had been someone she knew. Especially someone who was now dead. Uneasily, her hand went to the slash on her neck as another even more frightening thought occurred to her.

In a small voice, she asked, "Do you think the man who attacked me last night might have murdered Leyton?"

Grimly, Tony nodded. "I think it is a logical conclusion. While Natchez is noted for its criminal activities, most of them usually take place amongst the rougher element. I find it hard to believe that the attempted robbery, Leyton's murder, and your experience last night were simply unrelated acts of violence." He looked at her, the expression in his eyes hard to define. "You seem to be the key, my dear."

"How could I be? I don't know anything."

"Perhaps you know something or have seen something that is important, only you don't realize it," Tony offered.

Arabella started to protest, then closed her mouth with a snap. "There was someone else at Leyton's when I came to call," she said slowly. "He was hiding, but I saw his boots protruding from beneath the curtains in Leyton's office."

Tony sat up with a jerk. His gaze intent, he demanded, "Are you positive? That there was actually someone there—it wasn't simply an empty pair of boots placed behind the curtains?"

Arabella threw him a glance of scorn. "No, Tony, dear, it was not an empty pair of boots! Besides, Leyton was acting strangely. He was nervous, and he very definitely wanted me to leave. I thought it was simply because of the nature of my call, but now I wonder. And of course, once I spied the boots, and knew that someone was spying on us, I wanted out of there immediately." She gave a delicate shudder. "It was rather unnerving."

Liking what he was hearing less and less, Tony stood up and walked impatiently around the room. "We have to assume," he said thoughtfully, "that Leyton was in some sort of partnership with someone—your fellow with the boots—and that, for whatever reasons, they had a falling out and Boots, for want of another name, killed Leyton."

"And they fell out," Arabella guessed, "because of something that Leyton had, something Boots wanted and Leyton wouldn't give to him—because once he did . . ." Her voice lowered in horror as she said, "Because once he did, he knew Boots would kill him!" She swallowed. "I must have interrupted their meeting, and after I left, Leyton got it into his head that I had taken whatever it was they were arguing over. Which is why he later tried to rob me—he needed to get it back in order to protect himself from Boots." She frowned. "He must have planned once he had it back to put it somewhere safe and hold it over Boots. Only he failed." Her face went white. "And Boots knew it!"

"Which is why Boots paid you a visit last night," Tony ended grimly.

Arabella leaped up from her chair, clearly agitated. "Oh, Tony," she cried, "do you think that is what happened? That this Boots person believes that I have whatever it was that Leyton had?"

Pulling her into his arms, Tony sighed. "The tale hangs together, sweet. And it makes more sense than to believe that none of the incidents is connected. That they were just coincidence."

Her face buried in his shoulder, Arabella asked in muffled tones, "Then he'll be back, won't he? He'll try again, won't he?"

Tony's arms crushed her to him. "Not," he said fiercely, "if I have anything to say about it."

"But how can you stop him? We don't know who he is—or even what he wants!"

"And that should be our first step—finding out what it is he thinks you have."

Arabella shot him an irritated glance and reluctantly left the comfort of his arms.

"I've already told you—I don't have anything!"

"Let's just make certain, shall we?" Tony suggested with such reasonable calm that Arabella's palm ached to connect with his jaw.

"And how do you propose we do that?" she asked

acidly. "Take an inventory of all the contents at High-view and Greenleigh?"

Tony smiled and shook his head. "No, nothing that drastic. The whole affair seems to start with your visit to Leyton's. We can begin there. So tell me again everything that happened."

Succinctly Arabella did, not bothering to hide her annoyance.

"So you see," she said exasperatedly, "there is no way that I could have taken something that wasn't mine from Leyton's."

"Are you certain? What about when you gathered up the deeds from the floor? Could something of his have been amongst them?"

Arabella started to say no, but considering the incident, she admitted, "I suppose it's possible—there were already several papers lying on his desk when I arrived. If it were something small or just a piece of paper, I might not have noticed it when I put everything away."

"Where are the deeds now?"

"At Mr. Haight's. I left them in the portfolio and returned them to him for safekeeping yesterday, before I came to Greenleigh."

"It is too late to do it today, but I suggest that tomorrow you drive into Natchez and look inside that portfolio and see if there is anything mixed in with your papers."

Arabella made a face. What Tony was proposing made sense, but she was getting rather weary of driving into Natchez and seeing Mr. Haight. Still, it would answer once and for all the question of whether she had anything that didn't belong to her in that portfolio. If they found something, the object should give them a clue about Boots's identity. If there were nothing amongst her papers, then they would have to rethink the situation. She really didn't have a choice, Arabella thought wryly.

"Very well," she said unenthusiastically, "I shall do it."

"Shall I escort you?"

"If I say 'no,' will it deter you?"

Tony laughed. "Probably not."

"Since I don't seem to have a choice in the matter," she muttered, "I shall be resigned to your company tomorrow morning."

Having thoroughly assured himself that Arabella had taken adequate precautions against another nocturnal visit from Boots, they made plans to meet on Friday morning. After a bit more tidying of the lodge, they left. Tony led his horse and walked beside her until Greenleigh came into sight. From the concealment of the forest, Tony waited, watching her until he knew she was safe inside the house. Only then did he turn his horse aside and begin the ride back to Sweet Acres.

He was more worried about the situation than he had admitted to Arabella. None of it made sense, and he was aware that while their speculations held together, they could be entirely mistaken. The events might not even be connected. Worse, it was possible that they would find nothing in her papers that shouldn't be there. Which event, he thought sourly, would blow a very large hole in their web of suspicions.

Hot, dusty, and irritated, Tony was in no mood for visitors when he arrived at Sweet Acres half an hour later. The sight of a neat bay gelding tied to one of the black-iron hitching posts at the front of the house made him swear under his breath. Now who?

Entering the house, Tony brushed aside Billingsley's lofty announcement that a young gentleman caller was waiting to see him.

"Whoever it is," Tony muttered, "can damn well wait until I have washed some of the dirt from me and changed my shirt."

Ten minutes later, having refreshed himself, Tony descended the stairs.

Confronting his beak-nosed butler, he asked, "Who is it? And where have you put him?"

Billingsley sniffed, obviously put out by Tony's earlier brusque manner. "It is a Mister Jeremy Montgomery. I told him that you were out, but he insisted upon waiting for you. Having no idea," he said grandly, "where you had gone or when you would return, I placed him in the green saloon and provided him with refreshment."

If Tony was surprised to find that Arabella's brother had come to call, it was not evident when he pushed open the doors and walked into the green saloon. But he was surprised. *Very.* And wary. Had young Montgomery found out about the infamous bargain he had forced upon Arabella? He sighed. The very last thing he needed was to be issued a challenge by this young cub.

The two men shook hands, introducing themselves. Tony had never met Jeremy; Arabella's brother had only been sixteen at the time of their aborted engagement and had not yet begun to join adult society. And since Tony had not been exactly welcome at Highview, despite Arabella's professed determination to marry him, there had been little interaction between Tony and the rest of her family.

Tony was not at first inclined to like Jeremy—after all, the silly young fool had gambled away his inheritance and put his family in jeopardy. On the other hand, Tony admitted, everyone was entitled to their youthful mistakes. The Lord knew that he had made plenty of them—far more grievous ones and with fewer excuses for them than Jeremy. And, he reminded himself, he had Jeremy to thank for creating a situation that put Arabella in his arms once more. Taking that into account, Tony was inclined to give Jeremy the benefit of the doubt.

Jeremy's handshake was firm and Tony was favorably taken by the honest and direct way Jeremy's blue eyes met his and the boy's overall manner. Motioning him to a seat, Tony took a comfortable chair covered in a dark green patterned silk opposite him.

Having heard for years tales of Tony Daggett's many excesses and the rampant gossip of murder and despicable acts that followed the man, Jeremy was not prepared to like Tony. Most of the talk he might have brushed aside, were it not for what Daggett had done to Arabella—for that, Jeremy found himself unable to forgive the man.

And yet, Jeremy found himself in a great dilemma. Expecting to be confronted by a murderous, dishonorable, dissipated knave, he wouldn't have been surprised to find Sweet Acres a den of depravity, with Daggett roaring drunk and the house filled with all sorts of blackguards and lewd women. Instead he had found a gracious, well-run home and a neatly dressed gentleman whose manner and demeanor betrayed only good breeding and polite interest. Certainly the handsome, urbane man sitting across from him did not in any way resemble the ogre he had been anticipating. Reminding himself that Daggett had once disarmed Arabella and that appearances could be deceiving, he decided to withhold judgment.

Nervously clearing his throat, Jeremy began, "You are no doubt wondering why I have called, sir."

"The question had crossed my mind," Tony said easily, crossing one booted foot over the other. "The relationship between our two families has not been particularly, er, warm."

Jeremy's jaw tightened. Although he had told himself he would not bring up the past, he could not help himself. His blue eyes burning with resentment for the way Daggett had treated Arabella, he muttered, "Under the circumstances, I think our stance is understandable."

Tony sighed. Unless he wished to meet Jeremy on the dueling field, he had better pick his words with care. "I cannot argue with you," he said quietly. "It was a deplorable situation."

It was on the tip of Jeremy's tongue to demand an explanation for Tony's previous cruel treatment of Arabella, but recalling that they were in debt to this man, he stifled the words.

Contenting himself with a stiff nod, Jeremy said coolly, "I am not here to discuss what happened five years ago. I wish to talk to you about the agreement you made with my sister concerning the return of my vowels."

Tony stiffened. "She told you about it?" he asked warily, his heart sinking.

"Yes, and I want you to know that I am forever grateful that you have agreed to be so benevolent," Jeremy said forthrightly, "even if I do not know why you are being so kind and generous to us. As Arabella has no doubt told you, I was criminally foolish to drink so much and to gamble with such known scoundrels as Leyton and Walcott." He flushed. "I do not mean to make excuses for myself. What happened was entirely my fault. Nor do I mean to hide behind my sister's skirts." Awkwardly he added, "If I had known what she planned to do, I would have stopped her. And while I am gratified at the outcome of her interference, I will admit I was appalled when I first learned what she had done." He leaned forward, and said earnestly, "You must realize that I had no idea what she was up to until after she had concluded her dealings with you. I know that a man's word is his bond and you must believe me when I say that I would never have reneged on my vowels."

"I believe you," Tony said lightly, deciding that Arabella had not told Jeremy the true facts of their bargain. He had been a fool to think that she would. "And I admire your sentiments." He smiled engagingly at Jeremy. "Your sister does seem to have a way of taking the bit between her teeth, doesn't she?" Tony's expression invited Jeremy to share his opinion.

Torn between loyalty to his sister and Tony's likable ways, Jeremy was uncertain whether to be resentful at Daggett's easy familiarity or grateful that he was being so agreeable about the matter. In fact, he was finding it difficult not to respond to the man's effortless charm—Daggett was nothing like he had expected. He was inclined to believe that Daggett had been greatly maligned.

Coaxed by the faint smile that lurked at the comer of Daggett's mouth and remembering numerous times when Arabella had done just that, Jeremy abandoned his preconceived notions of Tony's villainy, and said with great feeling, "Indeed, sir, she does."

Tony laughed. "As her fiancé, I found her shockingly hot-at-hand—as her brother, I would not care to contemplate your fate."

Ignoring the faint pang of guilt that went through him, Jeremy joined in Tony's amusement, a smile breaking across his face. "Father always claimed that she was a handful from birth. Determined to do things her own way."

"Well, in this case," Tony admitted, "I think she did the right thing. As you stated, a man's word is his bond, and one's honor is a thing to be desired and protected above all else, but you were treated dishonorably by Leyton and Walcott. Your sister's actions may have been embarrassing and unconventional, but she had the correct reading of the situation."

"If our positions were reversed, would you have allowed your sister to save you?" Jeremy asked, obviously embarrassed.

"I am not fortunate enough to have a sister, but I would have been greatly honored if I'd one as loyal and caring as yours," Tony said gently, sidestepping the question. "She has only your best interests at heart."

"I know," Jeremy said, his features softening. "But sometimes, sir, it can be the very devil!"

They shared a knowing smile, and then Tony said, "But come now, tell me why you are here."

Jeremy tugged uneasily at his neatly tied stock. "It is about the vowels, sir." He nervously cleared his throat. "Uh, I was wondering when you planned to return them. Arabella was rather vague on that point."

I rather imagine, she was, Tony thought to himself with amusement. But deciding to put Jeremy out of his misery, Tony rose to his feet and walked to a velvet pull rope in one corner of the elegant room. Giving it a firm yank, he walked back to his seat.

"I agreed to the return of your vowels, but, er, we decided that I should hold the actual vowels for a period of six months." Gently he added, "It will allow you time to consider just how very ruinous your actions were."

Jeremy made a face. "I understand, sir. I shouldn't be allowed to escape totally unscathed."

Billingsley promptly answered Tony's ring and as promptly carried out Tony's request to bring him the folder lying on his desk. When the butler had returned with the folder and departed once more, Tony opened the folder and withdrew a piece of paper.

Handing the paper to Jeremy, he said, "I believe that this will allow you to sleep easier at night."

Swiftly Jeremy scanned the document, his expressive face revealing how very relieved he was to know that everything Tony had said was true. It was all there written out, signed and witnessed. On October 17, 1797, Anthony Daggett swore to return all vowels, dated April 16, 1797, by Jeremy Montgomery. If Anthony Daggett should die before the October 17 date, the vowels would immediately revert to Jeremy Montgomery's sole possession. Anthony Daggett was only to hold said vowels and would not taint them in any way.

His blue eyes shining, Jeremy looked at Tony and stammered, "Th-Thank y-y-you, sir! You do not know how cheered I am by this. It is such a weight lifted from me! I do not know what I would have done if you had not acted so graciously. I can never thank you enough. Never!"

"If you learn from it," Tony said dryly, "that will be thanks enough."

Jeremy did not linger. The precious document clutched tightly in his hands, vowing his eternal gratitude and swearing he would never be so foolish again, he soon took his leave. Tony was smiling when he finally waved him good-bye from the front steps of Sweet Acres, but his smile faded as he returned inside.

Though he hadn't shown it, Jeremy's visit had made him uncomfortable and had pointed out to him, just how base his bargain with Arabella was. Bedeviled by a nagging sense of guilt, he actually considered calling the whole thing off. It would be, he admitted sourly, the honorable thing to do, and honor was important, vital to Tony. Except where Arabella was concerned, he thought grimly, for her he was willing to seal a bargain that he would have normally, instantly condemned as the act of a blackguard in anyone else. That knowledge stung him, and he grimaced. His problem, and he faced it honestly, was that he wanted Arabella in his arms too badly to turn back now. She had agreed to his terms, and he firmly ignored the whisper in his brain that she had had no choice.

It wasn't, he told himself almost virtuously, as if she

was a young, innocent maid and he a lecherous, fat, old sot. They had been lovers once, and she had been warm and willing and eager in his arms—he intended that she would be so again. That thought eased his conscience somewhat, not entirely, but enough to let him turn his thoughts to the other problem he was going to face with Arabella.

She wasn't, he conceded wryly, going to be happy that he had given the letter to Jeremy instead of to her as planned. But dash it all! Jeremy was a grown man and the vowels were his. What else could he have done?

Chapter Ten

❧

"*Y*ou could have told him that the agreement was between you and me and that I was to receive the document," Arabella said tartly as they drove toward Natchez the next morning. Tony had explained what had transpired with Jeremy, and Arabella was obviously not pleased.

She had been even more displeased, when, ignoring their plan of Thursday afternoon, he had boldly ridden up to the front door of Greenleigh to call for her.

"And that's another thing," she muttered, looking across at him, as he sat beside her in the cart; his horse had been left behind at Greenleigh. "I thought it was understood between us that you were to meet me on the road, not at the house."

"You understood it to be so. I did not," Tony said amiably. He glanced at her charming profile. "I think I have behaved with great restraint so far, but I feel it only fair to warn you that I do not intend to let you relegate me to the shadows of your life."

Arabella's bosom swelled with indignation. Her hands tightened on the reins, and she shot him a furious look. "I thought we agreed our liaison was to be secret!"

"The liaison, yes, but not any other relationship we may have."

"We do not," she said from between gritted teeth, "have any other relationship."

"Then how are you going to explain my presence today to Mr. Haight?" Tony asked reasonably, settling his broad shoulders comfortably against the black-leather backrest of the cart.

"Since," Arabella muttered, "I hadn't intended for you to be with me when I went to Mr. Haight's, I didn't have to have an explanation."

"Ah, now let me see if I understand this correctly," Tony said blandly. "Not only was I not to show my face at Greenleigh this morning—or ever, for that matter—but once we reach Natchez, I am instantly to remove myself from your vicinity until such time as you conclude your business with Haight?" A definite note of sarcasm in his voice, he added, "And then I presume I am to come skulking back like a dog to his mistress's heels? Is that how you envision this morning's events?"

Arabella opened her mouth to protest, then shut it with a snap. Tony had the correct reading of the situation. Damn him! That was precisely how she had intended for the morning to go, and she was appalled at how cold and unfeeling it sounded.

Determined to protect her vulnerable heart and to keep him at arm's length for her own sake, she had not considered how her actions would affect him. How he felt shouldn't matter to her, she thought miserably. But it did. Terribly.

Her golden brown eyes troubled, she looked at him. "Tony, this situation is very difficult for me," she said huskily. "We parted under the worst conditions imaginable, and we are only together now because of the bargain we made." She glanced away. "If we are seen publicly to be on friendly terms, it will cause all sorts of gossip." She flushed. "I do not want to go through that again. A-A-After our engagement ended, you left immediately for England, so you don't know what it was like to be the subject of everyone's speculation, to have conversation stop when you entered a room, or to know that people were staring at you when you walked down the street or drove by." With a wealth of understatement, she added simply, "It was not pleasant."

He grimaced. *How did she do it?* he wondered bleakly. He had been prepared for a fight, in fact had looked forward to it, but with only a few words, she had utterly disarmed him and made him feel the greatest villain in nature. And yet she was wrong on one important point; he did know what it was like to be the cynosure of all eyes, to know that everything he did, every deed, small or great, was intimately examined in the hope that it would reveal another source for malicious gossip.

Wearily, he said, "I think you forget just how most of the inhabitants of Natchez view me. I have been their favorite fodder for gossip almost from my birth." He shot her a keen glance. "I'm sorry for what you had to face, Bella," he said quietly, "and that you had to face it alone."

She smiled ruefully. "I could have hardly faced it

with you at my side, so do not feel sorry for me. In retrospect I can see that your leaving was the best thing that could have happened. If you had remained, it would have only made the situation worse." She took a deep breath. "It was most unpleasant, but it is behind me now, and I hope that I am better for it."

"How very noble," Tony said dryly. "You did not used to care so much what people said—if you had, you never would have become engaged to me in the first place."

Keeping her eyes on the road ahead, she said softly, "And we both agree that I made a terrible mistake."

"No," Tony muttered, "the mistake was mine. I should have known that fate would find a way to destroy my only hope for happiness."

Arabella could think of nothing to say, nothing that wouldn't lead them closer to disinterring the corpse of their dead love. Her dead love, she reminded herself firmly. Tony's emotions had obviously never been fully engaged. If they had, she never would have found him in bed with Molly Dobson.

They were preoccupied with their own thoughts for most of the remainder of the journey to Natchez, although a few idle comments did pass between them.

When they reached the outskirts of Natchez, Tony said abruptly, "You may put me down here. Go see Haight and pick me up in this vicinity in an hour or so. I'm sure I can find some way in which to amuse myself."

Arabella's fine mouth tightened. "No. That won't be necessary. There was enough truth in what you said earlier to make me realize that I am being silly—and unkind.

I will not try to pretend any longer that we have nothing to do with each other. And, of course, you will go with me to Mr. Haight's." Beneath the brim of her saucy straw bonnet, her eyes met his gravely. "Don't read anything into it, Tony. It changes nothing between us."

Tony would have argued the point with her, but since he had won this round, he saw no reason to push his advantage. His spirits considerably lightened, he merely nodded, and said softly, "Whatever you say, sweetheart. Whatever you say."

Driving down the wide, tree-lined esplanade near the main plaza, they passed several people known to both of them. And if she hadn't felt so naked and exposed, Arabella might have found humor in the situation. Some of those passersby managed to acknowledge them with only polite nods, but others halted dead in their tracks, expressions of ludicrous astonishment and shock on their faces.

Pulling her horse to a stop in front of Mr. Haight's office, Arabella said resignedly, "After today I expect that we will be the topic of conversation in every house within ten miles of Natchez."

"Twenty miles," Tony corrected, a crooked smile curving his lips.

After he had jumped down and tied the horse to the hitching rail, he turned to help her down from the cart.

Once on the ground, Arabella shook out the crumpled skirts of her lavender-sprigged muslin gown. Taking a fortifying breath, she said, "Well, shall we go see what else may be mixed in with my deeds?"

"And Mr. Haight? How do you intend to explain my presence to him?"

Arabella's chin lifted. "I do not have to offer Mr. Haight any explanation. He is merely my attorney. Not my guardian."

Tony grinned, his blue eyes dancing, his white teeth flashing. "Ah, Bella! I knew that all that wonderful spirit of yours could not have died entirely—it was what made me fall in love with you in the first place."

Flustered, Arabella said nothing. Turning away from him, she hurried toward the door to Mr. Haight's office as if pursued by demons.

Mr. Haight hid his displeasure well at seeing Arabella Montgomery and Tony Daggett together once again. And if his manner was a bit cool, Arabella's was equally cool. He obeyed her request for the portfolio and frigidly showed them to a private room.

Staring hard at Arabella, his hand on the crystal doorknob, Mr. Haight asked, "I trust all is well?"

"Why, yes, it is." Arabella answered, reminding herself that he had only her best interest at heart.

Mr. Hight hesitated, then said, "I seem to be seeing a great deal of you Montgomerys of late. Your brother was in early this morning. He had a paper that he said was most important and he wanted to put it in my safe."

It was obvious that Mr. Haight was fishing, but Arabella merely gave him a sunny smile, and murmured, "If it was important, your safe is obviously the best place for it. I am glad that Jeremy is showing such good sense."

"It would make me happy if you showed as much good sense!" Mr. Haight muttered before he could stop himself.

Arabella looked at him frostily. "Thank you, Mr. Haight. That will be all."

His expression grim, Mr. Haight left the room, snapping the door shut behind him.

"Is it just me," Tony asked lightly, "or is it rather chilly in here?"

"You know very well that Mr. Haight doesn't like you. He never did," Arabella replied absently, as she opened the portfolio and began to leaf through the papers inside it.

A minute later, she lifted her eyes to Tony. "There is nothing here that shouldn't be."

Tony quickly double-checked the contents.

"You're right," he admitted, puzzled. "It seemed such a logical place for it to be."

"I know," Arabella agreed, her face troubled. "I was so hoping that our mystery would be solved now, but it appears that it is not." She sighed as she put away the documents and redid the black ribbon around the portfolio. "I still have no idea what Boots was after, and worse, we have eliminated the only logical place it could have been placed—if I had whatever he wanted in the first place!"

Mr. Haight said nothing when Arabella returned the portfolio to him, but as they were preparing to leave his office, he asked abruptly, "Have you heard the news about Daniel Leyton?"

It seemed wiser to Arabella to pretend ignorance about Leyton's fate than to admit she had already heard the news . . . from Tony. She hoped she looked suitably shocked when Mr. Haight informed her of Leyton's murder.

"Do they have any idea who could have done it?" she asked, after she had expressed appropriate horror and dismay. "It is terrible to think that there is a murderer wandering amongst us."

"No one has been identified as yet. But the authorities think it was someone he knew. Probably another gambler and flagrant womanizer like Leyton himself." Mr. Haight said, his gaze sliding suggestively in Tony's direction.

Arabella stiffened. Her eyes sparkling with temper, she said crisply, "Gossiping, Mr. Haight? How shocking! Do you think that it is wise for someone in your position? Just think what people might say if it became known that you cannot keep a discreet tongue in your head."

Mr. Haight glared at her, clearly thwarted. Arabella gave a toss of her head and sailed out of the office, closely followed by an amused Tony.

A few minutes later they were in the cart, driving out of Natchez. They passed more acquaintances, and this time Arabella was able to take their stares more in stride and actually be amused at the expressions on several faces. Perhaps it was as well, she told herself, that everyone saw for themselves that she and Tony were not at daggers-drawing with each other. At least this way the wild speculation about what would happen should they meet unexpectedly had been avoided.

They were just leaving the last buildings of Natchez behind them when they came abreast with a group of gentlemen riding into town. Recognizing them, Arabella's heart sank. Wonderful. Uncle Richard. Tony's most ardent critic.

Richard Kingsley was not alone, and Arabella wasn't thrilled to see the others either. She was surprised to see Vincent Walcott, Leyton's partner in fleecing Jeremy, with Richard, but then Richard didn't know what Leyton and Walcott had done to his nephew, and Richard did so like to gamble. Alfred Daggett, Tony's uncle and his two sons Franklin and Burgess, and Tony's boon companion, Patrick Blackburne, comprised the rest of the group.

A wave of bitterness swept through her at the sight of Tony's friend. Dear Patrick Blackburne, she thought viciously. The same dear Patrick who had made that infamous wager with Tony in the first place. The wager that had caused her so much pain.

There was no chance of avoiding a meeting. The men had spied them, and with varying degrees of displeasure, astonishment, and plain curiosity on their faces, they were already bringing their horses alongside the cart. Regretfully, Arabella pulled her horse to a stop.

Alfred Daggett did not even try to be polite. He gave a brief acknowledgment of Arabella's presence, and then muttered, "If you will excuse me, I'll wait for the rest of you down the road." And promptly put a discreet distance between himself and the others.

Richard Kingsley, as blond and blue-eyed as his sister, Mary, made little effort to hide his displeasure. His fair, attractive features stiff, he nodded curtly to Tony, and said to Arabella, "I had not expected you to be in town today." Left unsaid was the statement "with *him*!"

"Nor had I," Arabella answered easily. "But there was something that I wanted to see at Mr. Haight's office."

Looking across at the other gentlemen now gathered around the cart, she smiled, and said, "Good afternoon to you all."

There were polite murmurs and greetings, and doffing of their low-crowned hats. Conversation was stilted, and it was clear that everyone was a trifle constrained by the situation.

Patrick was the most at ease, and with a mocking smile on his strikingly handsome face, he murmured, "It is good to see you going out into society again, Tony. I worried that you would molder away at Sweet Acres."

"Yes, indeed," drawled Franklin Daggett, his indigo blue eyes, so like Tony's, full of sardonic humor, "you have been acting most reclusive since your return from England." He smiled unkindly. "You would not have it said that you were hiding out, now would you?"

Tony smiled grimly. He was not particularly fond of his cousin, Franklin, and he held only contemptuous affection for Franklin's brother, Burgess. At thirty-seven, Franklin was only a year younger than Tony. Burgess was thirty-five, and since they were all three close in age, and had grown up together, they should have had much in common. Unfortunately, they did not. Most of the time, Tony found Burgess, with his dandified ways, tolerable and frequently amusing, but Franklin's gibes and blatant envy did not endear him to Tony.

The discord between Tony and Franklin extended further back than the current generation. Alfred was not by any means considered poor, but from an early age he had harbored the feeling that Ramsey had cheated him. He had bitterly resented Ramsey's position as firstborn, and had always felt that it was palpably unfair that Ramsey, simply because he had emerged from the womb first, and by mere minutes at that! should have been blessed with the position, wealth, and power that were the entitlement of the heir to Sweet Acres. Regrettably, he had also passed on much of this attitude to his own son, Franklin.

Nor had it helped the situation that the tragically orphaned Tony had been the delight of his Daggett grandparents. Alfred had burned with jealousy at their doting on Tony, feeling that their affection for Tony was a slight against his own two sons. It was not surprising, having grown up hearing these oft-repeated sentiments from his father, that Franklin had taken this view, too.

Burgess remained indifferent to the fray. As Alfred's younger son, none of it made any difference to him. It might have if, like Franklin, he'd had to depend upon his father for his lifestyle. But as it was, Burgess was perfectly happy with the tidy little fortune he had inherited several years earlier from a great-aunt on his mother's side. He was much too involved in fashion and his own handsome self to be concerned about something that wouldn't have benefited him anyway.

It was Burgess, eyeing with admiration the cut of Tony's bottle green jacket, who said, "I say, Tony, is your coat by Weston? I hear he is all the rage in London these days."

Tony nodded, amusement obvious in his dark face. "You may be a fool, cousin, but you have a good eye. The coat is indeed by Weston."

Much pleased by his own perspicacity, Burgess beamed at him. "I thought I recognized his work. But considering the skill of our provincial tailors, it is not so surprising—the work of a master is unmistakable."

Franklin sent his brother a disgusted look, and muttered, "Sapskull."

Walcott, who had remained on the outer edge of the group, and who was a bit of a macaroni himself, remarked, "We hear that some army fellow, Brummell by name, is making quite a name for himself on the fashion scene."

Tony shrugged. "That may be. I wouldn't know. Fashion has never interested me overmuch."

"Not interest you!" exclaimed Burgess, scandalized by such an admission. His blue eyes earnest, he added, "My dear fellow, I must take you in hand. Why fashion is everything!"

Viewing Burgess's garb, the green-figured waistcoat of fine India dimity and the plum-colored jacket and pale yellow breeches, Tony shook his head. "Not to me, cousin," he said with a laugh. "Not to me."

"No," purred Richard, "your cousin prefers something a bit more challenging. Something such as murdering and seducing innocent—"

"I do not," interrupted Tony mildly, "think you want to finish that statement." He smiled charmingly. "I have not forgotten, even if you have, that there is a lady present."

Two angry spots of color burning high on his cheeks, Richard snapped, "And you would have done better to have had such concern for her five years ago."

"That's enough!" Arabella said sharply, worried that in another moment challenges would be thrown. Heedless of the others, she fixed Kingsley with an angry look. "I am quite capable of taking care of myself, Uncle, and of making decisions for myself. I do not appreciate it, nor do I need you taking up the cudgels in defense of what you perceive as past wrongs."

She gave a curt nod, and, picking up the reins, said regally, "Good day to you, gentlemen. I would like to say that it has been pleasant, but I am afraid that I cannot."

A slap of the reins, and the brown gelding leaped forward, leaving a red puff of dust in its wake.

As they drove smartly away, a muffled sound had her glancing at Tony, and she was astonished to see that he was laughing.

Frostily, she said, "I see nothing amusing about the situation. Richard's actions were deplorable."

"But then you were not the one being so valiantly defended by a red-haired elf, sweetheart."

"I was not defending you!"

"No? Then with your brave words, you were not trying to prevent Richard and me from hurling challenges at each other?"

"What if I was?" she muttered, a flush staining her cheeks as she kept her eyes firmly on the road in front of her.

"Bella, Richard holds no love for me," Tony began softly, "He never has, not since I—" Tony stopped, realizing that revealing the start of the animosity between himself and her uncle would not reflect well on him—or Richard. Hastily, he said, "Never mind the reasons why—we simply do not like each other. I have endured his baiting for almost as long as I have Franklin's, and if

I haven't allowed him to goad me into a duel before now, it isn't likely that I will."

Arabella sent him a thoughtful look. "Do you know I hadn't realized that before—despite what I am sure has been great provocation, you never did fight that many duels. Unless," she added curiously, "you have done so in England?"

Tony shook his head, a whimsical smile on his handsome face. "No, I am afraid not. Does that fact lessen my allure?"

Finding herself responding to that smile and the teasing note in his voice, Arabella looked once more at the road. "Naturally not!"

"Ah, but you do find me alluring?"

"Tony—" she warned.

He laughed. "Very well, sweet, I shall stop teasing you. For now."

Tony might have been laughing, but the gentleman he and Arabella had dubbed "Boots" was not. He watched the cart pull away with a narrow-eyed gaze. Seeing the two of them together had been unpleasant—and a shock. He had hoped that Tony's intervention in Leyton's robbery attempt on Tuesday night had been an isolated event, but if today was anything to go by, it was not.

Tony and Arabella had looked too cozy as they had sat together in the cart, and he didn't like it one bit. Individually they didn't alarm him, but together . . . He grimaced. Their engagement five years previously had only been brought to an end after a great deal of maneuvering on his part, and he didn't discount the notion that the pair of them were still as deeply in love as they had been in the first place. If that were the case, and he suspected it was, propinquity would swiftly undo all his hard work.

Thoughtfully he joined the others for the rest of the ride into Natchez. *I should have*, he decided calmly, *killed her the other night when I had the chance*.

Unobtrusively his fingers rose to touch his temple. He winced, but was grateful that the worst of the wound Arabella had given him with the glass pitcher was hidden beneath his hair and that there was only a little bruising that showed on his temple. A judicious use of rice powder had neatly concealed all outward signs of the attack.

One part of him was smiling and jesting with everyone else as they all dismounted in front of one of the hotels, while the other was busily considering the situation. Obviously, Arabella had not yet found the letter. And it didn't take a brilliant mind to deduce that the reason for her visit to Mr. Haight was probably to see if there was anything concealed within her deeds. Since neither she nor Tony had looked at him suspiciously, he had to assume that they had found nothing.

He frowned. But if they had found nothing, then where was the letter? He had been certain that the letter had been mixed in amongst her deeds, but it seemed he was wrong. Yet Arabella had to have it. Why else would Leyton have tried to rob her, if not to get the letter back?

Disturbed more than he cared to admit, he followed the others inside to the welcoming shadows of the lobby of the hotel. Their plan was to drink Madeira and play cards in the cool interior of the hotel until the heat of day dissipated. Once darkness fell, they were "going down the line," intending to spend the evening gaming and whoring in "Natchez-under-the-hill."

That plan no longer appealed to him, not since the meeting with Arabella and Tony. He wanted, needed, time alone to consider his next move.

Another attack on Arabella did not seem propitious at the moment. Besides, in retrospect, he had begun to think he had been incredibly foolish to have sought her out in the first place. If she had been ignorant about the letter, she certainly wasn't any longer—and he had only himself to blame for that. His lips thinned. Of course, she didn't know precisely what it was that he had wanted, but he had obviously set her to thinking. And Tony. Blast it!

Tony's presence at Arabella's side worried him a great deal. Tony was too damned quick and clever for his own good, and the last thing he wanted, at least at the moment, was to have to kill Tony. Arabella was another story, however.

Absently, he picked up the glass of Madeira before him and took a sip. Under the cover of the conversation swirling around him, as cards were cut and dealt, he brooded about the situation.

Perhaps it was not as bad as he feared. Perhaps Arabella had never had the letter. Perhaps he was merely chasing after will-o'-the-wisps.

Briefly he considered the possibility that Leyton had only been bluffing about having the letter. It was a pleasant notion, but he knew that he was only deluding himself. Leyton had to have had the letter—he would never have tried to blackmail him without it. Besides,

Leyton had been frightened witless when he had arrived unexpectedly to visit him on Tuesday afternoon. And from the way Leyton's gaze had constantly drifted to his desk and the restless movements of his hands, he was convinced that the bloody letter had been right there, right within his reach. If only that stupid chit Arabella had not interrupted them, he'd have the letter; he was positive of it. Now he was left to wonder who had the blasted thing, and where.

A frustrated expression crossed his face. He had, he admitted bitterly, mishandled this entire affair from the very beginning. He should have gotten the letter and then killed Leyton. He had behaved arrogantly and let his temper rule him, and he was paying the price. Daniel Leyton was dead, the letter had disappeared, and he couldn't even be certain that Arabella had it.

It was the mention of Leyton's name that brought him back to the present.

"Shame about Daniel," someone said.

"Could have knocked me over with a feather when I heard about it," exclaimed someone else.

"We all knew he was going to come to a bad end," said Patrick, as he picked up his cards and glanced at them.

"Well, yes," agreed Burgess, sipping his Madeira. "But *murdered*, my dear fellow! And in his own home. Doesn't happen to our kind."

Franklin snorted. "It could happen to anyone. Leyton knew the risks—I've heard that he has been rather friendly of late with a decidedly lawless crew."

"Which," Alfred Daggett said with a stern look at his

two sons, "shows you what can happen when you consort with scoundrels and blackguards."

"Oh, I wouldn't say that," said Walcott, nervously tugging at his softly tied stock. "I know several of the same fellows, and while they are not, er, respectable, they are not quite as black as one would think listening to gossip."

"And isn't that what we are doing?" inquired Richard Kingsley dryly. "Gossiping?"

Patrick laughed, his gray eyes gleaming. "Indeed not, my friend. When gentlemen gossip, is it called social commentary!"

The table burst into laughter, and they settled themselves comfortably and began to play cards in earnest. The remainder of the afternoon and evening passed predictably.

It was nearly two o'clock the next morning before Boots could detach himself from the others without comment. Leaving them all at a whorehouse on Silver Street, he had swiftly made his way to his home.

Once there he had settled himself comfortably in his study and was able finally to put his full attention on the nagging problem of the letter. It was possible, and Arabella's reaction to his attack and her visit to Haight's that morning rather confirmed it, that she did not have it or know precisely what he had been after. His mouth curved sardonically. She was looking for something now though, thanks to him. He cursed his folly.

At least, he reminded himself, she did not know that it was a letter for which she searched. But that was small comfort. If it surfaced and she read the letter, she would know it was what he had been after—and that

Molly's presence that fateful night had been arranged— by someone other than Tony.

He brooded over that for a while, but eventually he turned his thoughts to another more promising tack: Where had Daniel gotten the letter in the first place?

He sat up, damning himself for being so dense. Of course! There was only one person Daniel could have gotten the letter from, Molly Dobson.

Smiling now, he sat back in his chair. Dear sluttish Molly. Now that he thought of it, hadn't he heard something a few months ago about her being under Leyton's care?

Seeing Molly would answer one question for him. He'd know for certain whether Leyton had actually had the letter. Another even more pleasing thought occurred to him. It was possible that Molly still had the letter. That Leyton had left it with her for safekeeping.

That didn't explain Leyton's nervousness when he had come to call, but then Leyton had never struck him as a particularly pluck-hearted man. It was possible that Leyton had merely been reacting to his own guilty conscience about blackmailing him.

A visit to Molly is definitely called for, he thought happily. A few slaps and a little silver, and she would tell him whatever he wanted to know.

It occurred to him that it was rather clever of him to have remembered Molly. He might, he decided maliciously, as he stood up and prepared to walk to his bedchamber, be able to use her to once and for all destroy the budding intimacy between Tony and Arabella. Oh, not in exactly the same way as five years ago, but in some new fresh way. A notion came to him and he smiled widely. Of course. It would be perfect and would forever kill whatever tender emotions Arabella felt for Tony. His smile took on a vicious twist. And would naturally cause as much embarrassment as possible to Tony. Delightful.

Feeling extremely satisfied with himself, he made his way upstairs. Having disposed of his clothing, he climbed into bed. He would be busy on the morrow, but seeing Molly Dobson was his first task of the day. And making it painfully clear why it was to her advantage to do precisely as he said. He sighed. It was a pity, but of course, after she served her purpose this time, he would have to kill her.

Then he smiled. Perhaps, he could arrange it so that suspicion fell upon Tony once again. Only suspicion. He didn't want Tony to hang. Yet.

Chapter Eleven

*T*ony and Arabella spent most of the journey back to
Greenleigh speculating on the connection between the
attempted robbery, Leyton's murder, and the attack on
her. They also put forth various ideas about what her intruder had been after, both of them agreeing that it was
probably a letter, a note, or something of that ilk.

A frown on his face, Tony said, "It almost has to be
something written—because an object, even if readily
identified as belonging to your assailant, would not, in
and of itself, be incriminating—unless it was found next
to a body."

"But we found nothing in my papers at Mr. Haight's.
And if I came into possession of it at Leyton's, that's
where it would have been."

Tony scowled. "Since we didn't find anything useful
at your attorney's, I suppose the next thing for us to consider is the identity of Boots—assuming he is the person
behind all of this." Tony's eyes grew hard. "I'd like to

know," he said grimly, "who it was that paid you a visit."

For the remainder of the journey they considered the problem, but neither could come up with the name of a person who would have killed Leyton and then brazenly attacked Arabella.

"There are any number of people," Tony finally said, "who, no doubt, disliked Leyton intensely—perhaps, even enough to murder him. Jeremy is not the first young man who has suffered at his hands—and no one has ever been able to recover the fortunes they lost to Leyton. He has ruined more than one family." He shot Arabella a wry look. "If I didn't know for a fact that Jeremy had no reason to kill Leyton, he would be my most likely choice."

Arabella flashed him an outraged glance. "And I will have you know that my brother is no murderer—even if he hadn't gotten his vowels back. How dare you say such a thing!"

Tony smiled. "Do you know that you are very loyal to those you love?"

"Loyalty," she said gruffly, "is part and parcel of loving."

The first uncomfortable silence of the trip fell between them, and several more miles passed before Tony commented on the passing scenery and Arabella returned a light reply. After that, conversation flowed more easily between them, but they carefully avoided personal topics.

It was well after three o'clock in the afternoon when Arabella at last turned the brown gelding down the winding drive that led to Greenleigh. She was uneasily aware of the passage of time and mindful that she and Tony were to have met at two o'clock at the lodge to officially consummate their bargain. She was not quite certain how to bring up the subject.

She didn't have to. As she began to guide the horse around the graceful curving driveway in front of the house, Tony said abruptly, "I think we shall have to postpone our rendezvous today." He glanced at his gold pocket watch, and said, "It is now past the hour we set to meet and I am sure that you are tired after the long drive and in no mood for dalliance. We shall have to decide upon another day and time."

Arabella didn't know whether to be relieved or disappointed. In the time since she had made her rash bargain with Tony, there had been much opportunity to consider precisely what it was she had agreed to do. It had not seemed demeaning at the time, and she had even admitted to herself that she wanted to become Tony's lover for reasons that had nothing to do with Jeremy's vowels. Unfortunately, Tony's reasons for suggesting the bargain had everything to do with Jeremy's vowels, and she could not escape the reality that no matter what sort of face she tried to put on it, she was selling her body—whatever the reason. That knowledge left her feeling decidedly tawdry.

It was true they had made love yesterday afternoon, and she had felt nothing but gloriously, wondrously alive in Tony's arms, but that event seemed, in her mind, totally separate from the bargain they had made. Their lovemaking had been unplanned, untainted by any thought of trading her body for Jeremy's vowels. Such was not the case today. Today's planned meeting had seemed cold-blooded in comparison, and she did not like knowing that she was selling her favors as boldly as any woman of easy virtue. And yet, she thought unhappily, she could not renege on her word; the bargain had been struck, and Jeremy already had the paper that would return his vowels to him. She had no choice but to continue as she had begun.

Her face averted, she muttered, "Whatever you think is best. After all," she said bitterly, "I am at your disposal."

Tony bit back a curse and grasping her shoulders, swung her around to face him. "And that," he snapped, "is precisely how I do not want you feeling." He thrust her away from him, and growled, "I must have been mad to have made such a witless agreement."

"Are you saying you regret our bargain?" she asked stiffly.

He sent her a twisted smile. "Regret making love to you? Never that, sweetheart, never that."

His words made her heart jump, but before she could question him further, Tidmore came down the stairs and approached the cart. For the moment private conversation was ended between them.

Tony declined Arabella's invitation to come inside for refreshments. In fact he refused to come inside at all, bidding her a cool adieu and waiting impatiently on the front steps of the house for his horse to be brought round. With confusion evident on her face, she watched him ride away, wondering if she would ever understand him . . . or ever stop loving him.

There. She had admitted it. She loved Tony Daggett and probably always would. That he didn't deserve her love, she was well aware, but it still didn't change the fact that she did love him—in fact, had never stopped loving him.

It was unpalatable knowledge and did nothing to help her resolve the situation between them. Actually it made her all the more determined to resist any attempt by her rebellious heart to make excuses for him—or to let herself be seduced by him again. She might love him, *that* she had no control over, but she was not going to allow her silly heart to believe in him once more. He was only a charming rascal, too handsome and rich for his own good, and she had better not forget it! Nor forget the pain she had felt when she had discovered him in Molly Dobson's arms.

Someone else was also thinking of Molly Dobson, and Boots awoke the next morning determined to find her. He had not kept track of Molly, but it took him only a few minutes of casual conversation with a few friends the next morning to discover her lodgings. It didn't surprise him that the house where Molly was living was nearer the notorious Silver Street of "Natchez-under-the-hill" than the elegant mansions perched high above on the bluffs. She had, he thought, as he ascended the worn plank steps and knocked on the unpainted door, come down in the world.

A slattern wearing a ragged mobcap and apron answered his knock and, seeing a gentleman on the porch, bobbed and invited him inside. It appeared that Molly was obviously entertaining any man who could pay for her services rather than being kept exclusively by one gentleman.

Having been shown in to what passed for a parlor, he held his shallow-brimmed hat in his hands and wandered around the room. There were a few nice pieces scattered about the area, the blue-satin sofa, a pair of dainty satinwood tables, and a fine carpet thrown on the rough floor, but there was generally a forlorn air about the cramped room. He wondered what she had done with the handsome sum he had settled on her five years ago.

He hadn't long to wait. Molly, wearing a blue-silk gown that revealed a great deal of her lush charms, came tripping into the room with a welcoming smile on her still-pretty face. The smile faded immediately when she saw who had come to call.

Her mouth took on a sullen droop, and she shut the door behind her. Facing him, a wary flicker in the sky-blue eyes, she asked belligerently, "What are you doing here?"

"Why, Molly, my dear, why else would I be here but to see your own sweet self?"

"Still the silver tongue, I see," she said dryly, crossing her arms over her magnificent bosom.

He had not seen her in five years and rather thought that the time in between had not been kind. Oh, she was still a tempting armful to be sure, but nearer thirty-five than thirty. The signs of time, and a life of debauchery, which was her stock-in-trade, were beginning to be apparent. That golden hair was not quite as bright as it once had been, and those melting blue eyes had acquired a noticeably calculating cast; there was a hardness to her delicate features that had not been obvious previously. But that stunning figure had changed little.

If anything, it had improved, the waist still girlishly narrow, but above and below there was a ripeness that he found decidedly appealing.

He laughed at her words. "Come now, sweet, let us not spar." He dropped his gaze and crossed his booted feet. "I have a proposition for you. I'll pay you well for it."

Her hostile manner vanished. "How well?" she asked eagerly.

He cast a contemptuous glance around the room. "Well enough for you to find better quarters for one thing."

She seated herself in a chair across from him. "What do I have to do?"

"A few questions first," he said easily. Steepling his fingers in front of him, he regarded her. "I heard an interesting rumor a few months ago—that you were in the keeping of Daniel Leyton. Is it true?"

At the mention of Leyton's name, she started and looked uneasy. "So what if it is?" she demanded. "The money you gave me ran out, and a girl has to keep herself. I can't see that it is any concern of yours."

"Ran out? I seem to recall that it was enough to keep you and that brat of yours, indefinitely—if handled properly."

Molly sniffed and shrugged.

"You squandered it, didn't you?"

"I had gaming losses," she muttered. She looked at him archly. "You never struck me as a jealous man. I never suspected you'd care if I took up with someone else."

"Well you are wrong there, my dear," he said softly.

"Very wrong when the gentleman in question approaches me with a letter that he could have only gotten from you."

She paled. Weakly she asked, "Why, whatever do you mean?"

"I mean, the letter I wrote to you five years ago—the letter I remember distinctly telling you to destroy."

"Oh, that letter!" she said nervously. Pleating her gown with restless fingers, she added, "I meant to destroy it, I really did, but things were so confused just after . . . well you remember how it was. It, uh, slipped my mind." She smiled beguilingly at him. "Since everything had worked out as we planned, it didn't seem so important. I just, um, stuffed it away in a drawer and forgot about it. Really."

"I see. And how did the letter end up in Leyton's hands? He just happened to find it? When he was going through your things?"

She swallowed. She had always been a little afraid of him—even when she had briefly been his mistress. Briefly because while he was handsome and generous, he had tastes that were cruel and degrading, even for a woman in her position, and with little regret she had brought their liaison to a swift end. He had been quick with his fists in those days, and she didn't relish feeling them again.

Nervously watching him as he sat across from her, Molly turned the situation over in her mind. She had not heard from Leyton in almost a week . . . and sitting right there in her parlor was a gentleman whose fortune was far more secure than Leyton's. A gentleman who owed her and a gentleman, who for all his faults could be generous when it suited him. Far more generous than Leyton ever thought of being.

Her mind made up, she asked slowly, "How much are you willing to pay me to tell you about Leyton?"

His lips thinned. "As much as I think the information is worth."

It wasn't the answer she wanted, but deciding she would rather have money than a beating, she shrugged, and admitted, "He accidentally discovered the letter and wanted to know who had written it. I told him."

"Did you now? And why was that, hmm? Didn't I pay you enough to keep your mouth shut? You swore yourself to silence and vowed never to contact me again—for anything. It seems that I spent my money poorly, doesn't it?"

"It was an accident, I tell you! I never meant for him—or anyone to know about it," she said hastily, alarm in her blue eyes. "He came to visit when I had just moved here from my last lodgings, and he was teasing me about all the fripperies I had scattered about the place—I had not finished unpacking. He was pawing through one of my trunks and came across the letter—I swear I didn't know it was there!" The expression on his face was not encouraging, but she rushed on, "He teased me when he found it, he thought it was just a love note from a former lover, and he began to read it aloud—"

"And discovered it was a very odd sort of love letter, yes?"

She nodded. "Yes."

"And so you told him everything," he stated with an outward calm that belied the fury in his gaze.

She shook her golden head. "Not everything." Her

eyes dropped from his, and she admitted in a low voice, "Just enough."

"Just enough for him to try to blackmail me," he snapped, his temper riding him. "And what," he demanded, "were you to get out of this scheme?"

Too frightened of him not to tell truth, she muttered, "Enough to let me leave for New Orleans and set myself up there."

With an effort he quelled the urge to beat her. The stupid bitch! He took a deep, calming breath. He needed her just now. She had a job to do for him.

Dusting an imaginary bit of fluff off his immaculate jacket sleeve, he said casually, "I will match his offer and raise it. Not only will I arrange for you to go to New Orleans, my dear, but you will have enough to set yourself up there in a far nicer house than Leyton could afford. I shall also see to it that you have ample funds to keep yourself until you find a new protector. And since I am feeling particularly generous this morning, I shall add several new gowns for you." He smiled attractively. "You will be able to display your charms to great advantage."

Molly's eyes brightened. To her astonishment, he was proving to be quite reasonable about what amounted to blatant betrayal. She was even beginning to wonder why she had been afraid of him. She should have, she decided regretfully, approached him first and not allowed Leyton any part of the spoils. The thought of Leyton brought a little frown to her forehead.

"Er, what about Leyton?" she asked. "He might cause trouble—and he has the letter. He took it from me weeks ago."

Well, that answered one very important question for him, and he hadn't even had to ask it. "Do not worry your sweet head about Leyton. He won't trouble you . . . or anyone else again."

Molly stiffened. "What do you mean?"

"Haven't you heard? Poor Leyton was murdered just the other night. Tragic. Just tragic."

Like a bird mesmerized by a snake, Molly stared at him. His features revealed nothing but polite regret, but she was aware of an icy tingle down her spine.

"M-M-Murdered?" she finally got out.

He nodded. "Yes. So sad. But then that is the way of the world, isn't it? Here one day and gone the next." He smiled gently. "It is a good thing for you that I came along with my proposition just now, isn't it? With Leyton dead, you no longer have any sort of protector at all, do you?"

A sickly smile crossed her face. Surely he had not murdered Leyton? It was an unnerving thought, but she told herself that it was no concern of hers what happened between the gentlemen who paid for her favors— as long as money fell into her outstretched palm. With a shrug, Molly pushed aside her uncomfortable musings.

"Your offer is certainly better than Leyton's and"— she flashed him a seductive smile—"could not have come at a better time for me. Now what is it you want me to do?"

He quickly laid it all out for her.

She made a face when he had finished speaking, but nodded her agreement.

Rising to his feet, he stopped in front of her. Pinching

her chin with more force than necessary, he said softly, "Do not fail me, Molly. I make a very bad enemy."

She swallowed, her fear of him returning. "I know. I swear I shall not fail."

He smiled. "I knew I could count on you, my sweet. Get the boy, and I shall let you know when we shall spring our little surprise on Tony."

Arabella got a surprise of her own that same morning—one she could have done without. The hours after she had returned home from Natchez on Friday had passed uneventfully and she had walked upstairs to her bedroom, looking forward to a good night's sleep. Which to her great pleasure she received.

She woke on Saturday morning to brilliant yellow sunshine and clear blue sky, and having enjoyed a sound night's rest, the first in some time, she rose refreshed and eager for the day. After enjoying a leisurely breakfast in the sunny morning room, she and Mrs. Tidmore began seriously to consider the various changes to Greenleigh that they both felt were necessary.

Greenleigh had been built to her maternal grandfather's specifications thirteen years earlier, when he and his wife had left England and moved to Natchez in order to be near Arabella, their only grandchild. It was not a pretentious house. It was a comfortable home rather than a mansion like Highview, but the adequate number of rooms were large and spacious.

Arabella had always enjoyed staying at Greenleigh when her grandparents were alive, but she had never considered the day when she would own it. Her grandmother had died three years before from one of the prevalent fevers in the region, and Arabella had barely come to grips with that loss when it had been followed the next winter by her grandfather's unexpected death caused by a congestion in his lungs.

She had missed both of them dreadfully and for a great length of time had not been able to think of Greenleigh without pain. She certainly never thought of it as belonging to her. Hence she had installed the Tidmores and given the house and plantation little thought beyond necessary upkeep.

All that had changed, and it amazed her how quickly her life was revolutionizing itself. She had never considered not living at Highview, but in a matter of days, she had not only considered it, but moved from the only home she had known since she had left England almost fifteen years before.

True, the departure from Highview had been originally viewed as temporary, until Cousin Agatha's visit was over, but every day she was away from Highview confirmed Arabella's opinion that it was time to strike out on her own—past time.

At first Greenleigh had seemed too quiet and small after Highview, but she was coming to enjoy those very aspects of the place and she was excited about rejuvenating the house. Already she could picture the long windows of the main salon draped in soft, misty green fabric, and lying on the polished plank floors, a woven wool carpet in pale greens and rose shades.

She and Mrs. Tidmore were discussing that very thing when Tidmore entered the room, and said, "Miss, a carriage has just arrived. It is your stepmother."

"Mary? I wonder—" Arabella made a face. Hoping

her surmise was wrong, she smiled and said, "After you have shown her in here, will you see to some lemonade for us?"

He bowed and departed.

Mrs. Tidmore stood up, and remarked, "I shall see if cook has finished baking those pound cakes I ordered this morning. If she has, I shall have one sliced and sent in with some raspberry preserves!" Arabella smiled gratefully at her.

After Mrs. Tidmore had left the room, she rose and nervously patted the skirts of her amber gown of glazed cambric. She had worn an older garment because she had planned on going through some of the storage rooms once she and Mrs. Tidmore had finished their discussion. In anticipation of that, her hair had been caught back in a tidy chignon that rested on the back of her neck, and she was wearing a yellow-chintz mobcap. She felt dowdy and in no mood for visitors, but she could hardly tell Tidmore to state that she was not at home to her very own stepmother.

Sighing, she waited for Mary's entrance and the first words out of her stepmother's mouth told her that she had guessed correctly the reason for the unexpected call.

Rushing into the room, her lovely features frantic, Mary immediately pulled Arabella against her bosom, and cried, "Oh, Bella, tell me it is not true! Tell me that you have not taken up with *that man* again!"

Gently disengaging herself from Mary's convulsive embrace, Arabella sent her a small smile and said, "I see that your brother wasted no time in telling you that he had seen Tony and me together in Natchez."

"Then it's true?" Mary demanded, dismay and horror written all over her lovely face. "Bella! How could you? After what he did to you?"

Arabella opened her mouth but shut it with a snap when Agatha Rutledge trod majestically into the room. Spying Arabella, she shook a finger forcefully at Arabella and said in her carrying voice, "For shame! Look at how you have upset your sweet stepmama. Why she has been beside herself since dear Richard first brought us the news yesterday afternoon. It was all I could do to persuade her not to leap instantly into the carriage that very moment and fly to your side. The poor angel hardly slept a wink last night—and it is all your fault."

Standing nearly six feet tall, Agatha was an impressive figure of womanhood. She had the beautiful Kingsley blue eyes, although hers were a trifle protuberant, a strong nose, a wide mouth, and a determined chin. Surprisingly, her features all fit very well together and with a shapely form, elegant carriage, and fair locks, in her youth she had been considered quite a handsome girl. Now approaching sixty, she was still a striking woman. The years had added some flesh to her already Amazonian size, and the once-blond locks contained a silvery hue; but her features had stood the test of time, her chin and jawline still firm and her eyes still bright and lively.

Arabella had always wanted to like Agatha. Honestly. But somehow they could not be in each other's company five minutes before they were ready to pitch bricks at each other. This morning was a typical example, and Arabella could feel her hackles rise and a scathing retort was already forming on her lips when something suddenly occurred to her: Agatha wasn't angry with her for having been with the notorious Tony Daggett, but because she had upset Mary. . . . It was a stunning revelation. And realizing that if Agatha had been the one to cause Mary the distress her stepmother was obviously feeling that she would be equally angry, Arabella tried a different approach.

Weakly, she said, "Good morning, Cousin Agatha. I see that you have arrived safely." Taking a deep breath, she added, "I am sorry that my actions have created such an unpleasant disturbance for you so soon after your arrival."

Clearly expecting an angry reply, Agatha stared at her as if she had suddenly sprouted a second head. Arabella held her breath as Agatha regarded her suspiciously for a long moment. Then apparently deciding to accept the olive branch, Agatha snorted, and said, "You know how Mary frets about you. You should take better care not to cause her pain. Selfishness is not a desirable trait—as you should know at your age."

With an effort, Arabella kept a smile on her face, but her hands curled into little fists hidden by the folds of her skirt.

Tidmore entered the room, bearing a large tray of refreshments and, following Arabella's directions, set it down on a low mahogany table that stood in front of the sofa. The ladies were silent until he had left the room.

As the door closed behind him, Mary sank down into a chair covered in straw-striped silk. "Bella," she asked reproachfully, "is it true? You really were in Natchez with Tony Daggett yesterday?"

Gesturing politely for Agatha to be seated, Arabella began to pour tall glasses of lemonade for her guests.

Keeping her gaze on the task at hand, she said with far more calm than she felt, "Yes. I was with Tony yesterday in Natchez."

Mary gave a wounded cry. "Oh, darling! You are not going to allow that *monster* to break your heart again, are you?"

"He is not a monster," Arabella said coolly, serving both ladies.

"Oh, I knew it! I knew his return would cause no end of trouble. See! He has already cast his spell over you—you are defending him once again. And after all the pain and scandal he created for you last time. I cannot believe that you would be so . . . so . . ."

"Stupid? Foolish?" Arabella supplied with a twisted smile.

"Yes!"

"Perhaps," Agatha said unexpectedly, "before you fret yourself into a decline, my dear, you ought to hear what Arabella has to say. There could have been a good reason why she was with this man yesterday."

Arabella and Mary both regarded her with open-mouthed astonishment. Never in memory had Agatha spoken up in Arabella's favor. Looking a bit flustered, Agatha took a fortifying sip of her lemonade, and muttered, "Just a notion."

Mary blinked, and, looking at Arabella, asked, "Well? *Was* there a good reason?"

Arabella found herself debating how much to tell Mary. Her visits on Tuesday afternoon to Leyton and Tony, for obvious reasons, could not be mentioned, and that included the attempted robbery by the highwayman as she had traveled home that same evening. But she could think of no good excuse not to tell of the attack on Wednesday night—the Tidmores and too many other people knew about it, and realistically she knew that it was only a matter of time until the incident reached Mary's ears.

Reluctantly, she began, "I discovered a prowler with a knife in my room on Wednesday night."

Mary gasped, her blue eyes wide in horror. Agatha merely appeared interested.

"No one was hurt," Arabella added hastily, "but I was rather unnerved after finding him in my bedroom."

"A thief?" Mary cried. "A thief actually broke into the house while you were here? And he accosted you? Oh, my dear, weren't you terrified absolutely to death?"

Arabella smiled. "No, in fact, I was furious!"

Agatha nodded. "Exactly as I would have felt. Bold, pushing varmints!" She eyed Arabella expectantly. "I trust that you taught him a lesson?"

Further revising her opinion of Agatha, Arabella said grimly, "Indeed, I did. He got away, but not before I struck him a blow on the head with a pitcher." With satisfaction, she added, "When Tidmore and I and the others returned to my room, from which I had fled, he had vanished, but the pitcher had blood on it so we know that I wounded him."

"Arabella!" exclaimed Mary, clearly aghast at such savage behavior by her stepdaughter. "You actually fought with this felon?"

"Good gel!" boomed Agatha. "By gad, that is precisely what I would have done! Can't let these fellows think they can frighten innocent God-fearing women in their own homes. Just encourages them."

"Well, yes," Mary said a bit more calmly, now that she had thought about it, "but weren't you frightened at all?"

"At first," Arabella admitted. "But then I got so angry, that all I could think about was, how dare he do this to me!" Ruefully she added, "You know my temper—you have lectured me enough about it in the past."

Mary smiled fondly at her. "Well, this is one time that I think perhaps your temper stood you in good stead." She frowned slightly. "But what does your intruder have to do with going to Natchez with Tony Daggett?"

"Uh, well, I was a trifle uneasy after the event, as you can well imagine!" Hastily improvising as she went along, she continued gamely, "And, uh, on Friday I needed to drive into Natchez to see Mr. Haight. I was not looking forward to the drive as I was still somewhat, er, nervous after what had occurred and Tony just happened to call and learned of my journey. When he offered to escort me, I immediately accepted and was most relieved."

Having not a suspicious bone in her body, Mary nodded in complete understanding. From her point of view it made perfect sense—she would never stir from the house without some sort of escort, preferably male. But Agatha was made of sterner stuff, and the look she bent upon Arabella revealed that she knew a Banbury tale when she heard one. She raised a brow, sniffed, but said nothing.

"I see how it must have been," Mary finally said. "And under the circumstances, I think you had good reason to accept his company." Her expression troubled, she asked, "But Bella, you are not going to allow him back into your life again, are you?"

It was not Arabella's nature to lie. She would not willingly hurt Mary, nor cause her pain, but she had no choice in this matter. The events of yesterday had shown her that Tony was not going to allow her to shove him into the shadows whenever it suited her—and she was ashamed that she had ever thought that she could. Tony, deceiving wretch that he was, didn't deserve to be treated like a dirty secret, and while she wasn't about to trumpet their intimate liaison from the rooftops of Natchez, she was not going to pretend that she would have nothing to do with the infamous Mr. Daggett.

Arabella took a deep breath. "I do not intend to let him into my heart again," she said quietly, "but I shall neither avoid him nor snub him if we meet in public."

"Oh, Bella, no! Never say so!" cried Mary, her distress acute.

"She doesn't have any choice," said Agatha calmly. "Plain as the nose on your face that the gel is still in love with him!"

Chapter Twelve

The look of absolute horror on Mary's face almost made Arabella laugh. Almost. The situation was too serious for humor, though, and Arabella faced an uncomfortable dilemma: Did she lie or tell the truth?

Spilling out her feelings for Tony to her stepmother, or anyone else for that matter, was not something that she had ever considered doing. What was in her heart was her business and no one else's. Unfortunately, Agatha's blunt words forced the issue. Arabella sighed. It would be easier to lie, to let Mary think that Tony Daggett meant nothing to her, but something deep inside her rebelled at that idea. Was she ashamed of her love for him? Her lips twisted. No, but she couldn't deny that her life would be so much simpler if she didn't love him.

Arabella took a deep steadying breath, and, meeting Mary's gaze, she said softly, "She's right, you know. I do still love him."

"But you can't! He's an awful man! People think he killed both of his wives. How *can* you love him?"

It was an argument she had heard often enough from both Mary and her father five years ago, and she still could not explain how or why it was that Tony Daggett held her heart so completely. She only knew that he did and she feared that he always would.

Ruefully she admitted, "In my mind I agree with every sentiment you have expressed, but in my heart . . ." Her voice trailed away, and her face softened. "My heart," she finally said, "doesn't always listen to my head where Tony is concerned."

Of course, Mary promptly had hysterics, crying and sobbing that Arabella was ruining her life. That Tony would make a terrible husband—look at his past—and if she persisted in this foolishness, Tony would no doubt murder *her* and then where would they all be?

Mary's first gusty outburst gradually gave way to heart-wrenching sobs, which made Arabella's own heart ache—even more so, because she knew that it was only love for her that motivated her stepmother. She could hardly be angry with Mary for having her best interests at heart, but at the same time, she was irritated with her stepmother's reaction. It wasn't as if she were an innocent young girl throwing away her future on an irredeemable wastrel, Arabella thought wearily, even if Mary held exactly that view!

Arabella was in a difficult position, and it didn't help matters to have Agatha on the other side of her scolding and lecturing about how unhappy she was making Mary. Feeling like a doe running before the hounds, Arabella tried to calm Mary and at the same time not let Agatha's criticism make her lose her temper. It was not easy.

She was thoroughly exhausted and holding on to her temper by a thread by the time the worst of Mary's tears had dried.

With some semblance of normality, Arabella escorted them back to the carriage and waved them away, although her heart ached at Mary's drawn, unhappy face. Hurting those she loved was the last thing she wanted to do, but she also had to be true to herself. Sighing heavily, she walked up the steps slowly and entered the house. The headache that had been building all during Mary and Agatha's emotional visit finally burst forth, making her pale and dizzy from the blasting pain in her temples. Gone were any thoughts of going through the storerooms. Feeling like some silly heroine in a Minerva Press novel, she fled to her room and spent the rest of the afternoon lying limply on her bed.

By the evening, having enjoyed a long soak in the bath that Martha had ordered set up in the dressing room adjoining the bedroom, Arabella felt somewhat restored. After a light supper, eaten in solitary splendor in the large dining room at the side of the house, she took a stroll outside. It was not yet dark, and there was a soft breeze wafting up from the river that carried on it the haunting perfume of magnolia blossoms.

She didn't want to think about Tony or the unpleasant scene with Mary and Agatha, but her thoughts had a mind of their own. Since she had already admitted to herself that it was foolish and unwise to love Tony, Mary's arguments had not changed anything. If anything, they had clarified her emotions. God help her, she *did* still love Tony Daggett.

Because she loved him, it didn't mean that she was blind to his faults. He had betrayed her once, and she wasn't about to let him do it again. She might love him, but she would rather die than give him the slightest clue that he still held her heart. To do so would be compounding an already great folly.

It was probably for the best that Richard had tattled to Mary about seeing her and Tony together in Natchez, she decided resignedly. For all its diversity, Natchez was a tight-knit community, and if Richard had not told Mary, someone else would have. Her mouth quirked. Probably Mr. Haight.

The buzz of mosquitoes whirling around her prompted her return to the relative protection of the house. Having dismissed the Tidmores and Martha for the night, she wandered idly throughout the rooms, halfway considering the changes she would make in the future.

Her heart was not in it, however, and she went upstairs to seek out her bed at a much earlier hour than normal. After changing into her nightwear, she picked up a book of poems by the English poet, William Wordsworth, and settled comfortably in her bed to read. Within the hour, she was nodding over descriptive flights of scenes in Italy and France and put the book away. Blowing out the candle by her bed, she pulled up the covers and fell asleep with little trouble.

She dreamed of Tony—of his mouth brushing teasingly against her ear as he murmured soft endearments and his hands traveling tantalizingly over her body. It was such a wonderful dream, so real that she twisted wildly in her bed, arching up to meet those caressing hands as they moved over her, her body tingling in a most pleasurable way. When his lips began to nibble at the corner of her mouth, she sighed blissfully, the delight she felt so real, so intense that she was certain she could not be dreaming. She wasn't.

"Wake up, Elf," Tony said softly, as his, lips continued to travel here and there over her face. "I don't want to make love to you while you are asleep."

Her eyes flew open. In the darkness she could see nothing, but she could feel him, his long, lean body lying close beside hers on the bed, his hands gently, caressing her and his lips brushing against her cheek.

"T-T-Tony?" she asked stupidly, still half-asleep, as she reached blindly for him.

His hand closed around hers, and, lifting her fingers to his mouth, he tenderly kissed each one.

"You were, perhaps, expecting someone else?" he murmured against her fingertips.

Wide-awake finally, Arabella sat up, pushing him away. She fumbled to light the candle by her bedside and once it was lit, turned to stare incredulously at the man lying so confidently in her bed.

He was there. In her bedroom. On her bed. His black hair attractively tousled as he casually rested his head on one of her lace-edged pillows, he was wearing only a white-linen shirt carelessly opened at the throat and a pair of breeches. His feet were bare.

She blinked, certain she must be dreaming. Her wondering gaze fell upon his jacket thrown over the chair near the opened French doors and the black boots placed neatly nearby.

She looked at him again. He was still there. Grinning at her, amusement dancing in his indigo blue eyes.

"H-H-How? How did you—" She stopped, frowning. "There are men patrolling the grounds," she said slowly, becoming more awake by the minute. "How did you get in?"

Tony smiled. "It would take more than those four brutes to keep me from you," he murmured, his fingers moving lazily up and down her arm.

"Tony," she warned.

"It wasn't so very hard, sweetheart," he said dryly. "You forget, I knew they were there. After a careful reconnoiter, it wasn't difficult to time my arrival between their patrols." His voice grew even dryer. "Anyone could have slipped in here."

Arabella swallowed, unease crossing her face.

Annoyed with himself for frightening her, Tony said quickly, "Which is precisely why I am here—to test the efficiency of your precautions. They don't seem to be working very well."

"And I am to be grateful to you for pointing this out to me by crawling into my bed?" she asked tartly.

Tony merely smiled, his gaze lingering on the fiery halo of tumbled hair that fell around her face and shoulders before traveling leisurely down to the rise and fall of her unfettered bosom. The fabric of her night garment was delicately spun cotton, so fine it was almost transparent, and the outline of her rosy nipples could be seen clearly beneath it. As he stared, that voluptuous bosom of hers began to move up and down more rapidly.

Tearing his eyes away from her breasts, he glanced up at her face. Her lips were half-parted, her cheeks flushed, and her eyes were brilliant, almost gold. The desire that had been simmering within him burst into clawing need. Cupping her jaw, he brought her lips to his.

Huskily, he said, "If you want to call it gratitude, you may do so, but it is, my sweet, something much more elemental."

He kissed her, his mouth moving gently, persuasively over hers, and Arabella shuddered at the sweetness. Giving a helpless little moan, her arms closed around him, and she gave him the access he wanted, her lips parting to allow him to kiss her deeply, thoroughly.

Together they fell back against the pillows and, for the moment, were content merely to kiss and embrace, the wild urgency that had marked their joining at the lodge not evident this time. For a long time, their mouths simply mated and parted and mated again, their hands drifting dreamily over each other, touching, exploring, teasing.

Those gentle kisses and light touches had a definite effect, though, and soon enough, the need for more—for more explicit, more intimate caresses—rose inevitably within them. Arabella had no thought of resisting him, not even when her gown went flying to land on the floor beside the bed or Tony's clothes were disposed of as swiftly and carelessly.

The pale yellow candlelight flickered and danced over their naked bodies as they lay together on the bed. For Arabella this languid, delicious drift toward passion was a novel experience, and she delighted in it.

Dreamily aware of the sweetly nagging ache within herself, half-sitting, she stared down at Tony, marveling at the masculine beauty of his body. He was all sleek male muscle, from his broad shoulders to his narrow hips and handsomely tapered legs. In the past, there had never been the leisure to look her fill, to touch him, to explore and see the results of her actions.

The hard little nubs of his breasts fascinated her; his low groan of pleasure when she bent forward and ran her tongue delicately over them excited her, as did the pulsating swell of his organ when she clasped it and stroked its broad length. Arousing him aroused her. Heat massed in her loins, her breathing became irregular, and the ache between her thighs became almost painfully insistent.

Unable to bear not touching her as she was him, Tony reared up, pushing her down into the feather mattress. She was incredibly appealing in the soft candlelight, that glorious hair of hers flung out like a living blaze across the sheets, the shadows and dips of her lush body full of carnal promise as she stared up at him through half-closed eyes. He caught his breath, blind desire slamming through him at the invitation he found in their golden brown depths.

He kissed her hungrily, his hands cupping her breasts, fondling and caressing their warm fullness, teasing the nipples into plump points. She tasted so good, he thought hazily, like warm wine on a winter's eve. Felt so good, her skin like hot satin under his hands.

Intoxicating though her mouth was, other parts of her body sang a siren's song to him, and unerringly his lips found her swollen nipples. He suckled strongly, his teeth lightly grazing the puckered tips; Arabella's gasp and arching body incited him to greater efforts.

Eyes blissfully closed, her hands tangled in his black hair and she cradled his dark head even closer to her bosom. She could feel the damp heat of his mouth against her skin, the burning warmth of his body half-lying on hers and lower still, the heavy, insistent probe of his erection against her thigh. She felt utterly alive, full of eager anticipation for the pleasure she knew they would share. Her blood was humming, all her senses clamoring for the moment they would join together, become one. Every tug of his mouth on her nipple, every touch of his hands as they skimmed her body, only intensified the sensation.

When his head dipped lower, she sighed, twisting restlessly under his nipping teasing kisses. It was only when his questing mouth reached the V between her legs that her eyes flew open in shock.

"T-T-Tony?"

Her uncertainty was obvious, and, reaching up to kiss her mouth, Tony murmured against her lips, "Only a variation, my sweet. Nothing to frighten you."

But it did. The stunning sensation of his mouth moving hotly over that most intimate part of her was like nothing she had ever imagined. The wild, uncontrollable feelings that erupted through her at the flick of his tongue over that damp, aching flesh were terrifying and yet . . . A soft, shaken scream rose up through her as her body arched helplessly, sensations never dreamed of exploding through her. Her fist in her mouth to still the sound of that scream, she twisted and thrashed beneath

Tony's hungry mouth as she was assaulted by wave after wave of intense pleasure.

Her body was still throbbing and trembling when Tony slowly slid upward, a satisfied smile curving his mouth. Taking a nipple into his mouth, he bit down gently, and she shuddered, feeling that caress clear to her womb.

Looking up at her, he asked, "And did my heart enjoy herself?"

With wide, dilated eyes, Arabella stared at him. The stunned, dazzled look on her face told its own story, but the dazed nodding of her head confirmed it.

He smiled, an incredibly tender smile that made Arabella's heart melt.

"Good," he said simply. Slipping between her thighs, he murmured, "And now we shall do it again—only this time together."

Arabella gasped as he took her, her arms reaching convulsively for him as he joined their bodies and the magic between them began anew. And this time it was sweeter, more potent, because Tony was with her, his mouth capturing her cry of release, his own groans of satisfaction as he emptied himself into her intensifying her own completion.

They lay there locked together for several long moments, Tony lazily kissing her, his hands lightly cupping and fondling her breasts. Arabella was touching him, too, her fingers running up and down his long back, marveling at the pleasure they had just shared.

Her eyes were closed, and she was smiling dreamily when Tony kissed the tip of her nose, and said softly, "Marry me, Bella."

Her eyes flew open, and her smile vanished. Pushing him away, she sat up. "Marry you?" she asked incredulously, ignoring the eager beat of her heart. "Are you mad?"

Flinging himself back across the bed, his hands behind his head, he regarded her somberly. "No. I am not. Why would you think so?"

Flustered, suddenly embarrassed to be sitting naked on the bed with him, she scrambled after her gown. Finding it, she hastily pulled it on and turned to face him.

Tony had not moved. He lay on her bed, like a splendid jungle cat at leisure, his tousled black hair gleaming with blue glints in the candlelight, his sleek hide smooth and golden, as he coolly looked at her across the brief space that separated them.

His nakedness seemed not to disturb him one whit, and, averting her eyes from all that handsome masculinity, Arabella said weakly, "Tony, you can't have forgotten what happened the last time you asked me that question."

"You're wrong there, Elf. It is quite vivid in my mind," he said mildly. "You said yes."

Her mouth tightened. "And I paid for my foolishness."

He muttered a curse and, rising up in one fluid motion, found his breeches on the floor and dragged them on. Shrugging into his white-linen shirt, he snapped, "Must you always throw the past in my face? Won't you even give me a little credit for having learned from my mistakes?"

Sadly she stared at him, her heart splintering into tiny shards. Her eyes shimmering with tears, she said

painfully, "Tony, don't ask this of me. I did believe you
. . . once. I fought with my parents, I turned a deaf ear to
all their entreaties, to all the hints and lectures from
friends and relatives alike. I was so certain. So certain
you loved me. So positive that my love was strong
enough to overcome whatever troubles came our way.
So positive that everyone was wrong about you, and
then to find it was all a lie . . ." She swallowed, unable
to go on.

Fighting the urge to smash something, Tony took a
deep breath. "I loved you, Bella. I never lied about that.
Never."

Unable to look at him, she turned her head and put
out a hand, silently entreating him to stop, but he would
not.

Capturing that slender, protesting hand of hers, he
kissed it. "Elf, I never lied to you about anything. I
never denied that I had been as wild and spoiled as
everyone had ever thought I was." When Bella kept
her head averted from him, he went on desperately, "I
wasn't a good husband to either of my wives—I told
you that. I was young. I was selfish. I was arrogant. And
I married them both for all the wrong reasons. I did
things then that make me ashamed now." Heavily, he
added, "I can't undo my past, Bella. Nor can I pretend
that my reputation, black as it is, is not well earned."

She risked a glance at him and even though she knew
otherwise, needing to hear him say the words again,
needing to be reassured that she did not love a murderer,
she asked quietly, "Are you admitting then that what
everyone says is true? That you murdered them?"

He shook his head, ignoring the stab of anguish her

words gave him. "No. As I told you in the beginning, I did not murder either one of them." Letting go of her hand, he tiredly rubbed his forehead. "I married Mercy to please my grandparents—I told you that, too. They wanted to hold their grandchild and it seemed an easy thing to do for them." Simply, he explained, "I loved my grandparents—selfish as I was, and I don't deny that I was selfish, but I would have done much to please them. And when my grandmother suggested Mercy Dashwood, the granddaughter of her dearest friend, I saw no reason to object. Mercy was a taking little thing and I was conceited enough to believe that she would do very nicely for me. Why wouldn't I? I had been brought up to believe the world revolved around me, why wouldn't Mercy?"

He flashed Arabella a twisted smile. "The problem was that Mercy was as spoiled and selfish as I was, and in a relatively short time we were at each other's throat, neither one of us able to understand why the other wouldn't do precisely as we wanted. Our marriage was brief and stormy, and in just a few months we could hardly bear to be in each other's company. It wasn't my fault and it wasn't Mercy's fault. We were young—she, barely eighteen and I, twenty-one, and we had both been outrageously spoiled. She infuriated me, as I'm sure, as I look back, I did her, but I didn't kill her." He took a turn around the room, his face bleak.

"I have to live with the knowledge that in a way I *did* contribute to her death—if I hadn't been right on their heels, if they hadn't been trying to escape me, their carriage might not have plunged into the river. I shall regret it to the end of my days."

He gave Arabella a long, steady look. "I have many things to regret, many things I would do differently now. But I can't change the past. I can't pretend that I wasn't furious when I found out that she had taken Terrell as a lover, and I can't deny that when I was told they were running away together that I went after them with the express intention of dragging Mercy back to Sweet Acres. My pride demanded it. But cold-bloodedly drown Mercy and her lover?" He shook his head. "No. I'm as capable of killing someone as the next man—I will not lie. I could have shot Terrell down on the dueling field, if it had come to that, and not missed a wink of sleep. And if I had caught them . . . We would have faced each other over drawn pistols, I'll not deny that either—only one of us would have ridden away from that meeting.

"As for Mercy . . ." He looked pensive. "I suppose there could have been a set of circumstances that would have driven me over the edge, that would have had me murdering her with my bare hands. But for me to take cruel advantage of a terrible accident? For me to have waded into the river to the crumpled wreckage of their carriage and then held them under the water until they drowned? No. That I would not and could not do."

"Tony, whatever else is wrong between us, I never thought you murdered Mercy," Arabella said softly, her heart wrung by the expression on his face. Resisting the urge to go to him, to comfort him, was unbearably difficult, but the need to protect her own vulnerable heart was stronger.

Tony looked back at her where she stood by the bed.

"Ah, you believe me about Mercy, but you have doubts about Elizabeth?"

Before she could reply, he crossed to her, grasped her shoulders, and shook her.

"I admitted that I was blind drunk, out celebrating my twenty-fifth birthday, when I made that unfortunate wager to marry the first eligible woman who crossed my path that night," he said sharply. "And, God rest her soul, it was poor Elizabeth Fenton who did exactly that. But I didn't murder her to end a marriage that should never have happened in the first place."

"It doesn't matter," Arabella said desperately. "I've heard all this before—and it changes *nothing*."

Tony's face was grim. "Can you swear that you don't harbor doubts about the way she died? That you don't wonder if I didn't, as some people say, give myself an alibi, get Blackburne to lie for me? Do you wonder if I didn't really creep back to my own home and shoot her dead?"

"Tony, don't," Arabella whispered achingly, hurting and ashamed for having opened this old, painful wound. "Don't torture yourself this way. I know that you did nothing of the sort. And those who say that you did are petty and mean-spirited."

He gave a bitter laugh. "Well, thank you for that!" He looked away from her, his features pale and strained as remembered anguish tore through him. "She was carrying my child, Bella. No matter how I felt about her, I would never have harmed the mother of my child." He glanced back again at Arabella. "My marriage to Elizabeth wasn't a good marriage, you know that." He smiled grimly. "Hell, *everyone* knew it and the circumstances surrounding it. But it wasn't the terrible, acrimonious travesty that Mercy and I had shared. Elizabeth was content to be wife and mother—she was looking forward to the birth of our child—as I was. And though we were vastly different and had little deep emotion for each other, we rubbed along together tolerably well."

Hoping to distract him, aching for him, Arabella asked, "Have you ever wondered who did kill her?"

The blue eyes glittering menacingly, he muttered, "Only every day of my life. Elizabeth did not deserve to be murdered. Nor my unborn child; and someday, if God is kind, I will find the person who shot her down and show him as much mercy as they were shown."

Staring at him, at the savage promise in his face, Arabella believed him—with good reason. She knew he was fiercely protective. He had gone after Leyton because he had believed that Leyton had attempted to rob her; he would be even more driven to go after the person who had so brutally murdered his wife—even a wife he did not love.

A quiver of fear rippled through her at the image of Tony facing a man who had already murdered once, and she could not help blurting out, "If you find him, take care, Tony."

His lip curled. "Careful, Bella, say things like that and I might think you care."

"I do care! I just will not subject myself again to the pain of finding you in bed with whichever woman has taken your fancy."

He cursed under his breath and his hands tightened painfully on her arms. "I was not making love to Molly," he growled. "I had broken off from her months before that night." His voice thickened, "Once I had seen you, no one else mattered. I wanted no one else." At Arabella's disbelieving snort, he shook her. "I was at the lodge to meet you that night, and no one else, god-dammit! I knew you were coming. Why in the hell would I arrange to have a romp with Molly? Tell me that, if you dare!"

She wrenched herself from his grip. "I don't know!" she cried, angry and hurt all over again. "I only know that when I arrived, I found the two of you naked and in bed together." Accusingly, she glared at him. "She was draped all over you—your arms were around her. No one had to tell me what you were doing, Tony, I saw the pair of you with my own two eyes. It hurt me more than I have ever been hurt in my life." Her voice shaking with remembered fury and pain, she spit, "The only thing that hurt me worse was to find out that our entire betrothal had been a sham—that you'd only pursued me because of another damned wager!"

His mouth grim, Tony sat down on the chair near the French doors and began angrily to pull on his boots. "There is no talking to you," he said wearily. Standing up, he fastened his shirt and put on his jacket. Finding his stock where he had thrown it on the floor, he picked it up and stuffed it into the pocket of his coat.

"What are you doing?" Arabella asked uneasily from her position near the bed.

"I'm preparing to leave—there is no longer any point to this conversation," he said harshly.

Fighting back the urge to weep and an equal urge to slap his face, Arabella snapped, "Afraid to face your own sins, Tony? Afraid to admit to my face that you made the wager with Blackburne? It won't come as any shock, you know—Richard told my father, months after our parting, that Blackburne himself confessed to the wager one night when he'd had too much to drink. Am I to believe that Richard lied to my father and my father to me? Am I to pretend I did not see what I did? Can you deny any of it?"

"I *did* make the bloody wager with Patrick—I admit it," Tony snarled. "But once I'd met you . . . once I'd met you, I forgot all about it." Drearily, he added, "Patrick and I constantly made wagers. Half the time we couldn't remember what they were by the time we sobered up the next morning. Neither one of us is proud of the particular wager involving you—but neither one of us really knew you, and we were half-drunk—a usual state for us in those days. It seemed an uproarious jest at the time, to see if I could catch the interest of the, oh-so-cool-and-proper Arabella Montgomery. Everyone talked about how devoted you were to your dead fiancé, how inspiring it was the way you were so constant to his memory, unwilling to give the slightest encouragement to any of your worthy suitors. We thought it would be vastly amusing if an *un*worthy suitor could topple you from your pedestal." His gaze bleak, he said bluntly. "You were a challenge, sweetheart. But our wager was cruel and unkind—we never should have made it." He smiled painfully. "You'd think that I would learn, wouldn't you?"

When Arabella remained stonily silent, he said levelly, "I know that you found me in the most compromising position imaginable. I know that. But I also know that I had nothing to do with Molly Dobson since I had paid her off—handsomely, I might add—the day after I met you."

His eyes locked with hers, he said evenly, "I went to the lodge that night to meet you. Only you. I arrived early as I always did. You were running late, and I helped myself to a glass of wine from one of the bottles we kept there. That," he ended coolly, his features grim, "is the *last* thing I remember until I looked up and saw your horrified face staring down at me."

His words shook her, as much because she wanted to believe them, as the ring of truth about them, their very simplicity giving them credence. And yet the entire scenario was incredible.

Skepticism on her face, she demanded, "Are you telling me that someone knew we used the lodge to meet? That this person knew we were going to meet that particular night? That he or she arranged for me to be late? And drugged the wine? And brought Molly Dobson there? Is that what you're saying?"

He scowled. "I'm telling you what I remember—I can do no more than that."

"And I don't believe you," she shot back.

His lips tightened, and one hand clenched into a fist. Temper riding him, he snarled, "If you were a man, I would knock you down for that statement."

For the longest time they regarded each other across the short space that divided them. Both were angry and hurt, and neither was willing to give an inch.

"We seem to have reached an impasse," Tony finally said. "Obviously we have nothing more to say to each other."

There was a note of finality about his words that sent

a shaft of ice through Arabella's heart, but she merely said quietly, "I would say that you are right."

His head bent, his expression hidden from her, Tony smoothed an imaginary crease from the jacket of his sleeve.

"I must have been a fool," he said softly, almost to himself, "to think that this time I could make things work out right." He glanced across at her, his gaze frighteningly remote. "And since I see no happy outcome for us, I will cut my losses." His lips twisted. "Gambling, you know, it's in my blood."

"What do you mean?" Arabella asked, a flutter of panic deep in her belly.

"Why, only that you have won, sweetheart," he drawled. "Jeremy shall have his vowels and I"—his voice hardened—"I shall not subject you to my company again. You have what you wanted, Arabella. The vowels are yours with no conditions attached—I shall have them delivered to your brother tomorrow morning. And as for your mistress, ah, duties, I set you free. Consider our bargain at an end—I'll not sully you with my touch again."

He spun on his heel and walked to the French doors. Standing in the open doorway, he paused and looked back briefly, and then he was gone, leaving only a black empty hole where he had stood. A black, empty hole like the one that bloomed in Arabella's breast.

Chapter Thirteen

❧

*D*uring the remaining hours of the night and all the next day, Arabella constantly turned the events of the disastrous evening with Tony over in her mind, minutely examining every word, every gesture, trying painfully to discover the moment when everything had gone so very wrong. Bleakly, she wondered if and how she could have handled anything any differently.

She had never once doubted Tony's version of his two marriages, nor the circumstances surrounding the deaths of his two wives—despite all the stories to the contrary. She knew that he regretted bitterly his wild, debauched youth, that he was ashamed of the selfish way he had treated Mercy and the irresponsible way he had chosen both Mercy and Elizabeth to be his wives.

She had never held his past against him, aware of the way both sets of his grandparents had doted upon him. It would have been astonishing if he had been anything but arrogant and spoiled. The important thing, she had told herself, was that he hadn't stayed that way, that he had matured and tried to rectify his mistakes—she believed that truly, else she would never have been able to fall so completely in love with him.

But the affair with Molly Dobson had shown Arabella that he was still capable of acting with reckless arrogance. And the knowledge that another of those careless wagers had piqued his initial interest in her only added to his crimes.

Thinking about the past, brooding on their argument did nothing to lift her spirits and with an effort, she tried to put Tony Daggett and their briefly mingled lives away from her. It was not easy.

Jeremy came to call Monday afternoon, mystified and jubilant that the vowels had been returned to him that very morning. His blue eyes bright, he bounded into the room, where she was sitting listlessly mending a linen tablecloth, and exclaimed, "I say, Bella, Tony Daggett is not such a bad sort, after all. I don't know what changed his mind, but he rode slap up to the front door of Highview this morning, asked to speak to me, and, to my astonishment, handed me the vowels and told me to tear up that document he had signed."

His words stabbed her. Any hopes that Tony had not been serious were dashed. He obviously intended to have nothing to do with her—ever. How she smiled and acted thrilled for Jeremy she never knew. She was just grateful when, whistling merrily, he rode away from Greenleigh.

To Arabella's dismay, she discovered that she missed Tony dreadfully. He had been back in her life for such a short time and yet she found, as one week became two, that the ache in her heart only grew worse. She tried to bury herself in the refurbishing of Greenleigh, but somehow her enthusiasm had faded, and she only listened indifferently to the Tidmores' proposed changes, sometimes approving items for purchase and renovations, having no idea to what she had agreed.

The night of the Crockers' ball arrived, and since she had already written her acceptance weeks ago, reluctantly she dressed and ordered a carriage to take her to Broadmount, the Crocker plantation. She had hoped that being out with friends would lift her spirits and shake her out of the doldrums. Instead she came home more angry, depressed, and confused than she had started out.

Tony had been at the Crockers. She had been startled when she had spied him across the room, his dark head bent as he listened carefully to something that the eldest Crocker daughter, Margaret, was saying to him. The smile he flashed at Margaret's upturned dazzled face did nothing for Arabella's peace of mind.

She wasn't exactly surprised to see Tony at the Crocker ball. Despite his reputation, he *was* well-bred and wealthy, and his handsome face and charming manners opened many a door to him that might have remained steadfastly shut. People might deplore his actions and gossip happily about him, but only the highest sticklers, like her father and Mr. Haight, would turn their backs on the opportunity to align themselves with the Daggett fortune and name.

The elder Crockers were a genial couple, well-known for their hospitality and their long friendship with Tony's grandparents, so Tony's presence was not the shock it would have been at a ball given by someone else.

Deliberately, Arabella kept the width of the wide ballroom on the second floor of the gracious Crocker house between herself and Tony. It was relatively easy, since Tony appeared to be completely captivated by Margaret's speaking eyes and laughing mouth. Arabella told herself that she was *not* jealous, but having had a fondness for Margaret in the past, she suddenly decided that perhaps her affection for the young woman was misplaced. Margaret, she discovered, was a forward minx. Just look at the way she was hanging on Tony's every word and blatantly ogling him. Disgraceful!

Finding that watching Tony and Margaret flirting together was doing nothing for her temper, she quickly made her way through the handsomely garbed throng to one of the long refreshment tables in an adjoining room. Accepting a glass of lemonade punch, she looked at the array of food spread out before her but found that she was not hungry—not even for delicate pastries filled with creamed chicken and fresh peas.

She spied Mary and Agatha sitting together with several other older ladies against one wall of the ballroom and strolled over to join them. Greetings were exchanged; a chair was quickly brought for her, and she settled down to enjoy herself—even if it killed her.

For a while she did enjoy herself. Mary related an amusing story about the two younger boys and a baby raccoon they had brought home, and Agatha, continuing to astonish Arabella, unbent enough to give a lively account of her journey upstream to Natchez.

"I tell you," Agatha said, "that I feared every night that I would wake up to find that we had been attacked by bandits. There was a rumor that those terrible Harpes had been seen in the area." She gave a theatrical shudder. "And everyone knows what would have happened if we had crossed their paths."

Several of the ladies nodded. Tales of the atrocities committed by the Harpe brothers, Micajah, "Big Harpe," and Wiley, "Little Harpe," traveled all up and down the Natchez Trace, their usual hunting grounds. Though the Trace actually ended at Natchez, it was known that the Harpes sometimes traveled farther south, and Agatha's fears were not precisely unfounded. Stories of their many wanton killings and mutilations made for grisly talk, but there in the brightly lit ballroom of Broadmount, surrounded by a merry crowd of friends and families, the ladies thoroughly enjoyed exchanging lurid tidbits about "those dreadful Harpes."

Thinking of the long, dark drive home, with only Tidmore as company, Arabella was glad when the subject was changed to gossip about the courtship of a longtime widow and an elderly bachelor. Not really interested in the topic, her attention wandered, and her heart felt as if it had dropped right to her toes when her idle gaze happened to meet Tony's across the width of the ballroom.

He was staring at her intently, his brilliant blue eyes boldly holding her own, his mouth unsmiling, and his expression bleak. From the look on his face, if she had not known better, she would have thought him bitterly unhappy, even angry, but having seen him only moments before laughing and teasing with Margaret Crocker she was certain she was misreading his expression. Besides, she told herself as she wrenched her gaze from his to stare blindly at the various dancers moving around the floor, he had no reason to be unhappy, or angry—he was the one who had ended their affair.

For the remainder of the evening, she kept her eyes fixed firmly in front of her, not daring to risk encountering Tony's disturbing gaze again. She laughed and chatted gaily with friends and family, flirted amiably with Richard Kingsley and even danced with Burgess Daggett and then later with Richard and still later, Franklin. She even shared a few words with Alfred Daggett and managed to give Vincent Walcott a polite nod. Mr. Haight was also there with his plump little wife, and she spent time talking idly with them.

In addition to keeping the width of the ballroom between herself and Tony, she also managed to avoid Patrick Blackburne. To anyone watching her, it might be assumed that she was having a wonderful time. Certainly no one would have guessed that her heart was breaking and that she wished herself a thousand miles away.

How she got through the remainder of the dreadful evening she was never certain. She had considered leaving as soon as was polite, and only the bitter knowledge that Tony would view her early withdrawal as retreat kept her standing and smiling and talking long after she would have left. Just after one o'clock in the morning, out of the corner of her eye, she saw Tony taking his leave of the Crockers and knew that her torture was over. Tony had barely strolled out the door before she was saying her good-byes to the Crockers and asking for her carriage to be brought around to the front of the house.

Intent upon escape, she was almost at the door when

Richard caught her. Smiling down at her, he asked in a low voice, "May I have the honor of escorting you home this evening?"

With the tales of the Harpe brothers still fresh in her mind, Arabella gladly accepted his protection.

Kissing her hand politely, he said, "I shall be only a moment—I must take my leave of the Crockers and have my horse brought 'round."

Her green paisley shawl draped around her shoulders, she waited just inside the entrance of the house, wondering if she had been hasty in accepting his offer. Normally she would have kept Richard at arm's length, well aware that he harbored ideas of strengthening the existing tie between them by the simple expediency of marriage. Her father had approved of Richard's subtle courtship, and she could not say that marriage to Richard would be a terrible thing. There was much to recommend him; he was well-bred, handsome, wealthy, and not unkind. Arabella frowned. He was also vain, selfish, and held a high opinion of his own opinions. She didn't precisely dislike Richard, although he often irritated her intensely, and it was flattering to be courted, however tepidly, by a gentleman of Kingsley's station, but she had always been wary of him. His talk against Tony prior to and during their engagement had not endeared him to her—even if his motives were pure, which she doubted.

But that evening he had caught her in a weak moment, and she had been far more encouraging to him than she would have been under usual circumstances. Doubt about the wisdom of her actions gnawed at her, and she watched the approach of his tall form with growing apprehension. Well, she had only herself to blame she admitted sourly. *And so help me,* she thought grimly, *if he presses his suit or makes advances, I shall give his ears a boxing he'll not soon forget. I am in no mood for dalliance tonight—not even respectable dalliance!*

With a smile on her lips that gave no clue to her inner thoughts and her hand resting on Richard's arm, they began to walk across the broad veranda to where Tidmore was waiting in the carriageway with her vehicle; Richard's restive bay mount was being tied by a small black boy at the rear of the light carriage.

The veranda and wide steps that led to the carriageway were well lit by several lanterns, and they were almost halfway across the veranda when Arabella noticed Tony, his back to her, standing on the second step. She would have recognized those broad shoulders and that arrogantly held head anywhere, and she stiffened, uneasy about a possible confrontation.

Richard felt her tighten. Catching sight of Tony and guessing the cause of her reaction, he bent his head near hers, and murmured, "You have nothing to fear, my dear. I will not let him make a scene."

She smiled faintly, never thinking until that moment that there would be a time she would actually be grateful to Richard.

They changed their direction slightly, planning to descend on the far side of the steps, when the sound of a woman's voice rang through the night, stopping them in their tracks—as well as several other late-departing guests behind them.

"Oh, cruel, cruel seducer! To leave me penniless and alone! To abandon me, giving no thought to my future!"

Arabella instantly recognized Molly Dobson's voice and spied her immediately as Molly stood at the edge of the carriageway, the lantern's wavering light eerily revealing her blond beauty. Feeling as if she had plunged into a nightmare, Arabella stood frozen to the spot, unable to move. All the pain of the last, terrible time she had seen Molly came rushing back, and for a moment she thought she would faint.

Fighting back the black void that threatened to overcome her, she swayed, and Richard's arm quickly closed around her waist, cradling and supporting her. Her cheeks fiery red, furious with herself for her sign of weakness, she instantly recovered.

Standing bolt upright, she said quietly, "I am fine, thank you. I have no need of assistance."

"No, I agree—poor Tony is the one who needs help," Richard said with malicious pleasure.

Despite the anguish of the situation, Arabella couldn't help but feel a pang for Tony. To be confronted by one's past in such an embarrassing and public manner could not be pleasant—not even for someone like Tony Daggett.

"You left me with nothing!" cried Molly in a pitiful voice, her blue eyes brimming with tears, her features pale and strained. "Did you never wonder what would become of me?"

Whatever emotions he was experiencing, Tony gave no sign. His head held proudly, his legs spread as if prepared to repel an attack, he said coolly, "Hardly. As I recall you were paid and paid well for your services—months before I left Natchez."

"Oh, vile, vile creature! You ruined me!" Molly spit, anger giving the words the color of truth. "I was but a poor innocent until you seduced me and then heartlessly discarded me and left me to fend for myself in the only way I could!"

Tony laughed, real amusement in his voice. "That horse won't run, Molly, and you know it. You were no innocent." He smiled at her outraged features.

"How dare you say such lies about me!" she shrieked, her fists clenching at her sides, her face contorted with fury. This was not the reaction she had expected. He was supposed to be ashamed and embarrassed. He should be humiliated, eager to slink away.

Tony was none of those things. If anything, he appeared faintly amused by the scene. He certainly seemed unaware of the shocked and revolted faces of the guests who were reluctant spectators to this ugly scene. He was as self-possessed as ever, acting as if he and Molly were alone, discussing a minor disagreement, and that there were not a dozen or so prominent men and women, privy to his most intimate affairs.

"There is nothing to dare," Tony drawled. "Your profession is well-known. I was but one of many . . ." His voice hardened. "And I'd give a small fortune to know who put you up to this little charade."

"Charade!" Molly screeched. "Nay, nay! It is no charade—you deserted me, coldly abandoned me to my fate." Panting emotionally, her magnificent bosom fairly heaving, she moved nearer to the base of the steps. "Did you never think that when you abandoned me, that you might have left me with part of yourself?"

Tony stiffened, even from where she stood, Arabella could see the change in his stance.

"And what," he asked in grim tones, "do you mean by that?"

Molly smiled, pleased with his reaction. "Why only, good sir, that when you sailed away to England that you left me . . . with your child!" And reaching behind her, she suddenly thrust a small boy of about five years old in front of her. Appealing to the stunned onlookers, she sobbed, "What am I to do? How am I to keep his son and myself? What sort of man deserts his very own flesh and blood in such a cruel, uncaring way?"

"That's enough!" Tony snapped, all amusement gone. Leaping down the remaining steps, he took Molly by the arm and shook her slightly. "Keep up that sort of talk and I'm liable to ring your bloody neck—before it comes to that, I want to know why you are doing this? Who put you up to spreading these blatant lies? Tell me, damn you!"

Wrenching her arm free, Molly cried out, "You see how he threatens and abuses me? I ask you, is this the manner of a gentleman . . . or of a blackguard?"

There was low, angry murmur from the crowd at the top of the steps, and William Crocker, having been hastily informed of the trouble brewing on his veranda by Mr. Haight, hurriedly pushed his way through the throng. Putting his hand on Tony's shoulder, he murmured something into Tony's ear and Tony nodded curtly.

Under his breath, Tony growled, "Come along, Molly, we'll finish this privately."

Molly held her ground. Staring imploringly up at Mr. Crocker, she demanded, "Make him swear first! Make him swear that he will not hurt our son or me. Make him swear!"

Tony's teeth ground together audibly, and he snarled, "I do not attack children and I swear I'll not harm a hair on your head—tonight! Beyond that I'll not swear."

Smiling sweetly, Molly bowed her head. "It will do," she said softly. Grabbing the boy by the shoulder, she dragged him after her as she allowed Tony to hustle her away from the condemning and utterly fascinated stares of the onlookers.

The moment the little trio disappeared into the darkness beyond the glow of the lanterns, like waking from a trance, everyone seemed to shake themselves, blinking as if they could not believe what they had just seen. A moment later, a babble arose, its tone indignant and from the few words Arabella caught, clearly not complimentary of Tony Daggett.

"I'm sorry you had to see and hear that," Richard said, as he urged Arabella down the steps toward her carriage.

She smiled thinly. "Why? It certainly proved your oft-stated opinion of Tony, didn't it?"

Richard sighed. "It did indeed, but I would not for the world have had you see proof of his true character in such a painful manner."

"Nothing could be as painful as what he did to me five years ago," Arabella replied in clipped tones. "Now, may we drop the subject?"

"Of course. I know that it is an unpleasant topic for you."

Richard was on the point of helping her into the carriage when William Crocker came up to them. His craggy face unhappy, he took one of Arabella's hands in his, and said quietly, "I am sorrier than I can say that you were subjected to that ugly little scene, my dear, but I think that this time Tony was more sinned against than sinner."

"What do mean?" Arabella asked painfully, her eyes huge and unknowingly hopeful.

Mr. Crocker's mouth thinned. "It is not a subject I would normally discuss with a young lady like yourself, but considering your past association with Tony, I believe you should know that wild and reckless and yes, thoughtless, he may have been, but there is no power on this earth that will convince me that one word of that harpy's story is true." He looked deeply into Arabella's eyes. "She was his mistress—that much is true—but I know for a fact that he broke off with her and settled a handsome sum on her months before the pair of you ever became engaged." He smiled faintly. "Meeting you was a facer such as Tony had never suffered before in his life, and within days of your first introduction to him, he had rid himself of Molly Dobson." His expression grew grim. "But even if I personally did not know that he had sent Molly on her way, I will swear on my own children's heads that he would never have denied or abandoned *any* child of his."

"Oh, come now, Crocker," broke in Richard, his blue eyes glittering with annoyance, "aren't you letting your affection for him and his grandparents color your views?"

Crocker's jaw clenched. "No. One thing everyone generally agrees upon is that Tony Daggett is no liar, and if Tony says the child is not his, then I believe him," he said levelly, giving Richard a look that would have made another man suddenly find something more interesting to inspect a safe distance away. Glancing back at Arabella, he continued, "There is much said against Tony that is pure gossip and wild speculation—and Tony, I am pained to admit, does little to squelch it. I cannot deny that he was spoiled in his youth, but he has always, even then, had a good and kind heart, and he never lied or made any attempt to hide his many transgressions." He smiled thinly. "Tony would be far more likely to have flaunted his son before all the haughty matrons and stiff-rumped gentlemen than to have ignored him. If you know Tony at all, you know that I speak the truth."

Arabella didn't want to excuse Tony, but there was much in what Mr. Crocker said. Tony was far likelier to have thrown an illegitimate child in the face of all his detractors than to have hidden him. The fact that he had always been brazen about his less-than-respectable antics and indifferent to the disgraceful tales that swirled around him had been one of the reasons he had become such a favorite topic of gossip.

Giving Mr. Crocker a small, unhappy smile, Arabella took her hand from his, and said, "Thank you—but Tony and I have nothing to say to each other anymore."

Mr. Crocker nodded sadly. "Which is a shame—you would have been the making of him."

Leaving Arabella flustered and miserable, Mr.

Crocker turned away and strode up the steps. Richard helped her into the coach and joined her inside.

There was little conversation between them for the first few miles, Arabella wanting to take comfort from Mr. Crocker's words and yet unable to discover how they changed the situation between her and Tony. Tony had made it clear that he wanted nothing to do with her. She bit her lip. No, that wasn't true—he had offered her marriage, and, coward that she was, she had shied away from it.

She had hurt him—gravely, she realized, but she still could not see how she could have answered him any other way. The past firmly blocked any future between them.

Sitting beside her, Richard suddenly patted her hands where they lay in her lap, and said, "Do not dwell on it, my sweet. And do remember, please, that the Crockers have always defended Tony, even in the face of the most damning evidence. He is a bounder of the worst sort and certainly undeserving of their affection and loyalty."

Arabella kept her thoughts to herself. There was no use arguing with Richard about Tony. Richard had always held Tony in contempt, and tonight's offensive scene would not change his mind about him.

Despite her best intentions, she couldn't help herself from saying tartly, "Isn't it interesting, though, that Tony's, er, sins are little different from yours and those of many other gentlemen in Natchez, and yet no one seems to even raise an eyebrow about them?"

In the darkness of the coach, Richard flushed. "I don't know what you are talking about," he said stiffly. "I have never acted as Tony Daggett."

Her expression innocent, she asked, "Oh? You have never kept a mistress? I seem to remember that Molly was even once *your* mistress. Did you never gamble the night away? Never make a reckless wager? Never return to your home foxed?"

His voice hardened. "These are not subjects I care to discuss with you."

Arabella laughed. "Oh, come now. I am not some simple miss who does not know the way of the world. I am a woman grown and in charge of my own life. Besides, you are not just anybody—we have known each other for years and we are related by marriage. I promise you I shall not be shocked. Why shouldn't we discuss such things if we wish? It will be much more interesting than merely making polite conversation."

"It is unseemly," Richard muttered, "for a gently reared woman of *any* age to be talking about such matters. If you are not shocked, I am! And I certainly would not want as a wife a woman who gaily chatters about those sort of subjects."

Her voice cool, Arabella said, "Then it is a good thing that I am not under consideration for becoming your wife, isn't it?"

"Now, Bella," he began coaxingly, "I didn't mean to put your back up—and as for the other . . ." He reached for her hand and, lifting it to his lips, pressed an ardent kiss to the back of it. "You know how I feel about you."

Arabella snatched her hand away. "No, I don't, and I don't care to know. I appreciated your offer of an escort to Greenleigh, Richard, but if you are going to make a nuisance of yourself, and attempt to court me, I would just as soon you get on your horse and ride away."

"Your father," he snapped, "should be horsewhipped for allowing you to grow up so headstrong and with such a forward manner. You are unnatural, do you know that? At your age, it should be your most pressing desire to wed before you are branded a hopeless spinster. Instead of firing up at me, you should be gratified at my interest." Regaining his temper somewhat, he added confidently, "Without sounding vain, I could list you a dozen young women who would be overjoyed to accept a proposal from me."

"Then why don't you go escort one of them home?" Arabella asked sweetly.

Richard took a deep breath. "Bella, I don't want to fight with you."

"Then don't! Find a topic we can discuss peaceably, and we shall deal quite well together."

It was obvious that this was not the way he had expected the ride back to Greenleigh to go, but concealing his chagrin, Richard dutifully began to talk of mundane things: the Crocker ball, the weather, the hope for this year's crops, and several other perfectly respectable subjects. By the time the carriage pulled up to the steps of Greenleigh quite a bit later, Arabella was heartily bored and pleased to wave him good-bye.

Boots was feeling rather pleased with himself. Molly had played her part well, and the introduction of the boy had been a masterful touch. The crowd of onlookers had been large and varied, and Arabella's presence had made the entire scene absolutely perfect.

He frowned. He had not been pleased by Crocker's intervention—or his conversation with Arabella. The meddling old fool could have ruined everything. But all in all, he was feeling quite satisfied. And any worry that Tony and Arabella might renew their previous interest in each other had been firmly put to rest. Arabella was a proud woman and unlikely to forgive Tony's apparent cruelty to Molly. And, of course, the child was the final blow. Even if Arabella could stomach common knowledge of Tony's women, she would never be able to forget about the boy. Yes, the boy had been the crowning touch, the final wedge between any budding relationship between Tony and Arabella.

Boots erred in his thinking, and he would have been greatly irritated to know that what he considered a brilliant plan to ruin Tony once and for all had set Arabella to considering seriously what she had learned that night and to painful reexamining of the past.

William Crocker's words had made a huge impact on her, reminding her of important traits of Tony's that she had forgotten in the midst of all her pain and anger. Tony was many things, but he was *not* a liar. He was, as Mr. Crocker had stated, far more likely to flaunt his sins than to hide or deny them. Incredible as it seemed, and it did seem so, Tony might have been telling the truth about that night at the lodge with Molly Dobson. Certainly, after this length of time, and all that had occurred, one would wonder why he still so stubbornly persisted in denying having arranged to meet Molly that horrible night.

Arabella dismissed Tidmore for the evening and sought out her bedroom. She told Martha not to wait up for her, and so she was alone as she undressed and slipped on her nightclothes. Her bed was turned back invitingly, a candle glowed on the table nearby, but despite the late hour, she found herself oddly wakeful.

Her soft lawn gown floating around her bare feet, she wandered restlessly about the room, her mind filled with the most unsettling thoughts. She had always believe that Tony had lied, but suppose he had not? Suppose someone had set up the scene she had found?

She frowned. But why? Who would be so against their marriage that they would go to such lengths to destroy her belief in Tony? Obviously, someone who didn't want them to marry. But that, she admitted wearily, could have been half of Natchez! Her father and Mary had been violently opposed to the match. As had been Richard. Even Tony's uncle, Alfred, had made it clear that he considered her a fool for being willing to marry Tony; Franklin and Burgess had somewhat less vocally echoed his words. There were others, too: Mr. Haight, the Gayles, and the Dennings—the list was endless.

Arabella did not want to believe that someone, perhaps even a member of her family, had deliberately set out to destroy her engagement to Tony, and yet she found that she was seriously considering just that idea. Ever since the moment she had seen Tony and Molly together at the lodge, she had believed the evidence of her eyes. She had been, she realized now, too hurt and stunned really to think about it. It had been easier to block the sight of Tony and Molly in bed together from her thoughts and to believe that Tony was every bit as black as he had been painted. Humiliated, wounded beyond words, every time Tony had tried to explain that night, she had thrown his words back in his face. But what if Tony had been telling the truth? It was something she had never, ever considered. And she should have, she thought miserably. If she had loved him as much as she claimed, shouldn't she have at least given him the benefit of the doubt? Listened to him? Not allowed her shredded emotions to cloud her thoughts?

As she paced, struggling to see her way clear of the maze in which she found herself, one thing became clear in her mind. Mr. Crocker had been right: Tony was not a liar. So, if Tony had said, had *sworn,* that he had not arranged to meet Molly that night, then he had not. But if he had not, she mused uneasily, then who had?

Chapter Fourteen

❧

*W*hile Arabella and Richard Kingsley were driving away from Broadmount, Tony was hastily ushering Molly Dobson and her son into the small study that William Crocker had suggested he use for privacy. Shutting the door firmly behind them, Tony sourly observed Molly and the boy as they stood in the middle of the room facing him.

Barely acknowledging the small boy clinging to Molly's blue gown, his gaze fixed grimly on Molly, he said, "All right, we're alone now. There is no longer any need for you to continue with your act. I want to know what you think you can accomplish by spouting these damned lies. Of even more importance to me is the identity of the person who put this entire idea into that pretty head of yours."

Molly shrugged. "I don't know what you are talking about—no one gave me any ideas." Her blue eyes wouldn't meet his, and her fingers nervously toyed with the soft dark hair of her son.

"And I'm sure you'll continue to claim your story is true unless I pay you well enough to change it. How much," he asked wearily, "are you going to cost me this time? How much do I have pay you to find out the truth?"

"You think that money will solve everything, don't you?" Molly snapped. "Well, it won't! You heard what I said tonight, and I'm not taking any of it back."

His expression shuttered, Tony stared at her consideringly. Someone, he decided thoughtfully, must be paying her an enormous sum. The Molly he had known had possessed a passion for money; her silence could only be because she had been offered a sum he wasn't likely to match. He frowned. Unless, of course, she was afraid. And if that were the case, his hopes of getting the truth out of her were nonexistent.

Trying another tack, he asked, "Who is the boy's real father?" And when Molly started to answer, he added sharply, "And don't try to pawn him off as mine. No matter what sort of nonsense you just spouted for everybody, you know damn well that we parted over six months previously to your, ah, surprise visit to me five years ago at the Greenleigh lodge." He smiled mirthlessly. "I may have been half-drugged, but I was very familiar with your body, and it was impossible that you were several months pregnant when you staged that ugly scene at the lodge. And while others may think that we had been making love, *I* know that no such act occurred. The boy cannot be mine."

"So you say," Molly replied coolly, "but you cannot prove it, can you?"

Tony's eyes narrowed. "I see. You are determined, then, to persist in this blatant lie?"

Molly smiled. "You are the only one who claims that I am lying—no one else who heard my story tonight believed *your* protestation of innocence."

Tony glanced down at the boy, who still clung to his mother's skirts. The child looked sleepy and confused, his wide blue eyes drooping, his soft rosebud mouth suddenly stretching wide with a yawn. He appeared to be about five years old and from Tony's limited experience with children, he also looked like he would grow into a handsome youth, his features fine and even, his frame sturdy and straight. Tony could see some resemblance to Molly in the boy's face, but it was not striking. He supposed, because the child possessed dark hair and blue eyes, that the argument could be made that the child looked like him, but dark hair and blue eyes could be found in almost half the male population of Natchez.

"What is the child's name?" he asked quietly.

"Marcus."

The boy glanced up when he heard his name, and Tony sent him an encouraging smile. "It is a nice, strong name," Tony said softly to the child.

Marcus flashed him a singularly charming smile and then, apparently overcome with shyness, dropped his head.

Uncomfortably aware of the boy in a way that he had not been before, Tony said abruptly, "Now is no time for us to discuss this. Marcus should be in bed—should have been in bed hours ago. I shall make arrangements for—" He stopped. "How," he suddenly asked, "did you get here tonight? And how did you know that I would be here tonight?"

Molly looked mysterious. "I have my ways. And as for transportation, there is no need for you to worry about it—I hired my own wagon and a driver."

"Where are you living these days?" Tony asked, knowing that further questions about her story would gain him nothing.

"I will give you directions," she said, "for I am sure that this will not be our last conversation together."

After giving Tony directions to her house, Molly allowed herself and Marcus to be escorted out of the Crocker house and to a spot some distance down the main driveway, to where her wagon had been pulled off the road and parked. The flickering light of a small lantern at the side of the wagon revealed an old black man leaning against the worn sides of the vehicle.

At their approach the black man straightened up and watched silently as Tony first helped Molly and then Marcus into the rear seat of the wagon. At a nod from Tony, the black man untied the horse and climbed stiffly into the front seat.

His hand resting on the edge of Molly's seat, Tony said, "I shall come to see you tomorrow afternoon. Will three o'clock be convenient?"

"Yes. I shall look forward to your visit," Molly said demurely.

"I wouldn't if I were you," Tony muttered. "I may still decide to break your neck."

Scowling, he spun on his heels and walked back toward the lights of the Crocker house. The remainder of the guests had departed, and Tony found his host and Patrick Blackburne waiting for him on the veranda.

A wry smile on his lips, he walked up the steps toward them. "William, I cannot tell you how sorry I am that you and your guests had to be subjected to that unpleasant scene. I hope that I am not entirely covered with shame."

William smiled and dropped a comforting hand on Tony's broad shoulder. "Don't worry about it," he said calmly. "I haven't been so entertained since you left for England. By gad, it is good that you have come back and will enliven the neighborhood."

"You are a good friend to make so light of it," Tony said huskily, much moved by William's open support. "I trust that your lady is of the same mind?"

William nodded. "You know that you have Milly wrapped around your little finger and have since you first learned to smile. Now come along—let us go inside and enjoy a final drink."

William deliberately walked ahead, leaving Patrick and Tony alone for a few minutes.

Patrick quirked a brow at Tony. "How bad was it?"

"Imagine your worst nightmare," Tony said bleakly. "Even worse—Arabella had to hear and see it. Blast! I am truly damned when it comes to that woman. After tonight, she will *never* believe that I had nothing to do with Molly once we had met." He sighed, his expression bitter. "Not that she isn't already convinced that I have been lying about my involvement with Molly all along."

Arabella woke late the next morning, the painful image of Tony lying beneath Molly's sprawled form floating ceaselessly through her dreams. And though her sleep had been troubled, she found that, despite all the evidence to the contrary, her belief in Tony's innocence had solidified. She might be a fool, she thought grimly, as she bathed and dressed. She might even simply be blinding herself to the truth, but she hung on to one thought: Tony Daggett was many things, but his word was his bond.

And if Tony hadn't lied, then someone else had. Someone else who for five long years had gotten away with the destruction of her engagement. Arabella didn't want to consider the fact that her family might have been behind that ugly scene at the lodge with Tony, but she couldn't ignore the possibility. Her father had been livid at the engagement, and he would have done anything in his power to stop her from marrying a man he was convinced would lead her a terrible life. No matter what pain it caused her, he would have been convinced that he was doing it all for her own good. That he was *saving* her. She frowned. But her father had also been an honorable man. Would he have stooped so low? Would Mary? She sighed. Anything was possible.

Descending the staircase, she entered the morning room and sat down to eat a light repast. Only half-aware of what she was doing, Arabella tried to tear her mind away from her troubling thoughts, but to no avail. Of course, she admitted as she sipped her coffee and nibbled on the fruit and toast before her, Richard was the most likely suspect to have plotted against her and Tony—she would put little past Mary's brother. He had been almost as rabid against the engagement as her father. But then, even Tony's uncle, Alfred, or many others that she could name, could have done the same. Very few people had been happy about the courtship and engagement.

When Mrs. Tidmore entered the room a few minutes later, asking if Arabella would look over the menu for the week, Arabella firmly pushed aside her speculation. She and Mrs. Tidmore had made plans to take one last look at the items stored in the attic, before having anything they didn't feel was worth saving thrown on the burn pile out back. She was almost grateful that she would not have time to brood over the past.

Unfortunately, she was not able entirely to escape repercussions from the ugly scene at the Crocker ball. Dusk was just drifting down when Arabella was astonished to see her stepmother's carriage pull up in the driveway at the front of the house. She watched perplexed as Mary hastily stepped down from the coach, and exclaimed, "Oh my dear! I am so sorry that you were forced to endure more of *that* man's horrible antics. Last night must have been most painful for you. Everyone is talking about it. Agatha and I thought that our presence here at Greenleigh would keep the worst of the gossips away."

Stripping off her white-lace gloves, Mary continued to chatter away as a bemused Arabella walked up the steps with the two arrivals. "We would have been here earlier," Mary said, "but we had to pack, you know— and then there were the children. I had to make certain they understood how important it was for Agatha and me to be with you at this time." Mary smiled at Arabella. "They understood completely—and they send you their love."

Not certain whether to be touched or annoyed by their arrival, Arabella merely smiled and showed them into the main saloon. As they settled themselves comfortably, Mrs. Tidmore hustled into the room and left a tray of refreshments.

Looking anxiously across at Arabella, Mary asked, "How are you, darling? We were so worried about you. If it hadn't been so late when Jeremy related what had happened after we left the ball last night, I would have returned immediately to Broadmount and insisted you come home with us."

Thankful that she had at least been spared that, Arabella said lightly, "I appreciate your concern, but I am fine." She smiled ruefully. "You must remember that I am well aware of Tony's reputation, and I am sorry to say that last night's little scene is not the worst I have been forced to endure since I first met him."

Agatha sent Mary a satisfied glance. "I told you that she would be all right." She looked approvingly at Arabella. "Told her that I have been agreeably surprised by the good sense you have shown lately and that she shouldn't treat you like you were made of china."

Still somewhat at a loss about how to react to Agatha's approval, Arabella merely sent her an uncertain smile, and said, "Thank you." Looking at Mary, she added, "Agatha is right, you know—if I were going to shatter, it would have been five years ago."

Realizing that Arabella was not as upset by what had happened the previous night as she had assumed she would be, Mary said uncertainly, "Well, I am glad that you are taking it so well." She looked uncomfortable.

"Er, did what happened change how you feel about him?"

"Do you mean was I so disgusted by what happened that I have completely fallen out of love with him?" Arabella asked dryly.

Mary nodded.

"I know that you are not happy about my feelings for him," Arabella began quietly, "but last night didn't change anything—it may have wounded me a little, but my love would not be the deep emotion I feel it to be if I quailed at the first sign that Tony is not the stuff of heroes." She leaned toward Mary, and said earnestly, "I know that it pains you, but you must understand that I do love him, and that because I love him, I am willing to try to understand him—even to question some of the conclusions that everyone has about him."

"She's right, you know," interjected Agatha sagely. "Love is blind—but sometimes, it is also more discerning."

"How can you say that?" Mary demanded. "You know what a terrible person he is!"

To Mary and Arabella's utter confoundment, Agatha shook her head. "No, I don't. I know what you have told me. And you do not know for certain the reliability of what you have heard. You have merely repeated tales told to you by others—others who might have their own reasons for speaking ill of the young man. Besides, you must admit that you are not in a position to judge him fairly—you detest him, think him little better than a wicked demon determined to ruin Arabella's life."

Clearly upset at this blatant desertion, Mary glared at Agatha. "How can you say that? You don't know him at all. Don't tell me that you, too, have been taken in by his handsome face." Almost accusingly, she added, "I saw you watching him last night while he was flirting outrageously with that forward little hussy, Margaret Crocker." Stiffly she finished, "Personally, I would never let a daughter of mine carry on in such a way— and with such a depraved creature as Tony Daggett."

"Oh, he is a handsome devil, I'll grant you that," Agatha replied, not a bit disturbed by Mary's outburst. Giving Arabella a sly glance, she murmured, "If I were a few decades younger, I might make a push to fix his attention, but that isn't the point. The point is that Arabella is in love with him—and if she is as sensible and intelligent as you have always told me she is, shouldn't you stop and consider that you might have gotten the wrong impression of him?"

At Mary's expression of outrage, Agatha held up one hand, and said, "Listen to me. Even you admit that much of what you have told me about him is merely gossip. Do you really know that he murdered his two wives? Do you have proof of it?"

"Of course not!" Mary muttered. "But everybody knows—"

"How do they know?" Agatha interrupted, one slim brow cocked.

Mary opened her mouth, then shut it with a snap. For a tense moment, she looked at Agatha with pure dislike. Finally she admitted, "All right, some of the stories about him could just be gossip, but what about what he did to Arabella? That is something that we *know* he did." She looked at Arabella for confirmation. "Don't we?"

Having been a fascinated bystander to the exchange between Mary and Agatha, it took Arabella a moment to realize that the question had been directed at her. She hesitated a moment, and then said unhappily, "When I found Tony and Molly together that night at the lodge I know that it looked as if he were the vilest beast in nature . . . but lately, I've begun to wonder if I saw the true picture that night."

"What?" demanded Mary, her blue eyes wide and disbelieving. "Have you gone mad? What other explanation is there?"

Picking her words with care, Arabella said, "Before I say anything else you must understand one thing about Tony—something that I, myself, had forgotten. Tony is not a liar. He is far more likely to flaunt his vices than he is to hide them. And he doesn't lie about them— *ever."*

"Well, I won't argue with that!" Mary snapped. "He is the most flagrant, womanizing wastrel I have ever known—and he has never taken any pains to hide it. Nor that he gambles and drinks—excessively!"

Arabella smiled faintly. "But you'll agree that he does not go around telling untruths? In fact, have you ever known anyone to accuse him of being a liar?"

Reluctantly, Mary admitted, "No, that is one charge that has never been leveled against him. But is it probably the only crime he has not committed."

Ignoring Mary's gibe, Arabella went on, "If you agree that he is not a liar, then I ask you: Why does he persist in claiming his innocence about that night at the lodge? Why does he continue to swear, when it doesn't matter any longer, that he had not laid eyes on Molly

Dobson for months? That he did not arrange to meet her at the lodge that night?"

An uncomfortable silence fell, Mary suddenly becoming very interested in the pattern of the rose-and-cream rug on the floor. Arabella and Agatha both watched her, waiting for her answer. It was a long time coming, and Arabella was puzzled by the delay. She knew that it was going to be painful for Mary to admit that she might have been wrong about Tony, but having crossed the first hurdle in agreeing that he was not a liar, why didn't she simply answer the question?

"Well?" Agatha finally prompted.

"I don't know," Mary said crossly, not looking at either of the other two women.

"Couldn't it be," Arabella asked gently, "that he is telling the truth? That someone arranged for me to find him in such a compromising position?"

Mary flushed. "What an awful thing to say! Why would anyone do such a thing?"

"Because they wanted me to break off my engagement to him," Arabella said.

"Of all the ridiculous notions I have ever heard in my life. That man has bewitched you!" Mary said furiously. "Next, I suppose you'll accuse your father and me of doing the arranging."

"Did you?" Arabella asked, her eyes fixed on Mary's angry features.

Mary sprang to her feet, her blue eyes flashing. "Well! It only needed that. I am not going to stay here a moment longer and be insulted in this fashion." Glancing at Agatha, she said, "Come along. It is obvious that Arabella has been thoroughly beguiled by that man. She certainly doesn't need our help. I'm just sorry we wasted our time and effort in her behalf."

Her nose in the air, Mary was on the point of stalking from the room, when Agatha said bluntly, "Oh, come down out of the boughs, you silly creature. We are going nowhere at this time of night. You might relish dashing to and fro over confoundedly rough roads in the dark, but I do not. I am staying right here." She looked at Arabella. "That is, if you have a bedroom I may use."

"Of course," Arabella replied, rising to her feet. Looking at Mary's stiffly held back, she added softly, "And one for you, too, if you are willing to stay."

"Since Agatha seems determined to remain here, I don't seem to have any choice but to do the same," Mary said ungraciously, not changing her stance.

It was an odd position Arabella found herself in. For the first time in memory, she and Mary were having a serious falling-out. It was clear that her stepmother was deeply insulted and that she wasn't going to be in a forgiving mood anytime soon. That it was Agatha who seemed to be taking up her side of the argument was also a novelty. In a decidedly confused frame of mind, Arabella rang for Mrs. Tidmore, and when she appeared, quietly asked if the rooms for Mary and Agatha had been prepared. At Mrs. Tidmore's nod, the ladies retired for the night.

Arabella did not sleep well. She was upset by the chasm that had sprung up so shockingly and unexpectedly between herself and her stepmother, and she hoped that a night's sleep would return Mary to her usual sweet self. Mary's reaction to the possibility that Tony might have been innocent that night at the lodge made her question all over again her conclusions that he was indeed innocent of having arranged to meet Molly. But as the soft pink-and-gold light of dawn spilled into her room, she was still firmly of the opinion that Tony had not lied. And that if he had not lied, then who amongst their friends and family had plotted against them?

She would have liked to discuss the matter with Mary, but her hopes that Mary might have had a change of heart during the night were dashed when she was greeted by the news that Mary and Agatha were leaving for Highview immediately after breakfast.

"Are you certain I cannot prevail upon you to stay just for one more night?" Arabella asked almost desperately, as they finished their uncomfortable meal in the morning room. She and Mary had always had a close, loving relationship, and her heart ached at the estrangement between them.

"Why? So you can insult me further?" Mary asked sharply.

"I did not mean to insult you," Arabella said levelly, "and I am sorry that you feel that I have."

Mary merely sniffed and pushed away her cup of coffee. Rising to her feet, she glanced at Agatha, and asked, "Are you ready to leave?"

Agatha shrugged. "Whenever you are."

It was an uncomfortable leave-taking, Mary coolly presenting her cheek for Arabella's kiss and ignoring her thereafter. To Arabella's surprise, it was Agatha who gave her a hearty embrace, and whispered into her ear, "Don't fret, she'll soon regain her sweet temper—and be most ashamed of herself for the way she is acting right now. And as for that young man of yours, don't let others make up your mind for you—I did once and regretted it all my life."

Depressed and unhappy, Arabella watched the coach until it was out of sight. *Wonderful,* she thought miserably as she wandered back inside. Not only was Tony furious with her, but now she had also insulted and infuriated her stepmother. Could she do nothing right?

All during the following week as she tried to throw herself into making Greenleigh her home, she went over and over again the events leading up to the break with Tony, as well as the painful falling-out with Mary. And again she was left with the lowering opinion that she could have done nothing any differently. Why, she wondered miserably, did loving Tony always seem to bring with it such conflict and unhappiness with those who meant so much to her?

Tony had one supporter in her family however: Jeremy. He rode over on Friday afternoon to see how she was doing on her own. Arabella was delighted to see him and hoped that perhaps he had brought a conciliatory message from his mother. Such was not the case.

Having shown himself into the small room at the rear of the house where she had been busy with mending, Jeremy gave her a kiss and threw himself into a nearby chair. His legs sprawled out in front of him, he said by way of greeting, "I tell you, Bella, I don't know how I've kept my tongue between my teeth these past few days. Mother has nothing but bad things to say about Tony—she does nothing but rage about how he has ruined our family and that he is an awful creature." Moodily he stared at his boots. "I've been thinking of telling her just how much she owes him. Why, if it weren't for

Tony's generosity, we'd be living here at Greenleigh and falling all over each other."

Arabella looked fondly across at him. "That is entirely your choice, my dear. But I doubt it will change her opinion of him."

"I know that, but it just doesn't seem fair." His expression became a bit sheepish. "It doesn't help that the entire neighborhood is still all atwitter about the scene at Broadmount last week. And, of course, word quickly traveled that he had been to see that Molly Dobson at her home on Silver Street."

Ignoring the stab of pain in her heart, Arabella said lightly, "Oh, really? I hadn't heard that bit of gossip."

Jeremy snorted. "And you are not likely to, either, except from a loose-lipped fool like your brother. Everyone is determined to spare you further embarrassment."

"And you are not?" she asked quizzically.

"Thing is," Jeremy said with a grin, "unlike everybody else, I know you ain't likely to go off in a swoon, nor fall into a fit of the vapors after hearing such tales."

"Thank you," she said dryly, putting aside a linen tablecloth, the small tear that once marred its smooth surface now hidden by Arabella's neat little stitches. A thoughtful expression on her face, she mused, "I suppose he went there to try to persuade her to tell the truth."

Jeremy shrugged. "Gossip has it that he went there to pay her off—or murder her. Jim Gayle told me that he heard that they had a terrible row. It's being said everywhere that Tony left her place absolutely furious, vowing to ring her neck."

Arabella frowned, a feeling of unease sliding down her spine. If Molly was lying, she could certainly understand Tony's temper, but she wished he would take more care over what he said when he was in a rage. To Jeremy she merely said, "Well, that doesn't surprise me—I'm sure that Tony was furious about what happened." A wry smile curved her lips. "Molly Dobson seems to have a penchant for showing up at just the right time and place to put Tony in the blackest possible light."

"You think she's lying?"

Arabella nodded slowly. "I certainly think that there is a good possibility that she might be." She hesitated, then said, "I've also begun to think that perhaps Tony wasn't lying when he says that he did not arrange to meet Molly at the lodge five years ago. He has always sworn that he had not seen her in months. He openly admitted that she had been his mistress, but that he had paid her off—handsomely—and sent her on her way once we had met."

Jeremy sat up, his face intent. "Having met the man, do you know I find that easier to believe than the stories I have always heard about that night?" He frowned and looked across at her. Slowly, he said, "If what you believe is true, Bella, then it means . . ."

Arabella nodded. "Then it means that someone went to a great deal of trouble to create a situation that put Tony in the worst possible light—one that would drive me to break off our engagement—as I did. And, if what happened at Broadmount is anything to go by, then that person is trying to blacken Tony's reputation."

"But who could hate him that badly?" He paused and made a face. "I suppose the list is rather long, especially when you consider the families of his previous wives and the family of the young man who died with his first wife."

Arabella looked startled. "I hadn't thought of them, but I can't believe that they would choose such a round-about way of taking revenge. If an attempt had been made on his life—well, yes—but to destroy my happiness? Besides, why wait so long?"

Jeremy shrugged and made a face. "I can't hazard a guess, but who knows? Are the families still in Natchez?"

It was Arabella's turn to frown. "No, I don't think that they are. I seem to recall that Mercy's family went back to England after her death and that Terrell had no family, at least not here in the Mississippi Territory. I never really knew that much about him. And as for Elizabeth Fenton . . ." She shrugged. "Again, I don't know very much about her or her family."

"You know," Jeremy said slowly, "we keep ignoring the fact that Elizabeth was murdered. His first wife's death could be put down to a tragic accident, but his second wife was shot. I know that there are people who believe Tony got away with murdering her, but there never was any conclusive proof—one of the reasons Tony did not hang and is still walking around a free man. And if, as we believe, Tony didn't kill Elizabeth . . . and he didn't arrange for Molly to be at the lodge and isn't the father of her son. . . ."

Arabella's face paled. "Good heavens! Do you know what we are suggesting? That Tony has a deadly enemy who will stop at nothing to destroy him."

"I agree . . . but isn't it interesting that this enemy

seems determined to destroy him, but not kill him. I wonder why?"

Arabella stared at him for a long time, her mind racing. Jeremy had just asked a very interesting question. If it was revenge someone was after, why not simply kill Tony? If Elizabeth had been murdered in the hopes that Tony would hang for it, why, when that had failed, had there been no further attempts to implicate Tony in some other crime? Or even an attempt on his life? Elizabeth had been dead nearly eight years when she and Tony had met and fallen in love—why would anyone wait that long before striking again? And if Tony's death had been the object, what had they expected to happen that night at the lodge? That she would be so incensed at finding him and Molly in bed together that *she* would kill him? It hardly seemed reasonable, but then none of what she and Jeremy were thinking made obvious sense. And yet . . .

"What is it that he or she, whoever the person may be, hopes to gain?" Arabella finally asked. "Obviously not Tony's death. His ruination?"

Jeremy grimaced. "I certainly cannot explain it—but I do believe that someone is going to a great deal of effort to make life unhappy for Tony. Someone shot Elizabeth and killed her. Someone arranged for Molly to be at the lodge."

"And someone," Arabella said grimly, "more recently arranged for Molly to confront Tony at Broadmount."

"Which leaves us where?"

Arabella made a face. "With very little except for a belief in Tony's innocence and the awareness that things are not always what they seem."

Chapter Fifteen

❧

*B*oots would have been annoyed, but not necessarily worried, if he had realized that Tony had a pair of supporters in Arabella and Jeremy. As it was, unaware that the two siblings had begun to question Tony's guilt, he was quite happy with the way things were going.

Thanks to his fine hand, Tony had once again scandalized the neighborhood, and the confrontation between Tony, Molly, and her bastard child at Broadmount was the main topic of gossip everywhere one went. To make the situation even more delicious, Tony, as Boots had known he would, had gone to see Molly at her house on Silver Street the following afternoon and, if gossip was to be believed, a terrible fight had ensued.

Boots had heard the tale from a gentleman who had just happened to be passing by at the time when Tony had stormed out of Molly's and, from what the gentleman had imparted, it appeared that Tony had been in the devil's own temper. According to the story, Tony had left Molly's, his face contorted with rage and vowing to throttle her. And of course, the tale grew with each telling, soon taking on a life of its own. By the time Jeremy had come to see Arabella, it was being bantered about that Tony had to be forcibly pulled off of Molly, his fingers tightly clenched around her throat. It was firmly believed that only timely intervention had prevented Tony from murdering her at that very moment.

The truth was a great deal different. Tony *had* gone to see Molly. It had been an unpleasant interview, Molly sticking staunchly to her story, and he had left her place baffled and unhappy. He did have one source of satisfaction though as he had walked away that afternoon. Upon learning that Marcus did not live with Molly and that he lived with an old slattern of unsavory repute, one well-known for her drunkenness, Tony had been furious. He had demanded and had gotten, with suspicious ease, permission to take over the care of the child.

Throwing Molly a look of contempt, he snapped, "This does not mean that I am acknowledging the boy as mine—we both know that he is not, even if you will not admit it. I am merely showing him the same kindness that I would a poor abandoned pup."

Molly merely shrugged, and said carelessly, "You can't expect me to keep him here. This is no place for a child. You know how I make my living—a child would only be in the way."

Tony bit back a sharp reply. He knew that it was foolish on his part to take responsibility for the boy, but he could not in good conscience leave Marcus in his mother's obviously indifferent care.

Made uncomfortable by the expression in Tony's eyes, Molly added defensively, "I never wanted a child.

I do my best for him. Old Annie watches over him and sees that he comes to no harm—and I *do* see him when I can. He is not starving, and he does have a place to sleep at night. You can't expect me to do more than that."

"No, I certainly cannot," Tony said dryly, wondering how he had ever found her desirable.

Molly had balked when Tony had demanded that she put her permission for him to have the care of Marcus in writing, but in the end, after he had waved a small bag of silver coins under her nose, she had sullenly done what he wanted. Not content with that, he dragged two unfortunate souls off the street to witness her signature. Molly's capitulation had not surprised him—the Molly he had been familiar with would sell anything for money, even her own child. She had, however, refused to budge from her claim that Marcus was his child or to take back anything she had said the night of the Crocker ball—and this despite a handsome offer of more silver.

He had left her house frowning—that much of the gossip was true. Tony was angry and not a little puzzled by Molly's stubborn refusal to tell the truth, and it occurred to him again, that the only thing other than money that would keep her lips sealed was fear. But his thoughts had turned immediately to Marcus, and he had pushed Molly from his mind.

Tony was not known to be a model of discretion, but in the removal of Marcus Dobson from the filthy, ramshackle hut in which he had found the boy, he had proved himself to be at least prudent. He had waited until after dark and then slipped in and out of the area taking Marcus with him, before anyone was aware he had been in the vicinity.

Marcus had not seemed a bit disturbed at being spirited away by a stranger, but then considering the circumstances in which he found him, Tony was not surprised by the child's willingness to accompany him. His first instinct was to take the boy to Sweet Acres to live with him, but he realized that if he did, the cat would truly be amongst the pigeons. Instead, he placed Marcus in the care of his overseer, John Jackson.

Hiring John Jackson to act as overseer and manager of Sweet Acres a decade or so ago had been one of the wisest decisions Tony had ever made, and he often congratulated himself on having made at least *one* smart decision during his irresponsible youth. John and his wife, Sally, were honest, kind, hardworking, and as pleasant a couple as one could ask for. They were around Tony's age and childless, much to their regret. When Tony had approached them about Marcus and explained the situation, Sally had said instantly, "Of course, you may bring that poor, precious boy to us—how could you think otherwise? Imagine a woman treating her own child that way! John and I shall be delighted to look after him for you."

Marcus was a bit wary when he first met the Jacksons, but he seemed to be an adaptable child—no doubt life with his mother and Annie had seen to that. Tony remained at the comfortable Jackson home for a few hours that evening to make certain the Marcus was settling in. He needn't have worried. Marcus seemed to find his change in circumstances quite gratifying—especially the warm gingerbread cake that Sally baked just for him and the novelty of having a soft, clean bed of his own in which to sleep. When shown into the cheerful room that Sally had hastily prepared for him, Marcus looked around with astonishment.

"This is to be *mine*?" he asked, his big blue eyes incredulous.

"Indeed it is," Sally said gently. "And you needn't be afraid that you will be alone—John and I sleep just down the hall."

His little face solemn, Marcus looked up at the brown-haired woman who treated him so kindly. "Oh, I am never afraid. Annie says that she hasn't time for a frightened, whiny brat and that I am not to bother her. So I don't."

Having tucked Marcus into his bed and brushed a hand across his dark curls, Sally said huskily, "You may bother me anytime at all, Marcus."

Worn-out by the events of the evening, Marcus yawned and nodded sleepily. A moment later he was asleep.

The three adults did not say anything until they were once more in the tidy front parlor of the Jackson house. A glint in her eye, Sally looked at Tony, and said, "You will not let him return to that woman, will you?"

Tony shook his head. "No. And I took the precaution of having Molly give me her permission in writing."

"Excellent!" John said. "He seems a fine boy, and I know that Sally and I will quickly become very fond of him. I would not want to see him torn from us—for his sake, as well as ours."

"Do not worry," Tony said, "We will have the law on our side if Molly tries to go back on her word. And if all else fails, money usually has the effect of making Molly see sense. Our only worry, and I believe that it is unfounded, would be if the boy's father made a push to claim him."

Having done, for the present, all that he could for the boy, Tony still had Molly's accusations to face. The icy stares and contemptuous looks that greeted his arrival at the few social events he attended after the Crocker ball did not faze him in the least—he was well used to being considered a disgraceful wastrel. As long as his friends, Blackburne, the Crockers, and a few others knew the truth and did not turn their backs on him, Tony was content.

That Arabella believed him so vile as to abandon his own child bit viciously, but he could see no simple way of redeeming himself. As he had remarked to Blackburne, he had honestly begun to believe that any hope of a relationship with Arabella Montgomery was doomed.

Despite believing that there was no hope for him, he could not bring himself to abandon her completely, particularly since there was a definite possibility that she could still be in danger. Calling himself all kinds of fool, like a lovesick moonling, he spent the hours from midnight to almost dawn each night secretly patrolling the area around Greenleigh. No one, he thought tightly, was going to attack Arabella as she slept . . . without having to go through him first.

He did manage to see Arabella during this time, covertly watching her whenever they happened to attend the same social events. And every time he glimpsed that bright head of hers or caught sight of those elfin features, something ached in the region of his heart. Tony did have some comfort though—he was able to keep track of Arabella's comings and goings through Jeremy, who had taken to dogging his heels in a most flattering manner. In fact, it was because of Jeremy that he accepted those invitations that he knew Arabella had also received and accepted.

It was fairly obvious that Jeremy was hoping for a reconciliation of some sort between himself and Arabella, and while Jeremy, flushed and uncomfortable, had tried to encourage him to believe that Arabella's opinion of him had changed, Tony turned a deaf ear. She had made her position clear, and he was not leaving himself open to that kind of pain again. Besides, it might very well be Jeremy's own hopes for a happy resolution that colored his opinions. But even convinced that there was no chance at all for him and Arabella to resolve their differences, he could not, he admitted morosely, bring himself to stay away from her—even if the closest he came to her was the width of a ballroom.

April finally became May and the political state in Natchez was still tense. Gayoso continued to stay in Natchez despite Ellicott's demands that he leave. Daily there were new opinions about the outcome. Tony was pleased that at last the planters had something else to talk about beside his reputed wickedness.

Another American unit under the command of Captain Isaac Guion had also arrived and was stationed at Chickasaw Bluffs apparently with orders to move down to Natchez itself, if it became necessary. Speculation about what Gayoso intended to do was rampant, and there were worries amongst the Natchez residents that open warfare could break out between the Dons and the American troops. Fortunately, as Tony had said to Blackburne, neither claimant had a clear edge over the other, and he suspected that at the moment, both sides were merely posturing.

May slid nearer to June and the weather warmed predictably; the cotton was growing well and, in addition to the problems between Gayoso and Ellicott, there was talk of an extremely profitable year amongst the planters wherever they gathered. The fact that Gayoso, in an effort to strengthen his hand, had issued a moratorium on the planters' debts for the season added to their optimism—assuming, of course, that a war did not break out in their midst.

Satisfied with the results of his meddling and busy with his own affairs, Boots, beyond sending a few token payments, had delayed meeting with Molly and finalizing their bargain. Molly had proved useful, and he was not quite ready to end their liaison until he was certain that he had no further use for her. Consequently, having ignored her increasingly angry notes, it was the last week of May before he finally bestirred himself to go to her house on Silver Street.

He had not sent her word of his impending visit, as much because of a dislike of putting pen to paper, as he wanted her off guard. From the shadows of a nearby building he had watched her house for several hours, noting old Annie's arrival and departure a short while later with an expression of contempt. The old cow had probably come whining to Molly for money—money she would spend getting herself disgustingly drunk.

From his vantage point he observed that Molly

seemed to enjoy a brisk trade that evening, gentlemen arriving and leaving quite regularly. As the hour grew late, he considered putting off meeting with her, but when what was surely her last caller for the evening had toddled off somewhere after the hour of two o'clock that morning, he felt that it was safe to approach her house.

Taking care that no one observed his entrance, he slipped into the house through the back door. Making his way toward the front of the small house, he met Molly as she came down the narrow hall, heading for her bedroom.

His unexpected appearance shocked a small scream from her. Recognizing him, she quickly recovered herself, and said sharply, "I might have known that you would come creeping around at this hour of the morning."

He smiled thinly. "You should have been expecting me, my dear. After all, you have written me several rather demanding notes of late."

"What if I have? If you think you are going to pawn me off with those damned little dribs and drabs you've been sending, you had better think again. We had a bargain, you and I. I kept my part, but you've been damned slow about yours."

"Indeed I have," he said smoothly, "and I have come to make amends." He cast a glance around at the hallway, and suggested, "Perhaps we could remove ourselves to someplace more comfortable?"

She shrugged. "If you wish." She quickly made her way back to the shabby parlor at the front of the house.

Moving swiftly around the room, Molly lit a few

more candles and, after setting down the candle she had been carrying, turned to face him. "Well? How soon are you going to give me the rest of my money?"

Seating himself in a comfortable chair, he crossed one leg over the other and said airily, "Oh, whenever you want. If you like, you and the boy can be on your way to New Orleans tomorrow morning."

"The boy is not going with me," she said coolly. "Tony offered to take care of him, and I decided to let him."

Boots's mouth tightened. "That," he said evenly, "was not part of the bargain."

"So? You weren't around, and I had to make a decision. Besides, you know that I am no mother and that the boy will certainly be better off with Tony . . . unless, of course, *you* would like to see to his care?" Boots's scowl was her answer, and she smiled cynically.

Boots had never given the boy's fate much thought, but he had definitely never planned for the brat to be in Tony's care. It complicated matters, and he did not like complications. There was little he could do about it then, but it was possible that he could find a way to twist this new situation to his benefit, although nothing occurred to him at that precise moment.

"Yes, of course, you are right." He forced a smile. "So, you will be leaving for New Orleans, with no encumbrances. How wonderful for you."

Molly looked at him, the expression on her face making him wary. "There has been a slight change in my plans," Molly said slowly, her eyes never leaving his. At the questioning flick of his brow, she added, "I've decided that I would prefer to remain in Natchez."

"Have you, indeed?" he asked with an edge to his voice.

Molly hesitated, suddenly a little frightened of him. It had occurred to her during the time since they had last met that knowing what she did about him, she held a rather valuable hand. A hand worth much more than a new wardrobe and passage to New Orleans. Besides, leaving Natchez and everything that was familiar to her and starting over in a strange city didn't appeal to her. Natchez was home—no one was going to drive her from it. She'd never cared in the past what those stiff-rumped, *respectable*, old tabbies had thought about her, and she wasn't about ready to start caring. Not when she had the opportunity to make a fortune and flaunt her presence under the very noses of those who had looked down on her for so long. But first, she admitted uneasily, she had to make him see that she couldn't be bought off as cheaply as he had assumed.

In her thoughts it had seemed an easy thing to do—simply tell him that she wished to retire from her present trade and that he was going to make it possible. Molly had envisioned living very nicely for the rest of her days, knowing that he could not deny her demands—not if he didn't want his part in Tony's misfortunes to be exposed. But lost in her plans, she had forgotten one important thing: He was a very dangerous man—a man she had always found it prudent not to cross.

With a little less confidence than she had felt earlier, she pressed on. "Yes, I have." Gathering her courage, she stared at him, and said defiantly, "If it weren't for me, none of your plans would have worked. You owe me—and I intend for you to pay."

"Do you really?" he asked with a note of amusement. "Trying your hand at blackmail, my dear? How foolish of you." He rose to his feet and approached her.

Molly stepped back, but he followed her. "Do you honestly believe that I will let a common slut like you blackmail me?"

"Don't come any closer," Molly said breathlessly, suddenly wishing she had never embarked on this little scheme.

"Ah, having second thoughts are we?" he taunted, crowding her against the wall. "You should have taken the time to have third and fourth thoughts, my dear, because you have just shown me how very dangerous and foolish it was to trust a whore."

Before Molly had time to think, his hands were around her throat, the powerful fingers closing off her breathing, squeezing the life from her. She fought, fought hard, but her struggles were useless, her fingers clawing helplessly at the hands around her slender throat, waves of blackness flowing over her.

Moments later, Boots released her limp body and watched as she slid to the floor. She was very dead, and he was very pleased. This wasn't quite how he had planned it, but the result was the same: a minor problem dispensed with.

Blowing out the candles, he swiftly escaped out the back door. Depending upon her regular gentlemen callers, it would be tomorrow or the next day before her body was found. Quickly walking to where he had left his horse concealed, he remounted and stole away. He was frowning as he rode, realizing that he had acted rather precipitously. Tony would certainly be blamed for Molly's murder, and no doubt there would be those clamoring for him to hang, but he doubted that someone of Tony's stature would actually hang for the murder of a creature like Molly Dobson.

Poor, poor Tony, Boots thought with a titter. *How awful to be innocent as a newborn lamb and no way of proving it. What a jest!*

In that Boots erred. He was quite correct, however, in believing that suspicion would first fall upon Tony.

When Molly's body was found early the following morning by old Annie, Tony was instantly named as her killer. Annie had come to do chores and upon finding Molly's corpse, had run shrieking down Silver Street. As word of the murder passed from lip to lip, an angry crowd had gathered in front of Molly's home. Tony's threats to throttle her were still in everyone's mind, and no one doubted that he had murdered her. The news spread swiftly all through the Natchez area. Some who heard the news were pleased that at last Daggett would pay for his crimes, but when it became clear soon afterward that Tony could not possibly have murdered Molly Dobson, many were disappointed and even disbelieving.

But it was true. Tony had a number of eminently respectable citizens who could vouch for his innocence.

On the night that Molly was murdered, Tony had spent the evening dining at the Crocker household with the elder Crocker, as well as several other important gentlemen in the district—his uncle Alfred among them. It was strictly a male gathering, and after the meal, they had all retired to William's comfortable study and played cards until the pink-and-gold dawnlight was beginning to peek over the horizon. Most of the gentlemen departed at that time, but Tony and a few others, his uncle among them, had stayed to enjoy breakfast at Broadmount. Hence it was well after the hour of nine o'clock Thursday morning before Tony had said his good-byes and ridden home to Sweet Acres. By then Molly's body had been discovered and the hue and cry for Tony's neck raised. A mob with hanging on their minds set out for Sweet Acres.

On their way to Sweet Acres, the rowdy crowd rode past Willow Dale, the Blackburne estate, and from his excited servant, Patrick learned of Tony's danger. Astride a bareback horse, he arrived at Sweet Acres hard on the mob's heels, barely in time to prevent a tragedy.

The mob had surprised Tony abed and even Billingsley's and John Osgood's spirited defense had not been enough to prevent Tony from being dragged down the grand staircase of Sweet Acres and out onto the wide veranda at the front of the house. His hair disheveled and clothed in only a pair of breeches, which he had been allowed to don, Tony did not give his captors the satisfaction of begging for his life.

His head held proudly, he looked at the leader of the mob, and said evenly, "I did not murder Molly Dobson. I have not seen the woman for weeks."

The man spit contemptuously near Tony's bare feet, and an angry murmur arose from the crowd. A hemp rope around his neck, they were on the point of hustling him down the steps and toward the tree they had selected for his hanging when Patrick had ridden up. A pistol in each hand, he faced the crowd, a sneer on his handsome mouth, and said, "Which one of you brave fellows would like to die first? I assure you that I shall have no compunction in killing you if you do not step away from my friend. Now."

Almost as one, the crowd put a distance between themselves and Tony. Blackburne's accuracy with firearms was legendary, and, despite their numbers, it was obvious that at least two of them would die before they could overpower him. No one wanted to be one of the two.

Patrick leaped down from his horse and ascended the steps to stand at Tony's side. As he handed Tony one of the pistols, Tony grinned, and murmured, "Have I ever told you that you have impeccable timing?"

Patrick grinned back at him. "Indeed you have. But one never tires of compliments."

Billingsley and Osgood, armed by then and joined by John Jackson, added to Tony's reinforcements. Together the quintet stared down at the angry mob milling around in front of the house. The situation was still fraught with danger. The crowd was furious at being denied their prey, and there was the chance that they might gather enough courage to charge the small group on the veranda. At the moment, it was a standoff.

Before more violence erupted, the thunder of hooves was heard, and Alfred, Franklin, and Burgess galloped wildly up to the house, sending the crowd scurrying out of their path. If Tony was surprised to see his uncle and cousins, he showed no sign of it. The question in his mind was whether they had come to his rescue or to dance at his hanging.

Alfred, scowling and furious, swiftly set the mob straight. His nephew, blackguard that he was, had not murdered Molly Dobson and *he* could prove it! No other man's word would have carried as much weight: Alfred Daggett's outspoken criticism of Tony was common knowledge.

William Crocker as well as Jack Gayle, who had also attended the previous night's entertainment at Broadmount, rode up only seconds later, having heard the news of Molly's murder and the mob's intentions from their sons, who had heard the news from Vincent Walcott. Their sons had accompanied them. With these new arrivals, Tony's safety was assured, but it took several minutes for order to be restored.

Tony's innocence could not be doubted—not when so many highly respectable gentlemen were speaking out on his behalf. It was clearly established that Tony had arrived at the Crocker's home the previous evening long before the hour when Annie had last seen Molly alive. And since Tony had been in the company of a dozen or so leading citizens in the area from then until nine o'clock that morning, he could not possibly have murdered Molly.

With some grumbling, and many dark looks cast Tony's way, the mob finally departed. There would always be, Tony thought wearily as he watched the last of them disappear down the road, those who would believe that he had killed Molly.

Glancing at his uncle, Tony smiled crookedly, and said quietly, "I thank you for your timely intervention—

you helped save my life. It was good of you to speak out for me, and I know it cost you."

Alfred sent him a surly look. "Give Burgess your thanks—he is the one who learned what was afoot and told his brother and me." He paused, frowning darkly. "You may be a villain," he finally muttered, "but I could not stand by and see you hanged for something I knew you had not done—even if you have done things that certainly deserve hanging!" Having said all he was going to on the subject, he remounted, and, glaring at his sons, growled, "Well? Are you coming with me, or are you going to stay here gaping like a pair of beached flounders?"

Wordlessly, his sons mounted their own horses and the trio rode off, leaving Tony and the others standing on the front steps of Sweet Acres.

"You'd think," William Crocker said thoughtfully, "that what happened today would make Alfred rethink his opinion of you. It was a stroke of luck that you were with us last night and that we could establish your innocence so quickly. If, by chance, you had turned down my invitation you would more than likely be hanging from one of your own trees at this very moment."

"I know—and I can never thank all of you enough." Tony smiled thinly. "For once I am glad that gossip about me spread so swiftly."

There was a bit more small talk and then, except for Blackburne, the other gentlemen mounted their horses and followed the road taken by Alfred and his sons.

Looking over at his friend, Tony said, "Do you know, I never found life in England quite so full of, er, stirring events."

Blackburne smiled grimly. "I will admit that I find it rather interesting that it is only when you are in residence at Sweet Acres that such ugly events swirl around you." Only half-teasing, he asked, "Have you considered a permanent move to England?"

Tony's face tightened. "No. And I am not going to, either. This is my home, and I will not be driven from it."

"I would be surprised if you were, but I would warn you to take heed, for it appears to me that someone is determined to do just that—or see you hang."

"It is possible that you are right," Tony conceded, "but I wonder why, if someone wanted me dead, they have not simply murdered me and have done with it? Why go to all the lengths to paint me as black as Hades and yet let me live? It doesn't make sense."

Blackburne shrugged. "I have no answers, I would only warn you again—take care—someone does not like you very much, my friend."

They discussed the situation a few minutes longer, and then Patrick, too, departed, leaving Tony standing alone on the veranda at Sweet Acres. All thought of sleep vanished from his mind, Tony eventually turned and walked back inside the house, his mind on what had transpired . . . and how he was going to tell Marcus that his mother was dead. Not a pleasant task, but one that he must see to immediately.

Ten minutes later, having taken just enough time to throw water on his face and finish dressing, Tony walked up to the front door of the Jackson house. Sally and John met him at the door, their expressions tense.

"Have you told the boy?" Tony asked quietly as he entered the house.

John shook his head. "No, we felt it was best to wait and discuss the matter with you."

Quickly, Sally said, "He is presently still sleeping—he knows nothing of the mob or what nearly happened this morning."

Wearily Tony ran a hand through his hair. "There is no need to wake him—let him sleep for now." His mouth twisted. "He will have to learn the truth soon enough." Glancing at Sally, he flashed his most charming smile, and asked, "Will you mind if I wait here for him to awaken?"

"Of course not!" Sally exclaimed. "Oh, where are my manners? Please, please sit down and let me get you some coffee and perhaps some toast, for I am sure with everything that has happened this morning that you have not had a chance to eat. Would you like for me to cook you a proper breakfast?"

Tony declined the breakfast, but was grateful for the coffee. Seated in the Jacksons' pleasant parlor, he sipped his coffee, and the three of them discussed how best to tell Marcus of the tragedy that had overtaken him.

In the end, the adults were far more distressed by the situation than Marcus was. An hour later, watching Marcus as he happily ate his oatmeal at the scrubbed oak table in the kitchen, Tony was relieved that the child seemed so resilient.

But he was troubled and brushing a gentle hand across the back of Marcus's head he asked, "You do understand that your mother is dead—that you will never see her again? You will have to live here with the Jacksons."

Marcus gazed up at him with limpid blue eyes. Solemnly, he said, "I understand. I am sorry that Mama is dead, but she did not like me very much, and she was not kind to me." He flashed a warm look at the Jacksons, who hovered nearby. "John and Sally have been nicer to me than anyone ever has—I like it here."

That seemed to settle the question for Marcus, and, feeling relieved, Tony took his leave shortly. It was understood between the adults that at some point the Jacksons intended to adopt the boy.

Walking away from the Jackson home, Tony wondered if he would brush through the whole ugly, tragic situation as easily as it presently seemed. More importantly, he wondered what Arabella would make of it all. He gave a grimace. It didn't matter. She didn't trust him, and this latest scandal would not make her think any more kindly of him—even if he *was* innocent.

During the weeks that had passed since the Crocker ball, Arabella had heard nearly every black tale about Tony that had flown around the neighborhood—Mary, still rather cool to her, had made certain of that. Even though she knew that her stepmother had only her best interests at heart, Arabella was finding it increasingly difficult to maintain even a vestige of politeness between them.

Fortunately for their relationship, Mary did not come to call often, and Arabella was able to put aside her unhappy thoughts for long periods of time as she submerged herself in the refurbishing of Greenleigh.

Pushing the painful break with Tony to the back of her mind and ignoring Mary's gossip, she rediscovered her initial enthusiasm for the project and actually convinced herself, most of the time, that she was happy. But at night she slept poorly, her mind working tirelessly as she considered and reconsidered her conclusion that Tony had not lied about Molly five years ago. And that if he had not lied, then who amongst their friends and family had plotted against him?

There was no one, other than Jeremy, with whom she could discuss the situation and since he firmly believed Tony innocent, his opinion only confirmed her own.

As the weeks passed, her longing for Tony did not diminish. In fact, it grew, as did her certainty that he had told the truth. A dozen times she nearly sat down and wrote to him, begging him to come to call, but she hesitated, fearful of his rejection. She regretted bitterly that she had not accepted his second proposal of marriage. Regretted bitterly that she had not considered more carefully Tony's character; she loved him, she should have believed in him. Instead, she had sent him away and wounded him, his pride certainly, and even possibly his heart—not once, but twice. How could he ever forgive her?

On the morning of the discovery of Molly's body, Arabella was listless and depressed. Of late, the slightest exertion seemed to leave her feeling exhausted. Her stomach had been unsettled, too—the scent of even her favorite foods sending her fleeing to the privacy of her bedchamber, where she spent several minutes nearly overcome by nausea.

The arrival of Jeremy a scant half hour later lightened her spirits some, although the news about Molly's murder and Tony's near escape from hanging did not engender a merry mood.

His blue eyes bright with excitement, Jeremy exclaimed, "This proves, doesn't it, that our suspicions are correct? Tony has been innocent all along, but this time whoever is trying to make him look black made a mistake. Someone else murdered Molly, but they had planned on Tony being blamed for it. Only Tony's attendance at the Crocker's place last night saved him from hanging."

Arabella nodded slowly, her stomach roiling at the sent of coffee wafting from Jeremy's just-served cup. "Yes, that is how it appears to me." She leaned forward, her expression anxious. "Are you perfectly certain that Tony was not harmed? And that his innocence has been clearly established?"

"Oh yes. Without a doubt."

Jeremy picked up an anise-flavored cookie from the tray Mrs. Tidmore had served upon his arrival. As he bit into it, the strong odor of anise floated on the air, and Arabella felt her stomach heave.

Her face pale, her stomach in full revolt, she rose to her feet, muttered, "Excuse me," and bolted from the room.

She barely reached the privacy of her bedroom before she lost what little had remained in her stomach. The worst over, she sank down weakly on her bed and wiped her mouth with a damp cloth she had begun to keep handy.

A sound from the doorway made her glance in that

direction. Jeremy stood there as if turned to stone, his young face suddenly grim.

"Have you told him?" he asked harshly.

Arabella looked confused. "Told who what?"

His mouth tightened. "Told Tony that you are going to have his child."

Chapter Sixteen

❧

*H*er eyes huge, her mouth a round 0 of surprise Arabella stared at Jeremy. "Pregnant?" she finally gasped. "You think I'm pregnant?"

Jeremy looked wry. "Of course you are! Why else would you be casting up your accounts this way? And looking pale as a ghost? I thought you looked peaked when I arrived, but I put it down to the heat. I know differently now." His mouth twisted. "You may think of me as little more than a child, but I am old enough to remember Mama turning pale at the very sight of food and rushing from the room when she was pregnant with the two boys. You're pregnant, my girl, and don't try to gammon me into believing that Tony Daggett isn't the father!"

Arabella stared at him incredulously, her thoughts jostling wildly in her mind. *Pregnant*! The notion had never entered her head . . . though it should have, now that she considered it. Looking back over the past several weeks, he realized suddenly that she had not experienced her monthly flow and that she was displaying all the symptoms of early pregnancy. Jeremy's conclusions, she thought with a little flutter in her chest, were absolutely correct; she was pregnant with Tony's child.

"Well?" Jeremy demanded. "Am I right?"

Unaware of the silly grin on her face, Arabella nodded. She was going to have a baby! Tony's baby! Could there be anything more wonderful?

"And is the prospective father aware of the impending event?" he asked dryly.

"Uh, no," Arabella answered. At Jeremy's expression, she added, "Oh, take that disapproving look off your face—I just found out myself."

"That may be, but you had best tell Daggett immediately. If the babe is not to be labeled a bastard, getting the pair of you married is of the utmost importance."

With a thud Arabella came back down to earth. Under other circumstances, a hasty marriage would, of course, be the next step, but with the situation between herself and Tony so strained, she flinched away from the idea of suddenly becoming his wife. For all she knew, he no longer wanted to marry her. She didn't honestly believe that Tony would not marry her—especially once he learned of the coming child—but she discovered that she did not want to be married simply because she carried his baby. She definitely did not want Tony to feel that he was being forced to marry her, even if he had proposed marriage at one time. He might not feel the same still.

"There is no need for me to make a decision at this very minute," Arabella said finally. "Tony can be told soon enough." A dreamy expression flitted across her expressive features. "Right now, I simply want a little time to get used to the idea myself."

Jeremy snorted. One hand on his hip, he regarded her impatiently. "Time," he said grimly, "is something that you do not have. If I discovered your state so easily, how long do you think it will be before others do the same? Others such as Mama or Cousin Agatha—they, in case you have forgotten, have sharper eyes than mine. You cannot wait. You and Tony must be married before anyone else learns of this." He drew himself up. "As the head of our family, I must insist."

Arabella made a face. There were many times she had wanted Jeremy to act with more maturity and to take his duties as the eldest male in the family more seriously—she just wished that it wasn't at that precise moment he had decided to do so.

"Jeremy," she said gently, "I am a grown woman. I will celebrate my thirty-third birthday this fall. Don't you think that I am a little old for you to be dictating to me?"

"No, not if you are going to act irresponsibly. Do you realize the scandal that your pregnancy will bring down on the family if you are not married—instantly? Believe me, there is going to be enough counting on the fingers and raised eyebrows when the babe is born. Delaying your marriage to Tony will only add to the gossip— especially if you are standing there taking your vows with your belly sticking out like a ripe melon." He took an agitated step around the room. Glancing back to where Bella sat, he said, "I know that I do not have the power or influence that our father would have had over you and that you are no longer a *young* maid, but good gad, Bella, what where you thinking of? This is a dreadful affair. Our sort are not in the habit of producing children until at least nine months of marriage!"

He sighed and ran a hand through his golden locks. "I do not mean to lecture you—but having gotten yourself into this position, I cannot believe that you, of all people, are willing to put the family through the shame and gossip that will follow us if you are not married as soon as decently possible. And if our family disgrace is not enough to sway you, think of your babe—you know how all the old tabbies are—they will never allow you or your child to forget the circumstances of its birth. Remember our sisters, too—don't you think that your actions will reflect badly on Sara and Jane? It could even leave them open to the sort of advances that cannot be tolerated." Craftily, he added, "Why, I may be forced to fight a dozen duels before I have them safely married off. Have you thought of that?"

Arabella could not deny the force of any of Jeremy's arguments, but something inside of her stubbornly resisted the notion of racing to Tony and blurting out that she was pregnant and that he had better be prepared to marry her instantly. There had to be, she thought unhappily, another way to resolve this situation. It wasn't that she wasn't *ever* going to tell Tony, it was just that she did not want to tell him immediately. She wanted time. Her lips tightened. And she wasn't about to be hustled into marriage. The baby was hers; she would decide when she would marry—and who for that matter!

But Jeremy wasn't going to give her any choice. Correctly reading the expression on her face, he took matters into his own hands.

"Since you seem to have lost your wits," he said sharply, "I see that I shall have to act on my own."

Spinning on his heels, he stalked from the room.

"Jeremy!" Arabella shrieked, leaping up to follow him. "Wait. Where are you going?"

He tossed her a look over his shoulder as he bounded down the stairs. "To see the father of your child!"

"Oh, wait! You cannot!" she cried, hurrying after him, but she was too late. Jeremy was through the front door and down the front steps before she even reached the bottom of the staircase. She ran out onto the veranda in time to see him riding away.

Damn. Damn, she thought to herself, as she stood there biting her lip indecisively. Her fate, she decided grimly, was not going to be settled by two stubbornly determined males—despite her earlier thoughts, she had no doubt that once Jeremy told Tony about the baby that Tony would be just as insistent, in fact more insistent than her brother that they marry. Tony was, she realized uneasily, perfectly capable of carrying her off somewhere and holding her a virtual prisoner until she agreed to marry him. When Tony got an idea into his head, it was nigh impossible to stop him from seeing it to the end. There was only one thing she could do—she had to prevent the pair of them from making plans for her that would allow no escape.

Muttering under her breath, Arabella picked up her skirts and ran toward the stables at the back of the house. Ignoring the startled servants, she pulled out the little black mare from her stall and, taking only enough time to throw a bridle onto the sleek dark head, leaped upon the mare's back and careened away. Skirts flying, her trim ankles and bare calves shockingly exposed beneath her jumbled-up gown, she urged the mare into the green woods.

Jeremy had several minutes' head start on her, and Arabella, while a decent rider, was not known for her intrepidness in the saddle. Consequently, she concentrated more on staying upon the mare's back than speed as they galloped through the shadowy forest, the mare clearing fallen logs and gurgling streams with ease.

Knowing Jeremy had probably taken this same short-cut through the woods to Sweet Acres, she hoped to overtake him, but despite her efforts, she arrived at her destination several minutes behind her brother. She had just broken from the woods and come galloping up to the front of the big house as Jeremy and Tony prepared to mount their horses. That they had already reached some sort of agreement was obvious from their satisfied expressions; that and the fact that they were apparently on the point of riding back to Greenleigh to confront her.

Arabella's face was red from her exertions and the brush and trees had liberally snagged her gown and torn her hair loose from its normally neat chignon. Bright waves of fire tumbled around her shoulders as she halted her horse. Her blue-muslin gown was ripped in several places, and a series of nasty scratches marred the smooth paleness of her calves. Tony took one look at her and in two swift strides reached her side. With less-than-gentle action, he pulled her from the heaving horse.

"Blast it, Bella!" Tony said sharply, his expression half-angry, half-anxious as he cradled her next to him.

"Have you no sense? There is our babe to think of now—you should have waited for us—you had to know that I would come to you."

Breathless and a little more shaken from her wild ride than she would have liked to admit, Arabella was grateful for Tony's strong arms around her. For just a moment she let herself relax against him, savoring the warmth of his body, the stirring masculine scent that was Tony's alone.

Pushing back a lock of fiery hair that had fallen across her eye, she finally straightened up and stepped away from him. She met his indigo-eyed gaze, and said quietly, "Yes, I knew that you would come to me—but only because of the baby and because Jeremy had coerced you into doing it."

Tony bit back an oath. Glaring at her, he demanded, "Is that what you really think? That I only want to marry you because of the child? Or that your brother could make me do anything that I did not want to?" He gave a bitter laugh. "You seem to forget that when we last parted I had asked you to marry me." He looked wry. "And as for Jeremy . . . when, my pet, have I ever allowed anyone to coerce me to do anything?

They both knew the answer to that question, and Tony did not wait for her to reply. One hand firmly around her upper arm, he hustled her toward the broad steps of the house. "Come along now. This is no place for this discussion. Let me get you inside out of the sun and have Billingsley bring us some refreshments. I think that a tall glass of lemonade will make you feel cooler and more comfortable."

There was no arguing with Tony, and, quite frankly,

the idea of sitting down and allowing him to coddle her for a few minutes was vastly appealing. Meekly, Arabella let him guide her up the steps and into the welcoming shadows of the house.

It was only after she was seated and had drunk half a glass of the lemonade that the niceties were put aside.

Standing in front of her, his blue eyes dark with emotion, Tony made her heart turn right over her chest when he asked softly, "You are going to marry me, aren't you, Bella? I know that there is much between us that must be resolved, but surely it is nothing that we cannot overcome—at least for the sake of our child." He sank down onto one knee and taking her hand in his, he dropped a kiss on the back of it. Oblivious to Jeremy, who suddenly became very interested in the shine on his boots, Tony said huskily, "I want to marry you—I always have—since the first moment I met you. To have you for my wife is my dearest wish." His voice thickened. "To have you *and* our child is something I never dreamed would happen." He smiled whimsically. "Will you deny me my dearest dream?"

"Oh, Tony, you perfectly wretched creature!" Arabella cried, all her reservations fleeing at his first touch, her entire body turning shamelessly into a puddle of warm, quaking pudding at his words and the look in his eyes. "You know that I have never been able to deny you anything."

His expression boyish and eager, he bent forward. "Then you *will* marry me? As soon as it can be arranged?"

Arabella tried to recall all her reasons for wishing to delay marrying Tony, but it was impossible. She wanted to marry Tony Daggett. She had loved him for years. She was carrying his babe. He wanted to marry her. Thoroughly convinced that if not for the wicked intervention of some enemy five years before, they would already be married, she was having a hard time finding any excuse—reasonable or otherwise—not to marry Tony immediately. One thing was clear: She would be a fool if she let pride or anything else stand in the way of marrying him this time.

Her lovely eyes shining, she said gently, "Of course I shall marry you. Whenever you want."

"Bella!"

Jeremy forgotten, his hard face alight with joy, Tony swept her exuberantly up into his arms. Arabella was never certain how it came to be, but she next found herself seated in Tony's lap, his arms around her, her head pressed against his shoulder as he rained kiss after kiss upon her upturned face.

"You have just made me the happiest man in the world, sweetheart," Tony murmured between kisses. "I swear to you that I shall be a good husband to you and a good father to our child. I swear it."

Dreamily Arabella caressed his lean cheek. "I know you will be—I would not have agreed to marry you otherwise."

He looked down at her, his expression grave. "You know that I love you more than life itself, don't you?"

She smiled. "Probably. But I confess to liking to hear you say it."

"Then you shall—every day of our lives together."

"Oh, Tony!"

There was another spell of kisses and gentle murmuring between the lovers. This exceedingly gratifying time might have gone on indefinitely, if Jeremy, while agreeing privately that it was all very affecting, hadn't decided that it had gone on long enough. He cleared his throat, and muttered, "Uh, don't you think that we should start planning the wedding?"

Recalled to his presence, the two lovers stared blankly at him for a second and then, with identical bemused smiles on their faces, nodded.

"Yes, of course," Tony said briskly, still keeping Arabella possessively clasped in his arms.

"Mama will have to be told," Jeremy said unhappily. "And she will not like it." He straightened his shoulders and, looking at Arabella, said manfully, "As head of our family, I should be the one to tell her—she will probably take it better from me anyway. And I will arrange for a notice to be posted." He glanced to Tony. "Today is Tuesday. Shall we try to have the wedding on Friday at Highview? That will give Mama time enough to get over her hysterics and to make a few plans for the actual marriage." He frowned, looking again at Arabella. "Mama will, no doubt, be difficult at first, but she shall see reason. Cousin Agatha, I am sure, will help her to be sensible. And, of course, waiting until Friday will also give us time to invite a few intimate friends to the wedding—the Crockers, the Gayles, Blackburne, and perhaps even Tony's uncle and cousins. We do not want your marriage to seem to be a ragtag affair." Jeremy sighed and grimaced. "As for the babe . . . we shall just have to claim it as a seven-months child."

Tony had listened quietly to everything Jeremy had to say, and while he agreed, he could not shake a nagging feeling of impending danger. His heart brimming with love, he glanced down at Arabella where she rested confidingly against him. He had lost two wives already. Two wives he had not loved, but he had, in his own fashion, mourned them. Even spoiled, reckless Mercy. Adoring Arabella as he did, he could not envision life without her.

Uneasily, he reminded himself that someone had already cost them five years, that someone had once gone to incredible lengths to prevent their marriage—and nothing had changed that he could see. Why someone had wanted him and Arabella parted had always baffled him. His lips pursed thoughtfully. No, that wasn't true. He had known that Arabella's family had been adamantly opposed to their marriage, and he supposed that he could not blame them for feeling as they did— his black reputation was not *all* a lie. Even so, he still could not envision Arabella's father being part of the ugly plot that had torn them apart. William Montgomery had loved his daughter and, even more importantly, had always struck Tony as an honorable man, not someone who would stoop to blatant trickery.

Yet the fact remained, that *someone* had gone to a great deal of effort to effect that parting. And though five years had passed . . . someone still might not want him and Arabella to marry. And this time, they might not be willing to settle simply for a broken engagement. What if they were to decide that Arabella must die? Die as Elizabeth had, and her babe with her?

He tensed as a knife blade of pain and fear cut through him. Instinctively his arms tightened around Arabella. He could not bear it if she were to come to danger. He loved her. Beyond reason. Beyond life. He would not dare to be the cause of putting her life, and that of their child, in danger. By simply becoming his wife, he admitted grimly, she might be in very grave danger.

"I have no real argument with your plans," Tony said slowly, "but I would remind both of you that someone went to great lengths to prevent Arabella and me from marrying five years ago. The purpose behind destroying our engagement has always eluded me, but clearly, someone did not want us to marry. I cannot think of anything that has changed during these past years that would guarantee that this person will not try again to stop our marriage." His mouth thinned. "And this time, whoever it is, might not be content with merely a broken engagement."

"You think that Arabella will be in danger if she marries you?" Jeremy asked, his face suddenly pale and very young.

Tony nodded. "I do, which is why, though I will marry Arabella, and just as soon as it can be arranged, I want it kept secret. We three and Blackburne should be the only ones who know that she has become my wife."

Arabella's first instinct was to argue. It was bad enough that they were going to have to have a hasty wedding, but to have no wedding at all? To marry secretly? But as she turned Tony's words over in her mind, she realized that he was right. There was a hidden enemy out there, and while she did not fear for her life, she could see the wisdom in not broadcasting their marriage. Not until the enemy had been unmasked.

She frowned. "Tony," she began, "there is much in

what you say, but there is something else that is inescapable—we cannot keep our marriage hidden forever." A rueful smile lit her face. "Soon enough my expanding belly will declare my state for all to see—and only a fool would think that you are not the father."

"I know—the babe makes haste imperative, and I don't intend for our marriage to remain secret any longer than it has to. I want to let everyone know that I am lucky enough to be your husband." His features twisted. "But I am also afraid—for you. Someone murdered Elizabeth. Someone prevented our marriage once before. And don't forget that Molly's body was found only this morning. It is the devil's own luck that I was not hanged for it—and from one of my own oak trees. I think my enemy is still very much at large."

Her eyes wide, Arabella gasped, "You think that whoever murdered Molly might have murdered Elizabeth and caused our broken engagement?"

"I don't know," Tony said helplessly. "I only know that the women in my life seem to come to a bad end." His expression was fierce. "I do not want that to happen to you."

"Tony's right," Jeremy said abruptly. "There is someone out there who seems determined to ruin Tony one way or another. And while I don't like it, I think that we should keep the marriage a secret for the time being—and try to discover just who arranged for Molly to be at the lodge five years ago—and, more recently, at the Crocker ball. We discover that, and we will know who caused her to be murdered. Once we have exposed that villain, the fact that the pair of you are married can safely be announced." He made a face. "There is going to be a devil of a storm over the news of your marriage whenever we do reveal it, so I see no great harm in delaying its announcement." He sighed heavily. "There is no way we are going to brush through this whole affair without some gossip."

Anxiously, Arabella asked Tony, "What do you plan for us to do? How are we to discover the person who murdered Molly? And if our wedding is to be secret for the time being, it cannot be here."

Rising to his feet, Tony carefully settled Arabella back into the chair he had just vacated. Frowning, he paced the room.

"Getting us married is the first priority," Tony muttered, as he strode back and forth across the room. "I will not have our child labeled a bastard, and if it should come about that some mischance overtakes me, I want to know that you and our babe are safely taken care of."

"Oh, Tony, do not say that something will happen to you! I could not bear it—not now when we are finally going to be together," Arabella cried, her expression stricken.

"I do not intend for anything to happen to either one of us, but we have to think clearly. We have no margin for error. Too much is at stake. Our lives together and that of our child."

Tony took another turn around the room. "As you said, we cannot be married in Natchez—which means that you and I and Jeremy and Blackburne will have to be gone, at least overnight." He looked at Jeremy. "Can you arrange to be away from Highview for a few days? Perhaps, tell your mother that I have invited you stay with me for a while?"

Jeremy grimaced. "She won't like it, but she cannot prevent me. What about Blackburne?"

"Blackburne owns a tract of land several miles north of here, near Greenville—he can give it out that he is going to inspect it. No one is likely to question his whereabouts."

Both men looked at Arabella. "You, my love," Tony said lightly, "are going to be our problem. Unlike us superior males, you cannot just up and take off, or be away from home overnight without speculation and questions being raised—even if just amongst your servants—something we cannot afford."

Arabella sighed. What Tony said was certainly true. The gentlemen could racket about the countryside, letting no one know of their plans or whereabouts, and not one brow would be lifted. However, just let her, or any woman, decide to be away from home by herself for one night, and whispers and scandalous looks would follow her to the end of her days. The fact that she lived alone at Greenleigh, even at her age, was already considered slightly shocking by some of her neighbors. And as for being gone overnight . . . She frowned. Surely she could think of something!

"Instead of coming to stay with you," Arabella said slowly, gathering her thoughts, as she talked, "why can't we give it out that Jeremy will be staying with me? No one will think it odd. And if my brother and I go out for a drive in the direction of Greenville and due to, er, a thrown wheel, we are forced to spend the night on the road, who could prove any differently? Or object to my being alone with my brother?"

"It might work," Tony admitted thoughtfully, rubbing

his chin. "But someone will have to tell the staff at Greenleigh what happened to you—else when the pair of you do not return, they will raise the alarm."

Arabella made a face. "You're right, I hadn't thought of that."

Tony smiled at her. "Do not fret, my love, we shall overcome all difficulties. I am not letting anything stand in the way of my marrying you this time."

"I take it," Jeremy asked, "that we are decided that the marriage will take place at Greenville?"

Tony nodded. "It is the most logical place. It is nearly thirty miles away and, while not large, of a size that we should be able to find an itinerant preacher in the neighborhood—there have been a few passing through Natchez lately." He frowned. "But before that, I think I had best make certain that there *is* someone there to marry us." He made a face. "I shall talk to Blackburne about it."

He took another turn around the room. He glanced over at Arabella. "For now, I think the best thing is for Jeremy to escort you back to Greenleigh." He looked rueful. "I would take great pleasure in doing it myself, my love, but if we are to keep our enemy guessing, I think the less we are seen in each other's company, the better."

At the expression on Arabella's face, he crossed to her and knelt before her once again. "Do not look so, sweetheart. It is only for a short while. Soon enough, we shall be together forever, and no one will be able to keep us apart. Remember that, won't you?"

Arabella sighed and nodded. "Of course. You are

right. It is just that this is not quite how I envisioned my wedding."

"At least there will be a wedding this time," Jeremy said cheerfully. "Now let us return to Greenleigh. I have to send a note to Mama telling her that I am staying with you for a few days and asking her to have my man send along several changes of clothing." He glanced back at Tony. "We shall leave everything in your hands."

"Good," Tony said. "As soon as you are on your way to Greenleigh, I shall ride over and see Blackburne immediately. Once I have made all the preparations, I will find a way to let you know. In the meantime," he said with a smile, "I think that tomorrow morning Arabella should wake expressing a strong desire to go for a long ride in the country, oh, say in the direction of Greenville?"

Tony stood up and helped Arabella to her feet. He glanced over at Jeremy and said, "May we have a moment alone?"

Jeremy blushed. "Oh, er, naturally."

Alone together, Tony gently pulled Arabella into his arms. His mouth traveled in butterfly light kisses over her face, as he murmured, "Do not worry, sweetheart. I meant what I said—nothing and no one will prevent us from being married."

She smiled mistily at him. "I believe you, but Tony, what about later? How are we to find out who murdered Molly and who sent her to the lodge five years ago?" Her beautiful eyes darkened. "And who murdered Elizabeth?"

Tony's grip on her arms tightened. "We will unmask him, never fear, but at the moment, all I want is for you and my child to be safe. Once we are married we will begin to look more closely into the past and more recent events."

His eyes on hers, he asked quietly, "When did you decide that I was telling the truth about Molly? I seem to recall that the last time we were together you did not believe my version of what happened that night."

She toyed with the button on his jacket. "I have been miserable since we parted and—and I began to think about you and what I knew about you." She met his gaze. "There are many things that you are," she said dryly, "but a liar is not one of them. Even your detractors admit that you do not lie. And it occurred to me, knowing you as I do, that you were far more likely to flaunt your sins than to deny them. So then I had to face the fact that you were not lying about Molly—that someone did entrap you and arranged for me to find you in the most incriminating circumstances possible." She looked rueful. "My pride was hurt, and it didn't help any to hear about that wretched wager with Blackburne. I don't know which hurt me more—finding you in bed with Molly or finding out that you only courted me because of a wager."

"That blasted wager!" Tony growled. "Sweetheart, it is as I told you—I *did* make the damned wager, but it was before I knew you." His face softened. "Once I met you, once I had gazed into those lovely eyes of yours and seen that enchanting smile of yours, the wager was the last thing on my mind. I only knew that I had fallen in love for the first time in my life and that with one look, you had snared my heart."

"Oh, Tony! What a lovely thing to say."

He kissed her. "All the more so because it is true. And I intend to spend a great deal of our life together telling you many more lovely things." He kissed her again, passion inevitably rising within him. But remembering that Jeremy waited outside in the hall and that there would time enough to make love to her, he reluctantly pushed her from him.

His breathing slightly labored, his eyes bright with desire, he dropped one more kiss on her nose, and muttered, "Now, let us get you to your brother, before I forget what I am about and ravish you on this very floor."

Suppressing a giggle, Arabella allowed him to usher her to the door. A few minutes later, once again on her little black mare, Arabella and Jeremy rode sedately away from Sweet Acres.

Tony watched them until they disappeared into the forest, then he swung up onto the back of his own mount. Seeing Blackburne was the first order of business.

It was by now late afternoon, and as he rode the miles that separated his home from the Blackburne plantation, Tony considered all that had happened. He tried to concentrate on the business at hand, but his thoughts drifted always to Arabella; to the brightness of her hair, the enchanting tilt to her mouth when she smiled, the color of her eyes, the shape of her nose . . . their baby that grew in her womb. . . .

Lost in his thoughts, he was almost surprised when Sugar stopped in front of the wide steps of Willow Dale. For a moment, he had no idea where he was or why he was there.

If Patrick was surprised to see Tony so soon after the

events of the morning, he gave no sign other than a kick-up of one black brow. Lounging in a pair of comfortable chairs across from each other in Blackburne's study, Patrick's expression of lazy interest changed only marginally when Tony laid the whole tale out before him.

When Tony had finally finished speaking, Patrick stared at him for a long minute, his handsome features giving nothing away. Then he nodded, as if confirming some inner speculations.

"Well?" Tony asked testily. "Are you going to help us or not?"

Patrick smiled, a singularly beguiling smile on such a hard, cynical face. "Did you ever doubt it, my friend?"

A weight let loose in Tony's chest. "No, I knew I could count on you. In fact, you are the only one I can count on."

Patrick waved away Tony's words. "Enough of that. We must make our plans."

The two men talked for several minutes, deciding on the best way to proceed. An hour later, both men were smiling as Patrick walked with Tony to where Sugar stood tied.

"My man, Robertson, and I shall leave for Greenville at dawn, and as soon as I have made all the arrangements," Patrick said, "I shall send Robertson to you." Clapping Tony on the back, he added, "Expect to hear something from me no later than Thursday afternoon."

Mounted on Sugar, Tony glanced down at him. "It seems incredible that before the week is done, I shall be a married man with a child on the way."

Patrick shook his head, smiling. "No, my friend, not

incredible—anyone who has seen you and Arabella together would know that it was inevitable." His face hardened. "And this time, there is going to be a very different ending than there was the last time the pair of you thought to marry. I swear it."

Chapter Seventeen

It wasn't the wedding of her dreams, and yet Arabella felt decidedly dreamy as she stood next to Tony on that Friday evening, in a small shady, green glen on the outskirts of Greenville, and said the words that made her his wife. Jeremy and Patrick Blackburne were the only witnesses to the wedding—they and the raffish-looking itinerant preacher who married them.

The time between leaving Tony and actually standing at his side had been anxious and frantic. Anxious, only for fear that something once again would prevent their marriage; frantic, as she and Jeremy had set events in motion and made their preparations to leave for Greenville the instant that Tony sent them word that everything had been arranged.

In the end, it had all come about with surprising ease. Mary had not questioned Jeremy's desire to spend time with his sister; Patrick had found Preacher Hattersfield almost as soon as he had arrived in Greenville; and by late Thursday afternoon, Tony had sent word to Jeremy that all was in place. Even Arabella and Jeremy's decision to take a long ride into the country Friday morning had raised nary a ripple of curiosity with the Tidmores. Nor did Arabella's airy statement for them not to worry if she and Jeremy did not return that evening—they might stay the night with friends if the hour grew too late. Just which friends and where Ambella had left deliberately vague.

Tony had left the arrangements for the actual wedding in Patrick's hands and Patrick had thought of everything—including a few things the others had not. When confronted, shortly before the wedding, with the floppy-brimmed, old-fashioned bonnet and worn green-and-white gingham gown that he insisted she wear, Arabella had wrinkled her nose.

"Must I?"

Patrick grinned at her, his cool gray eyes dancing with laughter. "Indeed you must. For the marriage to be valid you and Tony must use your legal names—we all must. We do not, however, want our preacher to be able to recognize you easily should your paths happen to cross before your marriage is made public—which is highly unlikely, but we'll not take the chance. That offending bonnet is most necessary—and I do not want one strand of that remarkable and memorable red hair of yours showing. The large brim also conceals your features somewhat. Besides, I have told Hattersfield that you and Tony are my tenants. You must look the part, my dear."

Tony grinned and held up the shabby, homespun garments and decidedly worse-for-wear black hat Patrick had provided for him. "Mine are no better, sweetheart. We shall make a matched pair."

"Well, damned if I see anything to laugh about,"Jeremy complained, shaking out a truly horrible pair of patched pants and ragged shirt. Warily he eyed the battered too-large straw hat that was included in his pile of clothing. But it was the unclean state of the clothing that aroused his greatest reluctance. "Couldn't you have at least had these vermin-infested rags washed?" he asked plaintively as he scratched uneasily at his shoulder.

"No, you have to look the part. And I expect a little gratitude—I'll have you know it took me the better part of a day to find, er, suitable garments," Patrick said, his amusement obvious. "I took great pains to get hats that are deliberately large. We want to hide as much of your features as we can—remember that and resist the urge to take it off or push it back. We don't want you recognized. Our preacher must see a trio of poor, hardworking tenants—sartorial elegance is not what we are worried about right now."

Jeremy eyed him almost with dislike. "I notice that you aren't wearing anything as nasty as we are. Why not?"

Despite the laughter glinting in his eyes, Patrick put on a most superior expression. "You must remember that I am your overlord—the master." He grinned, adding irrepressibly, "I could not possibly be seen in such wretched clothing."

The tale Patrick had concocted for the clandestine wedding was plausible. One of his tenants had gotten the daughter of another of his other tenants pregnant. The erring pair must be married before the woman's hot-tempered father discovered all—else there would be bloodshed. Fortunately, her brother was a good lad and had agreed to help in getting them safely married, and to run interference with the woman's father when the time came to tell all. Patrick was simply lending them his aid in order to keep the peace—and good tenants.

And so it was that Anthony Daggett married Arabella Montgomery on the sixteenth of June of 1797 near the town of Greenville in the Mississippi Territory. The ceremony was brief but legal—Arabella was Tony's wife.

It might have been clandestine, her only attendants her brother and Tony's friend Patrick Blackburne, the preacher bewhiskered and smelling faintly of whiskey, but the ceremony was utterly magical for Arabella. The dappled green glen might not have been the stately church in Natchez where she had once planned to marry, and she held no bridal bouquet of rare and beautiful blossoms in her hands, yet none of that mattered—she was marrying the man she loved. Standing close to Tony, feeling the warmth radiating from his big body, listening to his deep voice recite their vows, Arabella was certain she had never been happier in her life. And when the ceremony was over and Tony tenderly took her into his arms and kissed her, she thought her heart was going to burst with pure happiness.

If their wedding was unorthodox, so was their first night as man and wife. It was imperative that they not linger in the vicinity of Greenville, and so the vows had hardly been said and the bride kissed, before the quartet left the preacher with a mumble of thanks and the silver coins Patrick hastily pressed into his grubby hand.

Patrick had been adamant about them leaving their

own horses safely with his man, Robertson, several miles farther down the Natchez Trace. They had come on ahead in a rickety wagon pulled by a pair of nondescript nags he'd had waiting for them at the place of rendezvous. And so they began the ride home in the same shabby wagon in which they had arrived. Even Patrick was astride the most nondescript horse in his stables— along the Trace, a handsome horse could get one killed.

Given a choice, none of them would have spent the night camped on the notorious Natchez Trace, but there was no other alternative. The Trace was dangerous even during the daylight hours, and the notion of traveling along its narrow, twisting width in the dark, with the possibility of robbers and murderers lurking in the concealing forests and canebrakes along its snaky length, was not something any of them relished. And there was Arabella to consider. She'd already had a long, grueling day's ride in the saddle, and the gentlemen decided that it would likely be more harmful to have her ride through the night, despite her protestations that she felt perfectly well, than to camp along the Trace.

They met up with Robertson an hour before dusk and swiftly changed back into their regular clothing and exchanged the wagon and plodding farm horses for their original mounts. Leaving Robertson to dispose of the clothing, wagon, and horse before catching up with them, the quartet pushed on down the Trace until nearly the last ray of sunlight had vanished.

Arabella had not realized how bone-tired she was until Tony lifted her down from her horse. Anticipation and nerves had kept her going all day, since long before dawn, and now that she was safely married to Tony and

they were actually on their way home, she suddenly felt
like a squashed egg.

Tony smiled at her as he guided her to an old stump
at the edge of the clearing in which they had chosen to
camp; a small stream of water gurgled nearby. "It has
been a hard day for you, I know. Made more so by the
fact that you are not a frequent rider. Are you very tired,
my love?"

Having checked out the stump for any lurking visitors, Arabella sat down and let out a sigh of sheer bliss.
"I did not want to complain or delay us, but I do believe," she said wryly, "that if I had been forced to ride
for another five minutes, I would have fallen into a fit of
hysterics."

Jeremy, busy getting a fire started five feet in front of
her, grinned over his shoulder at her. "I confess that I
have been most impressed by your fortitude today. You
have been in the saddle for hours, riding at a banging
pace—you, Bella, who usually swoons at the notion of
using any other form of transportation than a well-
sprung vehicle pulled by a sedate animal."

Arabella's expression was haughty and at a distinct
variance with the twinkle in her eyes. "I'll have you
know that in my, er, youth, I was quite an intrepid
rider."

"Ah, and you are such an old pair of boots now,"
Tony teased.

Blackburne, who had been seeing to the horses,
looked over at them and said, "Do not allow them to
badger you, my dear Mrs. Daggett. You did splendidly
today."

"Indeed she did," Tony concurred proudly. Reaching

for her hand, he kissed it. His eyes warm and loving, he murmured, "Most splendidly."

Arabella beamed at him, her face aglow, the two of them suddenly aware of nothing but each other.

Jeremy and Blackburne exchanged a look and immediately became very intent upon their different tasks. But Tony and Arabella were not so lost to decorum that they did not almost instantly recall themselves to their surroundings. A moment later, having recovered her energy somewhat, Arabella began to help Jeremy make a pot of coffee and Tony helped Patrick finish unsaddling and watering and feeding the horses.

Robertson, his horse blowing and sweating from the mad gallop down the Trace, arrived within the hour. Fifteen minutes later, they were gathered around the glowing fire, sipping coffee and eating the biscuits and dried venison Patrick had packed in his saddlebags.

Nestled next to Tony where they sat together on a blanket on the ground, the strong bite of boiled coffee and salty venison lingering on her tongue, Arabella decided her wedding feast was just perfect. To be sure, the biscuits had been tough and the night air full of the whine of insects, but this was compensated for by the satisfying crunch of those same biscuits between her teeth and the aromatic woodsmoke that drifted over them and drove off the worst of the pests.

And later, as she and Tony lay in each other's arms near the dying fire, Patrick, Jeremy, and Robertson taking turns guarding the camp through the night, she was certain that *her* wedding night was far more memorable than most. It didn't matter that she and Tony could not make love—they would have all the rest of their lives for that part of their marriage. That night was special and unique for both of them though; for the first time, they would spend the night, the entire night, in each other's arms, knowing without any doubts that they loved and were loved in return.

Forty-five minutes after dawn the next morning, after a hasty breakfast that was the duplicate of their evening meal, they were on the road again. Speed was imperative if suspicions were not to be aroused.

Arabella couldn't help the small groan that escaped from her when she swung into the saddle that morning. And there was another hard day in the saddle ahead of her.

Hearing her groan, Tony threw her a commiserating look. "Sore?"

Arabella nodded. "Very. I shall be glad to be home."

And while she longed for a hot bath and a long uninterrupted nap on her soft bed, when they finally reached that part of their journey where their paths parted, she suddenly wished the ride could go on forever. It was late afternoon, and the day had been another grueling one, but she had dreaded this moment.

Leaving Tony and Arabella near a fork in the road, the other three companions discreetly withdrew to give the lovers privacy for a few minutes.

Bringing his horse alongside of hers, Tony said softly, "I will not come to you until tomorrow night—you need to rest." His eyes gleamed. "But do not expect to sleep a great deal tomorrow night."

Despite herself, Arabella blushed, and Tony laughed. His expression sobered almost immediately. "Do you still have those men guarding the house?"

Arabella shook her head "No. There has never been another intrusion, and a few weeks ago, I decided that my visitor was probably not coming back and dispensed with the patrol." She made a face. "I felt silly having them wandering about at night."

Tony frowned slightly. "Silly or not, I would feel better if I knew they were watching the house. Their absence would certainly make it easier for me to visit you undetected, but until we have managed to unmask Molly's killer, I think you should have them around at night."

"Do you really believe that I am in danger?" she asked, her beautiful eyes troubled.

Tony shrugged. "Probably not as long as the fact that you are married to me remains a secret, but I don't want to risk anything happening to you." He flashed her a smile that melted her very bones. "Indulge me, sweetheart—start the damned patrol again."

Arabella agreed, and they spoke for a few minutes longer, the subject of interest only to lovers, and then Tony kissed her, and they rejoined the others.

It was difficult for Tony to watch her ride away with Jeremy, every instinct within him clamoring to whisk her away to Sweet Acres and to announce to the world that she was his bride. But he dared not. Two wives were dead, one murdered, and he would rather die than allow the slightest hint of danger to come Arabella's way.

Bringing his horse alongside Tony's, Patrick said quietly, "She will be safe. Do not worry."

"I wish I was as confident as you," Tony said grimly, his eyes fixed on Arabella's departing shape.

"Now have I ever misled you?" Patrick asked lightly, attempting to distract him.

Tony threw him a look, laughter gleaming in his blue eyes. "Frequently!"

"Untrue. You malign me," Patrick protested virtuously. "Name me just one time."

Followed discreetly by Robertson, they fell into a friendly wrangle that lasted until their paths diverged.

Pulling his horse to a halt, Tony said, "Do you think it would be suspicious if you came to call on me this evening?"

Patrick considered it. "I don't see any reason why not. In fact, it would be logical, that in my case, having been gone for a few days and not having seen you, I would come to call."

That point settled, they parted ways; Tony to Sweet Acres and Patrick to Willowdale.

Upon his return home, Tony's first acts were to order a hot bath and a tray of sandwiches and ale. An hour and a half later, freshly shaved, bathed, and his stomach pleasantly full, Tony felt ready to face whatever came his way.

Having descended the main staircase, a preoccupied expression on his face, he walked slowly to his study. Seated behind his desk, he dwelt first on what he considered the most important thing for Arabella's future—his will. He wanted her future secure, and so he spent several minutes listing the various points he wished to remember when he had the document drawn up first thing the next morning.

His demise was not something upon which he wished to linger—especially not when he finally had everything to live for, and he soon laid aside his scribbling. He would have preferred to spend the time thinking about Arabella, their child, and the future they would have together, but he was bleakly aware that until Molly's murderer was found the future for all of them would be dicey.

The brief conversation he'd had with Billingsley while he had eaten had informed him that no one had come to call while he had been away and that nothing unusual or significant had occurred during his absence. He should have been reassured by this news, and to a point, he was. No one, except for a few trusted servants, even knew that he had been away, and they would not gossip. So that put to rest one fear. And it was unlikely that Arabella and Jeremy's overnight trip would be found remarkable by anyone—he hoped. Blackburne's absence should not arouse any particular attention either, and if it did, why would anyone connect it to Arabella and Jeremy's sojourn? Which left them with one obvious problem: Who had murdered Molly? And why?

He sat there for a long time, turning the problem over in his mind, trying to come up with some explanation that made sense. It was inevitable that thinking about Molly's murder his thoughts should stray to Leyton's death. Murders and robberies were common along the Natchez Trace and even in the infamous "Natchez-under-the-hill," but it was *not* common for someone of Leyton's ilk to be cold-bloodedly murdered in his very home. There was no obvious connection between Molly's murder and Leyton's, but he could not shake the growing certainty that somehow they were linked together, and that link led to him.

Tony conceded that a jealous lover could have murdered Molly. Or it was possible her death had come about simply because of the vicinity in which she lived and that her death had had absolutely nothing to do with Leyton's murder several weeks ago. And yet the notion, once considered, proved hard to dislodge.

He scowled. Hadn't he heard some rumor or gossip that Molly had been in Leyton's keeping? Hell! Over the years, she'd been in the keeping at one time or another of a half dozen men he knew—including Alfred Daggett and his sons, as well as that pompous fool, Kingsley. But if recently she had been in Leyton's keeping, perhaps even under his protection at the time of his death, it was almost too much of a coincidence that the pair of them should be murdered within just a few months of each other. Of course, he admitted wryly, it could simply be a coincidence—Leyton had certainly made enough enemies. So, had the same person murdered Molly and Leyton? And that led him to wonder what it was that Molly and Leyton had known or done that had gotten them murdered? And how, if at all, did it affect him?

Staring blankly at the top of his desk, the fingers of one hand absently tapped the paper on which he had written out the notes to his will. His lips twisted. Newly married and instead of spending his time in his wife's bed, he was considering his will. He sighed. If past experience was anything to go by, it was *Arabella* who should be making out a will!

He did, he admitted grimly, seem to have very bad luck in keeping his wives alive. Not only keeping his wives alive, he thought slowly, but also in getting a prospective bride to the altar. But was it just bad luck, or something else? He had always assumed that it was so, but thinking about the past, it suddenly occurred to him that it was rather odd that he'd had such a run of ill fortune when it came to the women in his life. And now another woman, Molly, the woman who had played such a major part in the destruction of his engagement to Arabella five years ago was also dead, murdered. Was it simply the luck of the draw, or something else at work?

Several people had been against his engagement to Arabella and any one of them might have arranged for Molly to play her part, but had strictly altruistic motives been behind the actions? Or was there some other reason? A reason that had more to do with keeping him unmarried and unencumbered than with sparing Arabella the ordeal of being married to him?

It was an intriguing thought but one that made little sense to him. There was, as far as he could see, only one reason to keep him without a wife or heirs: Under the terms of his Grandfather Daggett's will, should he die without issue, his uncle and cousins would inherit the Daggett fortune. But if that was the case, why didn't they just kill him? Why keep him alive?

He brooded over the idea that one or all of his Daggett relatives wanted him dead. It was an unpleasant notion, but not without merit. Except, he reminded himself bleakly, he was still alive.

Almost idly his gaze dropped to the paper where he had jotted down the main points he wanted to remember when he drew up his own will the next day. His attention sharpened, as one item seemed to leap off the paper at him. He sucked in his breath as the full import hit him. Of course. There was a very good reason for keeping him alive if one wanted the biggest prize of all.

During the hours while he waited for Blackburne to arrive at Sweet Acres, Tony examined his stunning conclusions from all angles. He could be wrong, grasping at straws, and yet it all made a frightening sort of sense.

Blackburne arrived promptly at eight o'clock that evening and found Tony still in his study. Greetings were exchanged and refreshment served.

Seconds later, seated comfortably across from Tony, a glass of whiskey at his elbow, Patrick looked at him a long moment before asking, "Why such a bleak expression, my friend? We accomplished what we set out to do—and with no one the wiser. You should be a happy man tonight."

"I will be once I know who murdered Molly—and Elizabeth," he said grimly.

Blackburne appeared startled. "Surely you do not think—"

"I have done nothing but *think* since I returned home this afternoon! And I can't say that my thoughts have brought me any solace." He took a swallow of his own whiskey. "I did come to one conclusion though—either I am a cursed man, or someone has been going to a great deal of trouble to make my life a living hell."

"Oh, come now," Blackburne protested. "I will agree that there have been some tragic circumstances in your life, but they have just been plain bad luck."

"Have they? I'll grant you that simple bad luck could have caused Mercy's death—if I hadn't been so determined to wrest her from Terrell and gone chasing after them, I am certain that she would probably be alive

today. But with Elizabeth . . ." He looked across at
Blackburne. "When Elizabeth was killed, she was here,
at her home. It was not yet nine o'clock in the
evening—not a time that any self-respecting house-
breaker would choose to enter and rob a place, especially not a place like Sweet Acres. It wasn't as if she
had been coming home late on some dark country lane
and tragically crossed the path of a murderous bandit;
nor was it a case of her having been somewhere she
should not have been. She was *here*," Tony said bitterly.
"The one place she should have been safe."

An unhappy silence fell and then after taking another
sip of his whiskey, Tony asked quietly, "Did I ever mention that there was never any sign of anything being
taken?"

Blackburne nodded. "Yes, which fact counted against
you—that and the hour." Blackburne frowned in con-
centration. "As I recall, the French doors leading from
her sitting room to the veranda were found open when
Billingsley, alarmed at having heard the sound of a shot
coming from upstairs, arrived in the room and found her
dead. You were not at home—having been invited to
dine at my house that night." Blackburne made a face.
"Which, of course, no one believed. Gossip has always
maintained that I lied about your whereabouts to save
your neck."

Tony lifted his crystal glass in a mock toast. "It
seems that I owe my life to you twice—a debt I shall
never be able to repay."

"Name your first child after me, and we shall be
even," Blackburne said, the expression in his gray eyes
only half-teasing.

"Done!"

The light moment vanished almost immediately, and his brows creased in a frown, Blackburne asked, "But what does Elizabeth's death have to do with Molly's? You don't believe that they are connected, do you?"

Tony nodded slowly. "As I said, either I have had the most damnable luck with women as any man I have ever known, or someone has gone to a great deal of trouble to make it appear that way. More to the point, have you noticed that it is only the *women* in my life who suffer the most?" Painfully Tony ticked them off. "My first two wives, Mercy and Elizabeth, are dead. Mercy's death, I honestly believe, was just bad luck. But obviously not Elizabeth's since she was murdered. And five years ago, my fiancée, Arabella, found me in deplorable circumstances and broke off our engagement. Now Molly is dead, murdered. Molly, the very woman whose antics brought about my broken engagement to Arabella. The same Molly who less than a month ago named me the father of her bastard child. Incidentally, the latter, once again in front of Arabella. Which, if there were any possibility of us renewing our prior attachment, certainly would have destroyed any new beginnings between us. Don't you find that interesting? I do."

Patrick frowned. "But I understood you to say that Arabella had already realized that you hadn't been lying about Molly's appearance at the lodge five years ago. Isn't that one of the reasons she agreed to marry you? She believed you innocent?"

Tony's face softened. "Yes. But that was something no one else knew. And if someone was determined to keep us apart, what better way than to have the woman who had led directly to our parting five years ago name me as the father of her child—a child supposedly conceived while I was originally engaged to Arabella! Few, if any, women would be able to forgive *that* betrayal." Tony's features grew intent. "Think about it, Patrick! Mercy's death was probably simple chance, but anyone with a lick of sense would have known that once I found out she was running away with Terrell I would have gone after her. And if someone was up to mischief, curious, perhaps, to see what would happen, and at no cost to himself, which I believe was the case at the time, seeing that I went haring off after the pair of them was one way of doing so. Anything could have happened. I could have died—leaving, I might add, the Daggett fortune for my nearest relative to inherit." When Blackburne looked skeptical, Tony said, "Don't forget that Terrell was just as hot-tempered as I was and just as quick and accurate with his pistol—there was a good chance that one or both of us could have ended up dead." His face tightened. "Unfortunately, it was Mercy and Terrell who died."

"If your uncle Albert was set on inheriting your fortune, why didn't he just kill you and have done with it?"

Tony stood up and took a turn around the room. His brow furrowed in thought, he said, "I don't think in the beginning there was any definite plan—I think it just evolved as time went by. Mercy's death was simply a side issue.

"Ah, but with Elizabeth it was different. Not only was I married, I was about to become a father. And it is then that I think our culprit became very serious about what he was doing. He killed Elizabeth and my child, in one blow, eliminating any heirs." Tony looked off, his jaw hard. "I'm certain that it was then, too, that our un-named villain began to take the long view, to realize that if he were patient, that if he waited and kept me unmar-ried, that there was an even greater prize to be had. He must have felt fairly safe, because with two disastrous marriages behind me, it was highly unlikely that I would consider taking such a risk again."

Tony smiled grimly. "He hadn't counted on me falling in love with Arabella—or she with me. But once our engagement was announced, he began to make plans to destroy our engagement." He glanced back at Patrick. "Don't you see? I haven't had bad luck—someone has merely made it seem so."

Patrick made a face. "You make a strong argument, and on the surface it does look rather damning. But, if I agree with your conclusions, and I'm not saying that I do, what would be the point of it all?"

"You know, the answer to that question has eluded me a long time. In fact, I never really put it all together before, but this afternoon, as I was considering revising my will to provide for Arabella and the babe, a bolt of insight came to me." He smiled mirthlessly, and asked, "Tell me, my friend, if I were to die, unmarried and with no legal heirs of my body, whom would it benefit?"

"Obviously your uncle and your cousins," Patrick said dryly. "Everyone knows that Albert has hungered for Sweet Acres and the rest of the Daggett fortune for years. Unfortunately, if it was your fortune they were after, why didn't one of them just murder you years ago and have done with it? Why go to all the trouble to keep you unmarried and childless—and alive?"

Tony nodded, looking pleased. "You have put your finger on the very obstacle that I faced, until I remembered one little fact."

"Do not, I beg you," Patrick drawled, "keep me in suspense any longer. What fact?"

Still looking very pleased, Tony sat back in his chair. "Did I ever tell you about my mother's father—Baron Westbrook?"

"You forget—I knew the man. Remember, you and I stayed at Brookhaven several times in our youth. I liked your English grandparents a great deal." Patrick glanced down at his whiskey. "Unlike myself, you may never have known your parents, but you were bloody lucky in *both* sets of your grandparents—even if they damned near ruined you by allowing you to think the world was yours for the asking."

Tony smiled ruefully. "You're right, of course. But before he died, Grandfather Westbrook realized what he had done, and he was determined that I not be allowed to play ducks and drakes with his fortune when I eventually inherited it. He tied up the bulk of the Westbrook fortune in a trust that placed it beyond my reach. But he also created some opportunities for me to, er, redeem myself, should I continue down the path that you and I were treading at that time."

Patrick grinned at him. "You mean our wild, misspent youth? We were rather wild and dangerous fellows, weren't we?"

"Indeed we were," Tony admitted wryly. "It makes me shudder now to think of the way we racketed about and gave nary a care to tomorrow. But back to Grandfather Westbrook." Tony sighed. "I was twenty-five and

Elizabeth had not been dead a week when he died. It was several months before I learned the terms of his will, and I'll admit that they came as something of a shock to me. I had already inherited the Daggett fortune and had just assumed that the Westbrook money would fall into my hands like ripe fruit from a tree."

"Never tell me, he left you a mere pittance?" Patrick exclaimed, startled. "You were his only child's only child. Who else would he leave that vast fortune to?"

"Oh, he left the fortune to me, all right—he merely made certain that I would not get my hands on the majority of it for years."

"What do you mean?"

"Simply that while I've had the free use of all of his various houses and the trust he set up has paid for the staff and upkeep, very little of that, ah, vast fortune has come into my hands. Everything, including the lands, the houses, and the money, has been held in trust—for me, to be sure, but with the provision that should I die, the fortune is to go to any legitimate child I might have had at the time. If I were to die without issue—then it is all to go to a distant cousin in England, Thomas Avery." He smiled faintly. "You met Avery once and thought him an arrogant fool."

"I still do. The man is a congenital idiot," Patrick said bluntly.

Tony shrugged. "I agree, but under the terms of Grandfather Westbrook's will, if I die without issue, Avery inherits." He looked pensive. "Grandfather worried that the way I was gambling and drinking in those days, if I didn't get myself killed in some silly duel or prank, I would quickly go through the Daggett fortune.

He didn't want me to do the same with his fortune when it became mine. And so he arranged for me to be able to live at Brookhaven or the London town house, but very little actual money crossed my palm." His eyes met Patrick's. "The trust ends on my fortieth birthday. On that date, I shall come into that vast fortune you mentioned earlier. Everything will be mine—the lands and the money. If I were to die before that date, however, without issue, Avery would inherit it all."

"Are you telling me that you think *Avery* has something to do with your unfortunate luck with women?" Patrick asked incredulously.

"No. If it were Avery, all he had to do was arrange for me to die. He'd get everything then."

Patrick frowned. "Then who?"

Tony smiled thinly. "Who else but one of my fond Daggett relatives? As my only surviving relatives, they would have a solid, nearly irrefutable claim—no matter what the terms of my will. And it embarrasses me to admit it, but despite their attitude toward me, I do honor the claim of blood. They *are* named in my will, since I have—had—no one else to consider. So, which one do you think it is? Albert? Franklin? Or Burgess?"

Chapter Eighteen

Patrick stared at him for a long time, the expression in his gray eyes hard to define. Finally, he took a deep breath, and asked, "You really believe this? That one of your relatives has plotted against you for *years,* in the hope of one day inheriting not only the Daggett fortune but the Westbrook one as well?"

Tony nodded curtly. "I know it may sound preposterous on the face of it, but blast it, Patrick! It also explains so much. And it makes more sense to me to believe that one of them is behind what has happened to me in the past decade than just to blame it all on fate." His mouth contorted. "It wasn't fate that murdered Elizabeth. And it wasn't fate that arranged for Molly to be at the lodge five years ago—and more recently at the Crocker ball."

"I agree, but it doesn't mean that it is the work of one person either."

"Ah, you don't think so? You find it easier to believe that several different people decided to make my life a tragedy? That someone else murdered Elizabeth? And that another person arranged for Molly's various appearances?" Sarcastically, he asked, "You do agree that it is unlikely that two different people arranged for Molly to play her different parts?"

"I'll concede that one person was probably behind that," Patrick admitted. "I'll even concede that it is more than probable that whoever arranged for Molly's, er, visits, is also the person who murdered her."

"But not Elizabeth and Leyton?"

Patrick scowled. "It's possible that they were killed by the same person, and I'll agree that it is not beyond reason that Leyton, at least, was killed by the same person who murdered Molly." He sighed and looked unhappily at Tony. "But you are really asking for a great leap of faith for me to believe that one of your relatives cold-bloodedly murdered Elizabeth in order to gain a fortune you wouldn't inherit for nearly fifteen years!"

"No, that would be asking too much, I agree. I think originally that Elizabeth was killed simply because she carried my child. My heir. The heir to the Daggett fortune." Tony took another turn around the room, his expression preoccupied. "It is not all clear in my own mind yet, and I do not think that it was clear at first in the mind of the killer. I think the plan, if you will, gradually evolved as time went by. Mercy's death was definitely an accident, but whether the events surrounding that accident had a little help from someone else remains to be seen. But I truly think, with Mercy so conveniently dead, that it was then that the idea of one day killing me and inheriting the Daggett fortune was born."

"So tell me, why weren't you murdered shortly thereafter," Patrick muttered.

Tony smiled grimly. "Two reasons, my friend. One, I think at that time, our villain had not crossed the line of actually dirtying his hands and committing murder himself. Mercy's death was an accident. As for the second reason—don't you remember? Mercy was hardly in the ground when I left for England. Unless he wished to follow me across the ocean, I was temporarily out of his reach. Remember, in the case of Franklin and Burgess, they were constrained by a lack of funds—Uncle Alfred kept them on a tight leash as far as money was concerned, and he is, to this day, a clutch-fisted old bastard. Sometimes I almost feel sorry for my cousins.

"But let us consider the notion that one of them could have followed me to England for the express purpose of murdering me. I am certain that if I had been murdered or even suffered a mysteriously fatal accident, suspicions might have been aroused. Especially since one of the men who would inherit the Daggett fortune from me would have just happened to be staying in London at the same time. Our villain wasn't, I suspect, willing to take the chance of having suspicion of *any* kind fall on him." Tony frowned.

"Since the idea of one person being behind my phenomenal run of bad luck first crossed my mind this afternoon, I've been trying to figure out what sort of person he might be. I don't think that he is a brave man, not necessarily a blatant coward, but a cautious man with his eye on the main chance. And I think, considering the life I used to lead, he was willing to sit back, remain safely in Natchez, and simply hope that I would manage to kill myself in England—something that was not out of the realm of possibility. I don't believe that he had thought out an entire plan. I think it was more of a wait-and-see attitude." He smiled cynically. "And if he got really desperate for some reason, he could always decide to speed up my demise."

"All right. I'll accept that much of your theory," Patrick said grudgingly. He flashed Tony a wry smile. "Damn you! You're beginning to make it all sound so reasonable and logical."

Tony was not certain whether to be cheered or depressed by Patrick's admission. Even he would admit that what he was proposing was far-fetched, and he had almost hoped that Patrick could convince him that it was all utter nonsense. It seemed that the opposite had happened.

Tony ran a hand tiredly through his dark hair. "I was both hoping and dreading that you would say exactly that. I'll confess, it would be easier just to blame fate than to believe that there is someone out there who is so diabolical that he would murder a woman and her unborn child simply to inherit a fortune."

There was a bleak silence as the two men considered the ugly situation before them. Even when Tony finally sat down and sipped his whiskey, the silence continued for several more minutes, each of them staring blankly into space.

It was Patrick who finally broke the silence. "If, and I'm only saying if, Elizabeth was killed simply because she was pregnant, and assuming that your relative is the man who killed her, having finally stained his hands with blood, why didn't he then come after you?"

Tony grimaced. "I'm guessing, but I imagine that he was rather unnerved after Elizabeth's murder, and I suspect he had to gather up his courage to strike again. I also don't think that he wanted the murders too close together. The last thing he would have wanted was for anyone to connect my murder with Elizabeth's—that would point suspicion in a direction he surely did not want it to go. He had no choice but to wait—and there was probably still the hope that I would do the job for him and manage either to break my neck or die in a duel." His jaw clenched, his eyes taking on a dangerous gleam. "It is one thing to kill a woman," he said harshly, "and another to kill a man—a man known to be handy with his fives and one known to be usually armed." He took a long swallow of his whiskey. "He had to wait. And by the time several months had passed, the situation had changed."

"The Westbrook fortune," Patrick said flatly.

Tony nodded. "Yes. The Westbrook fortune. He'd waited almost five years already—what harm was there in waiting several more? Especially, if at the end of that time, one would lay one's hands on a fortune that made the Daggett money look almost paltry?"

Patrick scratched his head. "I don't know, Tony. I still have trouble swallowing the notion that someone would wait that long. Nearly fifteen years is not five or six."

"I agree, and I don't think he planned, in the beginning, to wait five years, much less fifteen." Tony answered quietly. "I think he *did* plan to murder me, if I didn't do the job for him myself, just as soon as he felt it was safe to do so. Remember that he had time on his side—even with Uncle Alfred's tightfisted ways, none of them are penniless. Our villain probably thought to wait a year or two before killing me and probably even hoped to make it look like an accident." Tony's lips thinned. "A fall down my own stairs while drunk or, perhaps, a broken neck from a fall from my horse." Sardonically, he added, "History, one might say, tragically repeating itself when you recall how my father died."

"What changed his plans?"

Tony shrugged. "I don't know. I keep coming back to the Westbrook fortune." When Patrick started to protest, Tony held up a hand. "Wait. I gave you only the bare bones of Grandfather's Westbrook will: There are two significant provisions that I did not elaborate upon." He smiled ruefully. "My grandfather really couldn't bring himself to hold too tight a rein on me, even from the grave. Consequently, he ordered that at age thirty, no doubt hoping I would have matured somewhat, that fifteen percent of the portion held in the 'funds' should be dispersed to me—a rather handsome sum, I might add. The same amount would also be dispersed when I reached thirty-five."

Patrick sat back, absently brushing his steepled fingers against his lips. Nodding, he said slowly, "And so our villain decided that waiting until you were thirty would be greatly to his advantage—at the time only three or four years longer. Another advantage to waiting—by then, no one would ever think to connect Elizabeth's death with your own, no matter what the circumstances."

"That's what I think."

"And having waited until you were thirty, having invested, as it were, almost a decade in planning your demise, what was another five years—especially since you would be getting another fifteen percent? And as you say, our villain is not destitute. Greedy to be sure. But he could afford to wait."

Tony nodded again. "That's what I think. That the idea of gaining the entire Westbrook fortune only gradually occurred to him. And remember, over the years I have spent the majority of my time in England—well out of his reach, unless he wished to take a chance of being too-conveniently near at hand when I died. A chance he could not take, because though I am certain he would have arranged things to appear accidental, there was always the possibility that things could go wrong."

"He certainly didn't worry about covering up Leyton's murder or Molly's," Patrick commented grimly.

Tony smiled, not a very nice smile. "Ah, but you see, he considered himself to be their superior. They were nothing to him—he didn't *fear* them."

"And you think he fears you?"

"Why else am I still alive? He *could* have murdered me any number of times over the years if he were willing to take the chance. And again, I can think of only two reasons why he has not: the Westbrook fortune and his uneasiness—fear, if you will— in confronting me."

Patrick sighed, and muttered, "I know that there is a flaw in your reasoning, but blast if I can find it. Damme. Against my better judgment you have convinced me that you might be right."

The two men talked long into the wee hours of the morning, coming to no certain conclusions or solutions. They were both tired and not a little depressed when Tony finally escorted Patrick out of the house and to where his horse had been tied.

The light from the lanterns, which hung on several of the pillars at the front of the house, flickered weakly over them as they stood there talking. In view of the lateness of the hour, Tony had suggested that Patrick stay the night, but Patrick had declined.

Swinging up into the saddle, Patrick said, "You have me viewing my every action with an eye as to what our villain may think, and though we have often stayed the night at each other's home for no apparent reason, right now I am uneasy at the notion."

Tony grinned at him. "You just don't want to be in my vicinity, should he choose to murder me tonight."

Patrick laughed, but his gray eyes were serious. "Hardly that, but remember should you be murdered, *someone* must avenge you. And I swear to you that I shall see your murderer dead and that no harm comes to your lady and her child—or you—if it is in my power to do so."

"At least," Tony said grimly, "you will only have to narrow the choice of my killer down to one from three."

Patrick uttered the three names in a savage tone. "Albert. Franklin. Or Burgess."

"Precisely."

Tony waited until Patrick had turned his horse away and disappeared into the darkness before turning to mount the steps of the house. He was exhausted, and a few minutes later he was asleep within seconds of his head hitting the pillow.

Arabella and Jeremy's return to Greenleigh had been met with little fanfare. No one had come to call while they had been gone, and the Tidmores, like the well-trained servants they were, expressed no undue interest in their whereabouts during the preceding forty-eight hours.

Since she was exhausted after the events of the past two days, after taking a long, hot bath, and enjoying a light repast with Jeremy, she bid her brother an early good night and retired to her bedroom. She fell asleep almost as soon as she lay down on the welcoming softness of her feather bed.

Left to his own devices, Jeremy wandered about the downstairs, rather bored with his own company. Feeling let-down after the excitement of the stirring events of the past few days, he eventually sought out his own bed. While knowing that his lips were sealed for the time being, before sleep finally claimed him, he was just young enough to spend an enjoyable few minutes imagining the expressions of astonishment and envy on the faces of his friends when the truth became known.

Both Arabella and Jeremy woke the next morning refreshed. They shared a large breakfast together, and then Jeremy began to make plans to leave for Highview.

"I would stay," he said to Arabella as she walked him to his horse, "but I know that Tony will be riding over tonight." A slight flush stained his cheeks, and he suddenly seemed very interested in the shine of his boots. Clearing his throat, he mumbled, "Tonight will be your true wedding night, and I don't expect the pair of you would want me hanging about."

Arabella laughed and kissed him on his cheek. "So discreet, my dear. I must admit that you have surprised me lately, and you have developed into quite a diplomat."

"Well, dash it all, Bella! I ain't a child, you know."

"Of course not," she said soothingly, watching fondly as he mounted his horse and prepared to leave. He was so young and believed himself to be so very adult, she thought, affection mingling with amusement.

They spoke for a few minutes longer, and then Jeremy rode off in the direction of Highview.

Arabella spent the remainder of the day trying to act normal, but it was difficult, her thoughts wandering constantly to Tony and what the future might hold for them. By late afternoon, she gave up any pretense of normality and, telling Mrs. Tidmore that she was going to lie down for a while, escaped to her bedroom.

Time seemed to creep by for Arabella. She lingered over her bath, dutifully ate the savory meal prepared by the cook, then took a short stroll around the house in the deepening dusk. Though they tried to be unobtrusive, she had no trouble spying the four men she had set to watch the house. Their presence depressed her, pointing out as it did the fact that something exceedingly strange and dangerous was going on.

Not having any idea what time Tony would arrive, she eventually retired to her bedchamber. With care she donned a lovely pale yellow nightgown, the rounded neckline and little bell-shaped sleeves edged with fine lace. Lying alone in her bed, waiting impatiently for Tony's arrival, she did not think that she would be able to sleep a wink, but eventually her eyes closed, and she slept deeply.

The downstairs clock was chiming out the hour of midnight when Tony, having deftly avoided the men guarding the house, stepped into her room. Approaching her, he lit the candle that had been left on the small satinwood table near her bed, and, in the light from the dancing yellow flame, stared down at her.

She looked lovely, her red hair tumbling like silken fire around her shoulders, her long lashes resting like dark fans on her faintly flushed cheeks, and the soft swell of her generous breasts evident beneath the yellow gown. Tony sighed with pleasure, his heart suddenly so full of love for her that he thought it would surely explode.

After tossing aside his jacket and tugging off his boots, with nary a care for the smudges he left on their glossy surface, he slipped onto the bed beside her. Whisking a lock of hair from her forehead, he brushed a gentle kiss across her eyes.

"Wake up, sweetheart," he murmured. "Your husband has come to call." He kissed her again, this time softly on her rosy lips, and her eyelids fluttered.

She opened her eyes and stared sleepily at him. "Tony," she said happily, still half-asleep. "I was dreaming of you."

He smiled and nibbled on her earlobe. "Ah, but I am sure that you will enjoy reality far more than mere dreams."

Her arms slid around his neck, a teasing gleam in the golden brown depths of her eyes. "You are no doubt correct . . . but perhaps you would like to prove it?"

His own eyes suddenly darkened and, bending his head, heedless of the silky material of her gown, caught one nipple between his teeth and oh-so-gently bit it. Arabella gasped and arched up as desire, powerful and elemental, sprang to life within her.

His tongue and teeth busy with her nipple, with one tanned hand he pushed down the few covers that hid her body from him. Pleasing her as much as it did him, he ran a caressing hand from her thigh to her waist, his own passion rising with every passing second.

Lifting his head, he glanced down at her. "Well?" he asked mockingly. "Is reality better than dreams?"

Her fingers clenched in his dark hair. "I don't know," she teased. "Take off your clothes and let me see if memory has played me false."

"Witch!" he said with a laugh as he rolled off the bed and dispensed with his clothing.

Reality, Arabella thought breathlessly, as she stared at the broad chest and the rampant proof of his arousal between his muscular thighs, *is much,* much *better than dreams!*

She reached eagerly for him as he came back to the bed, but Tony caught her hands, and said, "Oh, no, you don't. First we get rid of your clothes."

Her gown was promptly whisked over her head and flung on the floor. Sinking down beside her, Tony's hands cupped her breasts, his thumbs moving rhymthically over her rapidly swelling nipples. Thickly, he said, "Every minute away from you has seemed an hour. All I have been able to think of the entire day is lying here like this with you."

Arabella moaned with pleasure, his clever hands on her breasts stoking the fire that burned low in her belly. "I, too," she muttered. "I could hardly wait for tonight to arrive." Flinging her arms around his neck, she pressed an urgent kiss to his cheek. "Oh, Tony, I do love you!"

"And I you, sweetheart. More than life itself."

Enraptured, they stared at each other, hardly daring to believe that at last they were man and wife. It was a precious moment, one to be savored.

"We are lucky, aren't we?" Arabella asked softly, her eyes shining like molten gold.

Tony slowly nodded. "Indeed we are, my love. We have each other and soon we shall have a child." He glanced down at her flat stomach, one hand almost reverently touching the area where their child grew. Dazedly, he said, "I can hardly believe that it is true. I fear that I shall wake and find that it is all a dream."

Arabella smiled mistily at him, her arms tightening around him. Lifting her mouth to his, she said huskily, "I am no dream, dear heart. I am your wife . . . and, oh-so-eager for your touch."

They kissed, their mouths melding together, tasting each other as their tongues tangled in a duet as old as the moon. Passion already simmering between them became a firestorm, consuming everything but the need to possess: he her and she him. And yet, despite the fierce emotions that drove them, there was an innate tenderness in the way they touched, love tempering the blind urge simply to mate.

Tony's hands were warm and gentle as they roved her voluptuous form, and the slow, languid exploration of her body made Arabella's breath catch in her throat. He touched her everywhere, her breasts, her slender waist, her taut belly, and the wet, aching place between her thighs. He stroked her there a long time, making her twist and pant beneath his caress. When his head dropped and he took one nipple into his hot mouth, tugging strongly on the hardened nub, Arabella could not suppress the primitive sound that erupted from deep within her.

Blindly, she reached for him, her hand closing around the bulging shaft she found between his legs. Tony groaned as her fingers grasped him and began slowly, torturously, to work him. Gasping with delight and pleasure, Tony endured the sweet anguish she evoked, straining to prolong this wondrous, intimate moment.

He found her mouth, kissing her with desperate urgency as his delving fingers sank even deeper within her. She writhed beneath him, her movements becoming wilder and more wanton as his tongue plunged fiercely into her welcoming mouth and mimicked the frantic movements of his hand buried between her thighs. He gave her no succor, not even when her hips reared up violently beneath his hand, telling him more clearly than words that she was as ready for their joining.

Fire humming in her veins, her body one long burning ache, Arabella tore her mouth from Tony's. "Please, Tony," she cried huskily. *"Please!"*

With a groan, Tony shifted and, cupping her buttocks, lifted her to meet his downward thrust. He sank heavily into her, the silken heat of her body closing tightly around him. Shaking with pleasure, Tony savored the moment. She was all sweet fire and soft silk beneath him, her nipples searing into his chest, her arms holding him tightly to her. It was pure carnal ecstasy.

Unbearably aroused, Arabella was nearly mindless with pleasure when Tony's lips captured hers and he began to thrust powerfully within her. Each deep thrust of his broad shaft, each blunt stab of his tongue, sent a bolt of sheer erotic sensation through her. Eagerly she kissed him back, her hand at the back of his head, holding him to her; her hips, guided by his hard hands, as well as her own spiraling pleasure, rose frantically to meet his every thrust. It was a desperate ride, the urgent demand for relief from the primeval urges that clawed through them both blotting out everything but the passion of the moment. And when that sweet release came, when ecstasy caught Arabella and she cried out, Tony's lips captured her cry.

Buried tightly within her, Tony felt her throb and clench around him. It was too much. Suddenly helpless in the wake of his own pleasure, with a great shuddering moan, he spilled himself into her and sank slowly, deliciously down onto her warm, silky body.

Nestled together, they lay there silent for a time, relishing the moment. Eventually Tony raised himself up on one elbow and, grinning down at Arabella, asked, "Well? Which do you prefer? Reality or dreams?"

Her eyes gleaming in the faint light of the candle near the bed, Arabella murmured, "Perhaps I should have another, ah, sample, before answering that question."

Tony laughed and dropped a hard kiss on her teasing mouth. "You shall have all the samples you desire, madam wife, but not, unfortunately, immediately."

Arabella smiled at him and stretched luxuriously, her hands over her head. "Hmm. Now that would be one area in which dreams are far better. No waiting."

"Why, you little witch!" Tony said, laughter dancing in his blue eyes. "I see that I shall have to show you that waiting has its own enjoyments."

"Oh? And what are they?"

"Allow me to show you," he said huskily, as he caught her hands in one of his and dropped his warm, seeking lips to her neck. And during the moments that followed, he showed her *precisely* just how enjoyable waiting could be.

They made love all through the night, their couplings growing more desperate and frantic as the hour approached for Tony to slip out of the house. Lying locked in each other's arms after their latest joining, they both heard the big clock in the downstairs entry hall strike the hour of four.

Tony sighed and gently disentangled himself from Arabella. "I have to go, sweetheart. I should have gone long before this."

Watching him pull on his clothing, dispiritedly Arabella found her nightgown and slipped the garment over her head. "I know. It is just very hard to have to meet so clandestinely. We *are* married, and yet we have to sneak around like we have something to hide."

Tony sat down on the bed beside her and took her hand in his. Pressing a kiss to the back of it, he said, "I know, sweetheart. It is exceedingly difficult for me to leave you. But for now we *do* have something to hide. I'll not have you placed in danger just so that I may sleep all night in your bed."

Arabella pushed back an errant lock of hair. Gravely her gaze met his. "I do not mind so very much that our marriage cannot be announced immediately, but how long are we to be in this invidious position?"

Tony shook his head. "I don't know." He smiled faintly and lightly patted her stomach. "We cannot delay too long, else our child will make the announcement for us."

She smiled, too, but her smile faded almost instantly. "Have you any ideas on how we are to resolve the situation?"

Tony shook his head. "No, but I have given it some thought." He hesitated and then, uneasily aware of the passing minutes, swiftly relayed his conclusions and the conversation with Patrick.

Arabella was frowning by the time he finished speaking. "You think everything is connected?"

"I do. It seems a much more logical conclusion than simply to rail at fate." His mouth tightened. "And until I am proven wrong, I am going on the assumption that one of my dear Daggett relatives has his eye on my fortune and is willing to stop at nothing to gain it."

"But why kill Leyton and Molly?" Arabella asked reasonably. "They do not stand in his way."

"No, but I think they knew something. Molly's connection is easy; she might even have threatened to expose him, to tell one of us who paid her to be at the lodge that night—and to make her damning announcement at the Crocker ball—which is why, I'm certain, that he killed her. And don't forget, Molly had been in Leyton's keeping." Tony frowned. "I'm speculating that Leyton learned something from Molly that made him dangerous to whoever is behind this."

"Boots?"

"For the present, he's my guess. It is possible that someone totally unrelated to my situation was there that day you came to call on Leyton, but I doubt it. I think, too, that he is the same fellow who paid you that unpleasant visit several weeks ago."

He shot her a keen look. "He wanted something—something he thought that you had. Are you certain you did not take anything else with you that day?"

Arabella shook her head. "Nothing except the portfolio containing the Greenleigh deeds, and we have already checked in it." She suddenly gasped. "Oh, and my reticule. But it was always in my hand." She frowned, trying to remember that afternoon at Leyton's. "Wait. When I placed the portfolio on his desk, I distinctly remember setting my reticule down beside it." Her eyes widened. "Oh, Tony, that has to be it! He was angry, or pretended to be, and he shoved the portfolio and my reticule on the floor. The portfolio and my reticule went flying, as well as several papers that had been on his desk. There were papers everywhere, and I was scrambling about trying to pick everything up. As soon as I could, I left."

"In your haste could you have put something in your reticule?"

"I suppose so." She grimaced ruefully. "And if that is what happened, its still in my reticule. Unfortunately that particular reticule is at Highview—I did not bring that one with me to Greenleigh."

Tony muffled a curse under his breath, an anxious eye on the dim light creeping into her room from the French doors. "There is nothing that we can do about it at the moment," he said unhappily. "And I have lingered too long already. Daylight is nearly upon us, and I must be gone."

Pulling Arabella into his arms, he kissed her almost

desperately. His expression fierce, he commanded, "Do not go to Highview. If there *is* something in that blasted reticule, I want to be with you when you find it." At the mulish look that crossed her face, he gave her a gentle shake. "Promise me, Bella. Promise me that you will not go to Highview and look for it yourself."

He wasn't leaving until he had her word, and as worried about the passing moments as he, she finally nodded "Very well," she said reluctantly. "I shall not go to Highview."

Tony didn't quite trust her, but he could not remain a second longer. Crushing her mouth beneath his one last time, he strode from the room and vanished into the misty mauve of first dawn.

After he had left, Arabella wandered morosely about her room, wishing she had not given Tony her word. It was frustrating to be able to do nothing, simply to wait, while she was almost certain that the answer to at least some of the recent, unpleasant events might be resting inside the reticule she had carried the afternoon she had gone to call on Leyton. And the blasted thing was at Highview! Momentarily out of her reach.

Then she brightened. Tony had made her promise not to go to Highview herself. There was nothing, she thought happily, to stop her from sending one of the servants to Highview to fetch her the reticule . . . and some other items of clothing in which to disguise the real purpose for wanting them.

Pleased with herself, she sat down to make a list of various pieces of clothing she had suddenly decided that she simply could not do without. The reticule was neither the first nor last item on her list, and being doubly careful, she had even listed a second reticule.

It was late in the morning before an opportunity to introduce the subject came about. She and Mrs. Tidmore had just finished cleaning out a cavernous wardrobe in one of the rarely used back bedrooms. Arabella was folding an old-fashioned gown to be given away to one of the other servants, when she said carelessly, "Oh, this reminds me, I shall have to send someone to Highview to bring back some more garments for me."

"Very well, miss," replied Mrs. Tidmore. "If you give me a list of what you want, I shall see that someone leaves immediately for Highview."

A half hour later the list was safely on its way. Suddenly nervous about having circumvented the promise she had made to Tony, Arabella began to pace in the privacy of her room. Tony was going to be angry, she thought uneasily, biting her lip. She knew it was only fear for her that prompted his cautiousness, and that knowledge warmed her even as it made her frown.

She straightened her shoulders and her chin lifted. Tony was her husband now, but that did not mean that she had suddenly become helpless or unable to make a decision without his approval—even one that might involve danger. He was, she thought warily, just going to have to learn that she could take care of herself and make some decisions on her own. And there was no denying that she had a compelling argument on her side—what she had done was probably the quickest and easiest way for them to get their hands on her reticule . . . and what it might or might not contain.

Chapter Nineteen

As Arabella had suspected, Tony was angry that night when he learned what she had done. But as she had also already guessed, once he realized that she had placed herself in no danger and that the reticule would be in their hands on the morrow, he admired her quick action.

They were lying in bed together, the hour sometime after two o'clock in the morning, and they had just finished making love. Tony had been too impatient and hungry for her for there to have been much conversation between them—other than fervent avowals of undying love. But having sated the most urgent of his needs, he was, for the moment, willing to relax and exchange news of each other's day.

It wasn't as easy to blurt out what she had done as she had first thought it would be. Glad to postpone the moment, she listened as he spoke of his day, including the depressing information that he had seen to the making of his will and that it currently resided in the office of a very disapproving Mr. Haight.

Tony grinned as he told her about leaving the document with him. "He would have had an apoplectic fit if he had known what was in it—especially the fact that we are married." Dropping a kiss on her temple, he added, "I wrote it out myself and had Patrick and my overseer, John Jackson, witness it. Once we have discovered the identity of Boots and presumably, the villain who murdered Elizabeth, I shall have your purse-lipped Mr. Haight draw up a new one, full of all those phrases that are so dear to lawyers. Perhaps when he knows that I have made an honest woman of you, he will unbend enough to smile at me—sour though I am sure it will be."

They spoke idly for some minutes, but inevitably the conversation turned to her day and plans to fetch the reticule. Taking a deep breath, Arabella said carefully, "There is no need for us to retrieve my reticule from Highview. I sent for it today . . . yesterday actually."

Tony jerked upright, his blue eyes darkening dangerously. "You did what?" he asked incredulously, anger not far. "Didn't you listen to a word I said last night?"

She looked demure and brushed a finger across his lips. "You said several rather interesting things last night, my love."

"Don't try to distract me," he growled. "Blast it, Arabella! You may have placed yourself in danger." His gaze narrowed. "And if I remember correctly, you swore you would not go Highview."

"And I've kept my word," she replied calmly. "I did not go to Highview. I did, however, write a note to Mary requesting that several items of clothing be sent here—amongst them the reticule. If all goes well, Martha and my reticule should arrive here tomorrow afternoon with no one the wiser as to the real purpose behind my request."

Tony frowned, his eyes on hers. "Hmm, that might work," he finally admitted grudgingly.

She flashed him a grin. "Thank you, kind sir."

"Which doesn't mean that I don't realize that you have outmaneuvered me," he said sternly.

"Oh Tony, don't be so stuffy. If I had thought of it while you were still here, I would have discussed the idea with you before taking action. But you weren't here, and I didn't want to wait until I had talked it over with you before sending the note off." She sent him a look. "I *am,* you might remember, perfectly capable of making a decision on my own—I have been doing so for years. The fact that I am your wife does not mean that my brain has atrophied."

Tony smiled ruefully. "Point taken, my dear. It is only that—"

"It is only that you worry about me," she said softly. "I know that. But there is no danger in what I did, and you must admit that it was the swiftest and least suspicious way to get our hands on the reticule."

"Tomorrow afternoon, you say?"

She nodded.

"Then I shall just have to come to call tomorrow afternoon, won't I?" he murmured with a smile that made her heart thud.

Putting her arms around his neck, she kissed him warmly on the lips. "You may call upon me anytime you wish, dear sir," she said teasingly. "But remember, as far as anyone is concerned I am still an unmarried woman—have care that you do not set tongues wagging about us."

Tony muttered something profane under his breath and, pulling her beneath him, proceeded to treat her in a fashion that would have indeed set tongues wagging. Not content with that, he did it again before he finally forced himself to leave her bed and begin to put on his clothing.

Her features flushed and rosy from his lovemaking, Arabella trailed him disconsolately to the French doors.

"I know this is all necessary, but I hate it," she said, as Tony opened the doors and glanced outside at the fading darkness.

He turned back to her and pulled her into his arms. "I, too, my sweet," he said huskily. "But it will not be for too long. Let us hope that your reticule holds some answers for us."

When Martha and the cart arrived just before noon the next day, Arabella forced herself to act calmly. Smiling at Martha as her maid entered the house, she asked, "Did you have a good trip?"

Martha nodded, and the two women exchanged a few words before Arabella dismissed Martha, saying, "Go eat something and rest a bit. I can have one of the other servants unpack and put things away."

It was difficult not to tag at Tidmore's heels as he dragged the leather trunk upstairs to her room. It was even more difficult to turn away and pretend she had nothing more on her mind than the arrangement of roses and sweet peas she had been working on when Martha had arrived. Every instinct she possessed was screaming for her to race up those stairs, fling open that trunk, and search for the reticule—and more importantly, for what the reticule might hold.

It wasn't until an hour later that she finally allowed herself to climb the stairs casually and enter her bedroom. Everything had already been put away, but it took her only a moment to find the little reticule she had taken with her the day she had called on Leyton.

Heart pounding, she finally opened the reticule. It was empty. Disappointment crashed through her. She had been counting so much on finding something significant, some clue that would lead to an explanation behind some of the recent events. She looked again, her fingers desperately seeking out every little cranny, but there was nothing.

Totally dispirited, she flung the offending item on her bed and left her room. There was nothing but to wait for Tony.

When Tony, accompanied by Patrick, rode up a short while later, he had only to take one look at her long face to know that the reticule had held nothing of importance. A black hole seemed to open up in the middle of his chest. He hadn't realized until that moment how much hope he had placed in something of significance being in the reticule. As disappointed and dispirited as Arabella, he forced a smile on his lips and, after dismounting from Sugar, strode up the steps to where she stood waiting for him on the front veranda.

"How do you do, Miss Montgomery," he said politely. "Mr. Blackburne and I were riding in the area and thought that we would call upon you and see how you did. I trust that you are settling in well?"

She made an equally polite reply, some of her usual good humor returning at Tony's ridiculously formal speech. Even though she knew the reasons for his stilted manner, she could not help but be amused by it—after all, she had lain naked in his arms less than twelve hours ago!

Patrick was just as formal, and, quelling an urge to giggle, Arabella replied in the same cool manner as she invited them inside and offered refreshments.

It wasn't until they were in the east parlor and Tidmore had served refreshments and departed that Arabella spoke freely. Putting down the tall glass of lemonade she had taken for form's sake, she said unhappily, "It was empty. There was nothing in it. Nothing at all."

Tony shrugged, keeping his own disappointment in check. "Well, it was a thought. Too bad for us that it came to nothing."

"At least," Patrick murmured, "you have eliminated that possibility."

"But it was such a *promising* possibility," Arabella said mournfully. "I was so certain—" She stopped and made a face. "Patrick is right, it does eliminate one possibility." She looked at Tony. "What do we do now?"

Before he could speak there was a gentle rap on the door and at Arabella's command to enter, Martha opened the door and came into the room. She flushed when she realized that she had interrupted her mistress entertaining guests. Dropping a quick curtsy, she said apologetically, "Oh miss! I am sorry to have bothered you—I didn't realize that you had company. I can speak to you later."

Arabella smiled at her and walking over to her, said quietly, "Do not worry—you have disturbed nothing but idle chatter. What is it you wanted?"

"Only to give you this," Martha replied, handing Arabella a piece of paper. "When I went through your things as I was packing them, I discovered this tucked down inside one of your reticules. I meant to give it to you earlier, but I forgot."

A thrill surging through her, Arabella's fingers only shook slightly when she took the slip of paper from Martha. "Thank you," she said with the merest tremor of excitement in her voice.

Clutching the paper for dear life, Arabella waited until the door had shut behind her maid before she turned to face the frozen gentlemen. "I never," she said weakly, "thought to ask Martha if she had gone through the reticule before packing it."

"It doesn't matter," Tony growled. "Let us see what is written on that damned piece of paper."

Crowding around Arabella as she opened the folded paper, the two gentlemen read the contents right along with her.

Molly, my love,
I have arranged all for tonight. You know the time and place. Tony will be waiting for you. Of course he is expecting Arabella—you shall convince him, I am sure, that your charms are far more alluring. I would suggest that you not drink any of the wine . . . not if you want to keep your wits about you. I will leave the arrangements for the guest of honor's surprise to you. I shall see to it that she is, shall we say, fashionably late. Enjoy yourself

D.

When they had finished reading the brief note, the three of them exchanged glances.

"He certainly didn't give us much to work with, did he?" Patrick observed dryly.

Tony nodded slowly. "But then it is nothing less than I would have expected from him—Boots, as Arabella and I call him, is not a stupid man. He covers his tracks well, and if we didn't know that this little note refers to the night that Arabella found me in such a compromising position with Molly, it would seem innocuous."

"Oh, Tony," Arabella said contritely. "To think that you were telling the truth all along, and I did not believe you. No one believed you. I am so ashamed of myself." Her bottom lip drooped. "We lost five years. Five whole years during which we could have been married."

Tony pulled her against him and dropping a kiss on the top of her fiery curls, said, "It doesn't matter, sweetheart—the lost years, yes, but as for the rest of it—we have each other now, and that is all that counts." He looked grim. "The important thing now is that we finally have something tangible with which to work. This note *proves* that the breaking of our engagement was definitely planned. And I'll wager a small fortune that it was because of this note that Boots came to call on you that night. Leyton had somehow gotten his hands on the note, and it inadvertently got mixed up with your papers. Boots wanted it back."

Frowning, Patrick took the note from Arabella's hand and reread it. "It certainly doesn't give us much to go on." He shot Tony a keen glance. "You have damn little proof to link this to what happened five years ago—or that it was ever in Leyton's hands. The thing isn't even dated."

"I know that," Tony replied tightly. "But I also *know* that the note has to be the one that was sent to Molly to get her to the lodge in time to set up the scene that Arabella found when she arrived. And the mention of the wine is telling—it had to have been drugged, which was why I didn't toss Molly out on her fetching rear when she first showed up. I remember drinking a glass of wine as I waited for Arabella, but I remember nothing after that until I woke up naked in the bed with Molly pawing me and Arabella staring horrified at me."

Tony's gaze narrowed, and he looked at Arabella. "You were late that night. Why?"

"Oh, it was the stupidest thing. Several people came to call on Grandfather and I had just offered my excuses and was planning to slip away to meet you when someone stepped on my gown and tore one of the flounces. Mary offered to sew it up for me. You might not remember, but Mary and I and the children were staying with Grandfather for a few days hoping to cheer him up. Grandmother had been gone several weeks to visit friends in New Orleans, and he was lonely." She looked guilty as she added, "I had been staying with him frequently those days—as much to keep him company as to be able to meet you at the lodge. That particular visit, Mary had decided that he might enjoy having the children around and, much to my dismay, they had accompanied me."

"I wonder," Patrick said to no one in particular, "if that isn't significant. Had she ever come with you before?"

Arabella shook her head, her expression troubled. "No. There had never been any reason for her to do so." She frowned. "In fact, as I recall she complained the entire visit about how small and cramped the house was compared to Highview."

"Which makes one wonder why she decided to come and visit in the first place, doesn't it? After all, she and her children were nothing to your grandfather," Tony said, his blue eyes narrowed.

"Well, no, but it did seem like a good idea. Grandfather enjoyed the children—they made him smile, and he said to me, more than once during that visit, that it was wonderful to hear the house ringing with the laughter of children." Unconsciously she touched the spot where her child grew. "This child would have pleased him enormously." Her eyes twinkled. "Once he was assured that I was a properly wedded wife."

"And you would have been five years ago," Tony said grimly, "if it hadn't been for someone's interference." He frowned and returned to the original subject. "It was simply a torn flounce that delayed you that night?"

"Well, actually," she began slowly, "it wasn't the torn flounce itself. It was because of—" She stopped and bit her lip. "It was because of Mary," she said unhappily. "I never considered it before, but I realize now that she took forever to mend the flounce—I wouldn't have bothered with it, but she insisted. There were dozens of reasons for the delay that I did not really think about at that time: Her maid took forever to bring her the sewing box; then she couldn't find the right color of thread, and I remember thinking that she would *never* get the needle threaded. And when all of those aggravations were done, it took her an eon finally to sew up the flounce. I was nearly dancing with vexation by the time she finished—the arrival of the gentlemen to visit grandfather had delayed me from slipping away in the first place, and then the mending of my gown seemed to take forever." She looked at Tony. "My mind was on meeting you. While Mary dithered and dathered, I was afraid that you would think I wasn't coming that evening and would leave before I could get there."

"Do you think her actions were deliberate?" asked Patrick quietly. "Or just a simple case of nothing going right?"

"I don't know," Arabella answered in a troubled tone. "It does seem suspicious, doesn't it, considering what happened because I was delayed?"

"I agree, but it doesn't prove that Mary was being anything other than solicitous . . . and clumsy," Patrick replied.

"Well, I for one," Tony sad harshly, "am of the opinion that Mary was being a damned sight more than just clumsy! It ties together too nicely for my liking." He glanced at Arabella. "Who were the gentlemen who came to call—especially the one who stepped on your gown?"

"I don't know who stepped on my gown. I didn't discover it until—" She looked even more unhappy. "Until Mary pointed it out to me," she said in a low tone.

"Ah-ha!" Tony exclaimed. "She had to be part of the plot. And I'll wager that she was the one who found out when we were to meet and passed it on to her cohort."

"Oh, Tony! I hate to believe such underhanded activity of her."

"She didn't want us to marry," he said tightly. "She knew your father was adamant against our marriage. He could not prevent it though—you were of age and had your own fortune. I doubt your father, even as much as he disliked me, would have been a party to such a cruel and dishonorable way of parting us, but I don't have the least trouble believing that Mary would have stopped at nothing to bring about the end of our engagement." Tony took a deep breath, holding onto his temper. "Everyone knows she adored your father," he continued in a more even tone, "and would have done anything to make him happy—even if it made you terribly *un*-happy."

"He's right, you know," Patrick said, his gray eyes kind. "Your stepmother's devotion to your father was well-known. She would not have wanted you to be hurt, but if she had to choose between you or your father . . ." His voice trailed off, and they all stared pensively at each other.

"You're right," Arabella said miserably. "She could have done it for him."

"If we assume that Mary was part of the plot to part us, then who was her partner?" Tony asked. "She could not have done it alone. I can't imagine her even knowing Molly Dobson, much less writing to Molly and enlisting her help. Nor can I imagine her arranging the scene that you found at the lodge that night. She had to have had help. A man."

"A man with the initial D." Patrick added, his gaze on Tony's hard face.

Tony flashed a twisted smile. "I think we are already agreed that Boots has to be one of my Daggett relatives. The question is—which one?"

"Well, I for one, vote for it being Franklin," said Arabella firmly. "He has never made any bones about the fact that he thinks it is the gravest injustice that his father, and hence himself, did not inherit Sweet Acres. You can't deny that he holds no love for you."

Tony shrugged. "That applies to all three of them, although Burgess at least appears to be indifferent to the situation. But then he would be—what happens with my grandfather's fortune doesn't affect him. He's the younger son—Sweet Acres and all that goes with it would not have come to him at any rate. Or the Westbrook fortune. I'll lay my money on either Alfred or Franklin being Boots."

"I think that we all agree that, ah, Boots is one of the Daggetts and," Patrick said slowly, "I think we can also agree that Boots is either Alfred or Franklin." He frowned and added, "I would also tend to agree with Arabella that our culprit is more than likely Franklin—although I wouldn't discount Alfred entirely."

"So how," Arabella asked softly, "do we expose him?"

"Through Mary," Tony said promptly. "If we let her know that we have the note and that we know of her part in what happened, I'll lay odds that she will give us his name."

Arabella shook her head, frowning. "She won't. She'll deny everything—I don't care how much evidence you lay in front of her." When Tony started to argue, she said firmly, "Listen to me. I know the woman. For five years she has considered herself safe from exposure. She is not, simply because you suddenly show up with this note and confront her, going to lay it all out for you." She made a face. "You may surprise a partial confession from her, but she is, in her way, very loyal, and if she knows that you have not identified Boots, she will not give him up to you."

"How can you call her loyal?" Tony demanded outraged. "She betrayed you."

Arabella sighed heavily. "Me, yes. But it was my father who had her first loyalty, and I can see that what she did, she did for my father. She adored my father—she would have done anything for him." She looked away. "And for that, I can't find it in my heart to condemn her totally."

At the expression on Tony's face, she added hastily, "She is my stepmother. I love her—with all her faults. She hurt me—us—horribly. I'll not easily forgive her, and I am just as angry as you are about the time she cost us, but she was doing what she thought was the right thing. Oh, Tony, don't you see—she was only doing her best to try and save me from making what she felt was a terrible mistake and at the same time trying to make my father happy, too. Can't we just leave her out of this?"

"Impossible." Tony said flatly. "You have a kinder heart than I, but putting that aside, remember—she is our only link. We have no choice but to use her."

The three discussed the situation at length, and, despite her misgivings and heavy heart, Arabella eventually agreed that there really was no choice but to use Mary to flush out Boots. With Arabella's assertion in mind that Mary would not simply give them Boots's name, they all agreed that somehow they were going to have to trick her into revealing Boots's identity. Precisely how that was to be accomplished had not been decided. The plan would simply have to evolve as they went along—which made none of them happy.

"Do you want me to approach her?" Arabella asked reluctantly, when they had decided to confront Mary.

Tony shook his head decisively. "Absolutely not! Whoever approaches Mary will automatically become a target for Boots. I do not want you in any more danger than you may be already."

He took a turn around the room. "I must be the one." When Patrick and Arabella started to protest, he held up a silencing hand. Looking at Arabella, he said somberly, "It cannot be you for obvious reasons. And," he continued, glancing across at Patrick, "having you approach her makes no sense. Our long friendship is no secret. She would more than likely guess that whatever you know, I know, and if she didn't, you can wager that Boots would. So your attempt to shield me would be fruitless and would only place you in danger. I *have* to be the one who approaches her."

"I don't like it," Patrick muttered. "We already suspect that you are his ultimate target—if the Westbrook fortune is his goal. If he feels that you are on the point of exposing him, he has no choice but to kill you." His chiseled mouth thinned.

"You'll just have to watch over me and see that he does not succeed, won't you?" Tony said with a mocking smile.

"How can you jest at a time like this?" Arabella

asked angrily, fear for Tony creating a cold void where her stomach used to be.

Tony took her into his arms. Kissing her lightly, he said, "Nothing is going to happen to me—I swear it."

"And, for what it is worth, madam, I swear that *I* shall not let anything happen to him," swore Patrick, his gray eyes dark with intent.

Arabella took a deep, shaken breath and stepped from the warmth of Tony's arms. "Very well, I shall hold you both to your promises. So, when and how are you going to approach my stepmother?"

"The sooner the better," Tony replied. "We cannot announce our marriage or begin our life together until we have exposed Boots." He glanced at the gold pocket watch he had taken from his waistcoat. Putting away the watch, his expression grim, he muttered, "If I leave now, there is time enough for me to pay a call on Mrs. Montgomery this afternoon."

Patrick discreetly withdrew to the far end of the room, giving them a moment's privacy.

Her eyes huge and worried, Arabella stared up into Tony's dark, beloved features. "You will be careful, won't you?" she asked huskily.

"Do you doubt it, sweetheart?" Tony murmured, his mouth inches from hers. "Now, when I have everything to live for? Everything I have ever wanted? Everything my heart desires?" His lips caught hers and he kissed her fervently, all the love and hunger he felt for her in that one, long, urgent melding of their mouths. His breathing erratic, Tony finally lifted his head. He smiled crookedly. "Nothing will happen to me, my love. Remember—I have the Devil's own luck."

Misty-eyed, fear an icy ball in her chest, Arabella waved them away a few minutes later from the front steps of Greenleigh. Telling herself firmly that Tony was right, that he *did* have the Devil's own luck, she went back inside and tried very hard not to think of all the things that could go wrong.

Tony and Patrick wasted no time once they were out of Arabella's sight. Kicking their horses into a distance-eating stride, they galloped down the dusty red road toward Highview. There was little to be said between the pair of them, and their pace made it nigh impossible to converse anyway. Taking a shortcut, they eventually left the main road and plunged into the green wilderness. Of necessity, their pace slowed somewhat as they careened through the verdant, vine-strewn, virgin forest, but it was still a silent ride, except for the thudding of their horses' hooves and the snap and crash of the brush, as they pushed onward. It was a half an hour later when they left the road and pulled their sweating, blowing horses to a stop a half mile away from Highview.

His expression grim, Patrick asked, "Is there no way I can convince you to let me be the one to approach Mary?"

"You know the answer to that question, my friend," Tony replied softly. "I *have* to do this."

Patrick sighed heavily. "And I am afraid," he said calmly, "that you leave me no choice—*I* have to do this—"

Before Tony could react, Patrick struck him with a hard right fist to the jaw. Reeling from the unexpected attack, Tony's head snapped back violently. Before he had time to recover, Patrick struck him again, this time on the temple with the butt of his pistol. Tony groaned and, nearly unseating himself, slumped unconscious in the saddle.

His expression cool and intent, Patrick dismounted and swiftly went to work. Shortly, he stepped away from Tony's horse and viewed his handiwork. Tony was well and truly gagged and trussed, his hands securely tied to the front of the saddle and his boots to the stirrups. *At least,* Patrick thought to himself, *he won't fall off—no matter how rough the ride home may be.* Reminding himself of one last thing, he reached inside Tony's waistcoat and found the damning note to Molly. His features set and dangerous, he carefully placed the note in his own waistcoat pocket.

Remounting his own horse and leading Tony's horse, Patrick pushed on cautiously toward Highview. Circling the extensive grounds that surrounded Highview, Patrick studied the layout, before finding a spot to leave Tony and his horse safely tied. That taken care of, he kicked his own horse into motion and trotted out from the concealing forests.

He rode up to the front of the house and tossed the reins to the little black boy who came scampering around the corner of the house. Swinging down from the saddle, he said, "Hold him. I won't be long."

Jeremy greeted him as he bounded up the steps. Puzzled and anxious by Patrick's unexpected arrival, Jeremy shook his hand, and hissed, "Everything all right?"

Patrick smiled reassuringly. "Couldn't be better." Putting his arm around Jeremy's shoulder, he said quietly, "Now don't jump and exclaim—just listen. I've left Tony around the back of the house in that small copse of locust trees. Go to him. But leave him just as you find him, hard as it may be." Patrick's fingers dug into Jeremy's shoulder. "Swear to it—on your honor."

Utterly at sea, his blue eyes big and confused, Jeremy nodded. "On my honor—I swear it."

Some of the tension ebbed from Patrick's body. "Good man! I will explain all when I return. I shan't be long—I'll join you as soon as I can. Now go!"

Jeremy was halfway to the copse before the strangeness of Patrick's actions really struck him. What in blazes was happening? Why did he have to go to Tony? Why hadn't *Tony* come with him? Worried and increasingly anxious, Jeremy increased his speed.

His handsome face giving nothing away, Patrick strolled into the charming sitting room where the butler Lawrence had shown him. Pleased to have found the lady of the house alone, a dazzling smile lit his face. Bowing extravagantly over her hand, he murmured, "Good afternoon, madam. I trust my call does not inconvenience you?"

Obviously puzzled by the visit of a gentleman she barely knew and whose reputation was rather alarming, Mary said with cool politeness, "No. Of course not, but I must confess that I was surprised when Lawrence announced you."

"Indeed," Patrick said, as he took the seat across from her she had indicated. Placing his riding gloves on his thigh, he glanced at her. "Actually," he said, "you should have been expecting me to come calling eventually." When Mary looked blank, he shook a teasing finger in front of her. "Oh come now, surely you did not expect your part in the fiasco five years ago to go undetected? You must have known that sooner or later, I, or someone very like me, would appear on your doorstep."

Mary's lovely face paled and one hand went to her throat. "W-W-What do you mean?"

Patrick smiled, not nicely. "Why only, madam, that the time to pay the piper has come. You've had five years in which to enjoy the results of your little escapade, and now I'm afraid that it is going to cost you."

"I do not know what you are talking about," Mary said weakly. Gathering some of her courage, she added more strongly, "And I find your words and attitude insulting. I wish you to leave—now, before I ring for my butler to throw you out."

Patrick leaned comfortably back in his chair. Pulling out the much creased and worn missive, he tossed it carelessly onto Mary's lap. "Read that," he said, "and then see if you still wish to ring for your butler."

Mary picked up the folded note and, opening it, read it. It seemed to take her a long time, and when she finally put it down and looked across at him, she seemed to have aged a decade.

At the open contempt and scorn in Patrick's gaze, her eyes dropped. She took a deep breath and, with all the serenity she could muster, said, "I am afraid that I still don't understand. What does this have to do with me?"

"I didn't come here to fence with you, Madam," Patrick replied grimly. "Continue to waste my time and my price will go up." Shrugging off his indolent pose, he leaned forward. His eyes were like chips of ice, his voice thick with fury, "I know the part you played in destroying Tony's engagement to Arabella five years ago. I know that you spied on her and once you discovered when and where she was meeting with Tony, you told Daggett, and he arranged the rest of it. That note in your lap is proof of it. The only thing you and I and he have to discuss is how much you are going to pay me to keep my mouth shut."

Mary started to protest, but the expression on his face stopped her. Sinking back into her chair, the fight seemed to go out of her, and she said miserably, "I never wanted to hurt Arabella. But her father was so opposed to the marriage and when . . . a way of stopping their marriage was suggested, I leaped at it." She buried her blond head in her hands. "You don't know how much I have suffered these past years, watching Arabella pine for that man and knowing that I was the cause of all her heartache. It has not been easy." She lifted her head to stare at him. "Believe me, I never wanted to hurt Arabella—I . . . I thought I was actually helping her." She gazed off in the distance beyond Patrick's shoulder. "But it was all for naught, wasn't it? Tony Daggett is back, and it is clear to me that she still loves him, and that given the opportunity she will marry him. And if that isn't bad enough, now you come to lay all my past sins at my feet."

Patrick rose to his feet. Plucking the note from her fingers and tucking it back into his waistcoat pocket, he said coolly, "I would offer you my condolences, but I am afraid that all my sympathies lie with Arabella and Tony. As for you—write your partner and tell him that his nasty secret is secret no more and that it will take a great deal of money for me to hold my tongue and not expose the pair of you for the vermin you are. I will let you know when and where we shall meet to make an exchange: You'll get the note, and I'll get the money. We'll both be happy. Tony and Arabella need never know of the viper in their midst."

A faint flush lit Mary's pale cheeks. "You can't prove anything,"

"I don't need to. But if I were to show the note to Arabella and tell her that you connived to tear her from Tony, which one of us," he asked with a mocking smile, "do you think she will believe, hmm?"

"Why are you doing this?" Mary demanded angrily. "The extent of your fortune is well-known. You don't need the money."

"Ah, but there you are wrong," he murmured. "Gentlemen of my reckless persuasions are always in need of money. Isn't it wonderful that I have found such an easy way to recoup my losses?"

Patrick bowed insultingly and walked toward the door. His hand on the silver knob, he said over his shoulder, "Write your friend. I am an impatient man—don't make me wait any longer."

Chapter Twenty

❧

When Patrick strolled up to where Jeremy and Tony awaited him, a stern-faced Jeremy greeted him. Jeremy was also pointing a pistol at him. A brief glance assured Patrick that Tony was still safely trussed on his horse, but from the blaze in the blue eyes that bored into his, it was apparent that not only was Tony no longer unconscious but he was also furious. Murderously so.

"I swore to you that I would not untie him, but before you come one step nearer, you have to explain to me what is going on," Jeremy growled.

"Oh, nothing very much," Patrick said easily. "I was merely keeping an oath that I, too, had sworn." His gaze met Tony's glare. Softly he said, "I swore to your wife and unborn child that I would see to it that no harm came to you." He flashed that dazzling grin of his. "You cannot hold it against a fellow for keeping his word, now can you?"

Still deeply puzzled, Jeremy regarded him suspiciously. "I don't understand any of this. Why is he tied up?"

"Put that damned thing down, and I shall tell you," Patrick said without heat, as he brushed past Jeremy and walked over to Tony's horse. He began to unfasten the leather strips that bound Tony to his mount.

Busy with the task of freeing Tony, Patrick explained over his shoulder to Jeremy, "Your new brother-in-law was determined to set himself up as a target for Boots. I disagreed."

His hands free, Tony ripped the gag from his mouth, and snarled, "Damn you Patrick! We had all decided that I was to be the one."

"No," Patrick said calmly, "*You* had decided. I had another idea. Perhaps not a better idea, but one that is more likely to keep you out of harm's way . . . for a while." He shot Tony a crooked grin. "And before you start swearing at me, answer me this: If our positions were reversed, would you have acted any differently than I did?"

Tony grimaced, knowing that Patrick had him there. He shook his head reluctantly. "No—and you damn well know it! But blast it, Patrick! We know Boots will come after me sooner or later, but now you've put yourself directly in his path. He'll have to take you out first."

"Precisely," Patrick said with a purr to his voice. "And then we shall have him." He cocked a brow at Tony. "After all, you will not let him kill me, will you?"

"You know the answer to that," Tony grumbled ungraciously.

Jeremy, who was still watching the two men with a perplexed expression on his face, finally spoke. "Would someone please tell me what is going on?"

Tony and Patrick exchanged a meaningful look;

telling Jeremy of his mother's part in what happened five years ago was not something either man wanted to do.

Smiling at Jeremy, Tony swung down from his horse. "There have been some developments since you left Greenleigh. We found what it was that Boots was after when he, er, visited your sister—it was a note he had written to Molly five years ago, making arrangements for the scene Arabella found at the lodge. We figure that Leyton got the note from Molly since he was one of her patrons. But whether she gave it to him or he took it, we don't know. It is more than probable that she and Leyton were in it together. *Someone* had to explain to Leyton what the note pertained to, and Molly is our only candidate for that.

"We're only guessing, but we think that they—or Leyton alone—tried to blackmail Boots. Boots wasn't having any of it and confronted Leyton, unfortunately on the same afternoon your sister went to call upon Leyton. It's all speculation, but we think Arabella interrupted them. The note got mixed in with her deeds when he shoved everything on the floor. It ended up in Arabella's reticule."

"And then," Jeremy said excitedly, "realizing what must have happened, he tried to steal it back that night when Arabella was driving home from seeing you!"

Tony nodded. "Exactly. And Boots, smart devil that he is, after killing Leyton that same night and not finding the note, concluded that Arabella had to have it." His face tight and grim, Tony added, "I don't even want to think about what would have happened to her if she had not fought him off."

"I wonder why he never made a second attempt,"

Patrick mused, frowning. "If our suspicions are correct, he'd already killed once trying to get it. Why stop?"

"I don't know," Tony admitted. "But I'll make a guess: The note had disappeared, and he couldn't be sure where it was. He'd looked for it at Leyton's place and couldn't find it. Arabella was his next best choice. But he'd taken a chance accosting Arabella, and I'm sure that he has cursed himself a dozen times for having made that foolish move."

"Why foolish?" Jeremy asked puzzled.

"Because if he had never paid Arabella that visit, we would never have become curious about what it was he thought she had. To be sure," Tony went on, "the note would have been found eventually, but that might have been months from now. It's possible that by then your sister might have forgotten the last time she used that particular reticule, and it's a good bet, she—or any of us—would never have connected it to Leyton or the attempt to hold her up that night on the road. Boots would have been wiser to let sleeping dogs lie, and hope that the note never surfaced."

Jeremy nodded, apparently satisfied with Tony's explanation. Tony and Patrick could see him turning the situation over in his mind and, both of them knew the moment the question they dreaded was formed in Jeremy's brain.

Frowning, Jeremy looked at them and asked slowly, "But why are you here?" His gaze fixed on Patrick. "You didn't come to see me, else you would not have sent me away from the house." An uneasy expression in his blue eyes he muttered, "There is only one other per-

son you could have come to see . . . It's Mother, isn't it?
How is she involved?"

"Ah, she is going to help us," Tony said quickly, after
a swift, unhappy glance at Patrick.

"How?" Jeremy demanded, obviously suspicious.

Patrick pulled on his ear. "It isn't easy to explain," he
began slowly. "But we think that Boots took advantage
of her—used her love of your father to benefit himself.
We think that she may know who Boots is. We've narrowed it down to one of Tony's Daggett relatives, but
we don't know which one."

"Does she?"

"Probably," Tony admitted reluctantly.

"And she told you who he is?" Jeremy asked looking
at Patrick.

Patrick looked at Tony, who made a face and
shrugged his shoulders.

"Well, not exactly," Patrick said lamely. "Actually, I
never asked her to name him."

"*What?* Why ever not?" demanded Jeremy, his blue
eyes incredulous. "If Mother knows who this villain is,
why didn't you simply ask her to tell you?"

"Because I didn't want her to know that we don't
know who he is—I acted as if I knew his identity,"
Patrick muttered uncomfortably.

So far Patrick had managed to skip around the complete truth, but keeping Mary's part in the debacle of
five years ago from her son was proving damned difficult. Patrick didn't know how Tony would have handled
the meeting with Mary, but he had managed the situation as best as he was able. Mary Montgomery had been
caught off guard and had confessed more than he had

hoped, but she was no fool and was likely to prove a wily adversary—as Arabella had warned. Even if he had ignored Arabella's advice and had simply asked Mary to name Boots, he didn't think she would have proven to be very cooperative. Everything else aside, she disliked and distrusted both him and Tony—why should she help them? If anything, she was more than likely to throw a rub their way.

He was convinced that Arabella's reading of her stepmother was correct; a demand for Boots's identity would have sealed Mary's lips and revealed the weakness in their own hand. His blackmail attempt and pretense about knowing who Boots was had seemed the likeliest way to find out who had been her partner in destroying the engagement between Tony and Arabella.

"But why? She would have told you. It seems to me," Jeremy said disgustedly, "that you have turned a simple matter into a complicated one."

"Dash it all!" Patrick exclaimed, stung by the criticism from the very man he was trying to protect. "She wouldn't have told me, you young fool!"

"But why not?" Jeremy asked bewildered. "You said she was helping you—why wouldn't she tell you his name?"

Patrick threw an agonized glance at Tony.

"Because she's afraid of him," Tony interjected quickly, improvising as he went. "He's threatened to hurt you and the children if she exposes him, but she's willing to help us trap him. Patrick has asked her to write to Boots, telling him that he has the note, and she has agreed to do so."

It was clear that Jeremy suspected that there was

something smoky about the story he was being told, but the main facts hung together and made a twisted kind of sense. He also discovered that, for the present at least, he preferred to leave the subject of his mother's involvement alone. She was helping them find Boots, and that was the important part.

"So what do we do now?" Jeremy asked quietly.

"We wait for Boots to try to kill me," Patrick said cheerfully, relieved that the heavy ground had been covered safely. "You and Tony shall have the pleasant task of seeing that I stay alive and that we catch Boots in the process of trying to murder me . . . hopefully, before he manages to put a period to my existence."

"I think it will be simpler and much safer, if we merely follow the servant who will be delivering the note that Mary is no doubt writing at this very moment," Tony said dryly. "Since Franklin has his own bachelor quarters in town and Uncle Albert is living at River's Bend, their home plantation, we shouldn't have any trouble identifying Boots."

Tony was correct in the fact that Mary was indeed writing a note to Boots at that very moment, but he miscalculated about her use of a servant to deliver it. Shaken and alarmed by Patrick's visit, it took her several moments to compose herself after he had left. When she finally had herself in hand, she sat down at her dainty writing table and swiftly wrote out her message. The existence of the note to Molly Dobson made her wary about entrusting her own note to a mere servant and after finishing it and sealing it, she decided to see that the missive reached the hand of its intended receiver herself. She could trust Daggett to see that it was destroyed. He was very careful that way. Her lips tightened. And he should have been more careful about what became of the note he had written to that slut Molly Dobson. She shrugged. There was nothing she could do about that now. Now all she had to worry about was seeing that her note reached him and that he could think of a way to pull the teeth from that detestable Blackburne's threats.

Delivering her note to its intended recipient proved relatively easy. It was simple enough for her to press the note into Daggett's hand that night when they met at a small soiree being held at the Gayle plantation. In this case, small meant thirty people or more, and as she wended her way through the gaily garbed group, nodded to this acquaintance and that, she was positive that no one had seen her pass on the note.

Despite Arabella and Jeremy's attendance at the same function and their discreet surveillance, neither one of them was able to report anything of interest back to Tony and Patrick when they met later that evening at Greenleigh.

They were gathered in the front saloon, the four of them scattered comfortably about the room. Tidmore had served the gentlemen whiskey and Arabella a cup of steaming mint tea. Leaving behind a full decanter and a silver pot with more tea, he bowed and departed. Like the good servant he was, his face gave no clue as to what he thought about the oddness of his mistress entertaining two well-known rogues at that hour of the night—even if her brother was present.

Her bronze satin slippers lying on the floor in front of the sofa, her bare feet tucked up under the skirts of her amber-hued silk gown, Arabella said wryly, "Tidmore is bound to wonder what is going on. It is shocking enough that I chose to live by myself, but after tonight, I am sure that he and his wife will be convinced that I am becoming quite fast."

"Will they talk, do you think?" Tony asked, a slight frown marring his forehead.

She shook her head. "No. They are loyal to me." She made a face. "They will just worry and fuss at me— very, very diplomatically and with great affection."

Seated beside her on the couch, his long legs sprawled in front of him, Tony lifted her hand and kissed it. "It is very easy, my love, to view you with great affection. I know I certainly do."

"Must you?" Patrick asked in a pained tone, though his gray eyes were twinkling. "We have important things to discuss—you may woo and court your wife at another time."

Arabella blushed, and Tony laughed.

"Of course," Tony said easily. "And you're right." He glanced across to where Jeremy stood in front of the fireplace, one arm resting on the mantel. "You saw nothing? Nothing at all?"

Jeremy made a disgusted face. "Oh, we saw plenty. All three of the Daggetts were there this evening and Mother greeted and chatted with each one of them. But I never saw her pass any note to one of them."

"Jeremy's right," Arabella added. "If I hadn't known better, I would never have thought she had anything on her mind but visiting and having a pleasant evening with friends. Cousin Agatha was by her side most of the time, and I don't remember there being any particular time Mary was alone with either your uncle or your cousin Franklin." She looked thoughtful. "Or Burgess for that matter. She spoke to each of them, but I couldn't see that she acted strange or different than she did with everyone else. I definitely did not see her pass on anything."

Patrick, who had been seated in the chair across from the sofa where Arabella and Tony sat, got up and took a brief turn around the room. "I was so certain," he said half-angrily, half-ruefully, as he came back to stand in front of the pair on the sofa, "that she would send the message to him by a servant. I thought by now we would know who he is."

"We can't be positive that she has even passed the message on to him," Jeremy said quietly. "While we are here speculating, one of the servants from Highview could be trotting down the road, the note clutched in his hand."

"Thank you very much for that observation, dear brother," Arabella said tartly. "It is so reassuring to me to know that the message that may send a murderer after my husband is at this very moment being delivered."

"Well dash it all, Bella! I was only trying to consider all the possibilities," he replied defensively. "Tony and Patrick spent the entire afternoon and evening lurking in the woods watching for one of the servants to leave, while at the soiree you and I hovered over Mama like a hawk over a rabbit. She probably thinks we've gone daft. I can tell you that Cousin Agatha sent me some deucedly odd looks." He grinned sheepishly. "She even complimented me on my care of my mama. Said I was a good boy to watch over my mother so solicitously."

Everyone smiled. A small silence fell, and they sipped their whiskey and tea and considered the situation.

"Well?" Jeremy finally asked. "What are we going to do now?"

Tony grimaced. "For now, we can do nothing but wait." He glanced at Patrick and grinned. "And as Patrick said earlier, wait for Boots to try to kill him."

Patrick bowed mockingly. "Anything for my friends, dear sir. Even my life." His teasing manner passed, and he mused aloud, "I wonder if Boots has even received the note. Or if, as Jeremy suggested, it is indeed being delivered at this very moment."

If Boots had been surprised when Mary had pressed the tightly folded slip of paper into his hand at the Gayle soiree that evening, he had given no sign of it. A charming smile fixed on his face, he had gone on as if nothing out of the ordinary had just occurred. But the small slip of paper burned in his hand, and even after he had carefully tucked it into his waistcoat pocket, he was uncomfortably aware of it.

It wasn't until after the soiree had ended and he had ridden home that he had any privacy in which to read it. The contents angered him more than they alarmed him, and the more he thought about it, the less disturbed he became. He was almost relieved.

So Blackburne has Molly's note, he thought slowly. *Now isn't that interesting! And he is attempting to black-mail Mrs. Montgomery and me. I wonder whose idea that was? Tony's or Blackburne's?* At any rate, he didn't believe Blackburne's threat for a moment. Or that Tony didn't know every move that Blackburne made. *They probably plotted it all out together,* he mused with a thin smile.

Absently tapping his bottom lip with the note from Mary, he wandered around the small room. It was obvious that he was going to have some major, er, tidying up to do. And rather smartly, too. Mary was no threat; she never had been—which was the only reason she was still alive. No, she'd keep her mouth shut. She had too much to lose if the truth came out. Basically proper ladies were so alarmed by even the merest hint of scandal being attached to their names that most, like Mary Montgomery, would rather die than openly admit having sailed too close to the wind, no matter the reason. So, for the time being at least, she wasn't a problem. But Tony and Patrick . . . They definitely had to be taken care of. And, of course, Arabella, too.

He frowned. He knew it had been a mistake when he had crept into Arabella's bedroom and tried to frighten the whereabouts of the note from her. Except for gaining her room and his undignified escape, nothing had gone right that night. Unconsciously he reached up and touched the spot where the pitcher had hit him. He was, he admitted, still furious at Arabella for having bested him—and with a water pitcher at that!

He had cursed himself for a fool a dozen times for having acted so recklessly that night, knowing that this present situation was his own damned fault. He couldn't have aroused Arabella's curiosity more than if he had sent a note himself, telling her to look for a mysterious object. He glanced at the note he held in his hand. Obviously she had found Molly's note and briefly he wondered where she had found it, but then he moved on to more pressing things.

Tony. Patrick. Arabella. Each one had to die. But how? Avoiding detection and suspicion had always been paramount in his mind—besides the fortune, of course.

He sighed. He certainly hadn't planned to become a murderer. In fact, he had planned nothing, he admitted frankly. It had all just come about.

Certainly he had never planned Mercy's death. He smiled. He had merely wanted to stir things up and see what would happen when Tony learned that she had run off with that Terrell fellow. And it had been so easy to drop the word into the ear of one of the biggest gossips in Natchez, knowing the fool would run straight to Tony with the tale—greatly embellished by that time.

No, he hadn't planned Mercy's death, but he had been pleased that things had worked out so providentially. After her death, he couldn't deny that he had hoped that Tony would drink himself into a stupor just as his father had done and kill himself, but that hadn't happened. Ah well, one couldn't have everything.

As for Elizabeth, well that, he freely admitted, had just been plain bad luck. Of course he hadn't been happy when Tony had remarried. After Mercy had died he had grown used to the idea of Tony breaking his neck someday and the Daggett fortune ending up in its rightful hands, but then *that* pleasing prospect hadn't happened. No, instead Tony had married again.

He had been reasonably content to wait, still not yet having committed himself to cold-blooded murder.

Having become obsessed with the notion of having all of the Daggett fortune—and not just the portion doled out to his side of the family—for his waiting game to pay off, it was imperative that Tony remain unencumbered. Elizabeth had to go, but he hadn't yet hit upon a way to remove her when she had surprised him rifling through her jewelry box that night.

Which one of them had been more surprised was hard to tell, but he at least had had the presence of mind to bring up his pistol and shoot her before escaping out the upper veranda doors. My God! But he had been terrified as he had fled over the railings of the veranda and ran for his horse, hidden nearby in the forest. His heart had pounded so violently he had been convinced that everyone within five miles of him could hear it. But no one did.

Elizabeth's murder had shaken him badly. He had never killed anyone in his life and he had been thoroughly shattered by what he had done—shattered enough that any notion of murdering Tony was temporarily pushed aside. As time had passed, however, he had become more used to the idea of murder to gain what he wanted, and viewed Elizabeth's murder as something that had been simply necessary.

It was the silly bitch's own fault, he thought disdainfully. *If she had gone with Tony to dinner at Blackburne's, as I'd assumed she had, none of it would have happened. Not then at any rate. But certainly before the brat she carried was born.*

It was probably just as well that he had been running so desperately low on cash at the time that he had even considered robbing Tony's rooms upstairs at Sweet

Acres. And he probably wouldn't have, if, when he had called earlier in the day, Tony hadn't mentioned that he was dining at Blackburne's that evening. It had been a mistake on his part, Boots admitted, just to assume that Elizabeth would be accompanying Tony, but it had all worked out in the end.

At least with Arabella, he hadn't had to resort to murder. Yet. He had been as shocked and startled as anyone else when Tony and Arabella had become engaged five years ago. Ironically, he had been nerving himself finally to kill Tony when the engagement had been announced. Used to thinking of the Daggett fortune as coming his way one day, it had been imperative that a wife or child was not in Tony's immediate future. Glad to put off the moment he would have to risk his own neck to kill Tony, he settled for destroying the betrothal. Considering the way her family felt about the engagement, it had been child's play to enlist Mary's help and set up the scene at the lodge. That, he decided with a reminiscent smile, had worked out perfectly.

Until recently. His smile vanished, and he scowled.

He'd invested a lot of time in his quest for Tony's portion of the Daggett fortune. In the beginning he'd never thought it would take so long—he'd certainly never planned to wait for more than a few years to get his hands on it, but he was not a brave and reckless soul like Tony. He had to be careful. Didn't want anyone to suspect *him*. And then, he thought with a smile, there was the Westbrook fortune. Ah, for that he could wait. It made the fortune held by both sides of the Daggett family look paltry in comparison.

In time his money problems had eased, and that had

made the wait more endurable. He would admit, however, that if Tony had managed to break his neck anytime during the past decade or so, he would not have shed any tears—even if it meant giving up a large part of the Westbrook money.

His expression grew sullen. Glancing at Mary's note he realized that he was not going to be able to wait until after Tony inherited the remainder of the Westbrook fortune to act. It was true Tony's current fortune was impressive, but combined with the Westbrook fortune . . . His lips thinned. To have come so close only to lose in the end was galling and a burning sense of angry, bitter resentment flashed through him. That damned Tony! The bloody bastard had ruined everything! He was, he admitted with an ugly smile, going to enjoy finally killing Tony. And his dear friend, Patrick Blackburne. And of course, sweet Arabella. He took a deep, calming breath. Now how, he wondered, was he going to kill the three of them without any hint of blame traveling his way?

Pacing the confines of his room, Boots gave it a great deal of thought. Dawn was just breaking when an idea occurred to him. *Oh, how delicious,* he thought smugly. *And it will work, with no one doubting the conclusion.*

Smiling to himself, he sat down and wrote three notes. Yawning, he stood up and stretched. Bed for a few hours, and then he would see to it that the notes were delivered. By this time the next day, it would all be over. He frowned slightly. There would be, of course, a few more details to take care of, but he didn't feel they were beyond his capabilities. After all, once one had murdered, what were a few more?

*   *   *

When the note was delivered to Arabella that evening, she was sitting on the veranda enjoying the faint, refreshing breeze coming up from the river. The sight of the small black servant astride a rather moth-eaten mule loping up her driveway had surprised her, and when she discovered that he had come expressly to deliver a note to her, she was aware of a flutter of anxiety in her stomach.

She recognized neither the servant, nor the animal, and by the time she had opened the note and read it, servant and mule were already disappearing into the shadows of dusk. Frowning, she reread the note.

Patrick wanted her to meet him at the lodge within the hour. Now why there? If he had just learned some vital information, why didn't he simply come to the house? What was so secret that he needed to meet with her privately? She didn't like it.

Still frowning, she went inside and sat down and wrote her own note. After handing it to Tidmore with the admonition that it was to be delivered immediately, she went upstairs and found her pistol. Tony had been forewarned; she would wait long enough for him to receive her note, making allowances also for him to have a head start before she left for the lodge. She had no secrets from Tony, and if Patrick had something to say, he could tell them both, at the same time. And just to give her an added edge, the pistol would be safely hidden in the folds of the fringed shawl she carried.

Patrick's reaction was much the same as Arabella's. Only he wondered what it was that Arabella had to tell him that could not be said in front of her husband and why she had selected the lodge as the location to meet. He, too, sent a note to Tony, informing him of Arabella's frantic request for a secret meeting at the lodge. And like Arabella, he, too, set out, suspicious and armed, for the lodge.

Boots had anticipated both their actions and to his list of murders he added the two servants sent by Patrick and Arabella. He'd had some wild riding to do and he was quite sweaty and breathless by the time he began his own journey to the lodge. With the two servants dead, their bodies hidden in the brush, he only had to see that his third and final note was delivered. And, of course, it would arrive in Tony's hands much too late to do any good.

It had been a hectic evening, but Boots had timed everything perfectly. He had known Arabella and Patrick would be suspicious, and he had known they would try to contact Tony before leaving for the lodge, so he had staggered the times that their individual notes had been delivered to give himself room in which to arrange things to his satisfaction.

Arriving at the lodge well ahead of the others, he tied his horse some distance away from the clearing where the lodge was situated. He wanted no snorting, neighing horse to disclose his presence.

Darkness had fallen and the silvery gleam from the half-moon overhead gave him just enough light to see his way. Slipping down the path that led from the lodge to Greenleigh, he waited concealed in the rank undergrowth that crowded the narrow pathway. Just when he began to worry that he had miscalculated, he heard Arabella's cautious approach. He smiled. Act One was about to begin.

Arabella had never liked this part of going to the lodge. In daylight, the lodge was a pleasant, scant ten-minute walk from the house, but at night, in near darkness, with thoughts of snakes and other feral creatures moving about, she found it not so pleasant. She had considered bringing a lantern but, not wishing to announce her position if there was something amiss, had discarded the idea.

Concentrating on where she was putting her feet, wishing the faint moonlight shone more clearly through the canopy of trees, she was unprepared when Boots sprang at her from his hiding place. She had only time for a startled cry and then there was a burst of pain and utter blackness.

Feeling very satisfied with himself, Boots half carried, half dragged her unconscious form to the lodge. Kicking open the door, having done his reconnoiter of the interior earlier, he moved confidently through the gaping blackness that greeted him.

Throwing Arabella on the bed, he turned and swiftly struck a flint and lit a candle. In the feeble, flickering light he stared at Arabella, as she lay sprawled across the bed, her fringed shawl tangled beneath her. She looked good, but he was going to make her look even better.

A few minutes later, he stepped back and admired his handiwork. She looked thoroughly disheveled now. Her hair tumbled in wild disarray across the pillows, her shoes and stockings were tossed on the floor and her gown was half-off, revealing a pair of charmingly plump breasts.

He frowned slightly and approaching her once more, arranged her gown so that one lovely thigh was exposed. She looked, he decided happily, quite wanton.

The next part of his plan was easy enough; he had been very careful to allow himself enough time to have events well in hand. Knowing Patrick should be arriving any minute, he secreted himself behind the door and waited for him.

Like Arabella, Patrick approached the lodge cautiously. The feeble, dancing light glimpsed through the cracks in the door did not reassure him. It occurred to him that it could simply be Arabella waiting for him and that she really did have some logical reason for requesting this mysterious meeting. A look of chagrin crossed his face. He was going to feel a complete fool if it turned out that the note was not a hoax.

Every nerve he possessed coiled tight, Patrick slowly pushed open the door. Silence greeted him. His pistol primed and ready in one hand, he inched into the doorway. In the flickering light, the sight of Arabella lying half-naked on the bed startled him, and he took two swift steps toward her before he stopped, his instincts screaming a warning. A warning that came a half second too late.

Like Arabella, Patrick felt only a burst of pain at the back of his head and then nothing. He crashed to the floor, the pistol falling from his hand.

Almost rubbing his hands together with glee, Boots surveyed Patrick's prone form. A perfect Act Two. Now to finish the scene and prepare for Act Three.

Boots was puffing and cursing by the time he had maneuvered Patrick's limp body on the bed next to Arabella. Disposing of Patrick's boots, jacket, cravat, and waistcoat added to his breathlessness, and getting Patrick out of his shirt took him longer than he had planned. But soon enough, all was arranged, and he smiled at the scene before him.

Arabella's head lay on Patrick's naked chest. One of his hands was resting on her equally naked breast. They looked, for all the world, like lovers—which was just what he planned.

Actually it was a very simple plan; the difficulty had been in making certain that each player arrived upon cue. So far, all had gone just as he had assumed it would, and he was feeling rather smug.

In less than a half hour, Tony would arrive, and the final act would take place. Tony would die, as would the other two. When the bodies were found, there would be no doubt in anyone's mind that Arabella had decided to pay Tony back for what had happened five years ago and had taken Patrick as her lover. It would be assumed that Tony surprised the pair of them in bed and in a jealous rage shot them both where they lay. And, of course, crazed by Arabella's betrayal and his own murderous actions, Tony would then turn the pistol on himself. A very neat and tidy ending if he did say so himself.

For a moment, he thought about shooting Arabella and Patrick immediately, before Tony arrived. He had hit them both soundly, and it was unlikely either would regain their senses before it was too late. It was tempting, and would remove a source of possible danger, but he decided against it. It was too close to the time for Tony's arrival, and he didn't want the sounds of pistol fire to scare off his prey.

Suppressing the urge to hum, Boots took another look at the scene he had created, then slipped out into the night. *Time for Act Three,* he thought happily as he crept away. *Come and take your bow, Tony.*

Chapter Twenty-one

❧

Scanning the note he'd just received, Tony scowled. Now what the devil! He didn't believe for one moment that Mary Montgomery had written *him* asking for a meeting at the Greenleigh lodge. There had to be some mistake. He looked again at the outside of the note and saw that it was clearly addressed to him.

He was not familiar with Mary's handwriting, so he couldn't discount the possibility that the note really did come from her, but he doubted it. And as for the servant that had delivered it, the fellow was already gone, disappeared into the night. Tony didn't like that either. There was something damned smoky going on.

Something was up, but what? Had Boots forced Mary to write this note to him? It was a possibility, but Tony doubted that, too.

Convinced that the note requesting him to be at the Greenleigh lodge that night at ten was a trap, Tony wandered restlessly about his study. It wasn't, he admitted, beyond the realm of probability that Mary *had* written

the note. She had to know that he could influence
Patrick and perhaps she planned on pleading with him
to intervene. He scowled again, even more blackly. It
didn't make sense, but it could be true. She would be
desperate, and desperate people did not always do the
sensible thing. But why had she chosen the lodge? That
was what made him doubly suspicious. A meeting at
Highview wouldn't have raised his eyebrow. But the
lodge?

He glanced at the gilt clock on the mantel. It was
nearly nine thirty, and if he intended to make the meeting, he had better get going.

It never entered Tony's mind not to go to the lodge. It
did enter his mind to take precautions and be on the alert
for anything that smelled of a trap.

Consequently, he tied his horse some distance from
the lodge and proceeded silently on foot the remainder
of the way. He found Patrick's horse tied to a young
sapling almost immediately, and the feeling that he was
walking into danger increased.

Like Patrick, he had his pistol primed and ready as he
crept toward the door of the lodge. The flicker of light
leaking around the edges of the door did not reassure
him either.

Tony hesitated for several minutes outside the shut
door. The windows were barred from inside, and there
was no way of seeing into the lodge. Except, he thought
with a grim twist of his lips, by opening the door.

Standing off to the side, his back pressed against the
wall of the lodge, he carefully lifted the latch and
pushed the door inward. The heavy wooden door
creaked as it opened, and Tony held his breath, wonder-

ing if he was to be met with pistol fire. When nothing happened, when only silence met his ears, he cautiously maneuvered to where he could glance inside.

The sight of Patrick and Arabella lying together half-naked on the bed caught his gaze and for one ugly, painful second, he actually believed what he was seeing. Fury and anguish knifed through him as the knowledge that Arabella and Patrick had betrayed him hit him. But that thought vanished almost as soon as it had been formed. No. Arabella loved him—he did not doubt it. And she would never betray him. Patrick was as loyal a friend as one could find and he, too, would never betray him. Knowing that he was staring at a carefully staged scene, he watched for several seconds more, the knot in his chest disappearing when he was able to discern the soft rise and fall of the chests of the two on the bed. They were alive!

Reassured that Arabella and Patrick were still alive, he smiled wolfishly. Someone, he decided contemptuously, had certainly gone to a lot of trouble—and all for naught. He wasn't about to be caught by such an obvious trick.

So what happens next? he wondered. That Boots had set the scene in the lodge was a certainty in his mind. *But where is the bastard and what does he expect me to do? Does he think that I will burst into the room and, presumably, driven mad by jealousy, shoot the pair on the bed?*

A long, slow glance around the portion of the interior that he could see revealed nothing. The lodge was small, and there were only so many places a man, or woman for that matter, could hide. In fact, there was only one place someone could hide, and, springing inside, Tony threw his entire weight against the door, slamming it back against the wall. Anyone concealed behind the door would have been crushed and from the crash of the door meeting the solid wall, Tony knew that only empty space lay behind the door. *Well, that took care of that place,* he thought dryly, as he stepped away.

Cold metal suddenly met his temple, and he heard a male voice purr behind him, "Very good, cousin. I knew that I would not catch you as easily as your friend there on the bed." The voice hardened, and the pistol pressed painfully into his skin. "Now drop your pistol, or I shall be forced to kill you as you stand."

Tony hesitated, knowing it was likely that he was a dead man, no matter what he did. Should he take his chances? Or follow directions, hoping for a better chance? A second jab with the pistol and a snapped, "Unless you want to see Arabella die this very moment, do it *now*!" had Tony's finger easing off the trigger and his pistol clattering to the floor.

Boots relaxed slightly, his pulse slowing. Catching Tony had been the most uncertain part of his plan, but the fool had acted predictably.

"Move," Boots ordered, pushing Tony farther into the room. Careful to keep himself behind Tony, he kicked the door shut with his foot.

Elated and excited at how easily his plan was unfolding, Boots was aware of an insane desire to giggle. Everything had gone so well! And in a few minutes, it would all be over—he would have won the biggest gamble of all. He frowned. Losing the rest of the Westbrook fortune was a blow, but he would manage to endure. The urge to giggle returned. Oh, yes, he would endure with a fortune that would open the eyes of everyone around him.

Giving Tony another shove, he said, "Sit there. At the table, and keep your hands where I can see them."

The sight of Tony meekly obeying him gave him a stab of pleasure, and, full of smug satisfaction, the tendency to gloat could not be entirely suppressed. Stepping in front of Tony, but keeping beyond the range of that powerful body, Burgess asked, "Did you really think you could best me, cuz? Did you?"

Tony stared at his younger cousin's gleeful face, his own face revealing only polite interest. He supposed that in some part of his mind he was shocked. Burgess had never really been considered seriously for the role of Boots, and yet, Tony admitted slowly, he should have, recalling now Burgess's jealousy of Franklin and his hunger to make a mark in the fashionable world—a hunger thwarted by Alfred's tightfisted ways.

"Obviously, I did," Tony said coolly, in reply to Burgess's taunt, "or I never would have come in answer to your little note." He nodded toward the bed. "Is that how you got them to come here, too?"

His blue eyes gleaming maliciously, Burgess replied, "You don't believe what is before your very own eyes? That Patrick and dear, sweet Arabella are lovers?"

Tony smiled wolfishly again. "No, I don't—you miscalculated there."

Burgess frowned. "I did not! Else you would not be where you are at this very moment."

Ignoring Burgess's comment, Tony went on easily, "You have been busy, I'll grant you that. Do you know that I did not really suspect you? I was certain that it had to be either your father or your brother."

"That pair!" Burgess said scathingly. "They are all talk. Neither one of them would have taken the risks that I have. As a matter of fact, since Molly's death and the knowledge that you could not have killed her, my father has actually begun to wonder about some of the other incidents in your past. Do you know, he had the gall to ask me just the other day if I thought you had killed Elizabeth?"

Tony's eyes narrowed. "And what did you tell him?" Tony asked silkily. "That no, I had not, but that you had?"

Burgess smiled and Tony's hands involuntarily clenched into fists. "Now, now," Burgess teased, "none of that. Put your hands back where they belong."

It was clear that Burgess wanted to preen and brag, and Tony was perfectly willing to allow him to do so. He was very aware of what would happen when his cousin had grown tired of bragging—his wife, his friend, and he would die. With that in mind, Tony asked with deceptive idleness, "Did you kill Elizabeth?"

"I did indeed. Although, I will confess that I had not planned to. It was an accident—she caught me rifling through her jewelry box, and I really had no choice but to shoot her." Burgess smiled at the murderous look in Tony's eyes, and he added with deliberate cruelty, "I'll confess that it was a rather fortunate accident for me; it showed me how easy murder could be. Do you know," he went on conversationally, "that if I had not been forced to kill Elizabeth that we might not be having this conversation right now? After I killed her, I realized that murder was a relatively simple thing to do—and that it solved so many problems."

Holding his fury at bay with an iron will, Tony fought to keep his features bland. Burgess was enjoying himself too much to consider that the prudent thing would have been to kill them and make his escape. And Tony certainly had no intention of pointing that out to him— or of letting the bastard know just how much his words clawed at Tony's very heart. As long as it kept them alive, Tony was willing to let him babble on. Time was the only asset they had. Given enough time, Tony reminded himself, Patrick or Arabella might regain consciousness. And if one of them did . . .

"Is that so?" Tony asked. "Is that how you plan to get rid of your father and brother? Murder them? I assume for your scheme to work that they will have to die. It *is* your plan to inherit everything, isn't it? All of it?"

"Yes, it is," Burgess replied, disappointed that Tony was taking things so calmly. "Father may save me the trouble—just as I kept hoping you would have the courtesy to break your neck, I am hopeful that Father will take himself off in a fit of apoplexy. Of course, if he doesn't, I may have to help him. And as for Franklin— do you know, I shall enjoy killing him?" Burgess's eyes gleamed. "He is so like you. Arrogant. Lording his position over me. Always letting me know that *he* is the eldest son and that he shall be the one to inherit the majority of Father's wealth."

Tony forced himself to look comfortable, stretching his long legs out in front of him, leaning back in the chair. His indolent posture disguised the coiled, poised strength of his body, the leashed power straining to explode. If only Burgess would come within striking range. All Tony needed was an opening. Just one tiny opening.

"What about Mary Montgomery? Is she to die, too?"

Burgess made a face. "Perhaps. It all depends upon how well she takes your deaths. I'm assuming that she will accept everything at face value—as will everyone else. After all, your reputation is well-known. I doubt anyone will have any trouble believing that you killed Arabella and Blackburne—they already think you killed Mercy and Elizabeth."

Tony cocked a brow, and asked, "Don't you think that some people might question the coincidence of my finding Arabella in a compromising position with my best friend? A position that bears marked resemblance to what she found five years ago in this very same place?"

Burgess shook his head decisively. "Don't be ridiculous! It would take a dunce not to see that Arabella was paying you back. No one would think any different."

The problem, Tony admitted darkly, was that Burgess was probably right. No one would likely question the findings. Except Jeremy, he thought suddenly. And Jeremy would be no match for Burgess. Unless he stopped him, Tony was bitterly aware that not only would he, Arabella and Patrick die, but Jeremy, too. Conscious of time slipping away from them, Tony slanted a covert glance at the pair on the bed. His heart nearly stopped when he realized that Arabella was stirring, that her lashes were fluttering, and that one of her hands was absently rubbing her temple.

He had hoped that it would be Patrick who regained

consciousness first. Filled with a gnawing sense of terror of what might happen if Burgess realized that Arabella was no longer insensible, Tony sat up straighter, and drawled, "It appears that you have it all figured out."

Burgess nodded. "Indeed I have. I have waited a long time for this moment. Of course, I never intended to wait this long. After Mercy died so providentially, I kept hoping you'd break your neck, and then I'd only have Father and Franklin to worry about. None of it was really planned," Burgess admitted idly. "It just seemed to fall in place—although I did grow tired occasionally of the waiting. If it weren't for my great-aunt's money and your Westbrook fortune, I would have killed you years ago. You should be quite grateful to Auntie Meg—if she hadn't left me her fortune, I would have been compelled to seek an earlier resolution to my financial difficulties. But dear Auntie Meg came to my rescue." Burgess grinned. "You might say you owe the last several years of life to dear Auntie."

"And for that I am exceedingly thankful," Tony said, risking another swift glance at the bed from underneath his lashes. Arabella's eyes were wide-open, staring at him in horror. She knew their danger, and his heart twisted at the knowledge that these might be their last moments together. There had to be a way out for them, he thought stubbornly. They had endured too much for it to end this way. For the moment, however, he was aware that all he could do was to keep Burgess talking. Taking a deep breath, he sought frantically for some way of continuing the conversation—if it could be called that.

"What about Mercy?" Tony asked abruptly. "How did you arrange that?"

On the bed, her head aching, her heart thumping madly, Arabella barely heard Burgess's reply. As she had gradually drifted up toward consciousness, Tony's voice was the first thing she recognized. For a moment, hearing his voice and the steady beat of a heart beneath her ear, she had thought that she was lying safely in her bed at Greenleigh with Tony. Burgess's voice had shattered that notion and brought memory crashing back. For several stunned seconds she had lain there, listening to the ugly story unfolding just a few feet away, trying desperately to take it all in—and equally desperately seeking a way to save them from certain death.

Aware that they had little time and that Tony's question was merely a ploy to keep Burgess's attention on himself, she fought to gather her scattered thoughts. Her head felt as if it had been stuffed with cotton wool, and her temples were throbbing out a vicious tempo, but she pushed those discomforts aside. She had known this was a trap, hadn't she? And she had taken precautions, hadn't she? The pistol! Had it fallen from her grasp when Burgess had hit her? Where was it? Heedless of the pain ripping through her head, she focused on trying to think clearly.

She moved slightly and when she did, she became aware of something digging into her back. She nearly groaned with relief when she realized what it had to be: the pistol. It was underneath her, tangled in the shawl.

Keeping her eyes half-shuttered in case Burgess happened to glance her way, she carefully, slowly, snaked a hand beneath herself. It seemed to take forever, but in a few blessed seconds her questing fingers touched the cool metal of the pistol. A feral grin curved her lips. Burgess was about to be very surprised.

Oblivious to anything but the pleasure of a captive audience, Burgess happily replied to Tony's question. "Mercy? Oh, I did no arranging. Well, perhaps a trifle. When I heard that she had run away with Terrell, I merely saw to it that the information reached your ears. I don't know what I expected to happen, but I can't say that I was displeased by the results of my meddling."

"And is that when you decided that my fortune would do you very nicely?"

"Oh, no. Not at first. In those days, I was simply trying to live on that miserable allowance Father thought was adequate for his youngest son." Almost meditatively, he added, "I had already considered killing Father and Franklin, but I hadn't quite brought myself to the sticking point." He smiled. "I hadn't yet discovered how simple it was to murder someone—it took dear Elizabeth's death for me to learn that lesson."

One part of his mind on Burgess, the other on Arabella's stealthy movements, Tony gibed, "And, of course, killing a grown man is not quite the same as killing a helpless woman."

An ugly expression contorted Burgess's features. "I killed Leyton. It wasn't much different than Elizabeth or Molly."

"Probably not," Tony said coldly, wondering if he could goad Burgess into making a false move. It was worth a try, and Burgess, Tony thought savagely, had had things too much his own way for long enough. "Like the little coward you are, you stabbed him in the back. Not quite the same as murdering a defenseless woman. But near enough."

"How d-d-dare you!" Burgess spluttered furiously. "I am no coward."

"Aren't you? You don't think it is cowardly to shoot down a pregnant woman in cold blood? To strangle a woman half your strength? To stab a man in the back?" Tony shook his head. "They certainly sound like the acts of a sniveling coward to me."

"Damn you!" Burgess spit, fury roaring through him. Stepping near Tony, the pistol wavering from its position slightly, he struck him a savage blow across the cheek. "Take it back!" he nearly screamed. "I am no coward. And now you'll see for yourself."

He raised his hand to strike Tony again, and it was the opening that Tony had been waiting for. Like a big cat springing upon its prey, Tony leaped at Burgess, one hand brutally clamping on the wrist of the hand in which Burgess held the pistol, the other closing around Burgess's neck.

Burgess's eyes bugged, and he gagged and clawed ineffectually at the hand crushing his throat. Tony smiled, and Burgess increased his efforts, terror cascading through him. Unable to escape the suffocating force at his throat, he twisted and fought to free his pistol hand.

At Tony's first move, Arabella, her own pistol held ready, struggled up from the bed. A wave of nausea swept over her as she stood and she swayed wildly on her feet. For one terrifying moment she feared she would black out, but she shoved away the darkness that threatened her.

Locked together in a dreadful parody of an embrace,

the two men rocked violently as if buffeted by a high wind. In the feeble light of that one candle, their shadows danced grotesquely on the walls. The air was filled with their labored breathing, their grunts muffled as each struggled to overpower the other. It was as ugly as it was primitive.

Stronger, coolheaded, knowing that all their lives lay in the balance, Tony fought with savage intensity. With explosive strength, he smashed the hand in which Burgess held the pistol against the wooden table, smiling fiercely at the scream that came from Burgess. He did it again and again, and finally he had the pleasure of hearing the pistol thump when it hit the floor.

Nearly blind with fury at the knowledge of all this man had cost him, Tony proceeded to take him apart inch by inch, every cry, every moan that came from Burgess a balm and blessing to his anguished heart. It was only Arabella's soft voice that brought him to his senses. "Don't, Tony. Stop. Don't kill him—he isn't worth it." With disgust, as much at his own loss of control, he let the man's bloodied body slump to the floor.

The next instant, Arabella was in his arms and his mouth buried in her bright curls, he muttered, "I love you. I love you. I will love you until the stars fade and forever ends."

"I know, I know, my love," she replied huskily, "I love you the same way—until forever ends."

He lifted his head and looked down at her glowing face. "You're not hurt?"

She smiled faintly. "My head aches, but it is nothing that a cool compress and time will not cure."

Shaken by how close they had come to death, Tony

jerked her next to him. "Jesus! Sweetheart, I do love you."

Absently putting the pistol in the deep pocket of her gown, Arabella reached up and gently touched his cheek. "Not more than I love you."

"If you two are through declaring yourselves," Patrick said with a muffled groan, as he sat up and put a hand to his head, "I would suggest that we do something about that vermin on the floor."

Over Arabella's head, Tony glanced at Patrick. "How badly are you hurt?"

Patrick made a face. "My pride, dear friend, far more than my head." He looked at Burgess, an expression of surprise crossing his handsome features. "Boots was Burgess?"

Tony nodded. "Yes. He fooled us all. I never considered him, mainly because I did not think that anyone would be cold-blooded enough to kill both father and brother." Dryly he added, "It seems that I was wrong. Almost fatally so."

Patrick struggled from the bed and, after picking up his shirt from the floor and shrugging into it, staggered over to sit on the chair so recently vacated by Tony. "I feel an utter fool. To think that I allowed that bit of frippery to best me. I shall not live the indignity of it down anytime soon." Patrick grimaced and gingerly rubbed the back of his head. "I knew it was a trap, but I thought that I was prepared for it." He cast a look at Tony. "It is a good thing that you got my message—else we would all be dead."

Tony frowned. "What message? The only message I received was supposedly from Arabella's stepmother."

Having been reminded of her own nakedness when Patrick had reached for his shirt, Arabella had turned away and swiftly rearranged her bodice. Rejoining the conversation, she said, "I sent you one, too. I knew that the note from Patrick could not be true, and I wrote you telling you that I was meeting him here at eight o'clock."

They all three looked at each other and then down at the softly groaning Burgess. "It would seem," Tony said grimly, "that my cousin planned for every contingency. I fear that both of your servants are dead."

Arabella pressed her face against Tony's chest. "I am almost sorry that I stopped you from killing him," she muttered.

"Which brings us to the question: what are we going to do with him?" Patrick inquired wearily. "If we are surprised at his identity, how are we going to convince anyone else of his villainy? We have little evidence but the note to Molly and, of course, our testimony as to what happened tonight." His lips twisted wryly. "The problem is, that with our reputations"—he glanced at Arabella—"with apologies to the lady, no one is likely to believe our telling of the tale." He looked at Tony. "I fear that everyone will think that she is lying to protect you."

"Oh, now I do wish I had not stopped Tony from killing him." Her eyes big and anxious, she asked, "Surely we cannot let him get away with all his evil deeds. I did not hear your entire conversation, but he *is* the person who killed Molly and Leyton, isn't he?"

"Yes, he confessed—bragged about both killings," Tony said wearily. "And Elizabeth's, too."

"So what are we going to do with him?" Patrick asked simply.

Involved in their own conversation, none of them were paying attention to Burgess. Keeping his eyes closed and feigning unconsciousness, he listened to them, waiting with deadly patience for a chance to turn the tables. He was, he reminded himself, *very* good at waiting. Knowing that he was no match for Tony and Patrick, he risked a swift glance in their direction, looking for his pistol. His pulse leaped. There, lying on the floor where he had dropped it, was the pistol. It was not more than two feet away.

Stealthily he inched toward the weapon, an ugly smile curving his battered lips when his fingers finally closed around it. The fools! Did they really think that they could best *him*?

Ignoring the aches of his beaten body, with a nearly maniacal will he surged to his feet, the pistol held firmly in his hand. At the incredulous expression on the other three faces, he giggled. "I told you," he boasted, "that I was the best. You cannot beat me."

With the pistol, he motioned Arabella away from Tony. "This isn't quite how I planned it, but it will do," he said with a terrifying smile on his bloodied face. "Yes, it will do very nicely, indeed." He pointed the pistol at Tony. "And you, dear cuz, will be the first to die."

Arabella didn't hesitate. Heedless of the danger, she hurled herself at Burgess, slamming into him like a small cannonball. Caught totally by surprise, Burgess staggered unsteadily and Tony was on him in a flash, his powerful grip forcing the hand in which Burgess held the pistol upward. Patrick sprang from his chair intent upon joining the fray, but a wave of blackness swept over him and he stumbled weakly to the floor.

Burgess and Tony were locked together in a deadly duel. There was no mercy in Tony's face as he fought for possession of the pistol. Both men knew that only one of them would survive this fight.

Horrified and furious, Arabella cast a desperate glance around the small room for a weapon. Then with a gasp at her own stupidity, she remembered the pistol in her own pocket. She snatched it free and swung it in the direction of the two men. Her skill with the pistol was minimal and she knew it. Even worse, staring at the intertwined bodies of Tony and Burgess as they strove violently to overpower the other, she was terrified of hitting Tony by mistake. Patrick was an excellent shot, but a swift look in his direction revealed him retching painfully at the side of the table—Burgess had hit him far more viciously than he had Arabella, and he was paying for it. He would be of little use for several more minutes—minutes they did not have.

Unable to stand by helplessly, yet afraid of shooting Tony, she was on the point of trying to get near to the struggling pair to be certain of her target when the pistol in Burgess's hand went spinning away. With a feral scream, Burgess smashed a fist into Tony's face. Tony staggered back and Burgess leaped into the shadowy darkness where the pistol had fallen.

Tony was blocking her line of fire and knowing there was not a moment to lose, Arabella shouted, *"Tony!"* and as he swung in her direction, tossed him the pistol.

The pistol sailed through the air, flashing silver in the flickering candlelight. Her aim had been true, and, with a thrill, she saw Tony's hand close round the weapon. He swung back around and in that instant Burgess came plunging out of the shadows.

Two shots rang out. An expression of astounded fury on his face, Burgess stared down at the widening splotch of blood that bloomed in his chest. "You shot me," he said accusingly, as he stared across at Tony.

"And you missed me," Tony said coolly, despite his ragged breathing.

Burgess slumped to the floor, a pool of blood spreading out from his body.

There was a stunned silence, then Arabella was in Tony's arms once more. Patrick weakly knelt beside Burgess and a second later looked at the other two. "He's dead," he said flatly.

Arabella shuddered. "Oh Tony," she cried, "I am ashamed to say it, but I am not the least sorry he is dead. He was a terrible man."

"That he was," Tony agreed, kissing her softly on the forehead and temples. He pushed her slightly away from him and smiled tenderly down at her. "You saved our lives, sweetheart. If you had not thrown me the pistol—"

With only the merest tremor in her voice she said, "Well, I am not a very good shot. It seemed only logical to get the pistol in the hands of someone who was."

Patrick and Tony both laughed, some of the tension of the night easing.

"So," Patrick said a few minutes later, "what are we going to do now? We can't leave him here. And, I think we are agreed that naming him as a cold-blooded killer will only rebound on us."

Tony looked thoughtful. "His horse has to be somewhere nearby. I think," he said slowly, "that Burgess will have suffered a tragic end at the hands of a murderous highwayman."

"Hmm, it might work," Patrick agreed. "Let's get busy."

Kissing Arabella, Tony said, "I'll see you back to Greenleigh, and then Patrick and I must be busy. We'll talk later tonight—after we have disposed of Burgess."

The discovery the next morning of the body of Burgess Daggett on the outskirts of Natchez had all of the area buzzing. Polite folk were outraged that such a dastardly act could occur so close to town and to such a prominent member of their society. There were calls for the beleaguered Governor Gayoso to *do* something. And if he wouldn't do something, then perhaps they would be better off under American rule. Everyone knew Americans *got things done*!

But the discovery of Burgess's body aroused none of the furor that the announcement of Arabella's marriage to Tony Daggett did. Everywhere one met, the topic of the stunning marriage was the first thing discussed—as well as their sordid parting five years ago. Some thought their marriage wildly romantic, others that Arabella was a fool. Some hardened gamblers even wagered on the odds of Arabella surviving the first year of married life. To all of it the newly wedded pair turned a deaf ear; they had each other, and that was all that mattered.

Before the announcement of their marriage had been

made public, Arabella and Tony had traveled to Highview to tell Mary. It had been an awkward meeting.

"I see," Mary said when Arabella had finished giving her an expurgated version of the circumstances of the secret marriage. No mention of Burgess's villainy was mentioned—or Mary's part in having helped part them years ago. "A runaway marriage is not what I would have wished for you, but you are old enough to make your own decisions—something I should have seen . . . years earlier." Her eyes painfully searched Arabella's. "You must love him very much."

"I do," Arabella replied quietly. "More than life itself."

Mary forced a smiled. "Then I wish you happy." She looked at Tony, who stood silently at Arabella's side. "Treat her well, she deserves great happiness."

"I intend to, madam." His voice hardening a little, he added, "And yes, she certainly does deserve happiness. We both do—after all, we've waited five years for this moment."

Mary flushed, and her gaze dropped.

In the hall, Arabella hissed, "Couldn't you have been more polite? You know she feels guilty and is sorry for her part in what happened."

"Not sorry enough for my liking," he muttered. "We might have been killed."

"She doesn't know that," Arabella said softly. "And she doesn't need to know it either. Her guilty conscience will be penance enough. Let it be."

His dark mood lifting, he glanced down at her. "You know I can deny you nothing. Very well, sweetheart— I'll *try* to be a more amenable son-in-law in the future."

Jeremy came bounding up to them just then. His expression eager, yet wary, he asked, "Did you tell her my part in it all?"

"Since you insisted that we do so, we could hardly have not done so," Tony said with a gleam of amusement in his eyes. "I am sure that your mother has no doubts where your feelings lie in regards to our marriage."

Jeremy nodded. "It will make it easier for her to accept," he said earnestly, "if she knows that I am firmly on your side."

"Thank you," Tony said quietly. "You have proven yourself to be a good and loyal friend."

Jeremy blushed. "T-T-Thank you," he stammered out. An expression of regret crossed his face. "I am only sorry that I was not there at the lodge when Burgess died."

There had been no attempt to keep the truth about Burgess's death from Jeremy. He had been as astonished as the others to learn the identity of Boots. Thinking of that he asked, "How is your uncle taking his death?"

Tony shrugged. "It is hard to say—there was certainly no love lost between them. I am sure he grieves, but how deeply or what he might suspect is not known to me." Tony grinned crookedly. "At least he has not accused me of murdering his son—yet."

Tony had been jesting, but that afternoon when Billingsley announced that Alfred had come to see him, he was aware of a sinking feeling. Tensely he waited for his uncle's entrance into the study.

Stiff greetings were exchanged, and when Tony offered a chair and refreshments, they bluntly were declined.

Standing rigidly before him, Alfred said, "You are no doubt wondering at my call."

Warily Tony nodded.

"I shall not keep you in suspense. Yesterday, that woman of Molly's—Annie—came to call upon me. She brought with her a small book that Molly had given her for safekeeping. It made for unpleasant reading. Among other things, Molly wrote of her liaison with Burgess—including his part in the destruction of your engagement five years ago. She also laid out the scheme she and Leyton concocted to blackmail him." Heavily, he said, "I suspect that Burgess may have murdered them because of that."

Alfred looked as uncomfortable as Tony had ever seen him. If fact, he looked damned embarrassed.

Clearing his throat, Alfred plunged on unhappily. "I have wronged you, and I give you my apologies. Not only were you not the blackguard I thought you then, but it seems my own son is far blacker than you ever were." Baldly, he added, "The boy Marcus is my grandson. Molly wrote that Burgess was his father."

"I would not," Tony said quietly, "want Marcus taken from the Jacksons. He is happy there."

Alfred nodded. "I am aware of that—and I am bitterly aware of my failings as a parent. That a son of mine—" He stopped, and, sighing gustily, said, "When it is appropriate, I would like the boy to know that I am his grandfather. And with your permission, I would like to arrange to visit him and have him visit with me.

Someday I will want him to have his father's share of my estate—even if he is illegitimate."

"I think that can be arranged," Tony said, thinking that perhaps Alfred's astonishing proposal was best for Marcus.

Alfred's eyes searched his. Painfully, he said, "I cannot say that we will ever be friends, but I am sorry for many of the things I thought of you in the past."

After Alfred had left, Tony stared out of the window for a long time. It was clear that Alfred did not know the full extent of Burgess's villainy, and while Alfred had guessed that Burgess had murdered Molly and Leyton, he would never know that Elizabeth's death lay at Burgess's door, too. And Tony was satisfied that it was so. The past was behind them.

That evening, Patrick came to dine with Tony and Arabella at Sweet Acres. The conversation was lively and amusing, and it was only when they had left the dining room and were seated in the gracious front saloon, the gentlemen enjoying brandy, Arabella a cup of tea, that the subject turned serious.

"Do you think we have brushed through the worst of it?" Patrick asked as he took a sip of his brandy.

Tony nodded. "It appears so. No one seems to doubt that Burgess's death was a tragedy."

Patrick's mouth twisted. "You know it really riles me that he has gone to his grave with everyone thinking he was such a nice fellow—even if his father knows part of the truth about him. But what irritates me even more is that you will be forever blamed for what happened to Elizabeth. It is flagrantly unfair."

Seated on the settee next to his wife, their clasped

hands lying between them, Tony merely smiled. "My shoulders are broad. Besides, just consider how well my black reputation will serve me when my daughters reach marriageable age. No gentleman would dare trifle with their tender hearts—I might be moved to murder them."

"Tony!" Arabella cried. "That is not amusing. And we may not have any daughters. What if we have only sons?"

"Oh, but I intend to have daughters," he said with a smile that made her pulse leap. "I shall settle for nothing less than at least two daughters with their mother's bright red hair and lovely eyes."

"And if fate does not cooperate?" she asked archly.

His eyes gleamed. "Then we shall just have to keep practicing until we get it right."

Arabella blushed and looked away.

Patrick laughed and stood up. "I think," he said lightly, "that it is time that I leave you alone—if I see the pair of you together and listen to you much longer, I might forsake my long-standing rule against marriage."

Smiling, Tony and Arabella walked him to the front veranda and watched him mount his horse.

"I shall stop in before I leave for London," Patrick said as he regarded the two of them standing nearby.

"You are determined then to go to England for a while?" Tony asked.

Patrick nodded, a lazy smile in his gray eyes. "There is nothing here for me, and you, my friend," he added with a sly glance in Arabella's direction, "are going to be preoccupied for some time. Years, perhaps."

Tony laughed, and they waved him away.

Returning to the house, Arabella asked as they

walked toward the salon, "What will happen to him? Do you think he will ever marry? Find the happiness we share?"

Shutting the door behind them, Tony pulled Arabella into his arms. Kissing her soundly, he said thickly a few seconds later, "The happiness that we share? Perhaps—and I wish him well if his heart is ever snared. Certainly I hope he does not travel the torturous path that we trod." He kissed her again more deeply. "Right now," he murmured, "I do not want talk about Patrick. I want to talk about us, our baby, how much I adore you and then . . ." He grinned wickedly. "And then I intend to make love to my beautiful wife."

"Oh, Tony, I *do* love you." Arabella sighed, her eyes shining like golden stars. "I will love you forever and ever and ever . . ."

"Yes," Tony said thickly, his hard face soft with love, "forever and ever . . . until forever ends."

More
Shirlee Busbee!

Please turn this page
for a
bonus excerpt
from

SWEAR BY THE MOON

available in
December 2001.

How long she stood there staring at Hirst's body sprawled on the floor, Thea never remembered, but finally something, some instinct for survival, made her move. She was aghast at what had happened, but the strongest emotion in her breast at that moment was a panicked urge to run—as far and as fast as she could.

With the marble statuette still clutched in her hand, she turned, not even certain what she intended to do, when she heard a noise. Fear flooded through her, and, unnerved and horrified by the situation, she could not even tell from whence the sound came—from the hall or somewhere in the room behind her. She only knew that she had heard something: a thump, a scrape, perhaps a gasp—she couldn't tell. In the state she was in, it could have been all three, but it galvanized her like nothing else could have, and she bolted into the darkened hallway.

Intent only on escape, she fled through the shadowy house, almost crying with relief when her hand touched the crystal knob of the front door. Flinging the door wide, she catapulted out onto the stoop and right into the arms of the gentleman who had just ascended the steps.

Strong hands caught her shoulders. Suppressing a scream, Thea gazed wide-eyed up into the dark, powerful face of a stranger. But not an utter stranger—she had seen him before, and even in her agitated state, she recognized him—it was the gray-eyed stranger from the park.

For a moment she stood there staring up at him, her raven hair swirling wildly around her shoulders, her eyes black with emotion, her face starkly white. Then she gasped, muttered something incoherent, and tore herself from his grip. The statuette fell from her hand and clattered at his feet as she half ran, half stumbled down the steps, her purple cloak rippling darkly behind her.

She heard him call out, but heedless of the coach pulled by a team of spirited horses bearing swiftly down on her, she darted out into the road and ran to the safety of her own coach.

Ignoring the startled glance of her servant, she scrambled into the vehicle, and blurted out, "Home. *Now.*"

Obediently the coachman did as she commanded. Feeling the comforting sway and bump of the moving vehicle, Thea sank back against the velvet interior shaking uncontrollably.

She buried her face in her hands. *I killed him*, she thought half-hysterically. *I killed him—my sister's own husband—I struck him and murdered him!*

*   *   *

Patrick stood on the stoop, staring astonished at the spot where Thea had plunged into the street, wondering if he had imagined the whole incident. He shook his head, knowing it had not been his imagination. Her shoulders had been warm and yielding beneath his hands, and he would never forget the stunning effect those huge dark eyes had had upon him.

Even now, he was still oddly breathless, could still remember the faint warmth that had radiated from her body . . . and the stark fear in her eyes. Thoughtfully, he watched the coach that had been parked on the other side of the street pull into the light traffic.

Of course, he recognized her: Thea Garrett. And what, he wondered, was she doing coming out of the house where he was to meet his mother's blackmailer? It crossed his mind that Thea could be the blackmailer, but he dismissed that thought as soon as it occurred. He could think of no connection between Thea and his mother's dead lover; more importantly, he could not even begin to name a reason why someone like Miss Garrett would stoop to blackmail . . . except perhaps the thrill of it?

As the coach disappeared out of sight, Patrick momentarily dismissed the mystery of Thea Garrett and turned back toward the house. The door was half-open. Something had obviously sent Thea Garrett running like a startled fawn, but what? And was whatever had frightened her waiting for him? Or rather for his mother?

His mouth tightened. Someone, he decided grimly, was in for a surprise. He strode purposefully forward, only to stop as his foot hit something. Bending down, he picked up the statuette that Thea had dropped. Curiouser and curiouser.

The statuette in his hand, he stepped gingerly through the opened doorway. As his eyes adjusted to the darkness, he noticed a light at the end of the hallway. Carefully shutting the door behind him, he walked slowly toward the light, deciding that he liked the heft of the statuette in his hand. Perhaps Miss Garrett had, too?

Just outside the lighted doorway, he stopped and listened. The hall narrowed at the point where he stood, half of its width taken up with a handsome staircase that led to the upper floor. Hearing nothing alarming, he looked into the room.

It was cheerful enough, a fire crackling nicely on the hearth, several branches of candles spreading light over the furniture that beckoned one to select a book from the shelves that lined the walls and settle down for a pleasant time. Without too much surprise he stared at the body of the man lying on the floor, blood trickling from the nasty wound on his head. Patrick glanced at the statuette and was even less surprised to see a faint smear of blood on its base.

He studied the fleshy features of the man on the floor. He was aware that he had seen the man about town and that he probably knew him, but at the moment, he could not call his name to mind. Was this his mother's blackmailer? Was the fellow blackmailing Thea Garrett, too? He doubted it. From what he had learned of the notorious Thea Garrett, there was little the public did not know about her. And since she seemed to care little what people thought, he would not have considered her a good prospect for blackmail.

He glanced again about the room. It was charming. Was it a love nest? Now that, he thought cynically, was far more likely. Had Miss Garrett come to meet a lover and they had had a falling-out? He smiled. The lady must be a fierce mistress if the condition of the man on the floor was anything to go by. Having decided that he had a fair idea of what had happened, he put down the statuette and bent down to check how badly the man on the floor had been hurt. His mouth tightened. It was obvious that the man was dead.

Stepping carefully over the corpse, Patrick wasted precious few minutes searching the room for any clue he could find. He found nothing. Nothing to identify the body on the floor, nor more importantly to him, nothing that led to his mother.

After one last thoughtful glance around, he quietly slipped out the back of the house. No use risking someone seeing him leaving the house. And he hoped to God that no one but Thea Garrett had seen him entering it.

Thea had other things to worry about than the gray-eyed stranger she had collided with on the stoop of the house. Reaching home, she dismissed the servants and hurried up the stairs to her room. Flinging off her cloak, she took several agitated steps around the room, her thoughts chaotic.

Pushing back her tumbled curls with a shaking hand, she continued to pace, frightened and appalled by what had happened.

What in heaven's name was she to do? Confess that she had murdered her sister's husband? She shuddered. She was brave, but not that brave, and the instinct for survival was very strong.

She closed her eyes, tears leaking from under her lids. She hadn't meant to kill him. She despised him, but she had never wished him dead. Away. Out of Edwina's life, yes. But not dead. And certainly she had never planned to murder him. But would she be believed? If she told the authorities, would they understand? Or would she, after a horribly public trial, be found guilty and hanged?

Another shudder went through her. Dare she risk it? Wouldn't the truth save her?

A light rap on the door interrupted her tortured thoughts, but before she could deny entrance, Modesty opened the door and walked into the room.

Modesty took one look at Thea's anguished features and immediately crossed the room to her side. Taking one of Thea's icy hands in hers, she demanded, "What is it? What happened?"

It would never have occurred to Thea not to tell Modesty, and the words came pouring out. Modesty listened intently, saying nothing, and when she judged that Thea had told her everything, she urged her to sit down on the bed.

Patting Thea's hands, she said, "I think a hot cup of tea, laced with a healthy dose of brandy, would be just the thing for you right now."

After ringing for a servant, Modesty walked back across the room and sat down on the bed beside Thea's forlorn figure. "It wasn't your fault, you know. He attacked you—you really had no choice." Modesty sighed. "It really is unfortunate that he died—I always said that he was an inconsiderate man. And look, he has just proven my point. Imagine letting himself be killed by a stupid little blow to the head! If that isn't just like him. Inconsiderate to the very last."

"I am very sure that he did not mean to be so inconsiderate," Thea replied dryly.

Modesty smiled at her, pleased to see that bleak look leaving her eyes. "Oh, you're wrong there. If he had planned it, he could not have been more inconsiderate."

There was a tap on the door and after Modesty gave orders for tea and brandy, she rejoined Thea on the bed. Patting Thea's hand again, she said, "I would tell you to put it from your mind, but I know that you will not. You must not, however, allow it to plague you unmercifully." She looked steadily into Thea's eyes. "You did not mean to kill him. It was an accident. A terrible accident to be sure, but an accident nonetheless." When Thea would have spoken, she raised an admonishing finger. "More importantly, there is nothing to be gained by your telling anyone else what happened. When his body is discovered, you will, if you are wise, be as surprised and astonished as anybody else."

Leaning forward, Modesty said urgently, "Thea, confessing what happened will change nothing. It will not bring him back. It will only ruin your life. While I would hope, that if the truth were known, you would not hang, you have to realize that being condemned to death is a very real possibility. Your contempt for him is well-known, and there would be those who would believe that you deliberately killed him——even though we know differently." Modesty's mouth tightened. "Alfred Hirst is not worth ruining yourself for again . . . or dying for. You must see that." When Thea's expression did not change, she added, "Think of Edwina! She has just lost her husband. Must she lose her sister, too? Must she know, no matter the circumstances, that you killed her husband? She will need you now more than ever. Think of that whenever you are moved to confess the truth. In this case, the truth would do far more damage than simply keeping your mouth shut."

"But it seems so wrong—so cowardly," Thea muttered, her features anxious and unhappy. "Oh, God! I do not know what to do. I killed him. I cannot deny it." Her eyes shut, and her hand closed into a fist. "But dear God, I did not mean to!"

"Of course you didn't! You are no murderess! Nor are you a fool, and for now, I strongly urge you to keep your mouth shut—at least wait until his body is discovered. If your conscience continues to bedevil you, you can always come forward and confess at a later time. But right now, tonight, I want you to think about the scandal and disgrace such a drastic step would bring down upon your entire family."

Thea nodded miserably. "I have thought of it. I have thought of nothing else. I've caused one ugly scandal already in my lifetime and cost my brother his life. Believe me, I certainly would prefer to pretend that tonight had not happened." She glanced at Modesty's concerned features. "But it did happen. I did kill him."

Another tap on the door sent Modesty to answer it. Taking

the tray from the servant, she shut the door behind her and, crossing the room, set the tray on a nearby table.

Pouring out a cup of steaming tea from the china pot and adding a generous dollop of brandy from the crystal decanter that had been set beside the teapot, Modesty brought it to Thea. "Drink this. It will make you feel better——at least momentarily."

Modesty was right. After several sips of the hot liquid, Thea could feel the terror and icy chill that had settled in her stomach easing.

Biting her lip, Thea glanced at Modesty who was also partaking of the same beverage, with an even bigger dose of brandy in her cup. Thea smiled faintly. If the amount of brandy Modesty was consuming was anything to go by, Modesty was more worried and perturbed than she had let on. A burst of love for her sometimes-astringent spinster cousin went through her. Modesty would stand by her . . . and understand and love her no matter what she did.

There was silence for several moments as both women drank their brandy-laced tea and thought about the death of Alfred Hirst. Neither came to any final conclusion.

Rising to her feet and walking to where the tray sat, Thea put down her cup. Turning back to face Modesty, she said unhappily, "I think for the time being that I shall do as you suggest and say nothing. As you said, I can always confess."

Modesty sighed with relief. "Thank goodness! I knew that you were a sensible gel."

Thea made a face. "Why does being sensible make me feel like a coward?"

"Because you are not a fool—you know you killed him, but you also know that it *was* a tragic accident—not something you planned or had even considered doing. Remember, too, that you were protecting yourself. It was not your fault—the fault, the entire fault, lies with Alfred." Modesty hesitated, then asked quietly, "I assume that no one else knows that you were there?"

That tight, pinched look returned to Thea's face. "Unfortunately," she said heavily, "someone else *does* know—remember I told you about the man I collided with as I was leaving the house."

Modesty uttered a decidedly unladylike curse. "I had forgotten about him. Are you positive that he recognized you?"

"I'm positive that he got a very good look at my face—and if he doesn't know who I am now, he soon will—especially since it appears that he is a member of the *ton*. He was with Lord Embry and that crowd when I saw him in the park."

"Hmm. Perhaps if we left town early and retired to the country until the spring, he wouldn't remember you, if you were to meet at a later date?"

Thea shrugged wearily. "It's possible. But I suspect that Nigel told him who I was—you know what a gossip he is." Sourly, she added, "Of course, we will have a perfectly legitimate excuse to go to the country—Hirst's death. I suspect that Edwina will not want to remain in London—she certainly will not be attending any balls or other entertainment for several months."

"Well, there you have it! I shall tell the servants first thing in the morning that we are packing and retiring to Halsted House for the winter."

Halsted House was the country estate Thea had purchased just two years ago. While Modesty much preferred London, there were times that Thea simply could not bear the noise and bustle a moment longer and would escape to the country, to Halsted House. She loved Halsted for another reason: It was located not five miles from Garrett Manor and living there, trampling through the three hundred acres that went with the estate, brought back all the happier moments of her childhood. Modesty's suggestion was tempting, but a thought occurred to her.

"Shouldn't we wait until after we are informed of Alfred's death before we begin packing?" Thea asked quietly.

Modesty looked vexed. "Of course. I can be such a fool sometimes." She stood up and said decisively, "Well, we can settle nothing more tonight and we will just have to wait until the news of his death is brought to us before we put our plans in motion."

A sudden rap on the door had both women exchanging a frightened glance. Taking a deep breath, Thea called out calmly enough, "Yes, what is it?"

The door opened and Tillman's bald head appeared as he peered around the door. "Miss, I know it is very late, but there is a gentleman downstairs who insists upon seeing you. I told him that you were not receiving visitors," he complained, "but he persisted." Walking into the room, he handed her a folded piece of paper. "He said that you would want this and that he would await your reply."

How she kept her features schooled, Thea never knew. Taking the paper with as much enthusiasm as she would have a live cobra, she opened the note and read it. Ignoring the fear that stabbed through her, she crumpled the note and said coolly, "Tell the gentleman that I shall be down in just a moment. Show him into the blue saloon—offer him refreshments if he wishes."

Tillman looked offended, but he said with only a hint of displeasure in his voice, "Very well, Miss, if you say so, but if you want my opinion—"

"I do not!" Thea said sharply. "Now do as you have been told."

Muttering, Tillman withdrew.

Thea glanced at Modesty. "It is the man I collided with as I left the house. He wants to talk with me."

"Should you meet with him alone? Should I come with you?"

Thea thought a moment, then shook her head. "No, I had better see him by myself." She smiled bitterly. "If I am to be exposed and condemned to hang, I do not want you involved. For the moment let him think that only he and I know what happened."

Her most haughty expression on her face, Thea entered the blue saloon a few minutes later. Telling herself that he could not *prove* that she had even been out of the house tonight—

her servants were loyal and would never give her away, Thea had decided that her best course, right now, was to deny everything and keep denying it.

Shutting the door behind her, she confronted the tall, gray-eyed stranger. Attacking immediately, she began crisply, "And what is the meaning of this unwarranted intrusion? I do not know who you think you are or what you hope to accomplish, but I'll not have you berating my servants and forcing your way into my home this way. I've a good mind to send for the Watch."

"Perhaps you should . . . considering what happened at Curzon Street this evening," Patrick drawled.

Thea's breath caught painfully. "And what," she demanded, "do you mean by that?"

Patrick had to admire her poise if not her manner, and under different circumstances, he would have enjoyed sparring with her. But not tonight. And not at this moment.

"I think you know very well what I mean," he said, his gray eyes steadily meeting hers.

Thea bit her lip. He did not appear to be a man who bluffed easily, but she had no choice but to continue on the path she had chosen. Her chin rising pugnaciously, she snapped, "It is very late. Even at the best of times, I have no taste for games and puzzles and I am afraid that you are trying my patience. I would suggest that you leave."

Across the width of the pleasant room that separated them, Patrick studied her. She was tall, but not as tall as he had first thought, and for a young woman with such a sordid past and wild reputation, she seemed oddly innocent and curiously vulnerable. The two times he had seen her had been so brief that he had been left with only a fleeting impression of flashing dark eyes and a soft crimson mouth. Reality did not change that impression much, her eyes were still just as dark and compelling and that red mouth . . . He frowned. Dalliance was *not* the reason for his visit, but he could not pretend that his only interest in her had to do with the dead man in the house on Curzon Street.

From his very first sight of her in the park, though he would have denied it hotly, he had been aware of feeling a spark of interest in her. He hadn't understood it then and he certainly did not understand it now. Knowing what he did about her, Patrick had expected to meet a calculating harpy—a harpy with whom closer acquaintance would kill whatever mad appeal she had aroused within him. Instead he was confronted with a slender, fairy-faced creature who looked as if she might have just left the schoolroom only a few years ago. She was also, he admitted uneasily, by far the most striking female he had seen in a very long time—if ever. To his alarm, he found her wide eyes and intriguing features much, much too attractive.

Still frowning, he said, "And that is your last word?" When she remained stubbornly silent, he added, "If you take this attitude, you may leave me with no alternative but to give evidence to the magistrate."

Her façade crumpled just a bit. Not meeting his gaze, Thea studied the pale blue and cream pattern of the finely woven rug that lay upon the floor.

She was in a terrible quandary. She dare not let him lay evidence, and yet she was terrified of admitting that she had reason to fear such an action by him.

Patrick watched her, wondering if she knew how appealing she appeared as she stood before him in her simple gown of finely spun rose-colored silk, her features hidden by the curve of her lustrous dark hair that tumbled around her bare shoulders. He had come prepared for battle, determined to wrest the truth out of her—no matter how brutal he had to be. His problem was that the reality of his opponent did not match the picture in his mind of a scheming, hard-hearted little harlot.

Sighing, Patrick said, "I doubt you'll believe me, but I don't honestly want to cause you trouble. I simply want to know why you were there, what happened, and the identity of the dead man." A coaxing note in his voice, he added, "I swear to you that anything you tell me shall remain between us. We might even be able to help each other."

"Why should I trust you? Why should I help you? You're a stranger—I don't even know your name."

Patrick smiled, a singularly attractive smile, the corners of his deceptively sleepy gray eyes crinkling. Bowing with exquisite grace, he murmured, "Allow me to introduce myself: I am Patrick Blackburne, late of the Mississippi Territory in America."

"That tells me nothing," Thea muttered, not willing to respond to his undeniable charm. Charming men in her view were particularly devious and dangerous—Hawley Randall had taught her that over a decade ago!

Patrick straightened, his smile fading just a little. "Perhaps, the name of Lady Caldecott is more familiar to you? She is my mother. The baron is her second husband."

"Of course, I know Lady Caldecott—everyone does," she admitted faintly, her heart sinking. Good God! Lady Caldecott—one of the most imperious society matrons in all of England, and this man was her son! Of all the gentlemen in London that she could have seen on Curzon Street tonight, Thea wondered despairingly, why did it have to have been him? If he even breathed a word to his mother about her presence there tonight, it would be all over London in a matter of hours. Ruination and scandal, possibly execution stared her in the face.

Patrick arched a brow. "Well? Does that make me a trifle more trustworthy?"

"Not very," she admitted, hiding her fear behind a cool expression. "I saw you with Lord Embry today, which means, I assume, that you are an intimate of his." Her voice hardened. "And Lord Embry and his cronies are as wild and as scapegrace a band of fellows as one can meet. Being friends with him does not raise you in my estimation."

Stung, Patrick snapped, "And I suppose your reputation is so spotless?" It was an unfair jab and he knew it as soon as the words left his mouth. A flash of distress crossed her face.

He walked over to her and grasped one of her hands. "Forgive me! That was uncalled for and ungentlemanly."

Gently slipping her hand from his, she smiled bitterly, "You have no reason to apologize—I know my reputation."

He glanced at her keenly. "And is it all deserved?" he asked softly.

"It doesn't matter," she said, stepping away from him, suddenly aware of how very attractive he was with his black hair and dark, handsome features. It had been a long time, in fact, not since Hawley Randall, that she had met a man who aroused anything within her other than amusement——or polite indifference. But there was something about this tall American that inexplicably pulled at her, something about him that made her aware of him in a way she had thought never to feel again, and she was at once unnerved and wary.

Once she had established a safe distance from him, she looked at him, her expression troubled. "This conversation is gaining us nothing. I'll grant you that you probably mean well, but I have nothing to say to you. I suggest that you leave."

Patrick stared at her, disturbed by how disappointed he was that she would not trust him, but not really surprised. After all, she didn't know him, and under the circumstances he didn't precisely blame her. But he had to have her help. Whoever was blackmailing his mother had used the same Curzon Street house where Thea had been and a man had been murdered. Whether she, or the dead man, had anything to do with his mother's plight he didn't know, but at the moment, Thea Garrett was his best chance of discovering the identity of the person who was demanding money from his mother.

Patrick pulled on his ear, his expression wry. He wanted her help, but there was only one way he could think of to get it, and he would have preferred not to reveal the only card that he held.

Especially since he wasn't positive of her reaction to it. It could tip the scales in his favor, and, then again, it could allow her to escape. He studied Thea a moment longer. From the stubborn tilt of that determined chin and the set of her mouth, it was obvious that she wasn't going to budge an inch. Blast!

Uneasy under his considering gaze, Thea said, "Mr. Blackburne, I do not mean to be rude, but I've asked you now several times to leave. Won't you please do so and save both of us an embarrassing scene?"

Patrick sighed. "I sympathize with your situation—I really do, but I'm rather in a pickle myself—you could help me." His eyes held hers. "We could help each other."

"I'm sorry, but your problems are really none of my concern," Thea said stiffly, desperate for him to leave, but frightened of what he might do when he did leave. Deny, deny, and *deny*, she reminded herself grimly, but heaven knew it was increasingly difficult. Her nerves felt as if they had been flayed with fire, and the strain of the night was telling on her. How much longer she could maintain her composure she didn't know—the American was very appealing, and when he offered help, she was almost bemused and frightened enough to take it. Increasingly, she feared that if he did not leave soon, she would break down and tell him everything, a move she was convinced would be fatal. But it was oh so tempting to give into the urge to do so—particularly when those gray eyes urged her warmly to do just that. "Please leave."

Patrick took a swift turn around the room, stopping immediately in front of her. Huskily, he said, "You've no reason on this earth to trust me, but I implore you to do so."

Her lovely dark eyes searched his. Oh, she wanted to trust him, and she was astonished at how much she wanted to, but she stubbornly shook her head. "I'm sorry," she muttered, "but you ask too much."

He sighed and smiled crookedly. "Would it help if I told you that you didn't kill him . . . that someone else did?"

To read more, look for *Swear by the Moon* by
Shirlee Busbee